# FEARFUL MASTER

*Arthur Lawrence*

Fearful Master

Copyright 2015 by Arthur Lawrence

All rights reserved. No part of this book may be used or reproduced in any matter without prior written permission.

Promontory Press
www.promontorypress.com

ISBN 978-1-927559-82-6

Typeset by One Owl Creative in 13pt Bembo Std
Cover design by Marla Thompson of Edge of Water Design

Printed in Canada
0987654321

How soon we forget history ... Government is not reason. Government is not eloquence. It is force. And, like fire, it is a dangerous servant and a fearful master.

— George Washington

# FEARFUL MASTER

# ONE

"HOW LONG WILL THIS TAKE?"

"Until your risk factor is determined."

"I was sent here by an agency of the Canadian government."

"We don't trust all our own agencies, let alone Canada's. What agency?"

"It's ... in our Department of Public Safety."

"Accident Prevention?" Heavy sarcasm.

"My friend is meeting me here at the airport."

"He will be paged and told you are delayed. A *courtesy* we provide." He pushes up his glasses, perhaps to be recognized for this accommodation, but immediately lowers them again to refocus on his monitor. Jason sees him as a man of fifty-something with an expression close to scornful. He wears the gray SECOR[1] uniform, the peaked cap on his desk. He would be one of a million men around the world, mostly in uniform, who are empowered by some authority—the state, the military, the church, the school—and who bar the way of travelers, refugees, applicants, students, any kind of supplicant. They are the gatekeepers of society.

"You went to Egypt last year." Spoken as an accusation.

"It's there—on my passport. To visit my aunt and uncle."

"You come from Egypt."

"You can see I was born in Canada. My parents came from Lebanon." He had expected a friendly welcome from SECOR. He still does, but this chilly guardian has to be bypassed first. Bil will have driven fifty miles to meet him and must now be fretting in uncertainty somewhere in the terminal.

He was peeled off right at the ramp. After the hours of encapsulation on the flights from Ottawa, pawing through the debris of his mind; after descending through clouds that he finally recognized were not just cloud but cloud thickened by smoke; after he noticed the wavering orange of brushfires below; after scanning the acres of lights before debarking, glassy-eyed, he was too numb to be surprised when he was elbowed by a pair of SECORs in gray and led through the back hallways on the perimeter of the terminal. A door had

---

1  SECOR: The United States Security Corps. The hugely expanded replacement of the Department of Homeland Security.

opened only after prompting from a keypad.

It had crossed his blurred mind that this must be an official, if private, welcome. He must be about to meet his new superior. He hesitated to ask, remembering his orders. After traversing several passages, all exuding the sterile atmosphere of any airport, they had turned into a subdued chamber like a great cave. Then a long wait. He had expected SECOR technique to be so immaculate, but not to be used on him. He's not a candidate for intimidation: he's clean. He works for an agency of his own government; he's been seconded now to an agency of an ally. Anyway, his psyche is bruised enough nowadays that these SECOR preliminaries are almost a welcome diversion.

He hasn't visited this country for years, but he knows something of what to expect. His own post in Ottawa falls under the umbrella of state security, and here it's far more intense. Crossing their border is touchy. You can't take your bags until SECOR verifies them as the same ones you checked in, duly tagged as having been sniffed by both dog and machine. Then the scrutiny in the Immigration line, where you look into a digital reader to compare your retina print to the one on your passport. SECOR scans all incoming passenger profiles. Since Canadians of foreign birth are so often shunted aside for interrogation, few now travel here. The country's inhospitable fence has reduced tourism to a trickle. Jason appreciates such vigilance; Canada is also less hospitable now toward visitors of questionable pedigree. But this Gray Man seems more than meticulous—he's hostile. The gray uniform gives him the heft of authority. If he wore a suit like a clerk, would he be so intimidating? As a clerk he might be courteous, even obsequious. In uniform, he's disdainful.

As Jason waits for him to finish punching keys and absorbing the hidden data on his monitor, he listens to the indistinct exchanges nearby, presumably shielded in cubicles like this one. He can just make out sharp voices questioning and muted responses, some hesitant, some overeager. A spurt of accented English is incomprehensible. A tang of fear infuses another reply. A group of applicants must be waiting nearby for another Gray Man to be freed up; he picks up a murmured exchange, several voices in a foreign cadence, suddenly silenced by *"Shut up there!"*

He looks back at his own Gray Man, who returns a flick of his eyes in Jason's direction. He can feel the hostility without understanding its origin. Perhaps just resentment for foreigners nurtured by the endless chain of them that serve up problems at his desk.

"Do you have dual citizenship?"

"No, just Canadian."

"Did you go to any other countries during your trips to the Middle East?"

"None. There would be a stamp on my passport."

"If you passed through a border checkpoint."

"You think I sneaked into some other country?"

The interrogator is unruffled. "You speak Arabic?"

"Enough to manage."

"So you communicated with your contacts in that language?"

"Contacts? I spoke with my relatives and friends. In Arabic. Also in English and French. They're mostly fluent in all three. Lots of educated Egyptians speak several languages."

"You Canadians are proud of all your languages, aren't you?"

"We only have two. And most people speak only one."

"Your religion?"

"Nothing to speak of. My parents are Maronites."

"Do you believe in God?"

"*Pardon?*" Only an intimate friend (or perhaps a minister) would ask such a question in Canada, and coming from an official it's just bizarre, like being asked your sexual inclination by a bank teller. He studies his interrogator—he's not sure whether he's being baited. Gray Man's mouth, tight-lipped, shows a hint of upturn at its corners, as if having scored a hit. "I suppose everyone accepts that there's some kind of pattern in the universe, whatever we call it," Jason says.

"Atheist." He appears to key that in, then looks up. "Lots of them in Canada, so I hear. We have to be careful about you people."

"We're less dangerous than you believers." But it gets no rise from this remote bureaucrat.

Jason is very tired. Not just from the long flight and arriving in the darkness, but from the accumulation of nights when his mind had run from sleep and then days when it crawled through the hours with half-lit attention, all of that ongoing for weeks.

"Canada is a friendly country," he says, almost whispering, disjointedly, losing focus.

"So you say. Some of us consider Canada rather unfriendly."

His frustration breaks through. "What if I just take the next plane home?"

Gray Man crows, not in amusement, rather in triumph at having caught him out. "You'd like to get *away* from here now, would you?" He taps a few more keys and then fixes Jason with a chilly smile. "You say your name is Currie?"

"It's on my passport."

"What was it in Lebanon? Not Currie."

"Our family name is Kouri." Jason spells it for him. "My father anglicized it when they immigrated into Canada."

"I thought so. I have a couple of Kouris."

"It's a common name. There are probably legions of Kouris in Lebanon."

"And one of them on my list is Jason Kouri." While Jason weighs the change in tone, the Gray Man touches some signal beside his desk. A buzzer sounds nearby.

"Perhaps I should mention that I'm here to work with General Hawk on special assignment." This is a desperate move; he's been told never to mention his mission.

"Never heard of him."

A different guard in SECOR uniform enters, wearing a

sidearm, his unfriendly stare piercing Jason. "Take Mr. Currie to the holding cells," his Gray Man says. "He's to be our guest for a while." He rattles a few more keys and looks with satisfaction at the screen. He gives Jason only a sidelong glance as he's whisked off. It says clearly, "One more disposed of."

As Jason is escorted across the Immigration hall, he looks toward the exit, which he had expected to clear hours earlier, and sees the illuminated greeting: *Welcome to the United States of America.*

# TWO

"WE CAN'T AFFORD TO GIVE YOU LEAVE. WE'RE SHORT OF Arabic analysts."

"We have tons—we're even loaning them to the Americans."

"Not analysts. Not like you. You can be a smartass, but at least you're good."

"But I'm not getting anything *real* …"

Ben Noble shifted in his chair. His irritation showed. It usually did when Jason made light of his own work. Noble glanced over his shoulder at a windowless wall, blank but for his framed credentials. It was a tic familiar to Jason. Maybe Noble looked over his shoulder in his dreams to be sure the A-D wasn't monitoring them.

"Come on, Jason. Every analyst has to work through a ton of shit to find the odd pearl." His other charcteristic was a voice so quiet that it barely rose above a whisper.

"I'm not finding any. I listen to voices. Mostly inarticulate. Then I create a story out of fragments. A daydream. These people will never blow up Parliament or bomb the American Embassy. They're just immature sociopaths who get off on apocalyptic visions. There's no red meat."

Noble tried to look shocked, but managed only uneasiness. Jason understood his discomfort: as the intersection and filter between management and staff—the middle manager—lacking the confidence of one and without the full respect of the other, defender of his people to the leadership, but translator of Authority to the foot soldiers, he was set up for abuse from either level, yet the essential fulcrum between.

When Jason wasn't preoccupied with his own needs, he felt genuinely sorry for Noble, even though he leaned on him even more than others. But now he dug in, waiting in silence. Noble said, "Jason, in this agency we have dozens—maybe hundreds—of divorcés or former live-ins, some multiple, all of them still able to translate and interpret and analyze without missing a comma. So how can I give you a month just to pine over your Ramona?"

"Pine? I'm just trying to stop thinking about her. She's fastened on my mind like a leech. I've been bled dry. I'm dysfunctional."

"One out of three marriages fails. It's not a tragedy; it's just modern times." Noble leaned back and studied Jason, who sensed a homily to be forthcoming. "What's happened to you, Jason? You're the sharpest analyst I've ever had in my department. You set the standards for the rest. You were more than enthusiastic—you were almost high on analysis. You worked your ass off and thought it was fun. Suddenly, you're fed up. We've got crises right and left and they bore you. Think about what's happened to you. Then get over it."

"Look, Ben, I just can't get what happened out of my mind. And I need to, just to be able to do this kind of work. I'm not enjoying work; I'm not doing it well. I know my marriage breakup is a joke to outsiders, but to me, it feels like a disease, it hangs on and hangs on, and I can't think clearly. You were divorced."

Noble absorbed the plea for a moment without commenting, maybe surprised at its intensity.

"I can't concentrate. Yesterday I misinterpreted an intercept."

"What intercept?"

"It's all right, I corrected it. I'm a threat to national security. I should resign."

Noble started at that chilling word. "Resignation is impossible under the Act. You have a contract with CSIS[2] and you can never resign. You can only be placed on indefinite leave.

---

2   CSIS: Canadian Secret Intelligence Service. It was formed when the domestic intelligence function was divorced from the RCMP (Royal Canadian Mounted Police) because of abuse of its powers. The two services have been fiercely competitive ever since. It's pronounced to rhyme with "thesis."

I could give you two days—a long weekend."

Jason was confident (as the best analyst of colloquial Arabic in his section) that he could never be allowed to walk away, certainly not nowadays with wars and threats of further wars animating the Arabic states. "Everyone says we're arranging a trade with SECOR's L.A. station."

"That's confidential." Noble looked more resigned than pained at the accuracy of the rumor mill.

"They say SECOR wants an analyst fluent in street-level Arabic."

"I know your qualifications. But they're asking for a senior officer. That's what they're sending us."

"None of our senior officers can say his own name in Arabic. Why do they need Arabic analysts anyway? There are plenty of Arabs in L.A."

"If you were a Muslim in California and your home country was under attack, would you volunteer to help SECOR?"

"I'm Christian. And this is a chance to work with a world-class intelligence operation." Noble still looked doubtful. "Ben, I'm not doing much for you in this state of mind. Can't you get me out of here just for a while? I can stay with my old friend, Bil Maron. I'll get over this and come back ready to be red-hot again."

Noble chewed on his lip, another familiar tic. "You'd be out of your depth at SECOR."

"SECOR is just like CSIS only bigger and better. I'm the best fit." He had to wait a long moment for Noble to bend.

"If you swear not to disgrace us … maybe I *could* nominate you … It would be a stretch. And you might not be at home with SECOR. If you fouled up I'd be in deep shit."

"Ben, I promise I won't get out of line." When Noble still hesitated, he added, "Not this time."

"All right, all right. I'll try it on the A-D. Let's be clear what they want. You'd be there to update them on Canadian technique and learn theirs. They're slotting their own advisor here in Ottawa. In practice he'll only be here to assess how dedicated CSIS people seem to be to American interests. They suspect some of our people are less than—committed. Listen, you could really help us there. We'd like to know more about the detention camps. They've advised us of some Canadians they're holding, but we suspect there are far more. Canadian travelers, missing, mostly Muslims."

"We've asked them if they're holding these people?"

"And they've stonewalled."

"Maybe they have good reason for holding them. SECOR has awesome humint[3]."

"And money we could only wish for. Of course, they might plant you in some back office where you'll never hear any-

---

3   Humint: Human Intelligence, as in old-fashioned spying. "Commint": communications intelligence, like intercepts and bugs. These terms do not exhaust the list; there is also "Sigint": signals intelligence; "photoint": photographic intelligence; and a few other combinations.

thing, but—look, Jason, DFAIT[4] is hounding us for some sort of leverage. You could make us look good. I'll try it with the A-D."

Assistant-Director McPherson was a retired general. He was referred to among senior staff as the A-D, but when the juniors learned that his nickname in the forces had been Bullet, presumed to be more for the shape of his shaved skull than the trajectory of his intellect, he became A-D Bulletproof to the foot soldiers of Jason's section, in recognition of his shield against any attacks of innovation.

Jason had been before him only once, not long after his appointment, before he knew better. With Jason's structured approach as a mathematician, he had quickly worked out certain shortcomings in the organization. Staff was encouraged (he had been assured) to comment via the suggestion box. He wrote a helpful memo pointing out that perhaps too heavy emphasis was placed on the analysts to follow up on daily highs rather than allowing them wider searches for the surprises over the horizon. The day after he dropped it in the box, he was surprised to be summoned to the office of the A-D. Noble was already there. Jason's suggestion lay dead center on the otherwise clear desktop.

"It's good of you to see me, General—"

---

4   DFAIT: Department of Foreign Affairs and International Trade: Canada's diplomatic corps.

A-D Bulletproof raised one hand from the desk to signal a halt. He owned a face as bland as an innocent but spoiled by rattlesnake eyes. He ran their gaze over Jason like a sensor, sucking the juice out of his enthusiasm. "I expect to tell you this once, Currie. I rarely ask the opinion of my superiors and I *never* need the advice of my subordinates. Further, I don't accept memos on our operating procedures." With one finger, he flicked the memo across to Jason. "This never existed."

Now Jason had a second chance. "Noble has recommended you for the SECOR exchange. I have some misgivings. He does mention you have a close friend in California, and in general you get on well with Americans." He waited while Jason realized it was a question.

"I certainly like the people I've met there, sir."

"Is that a sly way of saying that you don't like the administration?"

"Why ... I don't pay much attention to politics."

"Not pay attention to politics? And you're an *analyst*? Intelligence work is all about politics, Currie. Let's not forget that despots rule half the world and that only American determination is keeping the other half clear of them. That's politics and we're immersed in it. Are all your people like this, Noble?"

"No, sir," Noble barely muttered. "Currie is ... unique." When the A-D responded only with a cold stare, he added, "But he's our surest analyst."

"He needs to be. Who is this friend of yours, Currie?"

"Bil Maron. A former neighbor."

"In fact a Canadian. You said you liked Americans."

"Bil's been there so long I suppose I see him as American."

"Hmmm. Noble will check him out. Now then, let's be clear that their reason for this exchange is to feel out our level of commitment. The Americans see us as a satellite. They want more than token support. So they'll also be judging you as an indicator. D'you have any reservations about their policies, in the Middle East for example?"

Jason imagined Noble biting his lip but he avoided looking at him. "None at all, sir."

"Good. You must show them that we're a sound ally. That we're *committed*. If I had my way, we'd be there with them."

"I could mention that to General Hawk, sir."

The A-D fixed Jason with a thoughtful glare. His eyebrows twitched, a hint of suspicion. But the moment passed. "Currie, we're counting on your discretion. I hope you've got more of it than you've shown to date. That's all."

"You nearly blew that," Noble muttered as they reached his office. "Now listen to me, Jason: we liaise with SECOR, not any other agency. They all compete to the death. So be careful; don't talk to any other security people."

"Should I ask about detention camps?"

Noble gave this a moment. "No. That would get back to Hawk. Just keep your eyes and ears open. And don't do a number on SECOR the way you did on us in that memo." Leaning back in his chair, he considered Jason more thoughtfully. "How long since you've been to the States?"

"A few years."

"America has developed hardening of the arteries since then."

"I know what to expect."

"SECOR is about fifty times the size of CSIS. Maybe a hundred times."

"It's also the most efficient intelligence body in the world. So I hear."

"Just be careful. It's huge, it's efficient, but it also chews up people who don't fit. Make sure you're not one of them. I need you back here."

"Ben, I know you stuck your neck out on this. Don't worry. I'll fit right in."

Noble still looked skeptical but pushed a document across to Jason. "Sign it and I'll witness."

"Not read it, then perhaps sign it?"

"It's a waiver of extradition, undated. In case SECOR should charge you with revealing classified information or anything else they can think of. They insist on it. Just routine."

Jason was ready to sign anything to get on his way to a fresh assignment, so he did. He rose to leave, then hesitated. "Ben, I won't let you down."

Noble gave him an ambiguous look, but shook the offered hand. Jason paused at the door. "For the sake of argument, what if I do make some kind of innocent error and they detain me? After all, even SECOR must occasionally make mistakes."

"Then we'd try to get you out."

"With what hope of success?"

"As much as we've had finding our missing Arabs. Don't ever give them cause."

# THREE

JASON'S CELL IN A SUBTERRANEAN QUARTER OF THE TERMINAL is without bars, a plain little room with a solid door, its observation slide closed. There's a bench-cum-bed with no pillow or blankets and an uncovered porcelain toilet. No room to pace. All he can do is sit and try to hold down his anxiety. He's heard enough horror stories about American border crossings. Now that he's been plucked out of the line, he's not shocked, just unnerved.

His visit to the Middle East would have singled him out—he knows now that he might have foreseen that. He should have requested a clean passport from CSIS—they should have insisted on one! But that Gray Man—itching to humiliate him—he puts down to meanness rather than dubious admissibility. How could he not have heard of General Hawk?

Maybe some of them just resent Canadians for not buying into every American war.

Common sense reasserts itself as he cools. He shouldn't have challenged his interrogator. He should have seen the danger in a little man with great power. Noble tried to accommodate him—he'll be humiliated if SECOR now throws Jason out of the country. Then a flash of hope—SECOR is known for being out front of any problem. That's why there are no terrorist attempts nowadays within American borders (at least none that the public hears about). So L.A. Station should be looking for him by now. He quiets down, savoring the hope that he is now a datum on the screen of a meticulous data processor. They'll find him. He has a riff of malicious pleasure—Gray Man will be reprimanded! But how long will it all take? And meanwhile?

He's familiar with due process in Canada, where he would be brought before an officer in Immigration, represented by a lawyer if he chose, within forty-eight hours. All he knows of the American system is that it's changed now; it's much less welcoming. That thought stirs up his fears once more. He wills himself to let it rest—he no longer has control of his treatment.

But when he's quieted his fears and the monotony of the cell begins to weigh, his memories creep back in. Ramona materializes, loaded with deflating recollections. Now, spent from running his emotions on high, he slides into a trance and the whole sequence reruns like a looped tape.

She was overdone a shade—showy, with black hair, ripe lips, and a Mediterranean bronze complexion, busty and full-hipped, a figure to please the male eye. Their early days were an adventure, warm, unhesitating, and above all novel. She was a joy to be with, on his arm, across the table, seated against him in the car, soon wrapped around him in bed. His tight circle of friends, all securely coupled, among whom he was the outsider who seemed unable to maintain a relationship, was beguiled by his infatuation.

He was swept into her apartment in the flush of their first date, and she called him into her bedroom moments later. She lay prone with one jack-knifed leg pointing straight at him, reflecting its nylon sheath. She wore nothing else. He had to lean over her to peel it off with fumbling zeal. Then, she devoured him. They were married only a few weeks later.

After the heat subsided, little conflicts cropped up. Jason was disappointed that she shared none of his intellectual interests, while pressing him to share all of her physical ones. She wanted to get about, shop, dine out, meet people, go to parties. A certain amount of this was agreeable to him. With too much, he felt put upon. If he allowed it to show, she reacted sharply.

"You're showing your serious side. Again."

"Mathematics has hardly any funny bits."

"Well, life has lots of them. Forget math and just live a little."

Exchanges like this became more frequent, and the cuts

more wounding.

"I can't communicate with you!" The first time Ramona used that phrase, with nauseating repetitions to follow, their marriage began sliding over some crucial edge, then upending into freefall, but he recognized that only later, after it crashed.

He has only to close his eyes and the familiar pictures light up the walls of his memory. He knows that he had been spellbound, but now that he has cast off that enchantment, he cannot find his way back; he cannot recapitulate that Jason prior to Ramona. But he's already exhausted, so when he has flayed himself for a while, his mind suffers a kind of short-circuit; it breaks off and he sleeps. Not well, nor long. The door clangs open and the guard enters with a sort of breakfast.

"What happens to me now?"

"You're being transferred to a secure facility."

"A jail? But ... there must be some kind of review. Maybe a senior officer?"

"Oh, you're someone special? You'll have a chance to speak up when you get there."

"I've already spoken up but he wasn't listening."

"So you get a second chance."

Jason's desperate enough to violate his orders a second time. "Listen: do you know of General Hawk?"

"I only know General Motors."

There's another prisoner in the van, looking the way Jason

supposes he must himself after dozing in his clothes. Two guards stay up front but monitor them through a slide.

"D'you know where we're going?" the man asks. He's older, maybe sixty, dressed in work clothes. He looks as though he's never sat behind a desk. His beard is largely gray and trimmed without style; his hands are roughened. He speaks with an accent many years eroded from some unrecognizable origin.

"To some prison." This only adds to the man's anxiety. "Maybe just to answer more questions. Have you done anything that would make you seem … threatening?"

"Threatening?" He stares at Jason. "I'm a stonemason."

"Retired?"

"Fired. They didn't want any more Muslim stonemasons."

"Why not?"

"We're not good Americans."

"But … did you do something, say something?"

"I don't know. *I'm* an American. Forty years. My children born here. They've never even seen the Middle East. I didn't go back since I left. They've got my son. I came to find him. They took me. At the plane."

"What did your son do?"

"Only listened to his imam. At the mosque."

"Speaking against the Americans?"

"Aren't you an American?"

"Canadian."

"You sound like an American." He goes on, explaining—more to himself, it seems, than to Jason. "They say he said some things that he shouldn't have. It can't be true. He's quite wise, the imam. He wouldn't speak like a fool. He would know there were people there who could report him. So why was my son taken? I don't know. I don't where he is now. And now *I'm* going to prison. Can you understand it?"

Jason doesn't understand it either. "Has your son been to the Middle East?"

"Never been out of America."

CSIS knew the Americans were holding some of their own citizens (along with those missing Canadians) without due process. They were charged for some misstep on the gradient between activism and terrorism. Under the Revised Defense of America Act, hearings could be postponed indefinitely or forever. That was the screen beyond which DFAIT was unable to find Canada's disappeared. "Doesn't the imam know where he went?"

"Maybe in a camp, the imam said. He knows of such places. He says they torture Muslims."

"Torture? But ... how could he know that? Were some of his people released ...?"

"Maybe. But no one gets out now."

"I hope we do." Can CSIS know less about these American camps than does a sacked stonemason? Jason awakens to the likelihood that CSIS has kept him in the dark along with nearly all other Canadians.

The old man looks at him with a flicker of suspicion. "You haven't heard of the camps? In Canada?"

The knot in Jason's stomach begins tightening again. It's this easy to disappear into such a place? And no one gets out. If the Americans can't be bothered to cooperate with DFAIT, will they be just as dismissive of a missing CSIS analyst? He tries to reassert his faith in SECOR; they're bound to catch up to him. "D'you know of anyone else …?"

"The imam says others have asked him. About men who've gone missing." He quiets for a long moment, perhaps dwelling on an image of his son. "They let some go. The imam says so. I have to trust my imam. Wouldn't you?"

"I'm Christian."

"Ah!" He's startled but then embarrassed. "Then you'll be okay. They'll be easier on Christians."

They turn off the freeway onto a secondary route. There is only the one wired window in the rear door, but it's enough to see the road behind and the gravel waste on either side of it as they move steadily through a featureless stretch of desert. There's enough dust on the asphalt to raise little clouds that are whipped offline by the hot wind. There's nothing to catch the attention. Jason falls into a long conversation with his thoughts, now groveling in misery over his prospects, now brightening a little in hope as he gets back to SECOR's omnipotence.

The metal cabin gets steadily warmer. California's blistering summer has been newsworthy even in Canada, also suffering months of above-average temperatures. But here, he has seen on televised news, the effects have been more than an inconvenience—brushfires, dwindling irrigation, thinning crops, electrical grid failures. Like much of the continent, the gentle climate of southern California has calcified into extremes of dryness and wetness, months of soaking abruptly yielding to more months of searing sun, and flooding succeeded by firestorms. When he gets up to look through the wired porthole, he can see the effects on the desert, deep washes now baked and cracked in the oven of summer. They pass through a burnt zone, the Joshua trees reduced to charcoaled skeletons.

The old man removes his shirt. Jason is sweating as well in their capsule. After some hesitation—will he disgrace CSIS if he shows up shirtless?—he strips to the waist. The stonemason's upper body is heavily tanned and muscular, Jason's white and lean, a dispiriting contrast.

After a good while they pass a gate, seen by them only after they are beyond it. It's manned by a unit in SECOR gray, helmeted and bearing rifles, which inspects the prisoners before passing them through. The gate, the guards, and the guns all emphasize the impotence of the prisoners. As they drive off, they can see a barbwire barrier behind, stretching across the wasteland until it disappears over ridges in either direction. An armored vehicle crawls along the fence; overhead, a helicopter passes.

The old man edges beside him, staring back at the hostile fence. "We can never get out of here."

Jason's been avoiding the same conclusion. He sits and sweats and tries to hold down the doubt that keeps welling up like stomach acid. SECOR has lost him. He's en route to a prison—one where torture is legitimate. Hopefully, SECOR will catch up to him again. Maybe. Unless he's too unimportant to catch the attention of such a massive apparatus. Maybe some clerk (like his own Gray Man) will be tasked to find him in his own good time. His bowels grind.

Finally, the van brakes, gears down, and lurches to a stop. He shuffles to the grill. He's looking back at another high gate, now closing, and above it a watchtower, from whose balcony a gray guard stares down at him, his hand resting casually on the barrel of a mounted machine gun.

They totter out of the cabin into a blast of hot air. As Jason's sight adjusts in the piercing sunlight, he finds himself focusing on the chain-link fence, more than twenty feet high. He can follow it along to a distant corner and another guard station. When he turns to the interior of the camp, he fastens on a row of wire cages immediately in front of him, like chicken coops but with stouter netting. The whole line is protected by a long roof of corrugated plastic. A neighbor of theirs had raised canaries in such cages. Incongruously, Jason has a vision of the birds wafting about while multiple trills of song challenge each other. But these open cells each contain a man in a sort of orange coverall, and those men he can see are all watching their arrival. There's a lot of shouting in their honor, either to cheer them up or to defy SECOR.

"It's all fences here," the old man says.

Jason lifts his gaze and sweeps over the territory beyond—

row after row of cages. Beyond them squats a substantial building of cement block, windowless.

"So many ..." the stonemason mutters, awed, even horrified. Jason counts the rows he can see with the same thought. He gets a firm push from one of the guards. They stumble a few steps into an administrative center.

The young officer in the administrative center greets them with "What language?"

"English," says his companion, drawing a sharp look from the officer, who then hands him a printed sheet of rules.

"Do you have Arabic?" Jason asks and is given one without question. Glancing through it as a professional linguist, he finds the Arabic to be of mixed quality. Then on to the showers, where their clothes are consigned to bins and they are issued the orange suits—one shirt, one pair of shorts, and pants. No shoes—something like beach clogs.

"Personal kit in your unit," he's told. Then the ground rules from the SECOR lieutenant: twenty minutes daily of walks outside the cages ('units') in groups of ten with no talking. Two showers and a change of uniform per week. "You will be assessed for two weeks. Your level of risk will be determined, then a permanent site designated." They both react sharply to the word *permanent*. "Depending on how much cooperation you show, you will go on to one of four levels of incarceration. If you answer all questions honestly and fully you may be eligible for Level One. If you give us trouble or answer evasively or not at all, you will go to Level Four.

Understand?"

"What is *incarceration*?" the old man whispers to Jason. "Torture?"

"What's that?" the lieutenant asks. "What are you saying there?" The old man is frozen by the officer's tone.

"He didn't understand *incarceration*," Jason says.

"Well, perhaps you can explain it to him then." They're marched to adjacent cages, two empty ones in the middle of a row. Everyone is focused on the newcomers. He hears shouts of encouragement in English, in Arabic, in some unrecognized tongue. They both stare each way through the linked cages at the collage of faces staring back at them. Most look to be young, quite a few black, one or two Asian.

As soon as the guards march off, questions fly at them, some that he can hear from nearby, others passed along the row. These men must receive no news except from new arrivals.

"Do you know if anything is said about the camps?"

"Do people know what they're doing to Muslims?"

"Have there been any attacks on the Americans?"

He can hear the old man tell his other neighbor that Jason is Canadian. "Why isn't Canada speaking for us?" the man calls. Jason holds his hands up in resignation. "Do you know how the war is going?" He shakes his head.

The old man whispers that Jason is a Christian. This travels in both directions so that within seconds the cries sink to murmurs. He's no longer one of them; he's an outsider, even an enemy, and now he knows that they are all Muslims. He picks up a scrap of Arabic: "Be careful. He's not a believer."

The partitions have screening too fine for objects to be passed but allow voices and filtered sight along the row. The compartments are only about eight feet wide so many ears are in range. The back wall is solid metal; there's no communication between rows. The units contain a toilet—at floor level but with a flush handle—and a metal bench-bed attached to the wall and rather low. On it is a folded blanket, a roll that must be a prayer mat, two fresh towels, and a copy of the Koran.

Noble had said, "We'd like to know more about the camps." Maybe he'd meant, "Who is in those camps?" And how many.

There are Islamic militants in detention in Canada, but in regular penal institutions and in small numbers. He expected something similar if more extensive here. But this is a different level—not a couple of hundred, more like a couple of thousand. The cages are shocking. The numbers are more shocking. One, at least, is an American citizen—perhaps others are as well.

It's a chilling affirmation of American will. Here among thousands of caged—what?—terrorists? Dissidents? Or merely those foolish or angry enough to protest openly about America's campaigns? He is awed by the determination to control the security, and perhaps the mindset, of America. To a Canadian, it's wildly excessive, but maybe the Americans know better. If Canada were the leader of the Western world and had been seared by the same Islamic fundamentalism, might it be just as polarized?

The cages in this block—perhaps two-dozen—seem out of contact with the other blocks—so how does news get around? The stonemason begins passing along bulletins on camp culture. Their cages might be reassigned, "Because they don't like us to become friends. We'll be questioned tomorrow. If they think you're a terrorist you'll be sent to the building with no windows. Those men are tortured. They use dogs to attack them. Some go to other prisons where they have white clothes and are treated better, but you've got to give them names first. Unless you have names to give them, you don't get out. I don't know any names." All of this over the first hour or so, in brief installments after it's muttered along to his neighbor. Jason suspects some of this is fed by guards, perhaps to weaken resistance, perhaps only to taunt the prisoners. Finally, "You're a Christian. They tell me not to speak to you. You shouldn't be with us." After that, the old man leaves him be.

Waves of conversation still surge along the block, sometimes rising to a clamor as guards pass. Occasionally an inmate yells loudly enough to be heard from the next row, isolated from his by the rear metal wall, and some morsel of information is called back or shouted along to the next block.

In time there's a call to prayers at what must be the proper time. Jason notices then that the direction to Mecca is marked by an arrow etched on the concrete floor. Through the mesh he can see the ritual washing take place, then every man proceeding through the traditional positions on his prayer rug. The prayers are led by a voice from a far cell, sounding down the tunnel of netting.

With the prayers finished, a meal is handed in. A sort of truck crawls along the row and guards slide trays through slots at floor level. Jason's not sure what he's eating, but it's just palatable.

The desert night is encroaching; the sky beyond the floodlights is dark. But the compound continues to be bathed in white illumination. The light poles have been sited so that there are almost no shadows. At the setting of the sun there is no darkness here except high overhead or outside the perimeter. There will be no welcoming dawn either, only a little tempering of the white light.

Jason finds the murmur of the rituals immensely saddening. Each of these men must be remembering his family, his neighborhood mosque, the friends with whom he prayed, the comfort of his community. Here in the wasteland with the sweltering sun abruptly replaced by the desert chill, the lights holding off the darkness, only the prayers give any comfort. They have no hope here, except in those prayers. The guards are unseen during the ritual, perhaps to avoid provocation.

It's impossible not to feel sympathy for caged men in prayer. What if he did not have SECOR's tentacles reaching out to rescue him—how naked and abandoned might he feel? But then, what if SECOR hasn't even missed him yet? That stings him awake, and a cramp of panic follows. He has to fight it off for an uneasy stretch before he quiets down.

The old man is sitting on his bed, hands folded together and hanging between his knees, head down in despair.

Jason moves close to the screening. "How is it with you?"

He looks up, hesitant. "I shouldn't talk with you."

"In the neighborhood where we lived, quite a few were Muslim. Even some of our own cousins. And we all got along together."

"In Canada, maybe. It's different here."

"In this place?"

"In this country."

Jason tries a couple of times more—he badly needs reassurance himself. The old man won't be consoled. He seems close to tears. First his son, now himself in a wire cage, after forty years in America. Jason peers at the sad figure through the netting, brimming with compassion. How many stonemasons are there in these cages? How many of their sons? And where is it all leading America?

But then, America has its reasons. Burned enough by jihadist incandescence, America has wrapped itself in layers of fireproofing. Some of the men here, like his despondent neighbor, might be innocent of any act other than alienation; others are dedicated enemies. Jason's own experience has taught him how nearly impossible it is to sort one from the other. A security agency will inevitably take the safest fork in the process. How many prisoners would Canada be holding if due process could be sidestepped? And this is only a temporary prison. Two weeks evaluation, then on to … what, exactly? Permanent buildings with bars for high risks. For others? He ducks the speculation.

There is a settling down after the final round of prayers. He imagines this to be the most harrowing time of a prisoner's day, the alienation at its peak.

Watching and listening, he's been alert, involved. He's even feeling a little triumphant over cracking a detention camp for CSIS. Better to concentrate on this environment with all its threat than to paw over the entrails of his ruptured marriage. But when he's settled on his own metal shelf, padded by the prayer mat, his mind slips back into its obsession. Here comes the humiliation, the web of shame, crying out for analysis, itching to be picked over like a sore that refuses to heal.

He sleeps finally, and fitfully. It's never quiet. Guards pass and are jeered at, cages rattle, toilets flush, vehicles chug about nearby. Chilly gusts whip through the screening. He burrows in the single blanket. He can see his neighbors in the glare, similarly huddled. Just before dawn, anticipated only from the different quality of the light, prayers are signaled, and there's a reluctant crawling out of the devout, which is everybody but him in the block—maybe even in the camp. He feels left out again but wickedly comfortable in his blanket. After the communal devotions, a very quiet stretch. He can see the stonemason continuing with his private prayer. Jason nods to him and this time he gets a friendly nod back.

Breakfast arrives on the sliding trays—pita bread and rice with beans mixed in. A meal presumed compatible with traditional fare for Middle Easterners? But some, or many, or even all of these prisoners have lived in the United States for years, perhaps generations, so he imagines them more comfortable with American cuisine. It's lukewarm but welcome. He's feeling almost at peace with his screened world when word is passed along that "They're coming for the new ones." A detail of guards follows at once. He's shocked that they clamp on shackles as well as handcuffs—what can prisoners in handcuffs do to guards with guns? The stonemason looks at him like a comrade as they snap his in place. Religious difference aside, they're once more partners in fear. They move stiffly ahead.

As their slow march passes the pens, mutters and yells meet them, immediately joined by nearby blocks hurling defiance to overcome fear. Some prisoners shout in Arabic, "God is great!" The old stonemason squares his shoulders and marches with determination. That picks up Jason; his stride firms. He nods acknowledgement to the gallery. The shouting heightens.

The noise helps—the tightening in his solar plexus relaxes one notch. Insults in English and Arabic are shrieked at the soldiers. Then, as they pass further rows, the language mix changes. There's still English, but other tongues as well—maybe Farsi or Urdu. The guards bear themselves as if it's a familiar process. One of them raises his hand in a mocking acknowledgment and draws a heightening of abuse. The ground is soft as dust and the leg shackles suck Jason down into it. He tries not to slouch.

When they enter the windowless building, they're immediately separated, with only a quick look of fear between them. Jason and one guard enter a small room with a table and three chairs. The isolated chair is bolted to the floor. He sees that its metal arms have webbing attached to pinion the hands and feet of a prisoner. A flare of panic ignites.

Before he can be secured, two men enter, one in SECOR gray, the other regular army. "Good morning, Mr. Currie," says the one in gray. "I'm relieved to see you. I'm General Hawk and this is Colonel Werner. Soldier, release the prisoner from his restraints and leave us."

# FOUR

HE'S NOT AS OLD AS JASON EXPECTS A GENERAL TO BE, MAYBE under forty. He's trim, looking almost athletic in his tailored outfit. His face is thin, hollow-cheeked, with a narrow chin that just avoids the triangular. With pointed ears and a beard he could be a classic Satan. Very level gaze, the kind that seems interested but is not forthcoming.

He seats himself at the table, holding his eyes on Jason. "I thought I should come and extricate you personally." He waits for Jason to fill in his pause but Jason, finding himself nearly breathless with relief, says nothing.

"I hope you appreciate our screening. We use a very fine mesh to be certain no ... contaminants pass through. Maybe a little too fine in your case. You must have been assumed to be Muslim. Didn't they question that at LAX?"

"I mentioned Maronite, sir, but the interrogator didn't seem to pick up on it." Jason is so relieved to see Hawk—the head man, no less—that now he even makes light of his malicious Gray Man. "Perhaps he interpreted that as an Islamic sect."

"We know what a Maronite Christian is," Hawk says. "The officer who interviewed you says he was certain you were lying. He said you were defiant."

"Well. He was rather antagonistic."

"He's supposed to be."

"But he also told me he'd never heard of General Hawk."

Werner snickers and draws a sour glance from Hawk. "He has now."

"They sent me to this camp. But it seems to be just for Muslims." He's making conversation to work out his edginess, but Hawk seems to be measuring every word. "Maybe I should have been sent somewhere else."

"Somewhere else," Werner says. "That's where I think you should go after this stunt."

"We do it in their interest," Hawk says. "Separate religions. To observe their faith in company with their own kind." Their own kind? Jason lets that lie. "Of course," Hawk goes on, "anything you observe while you're working with us is subject to our regulations. And enforced by CSIS. The detention system is highly classified."

"The old man who was sent here with me is an American citizen. Maybe an oversight?"

Werner says, "If you Canadians were as vigilant as we are,

you'd have a few more of your own people in cages. Your agency knows about our camps." Jason's afraid to question this, but Noble didn't seem to know much ... "Our man in Ottawa may have had an easier time than you, Currie, but I doubt he will have picked up as much." Werner seems really aggravated, and the cause now breaks on Jason. His mission was compromised from the start. Not being a spy, merely an analyst, it had never occurred to him that his arrival in a detention camp could have been contrived. Now he grasps why he's feeling such hostility.

"I knew almost nothing about the camps, sir. Until they brought me here."

"Camps? Why plural?"

The question is so sharp that Jason chokes on his clumsiness. "Why ... I just assumed there must be another. For non-Muslims. You said 'with their own kind.'"

There is a look between the two officers, probably of mutual distrust. It clears his mind. When the A-D agreed to send a mere analyst on a senior mission, he must have known about the passport, about Egypt. Then Noble cautioned him not to mention his mission; they'd *counted* on a hostile reception, with a chance, however slim, to breach one camp. He recalls Noble—accepting his handshake, wishing him well—he chokes on it. His mind leaps ahead to visualize a hurried return home. Hawk's watching him intently. He just might be smothering a smile.

"Sir, I'm sorry I stumbled into classified territory. I just hadn't been made aware of … it wasn't by design."

"Certainly not by *your* design," Hawk says derisively.

Werner retreats into the background with the air of a man who has said his piece. Hawk goes on in a friendlier tone. "You do come highly recommended. For your Arabic analysis. Then you managed to get yourself arrested at LAX and sent to an off-limits operation. Now we're not sure what we're dealing with."

"Nobody prepped me to handle your screening."

"Really? It didn't occur to you *without prepping* that a command of Arabic and a visit to Egypt might set off an alarm?" Hawk's not quite laughing.

"I was zonked out from flying. I had a friend waiting for me. They told me not to expose myself. It all worked together to throw me in here. I guess I handled it like an amateur."

Hawk pauses after each response and continues to listen, his expression inquiring, *Anything else? That all?* Jason supposes this must be an interrogator's trick to draw out any trailers of information. Werner merely scowls at the excuses, though it's difficult to tell since his default expression is so similar. He's a chunkier man than Hawk and more forbidding, his body-set expressing disapproval. Or maybe scorn. Put-upon by Hawk and bitter over it? Contempt for any outsider who doesn't feel as hyper as an American officer who's privy to the national perils? He seems a forceful man, sure of himself, beyond the reach of doubt, who perhaps would expect to be a general himself at his age, forty-something.

Hawk's more intrigued than disapproving. "Well, either they've sent us a very artless analyst or a fraud." He folds his hands around each other at chest level, a preacher's gesture that signals a change in topic.

Werner says, "Your assignment would have been to work with voice intercepts. You were to take our upgrades home. If we'd kept you." So there's no doubt in his mind.

"I can handle any kind of voice intercepts, Colonel. I get all our tough nuts. Along with bushels of chaff, I suppose you have the same overload here? Lots of juvenile raving? We only get nuggets from about two percent." He wishes then that he hadn't overdone this. Werner's exasperated, but Hawk's expression suggests he's taking this babbling as an evasion.

Werner says. "Even juvenile raving can be useful. It gives us their tendencies."

"That's what my superiors say." He smiles to lighten the remark. "That assumption is what keeps hundreds of us at work."

Werner swears and turns to leave. "I'll be at the helicopter pad, *sir*. When you're finished with this asshole." He strides out the door, not without some dignity.

"You have an interesting style, Currie." Hawk speaks with detachment, but Jason catches the glimmer of mirth, as if he doesn't mind Werner being baited. "You're not creating a good impression on someone you'll have to work with." His watchfulness now dissipates. He becomes almost brusque. He's been working out what kind of person he has before him, he has him pegged; he isn't wasting any more time on appraisal. If he agrees with Werner, Jason may not have to unpack his bags.

"One more thing: what was your cover story?"

"Visiting an old friend."

Hawk's expression heightens to disdain. "Seriously? A questionable passport and a halfhearted cover. And not to reveal that you were seconded to SECOR. Certain to be picked up."

"It all seemed okay to me. But now I see—your screening is at a very different level from ours. I know I have a lot to learn, General. But maybe I can make some contribution. CSIS will be very disappointed if I'm not ... not really made use of. They expect a lot from your man in Ottawa."

Hawk does seem to pay attention to this last second pitch. "You're certainly questionable, but ..." He pauses. "I'll need the name and address of the man you claim to be visiting."

Jason reads off Bil's address from memory. "Sir, if I may: why was I singled out at the airport?" Why were they waiting for him at the ramp?

"You should know the answer. They had a scan of your passport."

"You interrogate *any* Canadian who's been to the Middle East?"

"Certainly. And various other places. And anyone who fits the profile of a Middle Easterner. We have other profiles as well."

"But that must be thousands ..."

"Tens of thousands."

"All treated like me?"

"They matched you with a suspect's name. You weren't cooperative. But when in doubt, yes, we'll hold anyone. We don't allow any more questionable people into this country except in detention."

"Even Canadian citizens?"

He looks Jason over with annoyance. "You know we're holding a couple of hundred Canadians, most of whom your people are glad to be rid of. Now you know what you've escaped. One more thing. CSIS may be a civilian agency, but SECOR is a military service, and the disciplinary code will be quite distinct from what you appear to be used to. You can work out the implications. One of them is that Colonel Werner is your superior officer."

"I'm sure he'll make that quite clear."

"But I want you to report directly to me. Throughout your stay, however brief it may be. My card. Our address in L.A. Nine hundred tomorrow. We have a chopper standing by. We'll drop you at LAX."

# FIVE

"YOU LOOK GREAT!" BIL SAYS, MANAGING NOT TO STARE AT the rumpled clothes and bristling chin. He looks better. That's always been so between them. Bil and his sister Miriam from early days had the kind of presence that draws attention, while Jason was just the neighbor who hung out with them. Now Bil shines as well with the patina of maturity. Confidence radiates from him, a handsome man who owns his place in the world. They cut a woeful contrast as they pass out of the terminal. Jason is limp with relief—free of detention, free of SECORs, and now about to find cover with his old champion.

"So where the hell have you been?"—as they pull away. "All I was told was that I would be contacted. But that was two days ago."

"It's quite a story, Bil. I was arrested by SECOR."

"*Arrested*? You mean—actually *held* by SECOR?" He's startled. The car slows abruptly, almost crawling. He turns from the wheel to stare at Jason.

"Just a foul-up. Just a communication breakdown." Jason's alarmed because Bil's alarmed. His old hero Bil should have found his arrest a sort of caper, maybe even something over which to share a full chortle. He reads a warning in Bil's reaction. "I got an explanation from a SECOR general, no less."

"It's just that … they're very sensitive to security. Where I work."

"You think this would get back to your office?"

"Oh, I'll have to tell them. They might hear it from SECOR. I can't take that chance. Mind you, we work under army intelligence—DIA—who can't stand SECOR. But I'd better mention it. Just in case."

Army intelligence? DIA? Jason smothers his uneasiness. He goes on carefully. "It's nothing at all, Bil. Just an old friend of yours who happened to be mishandled by SECOR."

"Let's hope it won't cause me … any problems." There's a disconnect between them.

Jason had been waiting in the terminal long enough to text a coded report to Noble, covering his detention and describing the camp. As he worked it out, half his attention was fretting over how much of it to share with Bil—none at all, if he hearkened to Hawk's warning. But he hungered to unload his experience, not just to be free of it but to hear whether

Bil (and Bil's world) have intuited the nature of America's hidden campsites. Could they really be that secret, or did people just avoid recognizing them? But now, Bil seems so uptight—better not to add any more doubt.

"So you've been seconded to some local agency?" Changing the subject, a relief for both of them.

"They wouldn't give me leave, but they did give me an assignment here in L.A."

"Wouldn't give you leave?"

"To get over the divorce."

"Right. Your divorce." He mouths that too evenly. Bil was married and later divorced, years past, but without any agonizing in his e-mails.

"I just need to rub out what led up to it. You got over your own in good time?"

"That's all it takes, just time." Then a deliberate pause.

Maybe Bil went through enough, then just sucked it in and got on with his world. Maybe he doesn't want to hear any whimpering, even from an old friend. Maybe he discovered that sympathy delays recovery. "So I thought it was a great chance to visit and share what's gone on in our lives. Ten years."

"I've been looking forward to it. Why not bring me up to date on your family?"

North Toronto was once a white and mostly Protestant enclave, but by the time the Curries and the Marons moved in, it had become international. Another Lebanese family wasn't so alien. Like Jason, Bil (his name Nabil was almost never used between them, though his mother always called him that) had been born in Canada to parents who were refugees from the endless Lebanese conflicts. They had then prospered in their adopted country. The parents all spoke Arabic, laboring in English in early days, the Curries more than the Marons, so that Jason became fully fluent in his parents' tongue.

The two boys, a year apart, became friends, united by non-conformance with the local culture. All kids played hockey; they were late starters so not as skilled as their age group and therefore passed over. Sunday was for worship at the local churches; their families were Maronite Christians separated from their church. The boys spent most of their time together and assimilated slowly.

Children of immigrants suffer the normal alienation of child from parents, but complicated further by their dislocation from the parental culture. Bil managed this gracefully; Jason picked his way painfully. Bil took up basketball and excelled; Jason was inconsistent and sidelined. Bil's friendly ways and easy smile allowed him to be accepted in time by the scions of old North Toronto, while Jason's artless manner left him on the perimeter. He learned how to survive random hassling, but when it got serious, Bil stepped in beside him.

Miriam was a couple of years younger than Jason. Young men could find their way into the folkways of the adopted country, even with parental misgivings, but young women only under tight supervision. Jason sometimes heard harsh words between Miriam and her mother, although to him she seemed far more restrained than most young women.

Bil and he went off to university and subsequent careers, Bil's in California. But they e-mailed each other at length several times a year. They never became aloof—they spoke to each other over time and distance as openly as ever. They kept their friendship alive. He sought Bil's advice sometimes, though Bil never seemed to need his.

Now they work hesitantly to resurrect their past as they head for Bil's home. Jason has seen pictures of the house, in some municipality adjacent to Santa Barbara, where Bil works.

"What is it you do there, Bil?"

"Right now it's related to the Internet." Interesting; Jason thought he was in electronic research on a university campus. "The department is off theoretical research. Temporarily." He pauses. "We have a contract with the Defense Department."

"Working for the Pentagon?"

"Not really. It's a kind of joint venture—major corporations and research institutes. Very high profile. They do documentaries on us. We're corporate leaders."

The reference to the Pentagon has annoyed him, like a breach of etiquette. Jason then compounds his error. "I didn't think they allowed foreigners in defense work anymore."

"Actually, I'm an American now. I took out citizenship a while ago."

Jason chokes off any response, but his silence may seem like an accusation; Bil stiffens slightly.

"I'm sorry, Bil. I'm tired and cranky and everything hits me the wrong way. I promise to be normal in the morning."

After an awkward moment, Bil says, "It never used to matter. Being Canadian. Lots of Canadians live here, tens of thousands. Of course, not many coming nowadays. Lately, it's become ... touchy. To be an alien."

"Touchy?"

"Especially with Middle Eastern ancestry."

"I knew they were sensitive to Muslims from the Mideast. But you're Christian and born in Canada."

"Nowadays Canada is just another foreign country."

"But would they even know? If you're a citizen or not? I mean—they gave you the appointment knowing you were Canadian."

Bil glances at him, irritated. "You don't understand how much things have changed down here. They're almost paranoid."

"I've already seen more ... sensitivity to Muslims."

"You must have heard about the church burnings? One right here in California."

"We heard enough about it."

"Americans were more than angry. They were ready to kill Muslims. Some did get lynched. None here. I felt just as mad about it as any American. I thought it was time to—to stand beside them. I didn't want to be an alien, an outsider. People here got to be a little skeptical about Canadians. We didn't seem to be onside about Islam."

The church riots had been heavily covered in Canada. Muslims there had also been targeted by the hysterical fringe. However, most Canadians connected Muslim anger to the American wars in Islamic countries, so the response was short-lived. "The story we got was that a church in Mississippi burned the Koran. Heaps of them."

"Well, Muslims retaliated by burning more than a heap of Bibles. They burned the churches with them."

"Bad time for you, with a Lebanese background?"

"I felt the looks coming my way. Management knew the difference between a Maronite and a Muslim but some of my colleagues were pretty frosty."

"Becoming an American, did it help?"

"With most people. Some still look at me as a foreigner with friends on the other side."

Jason breaks out a forced smile. "But that was years ago."

"It changed everything."

"Lots of Americans live in Canada. People who love America but don't much like what's happening."

"Well, they don't all feel that way. The president and the party are actually quite popular. They're very moral people, and Americans seem to be looking for that."

Jason doesn't want to comment. He's shelved his hope to share his divorce trauma. Maybe tomorrow. He chides himself for being so preoccupied with his own needs that he may have alienated his old friend, his schoolmate.

That brings on a flash of Bil on the basketball court. It's a pickup game. Jason's playing guard. He's run over by a taller, heavier attacker, and they square off, Jason willing but overmatched. Before the shoving can escalate, Bil pushes between them, hands to the chest of the bully, who backs off sullenly. Later, Bil and Jason walk home side by side. Jason can feel now the same flush of comradeship he felt that day. "Still shoot hoops?"

That brightens Bil. "Every day. We have a gym in-house."

"So that's how you've kept in shape." They're both more at ease now.

They pass through miles of a suburb with walled enclaves, no sidewalks, no one walking, neighborhoods designed to shelter the meritorious from the undeserving. Jason knows of Santa Barbara for its character, its waterfront, and its wealth. In this sterile quarter, only the latter is on offer.

"You haven't mentioned Miriam." Jason lost track of her but knows she settled here somewhere after marrying in Canada and then, like Bil, divorcing in California. "She live around here?"

Driving slowly now, they pass a little park, and Bil swings into the parking area. "Let's walk for a bit before we get to the house." He leads them down a graveled path. Jason waits patiently. "I can't talk about Miriam in the house. She caused a problem for me. She's on the Nonconformist List—the NCL."

"Miriam? How? Why?"

"I know it will sound innocent to you, coming from Canada, but it doesn't take much here. Not nowadays. She's living in Mexico, in Guadalajara, with a man named Manwaring. Professor Brendan Manwaring. He's there because he'd be in detention if he came back here."

Jason's heard a little of Manwaring. He's on a CSIS watch list as a potential refugee claimant. If he does cross the border, CSIS would ask that he be denied entry. If he got into Canada, he would then become another irritant between the two countries. "You say it doesn't take much. Just what does qualify for detention?"

"He accused the administration of invading Arab states that weren't attacking us. Also to indulge the Party's fundamentalist supporters, who want the Holy Land to be taken over entirely by Jews. He referred to the cabinet—seriously—as 'pious warmongers.'"

"That's considered serious enough for detention?"

"There's more. Miriam was active herself. Not enough to be detained. But it's a very short step from being antiwar to soft on terrorism. I'd be surprised if DIA doesn't have a file on her."

"*Why would they?*"

Bil stops and stares at him. "You don't understand. She's with Manwaring. He's a traitor so far as DIA is concerned."

"You said *you* were in trouble."

"Jason, please don't misunderstand me. I know how close you and Miriam were. We were a tight little group, weren't we? There was some wishful thinking in the family that you and she might get married."

A blast of icy regret sweeps through Jason, so fiercely that he stumbles. It carries him back to a fork in the road that he couldn't have been aware of at the time, one way leading into the Maron family with Miriam, the other, in time, to Ramona and tawdry betrayal.

"She never said anything to me." Bil watches Jason closely. "But I know Mom believed you were—well, more than friends …"

Jason's not sure what to say. He has assumed for ten years that his intimacy with Miriam was their well-kept secret. How to respond to a brother whose friendship would probably have been forfeited had he known at the time? He's dismayed over the mother's disappointment in him. In her daughter.

"I didn't mean to pry," Bil says. He sounds as uneasy as Jason feels.

"It only happened once. I felt … ashamed. Guilty. Because she was your sister. I had no idea she told your mom."

Bil's tone is more sympathetic than reproaching. "Mom just guessed. It's okay, Jason. It was long ago. We're all adults now. I'm not accusing you."

"She behaved … as if she'd forgotten it. So we went on as before."

"I understand. It's *okay*." The silence between them builds as their mutual past is revised. It takes some moments for stirred-up memories to begin settling into new patterns.

Jason says, "You brought me here to tell me this. Your house is bugged then?"

"All the senior staff probably are."

"By the people where you work?"

"By army intelligence. We're always under scrutiny. We're even forbidden to take holidays outside the country, to attend foreign seminars. But I wanted to explain about her." Jason follows Bil with only half of his attention, still dwelling on Miriam.

"So even in your own house—"

"Maybe even in my car. They know I don't share her ideas, but my work is highly classified."

"If you're under suspicion and Miriam's on that list, maybe it's time you both came back to Canada."

"Jason, I love my job. At least I did until I was replaced as head of research. My own work's been credited to my successor." Spoken with the bitterness of non-recognition, the vilest affront to a researcher.

"Why was that?"

"Probably because of Miriam."

"So you can't even get in touch with her?"

"One more contact with my sister would get me under fulltime surveillance. If I'm not there already." Jason's disapproval hangs in the silence between them. "I love my sister! I'm sick over this."

"But you'd rather get along with the people you work with.

That's your priority?"

"They're all patriots. They're dedicated to this country."

Jason feels the gap between them widening, so he keeps quiet. But he can't imagine the woman he remembers changing as much as Bil has.

Driving to his home, Bil goes on, without much conviction, selling his position. "You have to understand. We've all had to learn how to get along with this administration. It's not so bad if you just make up your mind. Forget about politics and get on with your work. You can't believe the resources they give us—virtually unlimited. You can make a good life here, you can do research or teach, you can submerge yourself in your work, you can be very successful. But you can't cross the administration."

NOW IN BIL'S HOUSE, THEY SHARE A BOTTLE OF WINE AND some hesitant memories. It's not a comfortable time. Jason finds himself listening to his own cautious words like an actor trying on a new role.

As Jason's eyes wander the room, they light on a picture of Miriam, with Bil and Jason at either shoulder, taken at the family cottage. He picks it up and studies it. He meets Bil's eyes: he looks stricken. He must see Jason's concern for Miriam as a rebuke. Jason puts the picture down without comment and smiles reassuringly. He's overcome by sympathy for his friend, trapped between dedication to his work and guilt for breaching his family loyalty, in an environment suddenly turned from welcoming to hostile.

"It's getting pretty late, Jason. You must be zonked." Bil

begins clearing up. As Jason helps, he finds another picture. It's a professional likeness of Anita Skye, the Vice President of the United States. Bil watches him as he reads the handwritten inscription: *With gratitude for your efforts. We owe our victory to volunteers like yourself.* Jason, whose political sophistication is so basic that he has to rely on the media to differentiate right from left, understands her to be arch conservative, only because more liberal Canadian media sometimes call her 'the Screeching Eagle' in recognition of her high-pitched diatribes. She's condemned Canada's sometime independence from American policies, especially its military crusades.

"We were all expected to pitch in," Bil says. "Everyone at work. I only stuffed envelopes."

"I heard she's not a great fan of Canada."

"She hates Canada. I mean, that's her politics." But his look warns Jason. "A lot of Americans think Canada should be fighting with us."

Jason only nods. They chat for a few more moments, skirting carefully around anything sensitive. When their eyes meet, Jason reads more than discomfort in Bil: he's scared.

For a sleepless while, Jason lies visualizing his lifelong friend and trying to reconcile him with this other Bil. Ever since hearing of Jason's coming visit, he must have been worried about how they could manage their private exchanges without being monitored. The little park was the solution, but it must have been very hard for Bil to expose himself to his old follower. When he did open up, Jason saw the familiar Bil once more, although without the confidence Jason had always envied. In this house he was again a stranger.

When he does sleep, he dreams. He struggles to pull that single blanket around his bare shoulders. A cold breeze is sifting through the netting, carrying the troubled moans of other inmates. The constant white light in the otherwise blackened desert mocks his attempts to shut down. He wakes up.

Now he tries to knit his thoughts together, but they refuse to gel into any useful pattern. Having come here to seek reassurance, he has found only uncertainty. America has changed; California has changed, even its climate. Bil has changed. Would Miriam be as much a stranger now as her brother? That thought is even more unsettling. He concentrates on recalling her as she was at about twenty, slim and sensual, when she had changed in his own eyes from near sister to potential lover. He falls asleep finally, soothed by the warmth of that image.

Jason borrows Bil's car to drive to L.A. and SECOR so they go together to Bil's workplace. The whole property is fenced, barbwire topping and all, within grounds the size of a golf course, with an entry post and a barrier manned by a pair of soldiers, the buildings hundreds of yards beyond. The guards raise their weapons to signal a stop. They block the car while a sergeant comes out of the security post.

"What's this place called, Bil?"

"California Research Laboratories. We're a cutting-edge

facility. You might have heard of us in Canada. We work with some of your agencies."

Jason knows of the company. Apart from research, they supervise the manufacture of advanced surveillance hardware, widely used in the States and now sought-after by CSIS.

"Your friend can't go in, sir," the sergeant says. "I'll call for transport for you." So Bil and Jason wait beside the car while a vehicle like an oversized golf cart ambles out from the distance.

"Very solid security," Jason says to bridge the silence.

"It *is* a top-secret facility, and we're at war."

"I'm finding a lot of things are top-secret in this country."

"Careful, Jason. I've already notified Security of your visit. You'll probably be interviewed shortly, maybe even today. Please be cautious with them."

"Bil, did I say anything in the house …?"

"I don't think so."

"I'll be more careful. When I get back tonight."

"Look, I'm sorry I haven't given you much of a welcome. Let's go out for dinner and let down our hair tonight."

Jason nods happily. "That's more what I was hoping for." Bil pats him on the shoulder as he leaves. They part like old friends.

As he drives in the slow lane, Jason resurrects his carefully hoarded secret. Miriam had asked him to squire her to a neighborhood party, where they stayed late and drank much, with Bil then away at college. They were both very high. They took the usual shortcut along the lane and into the Marons' backyard. When she waited at the door for a goodnight kiss, he was helpless. At least, that's how he preferred to think of it next day and ever since. They thrashed about on the grass locked in a coital trance. He had barely enough presence of mind to pull away at the instant of climax, terrified to impregnate her.

He didn't see her for a couple of days. Meanwhile he was wretched with remorse. She was Bil's sister—their parents were all close friends—she was untouchable. How would Bil react? Through the next day, he squirmed with anxiety. When he went to the Maron house at last, he had to work at composing himself as he stood hesitating over the doorbell.

She answered it and broke into a smile. He waited for some word to tell him where he stood—perhaps she had told her mother? He smiles now at his dread of parental fury. In fact, she said nothing out of the usual patter, seemed unchanged, acted like a sister—well, a cousin—warm, unchallenging. He wondered if she blamed herself. Perhaps was ashamed to bring it up.

That night was over ten years ago but the euphoria of the moment now wells up, pungent with the smell of dewy grass and feverish skin. He has always felt guilty when he allowed himself to remember that night. Bil's outing them, without condemnation, seems to have exorcised the guilt. He parades those heady moments, in the darkness of the Maron garden, several times through the lens of his memory, feeling only pleasure. Other moments with Miriam open now like links on a screen. How unspoiled those times! How innocent compared to his sordid history with Ramona. He hasn't seen Miriam since her wedding day, but now he longs to. In his mind she's as he saw her that day, her eyes speaking directly to his own.

Bil's a different person. Maybe not Miriam. He feels a flush of optimism. Thoughts of her flood his mind like fresh air, blowing away Ramona's ghost. Miriam can be the answer; she can restore him. If he can find her.

SECOR? If she's with Manwaring—that thought pauses him—SECOR can find Manwaring. There has to be a file on him; they must know everything about an activist.

Bil has to be protected. No mention of Manwaring or Miriam in that house. He becomes quite cheered up as this fantasy falls into place. Find a way to reach her, shielding Bil meanwhile. All it will take is a little cooperation from SECOR, where he's now headed. He speeds up.

A bottleneck ahead turns out to be a convoy of army vehicles grinding down the right-hand lane, with motorcycle outriders guiding traffic to merge left and ease by. As he lingers in the converging queue, he turns on the radio. "… our correspondent aboard the aircraft carrier …" catches his attention. A disjointed report from one of the war zones follows. At its conclusion, he finds out its origin. "That was a special report from the landing area in Sudan. We take you now to ..."

Sudan! *Another* front? American forces are already tied down in three Middle East campaigns, none flourishing, and are on watch against threats from still other quarters. Sudan is in a chronic state of confrontation with its own current and former peoples, in the west and south, Arabic against black Muslim, Muslim against Christian and animist. He creeps into the passing lane as he puzzles over the reasons for one more campaign. His eyes meet those of the driver merging beside him, who signals him with a triumphant fist pump, no doubt a reaction to the same news, and then a sour look as Jason fails to respond.

# SEVEN

"CANADIAN HOURS?" AFTER A METICULOUS CHECK AGAINST his passport at an entry secured by armed SECORs, Jason is sent directly into Hawk's office.

"Held up by your army, sir. They seem to be everywhere. Is there a major base?"

"They have smaller bases everywhere now. The old army posts are mainly used for draftees, teaching them to polish their boots and hate their sergeants. Graduate training is all about urban guerillas. You might see exercises right here in L.A. They use rundown neighborhoods to simulate war zones."

"And not to intimidate any local dissidents?" With a smile.

"Only those that need intimidating." Hawk's sharp tone matches the disapproval in his face. "I suppose that kind of comment is considered quite discerning in Ottawa. But you'll find that your co-workers here won't appreciate it." Jason's not just chastened; he's kicking himself for the flip remark. Getting off to a solid start with Hawk is a priority.

"Your assignment is timely. You've heard the war news? Our forces have landed in the Sudan. Paratroops followed up by landings from the Red Sea. After a missile attack on Khartoum. Bombardment of Port Sudan." Happily, Hawk's pique only lasts a few seconds and now he seems a little high, like a football fan after a breakout play.

"I thought the military had their hands full already, sir. Why Sudan?"

"Officially, the Sudanese community here has been infiltrated by terrorists from the home country. They're inciting their people against us. Also against our allies, like Canada. Unofficially, Sudan's supplying weapons and volunteers to the insurgents in Somalia and Yemen." He watches Jason in his intent way. "You don't seem very impressed. Thousands of Sudanese immigrants here will have to be vetted."

Jason is trying to stretch his memory around an image of the Sudan. "It's a huge country—can it really be occupied?"

"Course not. Not with all our other commitments. A secure base is probably all we want. They'll use drones and aircraft to keep the countryside under control. Never mind the strategy. We can expect a flood of new data. We need to isolate their contacts here. For detention. It's a good opportunity for you to see how we coordinate a military campaign with a sweep for collaborators."

"Collaborators, sir?" Jason has a flash of caged Muslims in the desert. "Aren't we looking for terrorists? Lots of people from the Sudan might have mixed feelings about America but no thought of terrorism."

"Damn it, Currie! We're now at war with these people. Do they teach you anything up there besides polite consideration? If a lot of the Sudanese here are cheering for the home team, then we want a good sample of them in detention. The rest will then reconsider their attitudes."

"Yes, sir. Just feeling out the parameters. We're not concerned that some of them will become more resentful?"

"We don't care if they resent us. Just so long as they fear us, and so long as we know what they're up to. That's what you'll be working on. I'll get Sid Margate in here—your section head. Now listen. You'll be working under Sid, but I expect to see you in here often enough that I know what you're picking up. And what you're thinking. You report to me."

"How often?"

"Every day for now. One more word: don't parade your experience in that camp. I told you, *everything* about the camps is classified." He slows down to a word-for-word command: "Don't discuss it with anyone."

Margate is a black man with a wrestler's belly and matching neck. He's not in uniform like Hawk, just casual clothes with an open collar. Jason receives a meaty handshake.

"This is a great opportunity, Sid. You people wrote the book on security."

"Nice to hear that someone appreciates us. Some people in our own country think we have too much security."

"We've got some of the same people in Canada. But there wouldn't be so many here?"

"Enough to be a pain. It was bad enough even when I was in private security."

"That's how you came to be here?"

"Fireproofing private companies. Twenty years. Mind you, in those days I didn't have to put up with temperamental analysts. You temperamental?"

"Insensitive. No feelings at all."

"Fine. We should get along."

"What sort of resources do you have?"

"My section's Middle Eastern. Several hundred analysts, fluent in Arabic and Farsi mainly. Some Pashto, Dari, Urdu. Still nowhere near enough."

"You must have lots of ethnics to recruit from in California."

"And lots to watch. Arab Americans especially. There are over three million Arabic speakers in the United States. Perhaps half a million in this state. Our targets are mostly among them."

"Then why the shortage?"

"Big swaths have no security clearance."

"Out of half a million?"

"They're practically all Muslims."

"All Muslims are off-limits as analysts?"

"We need some but we use a fine screen. Lots of ethnics pass through but not so many Arabs." He suddenly stops and squints at Jason. "You're not a Muslim?"

"Christian. At least my parents were."

"An Arabic-speaking Christian. And a Canadian. Canadians and Americans, we all have the same values. You we can trust."

Jason's not sure whether Hawk agrees as he gives them a curt wave of dismissal.

Margate shepherds Jason around the giant building, rattling off a blizzard of comments. "We draw intercepts by the million here. From the print media, from the Internet, from taps on the chokepoints of all communication traffic. Even undersea cables. Then all public data, down to scientific papers, all screened. Then voice downloads—all the switching points of fiber optic networks, satellites, radio. Video we get from the Net, especially social networks, from surveillance cameras, including satellites and UAVs, from telecasts. We have libraries of film taken from drones. This is where the data gets sifted."

"To match up with your keywords."

"Also for facial recognition. Ours is pretty sophisticated. The system coughs up matches with well over ninety percent accuracy. The keywords are so numerous the lists are called dictionaries—names, telephone numbers, addresses, IP designations, companies, places, and then anything else the

Corps thinks is hot."

"Sounds like thousands of keywords."

"Easily. Updated continuously. Like a swatch of Sudanese data just went in. What spews out is the feedstock for human analysts like you."

"My work has mostly been with voice intercepts."

"That's where we'll put you to work."

Sid leads him through layer after layer of intelligence activity, each segment working with its specialized tools to peel the covering from opaque data, to get at the core, to find the meaning among the seas of random bits.

"Just some of our computers—we have acres of them … Translating machines in this quarter … This section clears up dumb translations, going back to the original source … That area's soundproofed so the code-breakers won't be disturbed … and here are the analysts, the brains of the Corps, who make sense of it all. They can call up all the data feeds along with humint input." His comments are terse, but Jason catches sidelong glances to judge whether he's grasping the scale and the intricacy of the operation.

Jason starts the lengthy tour assuming he knows what to expect: another CSIS, but many times larger. But this is no multiple of CSIS. Doors open onto stadium-sized chambers where hundreds of men and women—white, black, brown, Asian—hunch over computer screens, with masses of bulky machines hiding the walls, a hum and whir of intense activity over all. His image of Gray Men dissolves. The human mix here reminds him more of multicultural Canada. The next room is the same, and the next. Up one floor, and the parade of people and machines continues. Lines of listeners, massive earphones in place, pods of scanners and printers spewing documentation by the truckload, one whole section packed with floor-to-ceiling rows of massive computers, lights blinking, and drives whirring, like a Hollywood set for space travel.

Jason is more than impressed; he's awed. By the wealth of resources, by the way in which they've been organized, and especially by the determination behind it all. Clearly, America will pay whatever it takes to protect herself. Few Canadians would say they're proud of CSIS; it simply does a necessary job. Here, he senses dedication, like that which inspired NASA in its early days. Not every door is open, however. Quite a few times he's guided past closed entries: when he asks what they hold, Sid waves off his query. Another time: "No entry to that floor," as their elevator ascends.

"Who can go there?" Jason ventures.

"Hawk." So there are limits to what CSIS can know of this colossal spying venture or even what its own workers can be told.

Finally, Sid leads him into his office, opening the door, like all the other closed doors, by placing his hand on a palm reader. "Coming from CSIS," he says, a little archly, "you won't be too impressed with it all."

"I'm afraid I am, Sid. CSIS is solid minor league. But this

is the majors."

"Thanks. And this is only one operation. We have lots of others like it. Hawk said I'm to give you access to the secure phone here in my office. To report in private to CSIS."

"Very decent of you."

"Don't get carried away thanking us. We insisted on a secure line for our own man in Ottawa. You're familiar with SCIP[5] technology? So you set it up with your opposite number and you can't be tapped, right?"

"In fact, I'm overdue. May I?"

"Be my guest."

Jason sets up a call to Noble. Noble's acknowledgement at LAX only said, "Call me on a secure line."

"These camps, Jason. I don't know how you got in, but what you think you saw is causing indigestion in the corner office."

"I got in because I was told to behave like a tourist with a passport stamp from the Middle East. The A-D set me up. You set me up. I might never have gotten out. What if Hawk didn't give a damn whether I showed up or not?"

The pseudo-anger is wasted on Noble. "Well, it worked," he says softly. "But now we know too much."

---

5   SCIP: Secure Communications Interoperability Protocol. One of the secure phone systems used by governments and military. Matching equipment is necessary for both parties.

"Why's the A-D so pissed-off?"

"Because it's the first solid bit we've had that SECOR's detaining numbers of American citizens. Big numbers. You also implied they were using torture. Good thing you didn't see any."

"Only because I was rescued just in time. A Muslim I met knew about the camps. So they must be widely known. Maybe *I* was surprised, but I'm just an analyst. The A-D couldn't have been surprised. SECOR told me CSIS knew about the camps."

"There've been stories …" Noble's near-whisper drifted off without an answer. "But when we've inquired through channels … they were … evasive. Some Middle Eastern insurgents, a few domestic terrorists. Now, why is a friendly ally asking these questions? Not much to give the Minister."

"You knew what I was getting into, didn't you?"

"I remind you, you *asked* for this assignment. Begged for it. As a favour. To run away from your divorce."

"So you and the A-D decided to let me blunder into that camp—"

"You're missing the point. Do you really think we would tell an American agency that we had information that contradicts their narrative? The Americans already look on us as limp-wristed. We can't tell them we'd rather believe a bunch of Arabs than their State Department."

"So now we know the truth."

"And that's what's giving the A-D heartburn. Canada is a

signatory to the Human Rights Convention. We take our obligations seriously. If the United States is violating the Convention, we're supposed to make an issue of it."

The light finally breaks on Jason. "The A-D's not concerned with what he always knew. He doesn't like having to tell the Minister that it's much worse. That there's not a few Americans in the camps—there are thousands."

"That's exactly the problem you've caused."

"So don't tell him. I hear we don't tell him lots of stuff."

"We have a statutory duty to report to the Minister."

"You're not telling me to forget what I saw, are you?"

"I'm reminding you that you signed an oath. You're forbidden to reveal anything whatsoever about your work. Forever. The penalty for disclosure is imprisonment."

"So you are telling me to forget."

"Jason, in our business, information is the coin of the realm. Yours is especially negotiable. We just have to wait to cash it in. It's too sensitive right now." Jason, a little sulky, doesn't respond, so Noble amplifies, "The administration has us in the penalty box just now, because too many Americans are emigrating to Canada. They imply we're giving shelter to an expatriate opposition. If we had to admit American Muslims as legitimate refugees, we could have thousands—tens of thousands." There's a pause as the implications to Ottawa multiply in step with the numbers. "So I'm telling you to *keep very quiet!*"

He hisses this at Jason, clearly savoring the opportunity, the climactic moment for which the call was framed. No wonder Hawk had also cautioned him back in the desert camp. He knew that CSIS was no threat as long as Jason was silenced. When he seemed sometimes to be laughing at Jason, he really *was* laughing at him.

"I'm waiting for your acknowledgement."

"I understand I'm not to talk about thousands of Muslims in wire cages. Except to CSIS, who aren't going to talk about them either."

"At times you have a distinctive touch, Jason. That's why the A-D thought you had the precise qualifications to break into that camp."

"Blind ignorance?"

Noble hangs up.

Margate introduces Jason to his second-in-command. "Bear. Archie Bear." He's a surprisingly young man who has a jaw-stretching, open-mouthed grin, almost like a clown. He radiates friendliness, so Jason can't help twitting, "Really? With a momma bear and a baby bear at home?"

"One and two."

"Archie, Currie's expertise is colloquial Arabic. We're told he's exceptional. So he'll work with you on highlighted voice downloads—the tough ones." He turns to Jason with a wicked grin. "If he's not exceptional, you should know pretty quick. He's cleared for everything in Analysis. Not the Sealed Sectors, of course."

Jason feels himself examined by many pairs of eyes as he's led to Archie's corner. The two settle down to scanning intercepts of Sudanese Americans, Jason with growing interest as he sloughs off his pique and morphs into his intelligence persona. The game pulls him in. America's at war and this prodigious machine is on the front line. He's finally getting his teeth into that red meat.

Archie surprises him. Jason gradually recognizes that this rather innocent-seeming and youthful analyst has a ready eye for any kind of dissimulation. He scans written or recorded words at warp speed but picks out faint leads as if they were stop signs. He reminds Jason of a hound in full flight when jerked off-trail by a hot scent. Jason speeds up to carry his share.

In late afternoon, Sid Margate comes by. "So how good is he, Archie?"

"Razor-sharp."

"Good, then you can keep him. We've arranged accommodation just down the road."

"No need, I'm staying with my friend. I have his car."

"Hawk says it's not on. We may want you at any hour. On your way out, Archie will set you up for your SECOR necklace, Class Three. They can be picked up by the sensors in the cameras."

"Class Three?"

"Class One: highest ranks, like the president. Like Hawk. Class Two: other officers, like Werner. Class Three: analysts like us. Class Four: other ranks. The filtering depends on the location of the camera and the Security Index level."

"I knew something of the cameras, but I didn't realize the sensors were universal. So you can sometimes identify the persons on camera?"

"If they're wearing a necklace. Even if they're carrying an Identity Card with a chip. Once the Identity Cards become compulsory."

"Is that really imminent? Compulsory identification?"

Margate's disdainful. "Why not? They've been doing something like it in Europe for a hundred years. Once we get it past the courts."

Archie volunteers to follow him to Bil's house. Driving there, with the window open, the welcome breeze is heavily tinged with the smell of smoke and once or twice a flush of orange on a distant ridge identifies its source. A convoy of military transports passes in the opposite lanes. Traffic is backed up behind them.

He knows it will be easier for both Bil—and himself—to abort his visit. They can't talk about anything that matters in the house, maybe not even in the car, and there's sure to be tension over Miriam—Bil can't discuss her without anger or guilt, and Jason can't leave her be. But he doesn't feel comfortable. Another alienation from someone who had been very close.

As he gets out of the car and starts for the house with reluctant steps, Bil comes out to meet him. "Bil—I'm sorry.

SECOR insists on me staying close by."

Bil doesn't seem surprised. "I was hoping you'd have a short stay and a quick exit. Believe me, the States is no place for Canadians just now. I always thought it was SECOR, your assignment. Well, we both know it's better if you don't stay with me." He manages a smile, but one full of pain. "We've come a long way to end up on opposite sides of the same street."

Jason could shed some tears if he let himself go. Instead he covers up by giving Bil a solid hug. "I promise to e-mail you every six months or so. Same as always." He steps away. "Think about coming home to us, Bil."

"Not now." As he turns away, Bil has one last word. "*Watch your step, for god's sake.*"

There's nothing further to say. As he and Archie drive away, he looks back over his shoulder at a receding Bil, gazing after them from the verge. Jason came to California hoping that sharing his misery with Bil would make it easier. Now he should feel worse off, but oddly, he's less conflicted. Just sad.

# EIGHT

JASON'S SMALL HOTEL IS WITHIN WALKING DISTANCE OF THE SECOR Station. Leaving early and returning late, he escapes the baking hours between in the air-conditioned tower. He has always remembered California as Mediterranean—sucking energy from a tireless sun, a network of valleys and deserts patched between the Sierra Nevada and the Pacific. A land of creation and consumption, as full of prospect as a newborn. Now, under a colorless sky, weighted with tendrils of smoke, it's just cheerless.

Approaching the tower he nearly always meets uniformed SECORs, sometimes en masse, arriving or departing, carloads of them, more in the lobby. The parade of gray uniforms fits with the weather, dispiriting, like a Canadian winter awaiting the radiance of fresh snow.

The office atmosphere picks him up. It's buzzing; it's upbeat. Nearly everyone seems absorbed by their work—Americans of every hyphenation, even some Canadian-Americans, men and women (but far more men), Protestants and Catholics and Jews, some Hindus and Buddhists, though very few Muslims. There's a heartening sense that they're doing something vital. He never hears, "Why are we doing this?" These people seem to waste little energy over *why*. Their concern is just *how*, how to find the shortest route to the target, and they're very good at working that out. Jason finds himself uplifted by the can-do attitude. He begins to enjoy his work more than he had at CSIS.

There's every kind of personality among them: zealots, who purr with pleasure at their work; engineering minds, fascinated by the mechanics of intelligence foraging; chess players, challenged to outmaneuver their terrorist adversaries; the somber; the clowns. There are a few don't-cares and those to whom it's just-a-job, but far more of the committed.

SECOR staff is bound by military code. There are ranks and a hierarchy, although in practice this group behaves like a group of civilians. While everybody owns a dress uniform for public duty or ceremony, they do their work in casual clothes. Except Werner, regular army, who always looks and behaves like a soldier. He spends a good deal of time with Sid and hardly any with Jason, which is a relief. Jason suspects the colonel, uniformed as for parade, despises an atmosphere like the plain-clothes division of an urban police department.

Werner's assignment is to keep his superiors informed on SECOR's work while nominally reporting to Hawk. An institutional spy. It's a miserable role and perhaps explains why he often seems out of temper. Maybe also why Hawk's attitude toward him is ambivalent.

"Werner always seems to be uptight."

"Maybe he has reason to be," Archie says. "Colonel Werner comes from a military family. His father taught at West Point. The family had generals in every war. His son is at West Point right now. So he's not always comfortable working under Hawk."

"Hawk doesn't come from a line of generals?"

Archie breaks into his wide smile. "No way! He's a lawyer."

"Then how …?"

"Appointed by the White House."

The testy relationship snaps into focus. "How could a lawyer get to be a general at one bound? No wonder Werner thinks he's been outflanked."

"Not only because of the rank." Archie lowers his voice. "His job here's a come-down. It shows he's not in the loop at the Pentagon. He's uncomfortable working for SECOR. Any of the military are."

"Because people like Hawk get jumped up to general?"

"SECOR is a security agency, not really army. Most of the leadership is civilian. Lawyers, law-enforcement pros. The top dogs are all political appointees."

"Werner is uptight because SECOR is so politicized?"

"Since George Washington, the army has been drilled to stay out of politics. SECOR is soaked in politics. They distrust us. And they don't like us having military uniforms and ranks."

Finding Archie in a discursive mood, Jason tries for more. "Archie, Sid led me past several departments and even one floor that was secret. What else is going on here? Are you permitted to go into these places?"

Archie holds his hands before his chest in full stop mode. He's alarmed. The easy smile disappears and his voice drops to conspiratorial level. "Hold on, Jason. Those are the 'Sealed Sectors' and they're no business of ours."

"Sealed why?"

"They're top secret agencies. We don't even know their names. They're just 'Sealed Sectors.' They're so secure only the people who work there can enter. And their numbers are limited. I don't who they are. Neither does anyone else around here. Hawk can enter any of those sectors. Not Sid. Not even Werner. Definitely not you and I."

"So what do they do there?"

"Some people say there are Sectors for regions—Europe, Mexico, and so on, maybe Canada. We don't really know. Others say they're counterintelligence. All I know is that we're not supposed to know anything. So don't ask again. And don't ask anyone else."

SECOR runs a national police force, in effect, superimposed over local forces, and it's difficult to pass a day in Los

Angeles without coming across some of their uniforms, sometimes in bunches. Even in his hotel. One evening he is just walking in when a squad of the Gray Horde bursts out of the elevator and frog-marches a prisoner across the lobby. He wears a white dress shirt open at the collar. He might be a businessman who has finished his day, doffed his tie, and poured his cocktail, just as the SECORs strike. He looks both confused and terrified. He gapes around at the few people in the lobby, perhaps in humiliation, perhaps hoping for support in some quarter, while those who return the stare may wonder who might be next. Jason, just through the entrance door, steadies himself with one hand on the jamb as the group brushes by him, meeting the eyes of the prisoner at intimate range, reading their fear, and their appeal. He half turns to see the procession bundled into an official car, the suspect flanked by two officers in the back. When he turns back to the lobby, everyone is avoiding eye contact with anyone else.

Jason's shocked to witness this crude incident, both the act and the withdrawal of the bystanders. Though he's in awe of SECOR's potency, yielding his approval the way a child defers to the dominance of a parent, this raw brutality doesn't fit his sense of America, especially when he sees the other witnesses fading into the background, unchallenging, uninvolved. He's taken back to the camp and its pathetic thousands; do people want to know?

Archie and he grow their confidence in each other as they work. Jason sees him as a total technocrat, interested only in finding what's findable and passing it on for action without pausing to judge the content. He's like a lively bird, probing dense brush for kernels of nourishment without any concern for what's happening beyond his sphere. Some of the morsels he turns up might be used or perhaps misused to imprison fathers or sons. They may reduce some threats to America, but arguably are as likely to inspire others. Archie does not allow himself to be sensitive to the implications. His people come and go, bits of information are tendered; they fit or they're discarded. The process rolls along like a digital vacuum cleaner, gobbling up bushels of bytes. His staff are like solid performers in any office; none of them questions either the ethic or the worth of what they're doing, just the mechanics.

The momentum of the process is awesome. It grinds out data twenty-fours a day. It never needs a starting pull; it never crashes; it's inexorable.

Jason feels comfortable with the atmosphere—while he's deep in his work. As he walks to his hotel, often in darkness, that comforting blanket begins to slip from his shoulders. He often reaches there with his mind in conflict.

When Jason trudges across the lobby one evening, the manager hails him. "Can you help with this child?"

A waif of six or seven lurks behind one corner of the reception desk, staring at them, looking frightened. "I know you speak Arabic," says the manager. "Perhaps he does too. Whatever he's saying, I can't follow."

"Where's your family?" Jason asks in Arabic. The boy is startled, but speechless. Jason repeats the question slowly, trying to sound as friendly as an uncle.

"Gone." In a whisper.

"Where did he come from?"

"He just popped up at the desk. He seemed … out of breath. Or terrified. We've called Social Services, but I thought you …"

"I'll take him into the snack bar. Maybe if he has something …"

When he signals, the boy dashes from the shelter of the counter to his side and clings to him. He's quite slight, olive-skinned, with jet-black hair, dressed only in a shirt and pants, his clothes damp. He's shivering.

"Can we find him something to warm him?" Jason asks.

He sits the boy in a corner, orders tea, and loads the boy's with sugar. The boy stares at him. He stares at the deserted tables; he stares at the manager when he brings a blanket; he stares at the waitress with her motherly smile, but he doesn't speak until after he has sipped his tea. Then he surprises Jason. "You live here?" he asks in Arabic. He might see Jason as the owner of the building because of the deference of the manager and the waitress. A powerful man who can help him.

"I live here. You must tell me what happened to your mother and father."

Abruptly, he explodes into speech, rattling off his story at a pace Jason can just follow. He picks out phrases: "took them—gray men—ran away …"

By the time Social Services arrive, the boy has settled into fries and a burger and more tea, thrown off the blanket, and is talking freely. SECORs have been scooping up his neighbors for several days. He's afraid to be taken away. Jason explains gently that these people can help find his family, and he goes reluctantly, always looking back at Jason.

"We have a number of kids from around here," one of the crew tells him. "Some even younger than him—with no English either. One of our staff speaks a little Arabic, but it's so hard to help them."

Jason ponders on the boy, on the seized families, for a good while, sleepless. Later, he wakes in the darkness, going over the whole sequence again. He has seen nothing yet at SECOR of family arrests, but then, he's just started there.

He brings it up with Archie (definitely not Sid). "We had a little boy hiding in the hotel last night. I got involved because he spoke only Arabic."

"What happened?" Archie's sympathetic. Heads pop up from nearby monitors.

"His family may have been arrested. He ran away."

"Arrested? A family dispute? Husband beating up the wife? Police took them in?"

"Not police. They were SECORs."

Archie stares at him, not so sympathetically. "You didn't get involved, did you?"

"Archie, there was a small boy wandering around on a rainy

night. Naturally I asked him—"

Archie's hands signal him to stop. "Jason, asking questions—that's okay here. But it's *not* okay outside the station. If SECOR is arresting anyone, they must have reasons. But it's *none* of our affair and if one of us pokes into it, it's sure to get back to Hawk."

"But everybody seems to know we're arresting …"

"Everybody does *not* know. The detentions are kept very quiet. No media. Hawk won't be happy. You should have stayed out of it."

"I thought you might at least know if we were picking up alarm signals …"

"You *can't* get involved in other operations. *Stay in your own back yard!* We hear that on our first day of training."

Jason can't leave it be. "Do they at least tell us where they're taking all these people?"

Archie's voice drops to the conspiratorial level. "Jason, listen to me: this is a need-to-know environment. Any intelligence service has to be. You can question me all day about our work. You can't ask about anything outside it. I won't know the answer anyway. Got it?"

"I've got it," Jason says. The inquisitive heads have sunk back to their screens.

He becomes a figure of interest, the Canadian alien. One or two sometimes snicker when he finishes a sentence with "eh?" Some resent Canada for not joining America's wars, but most know little of his country. His enthusiasm for SECOR provokes friendly smiles. He gets on well, mostly.

When he's not at work the doubts cannot quite be dislodged. SECOR on the prowl; desert camps full of American citizens; army intelligence lurking. Do Americans sign off on it all? He's careful not to share these reservations, not even with Archie, who shows none of his own. Like most Canadians, Jason has a deep respect for America, for its openness, for its world leadership. That respect keeps grinding against the reality of his everyday experience here. He gets more immersed in his work but his misgivings sit uneasily on his shoulder.

Archie reruns a clip for Jason: a group of half a dozen in front of their mosque after evening prayers. They've been monitored from a patrol car, called in when they were picked out by a UAV, several men, and no women. The muted conversation in Arabic suggests some imminent event—could be some kind of assault, in the opinion of the analyst. Jason hears it through three times. Archie summons Sid to hear his analysis:

"They're discussing a family occasion," Jason says. "There's no conspiracy here."

"Nothing subversive?"

"Oh well, a couple of curses directed at the government, but nothing you wouldn't expect from any Arabic speaker nowadays. Nobody hatching a plot would talk openly in front of a mosque. They had nothing to hide. If they'd spoken

English you would have laughed at your analyst."

"We'll pick up one of them for interrogation," Sid says.

"Sid, I thought the whole point of all this—" Jason flings out an arm to include the entire section, "—was to isolate the bad guys. These guys are okay."

"You don't get the point, Jason. We don't mind a few harmless citizens in detention. Even quite a few. If some of these people are angry with us, we want them to see they're tempting fate. We want to *paralyze* them. You're here to learn our business. *That's* our business."

"Intimidation."

"Security." Sid turns to walk away. "Pick your spots more carefully." They now have the attention of everyone in range. Jason sinks down beside Archie, who at least seems sympathetic.

During the ten-minute breaks analysts are encouraged to take, Jason sometimes escapes from SECOR with reveries of Miriam. The more he thinks of her, the greater his desire to find her. He might slip into Mexico for a weekend—if he can find Manwaring's address. He could ask Sid. He decides to wait until he's more established here.

Two men in suits knock at his hotel door one evening. "Mr. Currie? This is a routine follow-up of your visit to a secure installation."

They show their credentials: DIA, as Bil had warned. "If you mean that park where Nabil Maron works, I wouldn't call it a visit. I only got as far as the gate."

"Could you explain your relationship to Mr. Maron?"

"I suppose that's how you found me? From Bil?" He goes all the way back to their teens. They're an older man, unremarkable, observant, neutral, and a much younger one, polite but slightly aggressive. The older one makes a show of taking notes, but Jason's sure they're recording it.

"So you were simply visiting an old friend?"

He nods and the senior partner makes a note, probably because the recorder can't pick up nods. "But on your arrival at L.A. International you were held by Security?"

"They confused me with some Lebanese with a similar name."

The junior glares at him. "We know you were held at the airport." Jason waits for the follow-on, but the statement ends there. They have nothing further on him until he turned up at Bil's—no input from SECOR.

"It took a while before SECOR verified my identity." They wait for more. "But then they apologized for holding me."

They exchange a glance he interprets as, *He sounds pretty naïve but after all he's a Canadian*, and they soldier on. "Do you have business in California?"

"I work for the Canadian government. They've given me a routine assignment that will keep me here awhile."

"What government department?"

"Department of Public Safety—same thing as your Justice."

"You're a lawyer?"

"A technician."

"What sort of assignment?"

"Just routine, but our policy is never to discuss our assignments outside our units. It could start rumors, which affect reputations. I believe your Justice Department has a similar policy."

"When will you be returning to Canada?"

"I'm not required to be back for several weeks."

They don't like this. There's a moment of hesitation. "You know Maron's sister, Miriam Ashbury? Do you plan to visit her as well?" The older agent asks this as casually as if he accepts Jason's evasions.

"I wouldn't know where to find her. Bil mentioned that she lives in Mexico somewhere, but he hasn't seen or heard from her in years. Why do you ask?"

"You mentioned Maron was an old friend so we assumed she was also. Have you been trying to locate her?"

"I asked Bil if he was in touch, but he has no idea how to contact her. I'm not sure what else I could do. Any suggestions?"

The younger man ignores that. "Will you be visiting Maron again?"

"I'll be pretty busy with my assignment, but I might if I have a chance. It was great to see him. He must be doing well here, since he decided to take out citizenship."

Now the senior man, "What's the nature of your technical expertise, Mr. Currie? What profession?"

"I'm a mathematician."

"In that department?"

"We have many professions in Public Safety."

They seem ready to leave, but then try another tack. "How did you come to choose this hotel?" Making the connection with SECOR's tower?

Jason manages a smile. "If you knew what our travelling allowance is, you wouldn't ask. I used the Net to find a good rate."

"I see. Then you must have your own vehicle?"

"Just cabs for now. I'll probably rent one once I know where all my contacts are located."

"What sort of contacts, Mr. Currie?"

"The kind we don't discuss outside my office."

As they walk away he hears the younger one mutter, "Smartass." Perhaps that's their final take, but perhaps they already know who he is and his evasions have only stimulated more interest. He hopes that he hasn't added to Bil's vulnerability. He's alarmed that they were so interested in Miriam. She's more in harm's way than he'd assumed.

He hasn't seen her since the day in Toronto when she married an American, to be carried off then out of Canada. He wasn't even Catholic, let alone Maronite, so she had defied her family one more time in making her own choice. He can visualize her in her white dress as he passed down the reception line. She gave him only a token kiss, but a lingering handshake and a meeting of their eyes that prompted him to suspect that she had remembered their moment of passion after all.

But now he's concerned about the present Miriam. How serious have her protests been? After his own experience of arbitrary imprisonment, he imagines Miriam in such a camp—do they even have such places for women? If she returns to the States, some sort of detention beckons. He's hesitant to approach Hawk. He decides to try for her file himself.

All known protestors (and thousands of "persons of interest") have individual files. His computer is denied access. Sid summons him soon after.

"You tried to access a personal file?"

Jason shifts to enlisting Sid. "It's not CSIS business. Just personal. She's an old family friend. Well, more than that, really."

"You're a pro, Jason. You know there's no access to individual files without clearance."

"Come on, Sid. I've known this woman since we were kids. Looking at her file's not going to endanger security."

"It could reveal a source."

"Undercover informant?"

"It's possible."

"Sid, it's more than casual. I'm concerned because DIA asked me about her."

"What's she supposed to have done?"

"Her brother works in a very sensitive facility. He told me she's in Mexico. She was involved in a protest here. In a church." Sid takes this in without showing sympathy.

"If she's in Mexico, those army guys will already know where she is. They liaise with SEDENA."

"The Mexican Ministry of Defense?"

"They'll have tracked her down for the Pentagon."

"Can we find out where she can be reached? So I can alert her?"

"Alert her that DIA is interested in her?" His sharper interest is making Jason uneasy. "I expect we have a file on her."

"I'll ask General Hawk for permission to see it. He knows my relationship to the family."

Sid shrugs that off. "I'll have a look at the file."

# NINE

HAWK SUMMONS JASON TO HIS OFFICE THE NEXT MORNING. "CSIS doesn't require you to follow direct commands?"

He sounds so scornful that it snaps Jason to attention. "Sir?"

"I told you to report only to me. Now I find you were after Sid to access a classified file." His tone tells Jason that no explanation will be of much help.

"Yes, sir. Sid set me straight. It won't happen again."

"We concur on that." He relaxes about one notch, but Jason remains at attention. "Sid—and Archie—both understand that you'll be taking time away for your own assignments, those required by CSIS. They won't question you about your work outside SECOR, and you won't discuss it. Now, do you understand my orders *this* time?"

"Yes, sir."

Now he becomes a little more human. "Remember, Sid works with Werner every day. Werner reports to the Pentagon. Whatever he reports to his command goes straight to DIA. I don't want anything you're working on to turn up there."

"I understand."

"United States security is complex, Jason. Complex as in byzantine. We're responsible for preventing terrorist attacks. We should have absorbed any other agencies with parts of that. But Congress lost its nerve, thanks to heavy lobbying. DIA got to keep their authority over all their own people. Military staff. Then built on that. They got civilian staff at defense sites, like Maron's. They have foreign terrorists in their stockades—picked up in the war zones. We know they're also holding some Americans, picked up somehow. So they're now a full competitor. Then the FBI is always with us. CIA is supposed to be counterintelligence but they do surveillance at will. Then every arm of the services has its own intelligence branch. Plus the Secret Service, Justice, et cetera. Every one of them keeps its own files. None of them are easy to work with. Get the picture?"

As he adds agency to agency, Jason counts them off on his fingers. "My god. There must be hundreds of thousands of security people."

"If you leave out informants. Then you're into millions. Security has the biggest payroll in the country."

"It's like a baseball team with unlimited fielders. The only way to beat it is to hit home runs."

Hawk stares that down. "You were questioned by DIA. You should have come right to me. I suppose they were chafing over that project of Maron's?"

"Why's it so sensitive?"

"They've developed a proprietary internet that can be accessed from satellites by hand-held devices. We're not supposed to know about it yet."

CSIS knew of this research; even Jason has heard of it. It could allow a military unit (or a spy agency) to examine any area around them without exposing themselves in daylight or darkness. An individual could call down images on his unit of what lay around the corner, or in the darkness ahead, all on a secure network.

Hawk looks him over with a surge of suspicion. "You already knew of the Secure Net, didn't you? It's been discussed with CSIS. They expect it to be particularly useful in Canada, if they can get it. Because of your limited forces. Why pretend you've never heard of it? Is that the real reason you were visiting Maron?"

"The Secure Net is just a rumor to me. I was at Bil Maron's because he's my closest friend."

"What else did they want from you?"

"They asked if I knew where Miriam Ashbury is."

"Sid says you asked him to locate her. Was that for them?"

"Certainly not. It was for me. Bil hasn't heard from her in years. DIA is somehow interested in her. Sid assumes they know where she is. From SEDENA."

Hawk studies him without the offhandedness he sometimes affects.

"I don't often misread people, Jason. But I'm not sure I've got you right. You're using your position here to find Maron's sister, who happens to be the protégée of a man we consider a dangerous activist and who in fact escaped from detention. Then instead of asking me, you tried to get Sid to find her."

"Manwaring's just a name to me."

Hawk smiles, coldly, then his face relaxes into its usual set. "You never knew about Manwaring? Not credible. Professor Manwaring is on a do-not-admit list that CSIS passes on to your border patrol."

"I only knew his name. Because CSIS believes Manwaring might try to reach Canada. It's giving them fits. He might be a legitimate refugee. We couldn't refuse him a hearing."

"He's an escaped felon!"

"If he's seen as just a law professor with independent views, an IRO[6] would have to hear him out. The media would be all over it."

"He's not just a law professor. Anyway, he can't get to Canada. He may not be harmless in Mexico, though. We believe he's in touch with a network here. But we don't know how—we're not getting any sigint on it."

The small chance that Miriam could be safe now evapo-

---

6   IRO: Immigration Review Officer

rates. If Manwaring's seen as actively subversive and she's his companion—his need to reach her now becomes pressing.

"Did her brother ask you to see her?"

"He doesn't even want to hear about her."

"What else did DIA want?"

"They were mainly interested in Miriam. They wanted to know if I intended to visit her."

"You told them you were with SECOR?"

"Certainly not."

Hawk smiles. "Good. Never give away more than you need to. Maron must not have told them you're here. But that doesn't mean you're invisible. Werner will have reported your presence, so they know who you are and why you're here. If Werner hears from Sid that you asked for that woman's file, DIA will be taking even more interest in her."

"Why do they want her?"

"To get to Manwaring. She's living with him, isn't she?"

"If she's so important, why don't we beat DIA to the punch?"

They each settle into a watchful silence while Hawk thinks this over. "I'm not that easy to manipulate, Jason. You're trying to use me."

"Because it's in your interest as well as mine. You can offer her protection from DIA if she comes back here. She's only guilty of protesting in a church."

Hawk relaxes against the back of his chair. "I wouldn't have thought you were ready for another entanglement." So he knows about Ramona. "You're anxious about this woman, aren't you?"

"I wish you wouldn't refer to her as 'this woman.'"

"I know where *Ms. Ashbury* is. And Manwaring. Suppose we offer to protect her if she returns, providing she'll cooperate with our surveillance of radical elements."

"Cooperate?"

"We have no mandate to hold legitimate dissenters. Only criminal ones. I presume she doesn't support violence against the state. If her friends are only carrying placards and marching in demos, we're not interested. If they're planning to blow up government buildings, she should be happy to have them in detention before they kill someone and discredit the lawful opposition."

"She might accept that if it comes from me," Jason says, taking pains to avoid any hint of disbelief.

"The alternative is for us to have her snatched. Before DIA does."

"In Mexico? You said you can't operate outside the United States."

"We have friends in Mexico just as we have CSIS in Canada."

"Miriam wouldn't trust any offer from you. But she and I were … very close. Do I have your word that she wouldn't be detained if she came willingly?"

"You have my word." For a moment, Jason expects Hawk to offer a handshake. It's not forthcoming. "You've been to

Guadalajara?"

"Just coastal cities in Mexico."

"It's the city where the cartel bosses hope to retire if they survive. It also has a large American colony, especially retired army vets."

When he doesn't elaborate, Jason asks, "Is that significant in some way?"

"That's for you to find out. I'll tell Sid he has you until the weekend and then you're off on a CSIS assignment. If you get to speak to Manwaring, use a recorder."

# TEN

IT'S A LONG CAB RIDE ACROSS THE CITY TO THE ADDRESS HAWK has provided. Guadalajara is a mile-high center of five million in central Mexico and nothing like the resort towns in that country where he has spent a couple of vacations. It's a part of the old world—the great cathedral built four centuries ago—though of the new as well, modern industry and transport, a seat of higher education, world-class medicine. Unprepared, he's surprised to find himself in an ambience more like southern Europe than California.

He's also unprepared on how to present himself. "Miriam. I know it's been many years, but …" For a decade he's almost put her out of his mind; now she's a few steps away. He's so self-conscious he asks the driver to stop down the block so that he will not be seen hopping from a taxi as if expected. When he walks back, hesitantly, he finds the house hidden within an old wall, its solid wooden gate unpainted for years. Not a large property. The wall surrounds it completely. There's no other entrance and no bell. He raises his hand to knock.

The gate is flung open. A dog lunges out, barking at high volume. A large black dog, maybe a Doberman. He stands still. The dog sniffs him thoroughly and then is quiet.

"Zorra will not harm you. She wants only to be reassured." Framed in the gateway is a slim man in a white shirt with a dark tie. Jason is shocked to note the pistol hanging in the hand at his side. In the background is the recognizable figure of Professor Brendan Manwaring.

He's older than Jason has imagined from the one picture he's seen, a man over sixty, gray hair on top with white over the ears, and a neat triangular beard of the same mix. Frameless glasses. He's dressed like a laborer in a cotton shirt and trousers. As Jason scans him, Manwaring reciprocates, with neither hostility nor friendliness.

"You were looking for me?" he asks in a voice so quiet that it demands concentration to be heard.

"Professor Manwaring, my name is Jason Currie, and I—"

"I know who you are. You may come in." Within is a small garden, enclosed by the wall and the house. Among formations of rocks and a couple of boulders, plants are tucked, their colors the gray-greens of the desert. There is a hint of spice rising from some, and a faint smell of musty old stone simmering in the autumn sun. A shaded patio leads to the house beyond. It's laid out with a table and chairs, a half-empty cup, and a newspaper. He can see its Spanish headlines. He's interrupted Manwaring's post-lunch coffee.

"May I ask how you knew me?"

"Of course you may ask." He shares a glance with his associate—their private joke. "You can sit there."

"As if you were expecting me."

He doesn't answer that either. As they eye each other, Jason works out his impression of this rare bird: an unrestricted representative of whatever underground opposition the administration might fear. Manwaring must be figuring out whether Jason is a threat or merely a curiosity. The other man—clearly a bodyguard—goes to a bench against the house and continues to watch him intently. The dog trots over to Manwaring and sprawls at his feet, frequently rolling its eyes in Jason's direction.

"What is it you want here?"

"I'm a family friend of Miriam Ashbury, and I came to offer to help her."

"You're also an agent of the American political police?"

"No!" Rattled at being unveiled so quickly, he barks the response. "I'm a technician with the Canadian Security Intelligence Service. I analyze Arabic files."

"Oh yes. CSIS. Do they torture like the American agencies or is that still considered uncivil in Canada?" He doesn't sound sarcastic, only mocking.

"Torture? SECOR?"

"Certainly, among others." He waits to allow a challenge. "You say you came to offer help to Miriam. Is that the extent of your interest in her?" It occurs belatedly to Jason that if Miriam is living with Manwaring, he may have reason to resent offers from another man.

"I need to warn her that if she stays here she may be kidnapped and returned to the States." He had taken the precaution of sending a last-minute message to Ben Noble that he was to meet Manwaring. Is it possible that CSIS has been in communication with an American dissident? If not CSIS, what about SECOR? Hawk was very upset that Jason had approached Sid for Miriam's file. Sid? Or even Werner? *Sid works with Werner every day.* Jason has trouble sorting it out; he has an uncomfortable sense that he's being used—the way the A-D used him to penetrate that camp. He has been so focused on Miriam that visiting an enemy of the administration seemed to be the obvious next step. Now he feels a flush of uncertainty. The bodyguard has laid his pistol on the bench beside him, inches from his hand.

Manwaring is watching him, intently. "I've been here now for over a year, quite securely," he says. "Why do you think they could abduct her when they haven't been able to take me?" He sounds to be enjoying the exchange; he's in charge, Jason's on the defensive.

"She hasn't your profile. You're an accredited refugee; seizing you would offend Mexico. Miriam's just a foreign resident."

Manwaring continues to study Jason, not threatening but clearly suspicious. "I'd be surprised if she agrees to return. Under any circumstances. So if she's in danger here, as you say, how else could you help her?"

"I can offer her refuge in Canada."

"She doesn't need your help to get that. Why would she be safer there than here?"

"She's a Canadian citizen. So long as she's cooperative, the authorities will protect her."

"There's that 'cooperating with the authorities' again. I'm familiar with the process."

"Miriam wouldn't be detained in Canada. We have no Defense of America Act. Anyway, by Canadian standards, she's more a heroine than a troublemaker. Most of us distrust this administration."

"So you say. But Canada's an ally of the United States, and your own agency works with SECOR." He speaks gently, but both he and his guardian continue to eye Jason as if he were a potential assassin.

"Mexico is also an ally, and the Mexican agencies work with SECOR and the Pentagon."

"We know we're at risk, but we also have friends here."

"Miriam's been a friend of mine since childhood." He raises his hand to reach inside his shirt, but instantly the guard springs to his feet and grips Jason's wrist. He pats his chest, locates the recorder, and strips it away, adhesive tape dangling from it. He scans the device with a professional eye and then tosses it on the table. The professor merely glances at it. "SECOR told me to record our conversation, but I never intended to. I didn't even turn it on. I need you to trust me."

"And you don't care whether SECOR trusts you?" Manwaring seems less certain of himself. "That was an innovative approach," he says. He focuses on Jason like a man debating his decision. After a moment, he continues. "You could have two of them. Felipe will settle that while I get you some coffee."

He mutters to the other and leaves Jason under his gaze. The dog also stays. Felipe motions to him, twice, before he grasps that he's to remove his jacket. Felipe opens his shirt, lifts it to see his back, and then signals him to drop his pants. Manwaring returns, a carafe of coffee in hand, and stands watching this humiliation.

"So now we can proceed without speaking to your friends."

"May I see Miriam now?"

"She's not here at the moment." Jason feels he's lying. "If you will sit here?"

He places him next to the door leading into the house and sits across from him, stirring his coffee. Jason looks over his shoulder into the pleasant little garden, probably at its grayest now in the approach of fall, just catching the terse Felipe from the corner of his eye. Zorra, no longer interested in him, gives a great sigh and lies on her side in the sun.

"Why would you work for SECOR? CSIS is bad enough.

SECOR is ... abhorrent."

"To get to L.A. to see Bil and Miriam."

"CSIS sent you to rescue Miriam? Hah!"

The way to Miriam runs through Manwaring. Jason feels a touch of panic. "They refused me leave. I had to accept the transfer just to get to California."

"You visited her brother? No doubt he sends his affection. Such an ardent supporter of the regime."

"He works in a Pentagon installation, he has no choice."

"He had a choice. He chose to work with them. Does *he* want his sister to go to Canada?"

"He doesn't know I'm here."

Jason toys with his coffee cup while the little surge of emotion between them evaporates. Manwaring still seems uncertain, brooding. Thinking he may be turned away, Jason begins mapping out a note to leave for Miriam.

"She will be back in a day or two," Manwaring says. "She may decide to see you or she may not. She makes her own decisions. You're welcome to be my guest tonight. Now, it's my custom to take an afternoon rest. Felipe will show you to a room where you can do the same. He will call you for dinner." It's a command rather than a suggestion. Felipe takes Jason's bag and sets off into the house. Jason barely has time to note the spare interior—a tiled floor, old furniture, books on all flat surfaces, but otherwise rather barren. No pictures, no mementos. Maybe he left them all behind. Felipe leads him up a tight staircase and into a small bedroom.

He makes use of the privacy to connect his cell phone to the message center in Ottawa. *Permission refused; Mexico out of bounds.* It was entered early that morning while he was already at the airport. Noble sent this from home.

He muses on Manwaring, too well informed for a man in virtual house arrest. He catches a faint smell. Perfume, wafting faintly from the pillow. So Miriam sleeps in her own bed. At least some nights. He dwells on her relationship with Manwaring, on the difference in their ages. Finally he shakes that off and allows his travel weariness to subdue him, and he falls asleep.

# ELEVEN

AS HE WAKES UP, UNFOCUSED, HE HEARS SOFT FOOTSTEPS retreating. Likely, they awakened him. He moves about the room. There's a wardrobe rather than a closet. It holds a limited selection of jeans, shirts, jackets, and dresses. The plain chest of drawers contains underclothes and other items no man would wear. He comes across her picture. It's a shot of Bil and her, one he believes he took himself just before Bil left for college. Not long before one of them seduced the other, however that happened.

A longing to see her again swamps him. The perfume, the intimate garments, the photograph; one adds to another to lever up his desire. He sits on the bed and concentrates on the image of Miriam. He imagines spending hours and days with her free of the baggage of his marriage, back in that state they enjoyed when they were more than friends and less than lovers. He escapes from the present, into a state of lightness and warmth, even while knowing that it's transient. He prolongs it as long as he can while it subsides like a drawn-out breath. He feels better then, even as the present snaps back into focus with a knock on the door. He trips down the hall on nimble feet.

There is a guest for dinner. Señor Campobello is a wiry sixty-something, whose gaze absorbs Jason with some interest as they shake hands. He looks rather grim until he smiles, when his face opens like the streaks of sunlight from a cloudbank. He exchanges pleasantries with the professor. Felipe, who's apparently the domestic as well as bodyguard, serves a simple dinner and then joins the table. Jason can feel his constant scrutiny. He also catches Campobello's glances, sweeping him like sensors.

Manwaring notices the ongoing examination. He lights up with one of his rare smiles. "Sergio is in a similar line to yours."

"Oh, a mathematician?"

"Your other profession."

"It's not a profession. I just work there."

Campobello nods politely. "Same for me." Manwaring snorts. Campobello goes on in careful English. "I used to control a network in Mexico City, all about drugs. We were too successful, so they transferred me here, where they keep me out of the way."

"Sergio is curious about CSIS," Manwaring says. Jason exchanges glances with the Mexican, who's unreadable. "But as a professional, he won't ask you a direct question."

"So you're asking for him?"

Manwaring nods agreeably. "Are people at CSIS at all ... sympathetic to the reservations many of us have about this administration?"

"Canadians certainly are. CSIS is officially neutral."

Manwaring banters with them throughout the meal of local dishes. He poses questions, not pointed, just polite, about Canada, which he seems to know far better than most Americans. He makes up for his earlier coolness with relaxed civility. Campobello soaks everything in with little comment. Felipe sits in complete silence. Zorra's at the Professor's feet. He slips her tidbits occasionally. It's all a pleasant domestic scene, but there's no mention of Miriam.

Manwaring glances at his watch. "Would you mind if we watch the news? I'm afraid it's an addiction of mine. We have a satellite dish—American stations."

Jason has already seen, in comparing American programs with Canadian coverage, how sanitized the U.S. networks have become, so he's not surprised that the day's actions in the Middle East are covered by a tidy and bloodless communiqué spiced up with generic film clips from the Pentagon. The network soon moves on to the denser matter of Washington politics.

"You might be surprised by the different coverage in

Spanish. Or maybe not, if your national network hasn't been intimidated yet by Washington. Would you like to see?"

Manwaring translates some of the Spanish commentary, but it's hardly necessary. Burning buildings, burning vehicles, and burning people, military and even more civilian. Suicide bombing by Islamic martyrs, massive barrages by American forces. Since international correspondents are barred from the American side, this coverage comes through the Arabic media; sometimes the muted Arabic commentary can be heard under the Spanish translation.

Manwaring says, "It's the comparison that's striking."

"I'm familiar with Arabic news. It's on cable in Canada."

"Then you understand? What they've done to my country? This administration?" He comes to his feet, suddenly animated. "Censoring television—the *Times* lost its TV license! The rest saw the light. The Net? Controlled. Websites? Filtered, blocked. Domestic news—censored, censored, *censored*!" His hands move with his rapid speech, pointing, tapping on the table, spreading in despair. The graceful manners are overtaken by his intensity. The quiet voice is louder, harsh. His eyes gleam; he leans toward Jason as if he might pluck at his sleeve like the Ancient Mariner. Tears press from his eyes.

Jason is shaken. Is he just being tested? Campobello is unmoved—maybe he spouts like this all the time? Jason tries to stem the torrent. "You believe Americans are being misled?"

"Doesn't CSIS *know* what's going on?" Manwaring's voice breaks with frustration. "What sort of intelligence service are they?"

"Sorry. I'm not questioning what you say. My job is analyzing intercepts. I pay no attention to politics."

"But SECOR is all politics. Its primary mission is keeping the party in power."

He seems to be spoiling for confrontation. Jason picks his way. "I don't follow, sir. Everyone at SECOR seems dedicated to stopping terrorism."

"You think I'm a terrorist?"

"Sir, I didn't mean—"

"I know what you meant. Look, Jason, I could be happy teaching law at Harvard if I didn't give a damn what this administration is doing. You're with SECOR—you should know what's going on." It's better not to answer; Jason doesn't. "I'm a dissident, but I don't approve of violence against Americans. Or anyone else. I merely do what I can to encourage opposition. Yet *I* was in detention. And tortured."

"Not by SECOR."

"So it was DIA. The point is this administration won't accept opposition. Other than token. SECOR spies on Americans so that it can isolate critics. Especially if they're effective. Are you aware of the Sealed Sectors?"

"You know what they do?"

"They track people like me. Loyal Americans who believe this regime is both evil and un-American. Thousands of us, inside and outside the country. Expatriates! SECOR has paid informants in Canada. Reporting on Americans in Canada.

Same here in Mexico. Their mission is to identify threats. Not terrorists, political threats. Threats *to the regime*." Now he sits back, a certain satisfaction showing, and dares any counter. Jason can't contradict him, however wild his ideas. Manwaring's attack is not helping him to reach Miriam. She might even have come to live with him just because of his passion.

"Professor Manwaring, you seem to know more than I do about SECOR. I just arrived there. I know nothing about censorship. My interest is the Maron family. And my duty to them. They're very close to my own family, coming from Lebanon like my parents. They supported me when I needed friends. Bil stood up for me. Now I see that Miriam may be in danger, and Bil's hands are tied by his job. He can't even talk to her. So to uphold my family's obligations, I should do whatever I can to look after Miriam. At the very least I should talk to her, let her know what she's facing, and that I'm available to help if I'm needed. I understand you've been … sheltering her and that's very helpful. But if she's directly threatened she should have a safety valve."

Now he waits.

Manwaring may be impressed. His face relaxes into thoughtfulness. He takes some time to reply. "A safety valve should not consist of a flight to the United States."

"Understood. I've seen enough there to worry she might end up in detention if she returned."

"But SECOR expect you to bring her back."

"They've even assured me that she would be safe with them."

Manwaring jumps on that. "How could you help Miriam without compromising yourself?"

"I work *with* these people. I don't necessarily agree with them. My job is purely technical—making sense of Arabic intercepts. I don't feel any conflict."

Manwaring weighs that. "You understand, Jason, I'm very fond of Miriam." He shows it, in a softened expression and a quieter tone. The agitator dissolves into the committed partner. "At times, she's been my nurse. At times, she's been my helper. In my work."

How? If she's a party to his network, she's even more exposed. Jason says, "Of course. I do understand."

"I don't want to misjudge you, Jason. Miriam has talked of her brother and as much about you." He looks quite tired, subdued. Jason waits, carefully expressionless. "I will ask her if she wants to see you. You may return in a few days. Now I must say goodnight."

Manwaring trudges off. Jason accompanies Campobello to the gate, elated for the moment, but assuming that Manwaring will not try very hard to convince Miriam. Campobello shakes hands with him in his formal way.

"Did I get through to him? Am I going to see her?"

"You made your point. He understands that you're a close friend, but he also knows you're a member of an unfriendly agency. He will allow Miriam to meet you, if she agrees, but he would never want to see her under the thumb of CSIS. So when you speak of Canada, you worry him. He's very attached to her."

"You mean—like a daughter?"

"Like a man."

Jason doesn't respond for a moment, absorbing that cue. "He's an old man in his sixties."

Campobello's smile reflects the faint light. "He may not feel like an old man." Campobello is not prepared to leave without offering some advice. "You need to be careful when you come here again, señor, your presence has been noted."

"By a Mexican agency? You're one of them. You seem to be his friend."

"We are not hostile to every American dissident. Not if they are genuine. He can say what he likes about the United States, especially if it is true. With care. Not to encourage violence. We cannot tolerate an attack on America from a Mexican base. Like Canada. We hope the Americans will always be too busy to pay us more attention. We expect him to be prudent. There are those in our own government—you must know of whom I speak, the Ministry of Defense—who are collaborators with the Pentagon, who want to deport anyone like him."

"SEDENA?"

"And others. Many Americans live here, mostly quite loyal to the administration. Others, not so much."

"Then is it safe for the professor to speak this way?"

"My people watch this place. We sweep it—for bugs. The high wall is useful against directional mikes."

"Your agency protects him?"

"Felipe is one of my men."

"Mexican agencies seem to have conflicting roles."

"Your own mission has more than one motive."

"Not really, Señor Campobello. I came to help Miriam."

"You are a CSIS agent. You are here for SECOR. Neither is a friend. Maybe you can be trusted. Maybe not so much. *Buenas noches*, señor."

Jason lies awake fretting over Miriam and Manwaring. A serious entanglement may exist. Or maybe Campobello has misinterpreted the relationship. When he sees her, he will know.

Manwaring intrigues him; his dual news, his doomsday view of the administration. And of SECOR: *Its primary mission is keeping the party in power.* The only Americans with whom he's familiar nowadays, the SECOR staff, approve of the administration's militancy, subscribe to its wars, and applaud its obsessive defense of American soil. Probably most Americans are so compliant simply because they believe the administration is doing the right thing. This thought does not remove the toehold of doubt that the professor has planted. There can be another way to look at SECOR.

There's a breath of perfume from his pillow. He focuses on Miriam, hopefully to be brought to life soon. Ramona and her venom are in hibernation.

# TWELVE

ON THE FLIGHT NORTH, JASON CATCHES HIMSELF STARING PAST his newspaper as he dwells on Manwaring—not the man he had expected. His passion hadn't seemed to arise so much from bitterness over his detention, and now exile, as from frustration that the country for which he cares deeply is being hollowed out. He's also remarkably well informed. Hawk takes him as dangerous even though SECOR has seamless control of American security. There has to be more meat on these bones than a reclusive life in Mexico under the protection of a state agency. And again: Miriam, living with him, perhaps party to whatever he's up to.

From full sun over the high country and then the northern desert of Mexico, they have passed through accumulating murk as he broods. By the time they reach the border, the smoke and clouds have merged into a dark brew, down into which they sink like some doomed vessel.

A team of gray SECORs mans the immigration hall. He spots a pair that could be the same ones who marched him to his interrogation. His stomach muscles tighten. He still carries that same passport. His line moves steadily through the gate until the agent spots the entry stamps. "Please step aside. Take the last gate on the left."

The agent there is ready to dispose of him after one glance at the offending page. "These men will show you to Interrogation."

"One moment," Jason says. He pulls his necklace from his shirt neck and dangles it tauntingly under the agent's nose. "Class Three." What a moment!

"You should have shown that at the first gate." The agent is peeved, surly. "Please don't waste our time, sir!" Jason steps through the gate, tossing a wave at the agent and the two SECORs. He's determined now that he does recognize them.

He checks in with Hawk, who flings, "Well, is she coming?" at him as he enters.

"I haven't even seen her yet. He needed to size me up first."

"So." In full uniform, his cap on the side table, he looks quite military. Jason's edgy under the concentrated gaze. "I don't get the feeling you're so committed to bringing her here."

Jason treads with care. "I got on well enough. I think he accepts that I'm trying to help her. But Manwaring is manic over this administration. He doesn't trust SECOR either. So it may take a while."

Hawk watches him carefully, stroking his chin. "Manwaring. DIA really screwed up with him. We knew all about him. In time we would have found his contacts. We were patient. That's spy craft 101, patience. But DIA, they barged right in and grabbed him before they had a case. They didn't touch base with us. Then they worked him over. They got nothing worthwhile. Then he got away. Now he's got sanctuary in Mexico and a hard-on for the Pentagon. And we're tarnished by association."

Jason's sure this is self-serving but he's content to agree with Hawk. "How could he have escaped?"

"He wouldn't have from us. He overcame his guard."

Jason can't imagine that kind of desperation in the sixty-year-old. "He doesn't look like he could handle that."

Hawk hesitates as usual, deciding how much to tell him. "We interviewed the doctor. Manwaring had a severe groin injury. He must have had a hell of a time walking out of there."

"My god!" Jason's heard of the Americans' use of torture. It used to be arranged through rendition to friendly countries to circumvent American laws and their international treaties, but under the current Act, certain agencies can use 'enhanced interrogation' providing they're 'acting to avert an imminent threat,' so now they don't have to render prisoners anymore. "He just seemed like an opinionated old egghead, but he must be committed as hell."

Hawk grimaces. "I actually met him once. A lecture in law school. He was on his constitutional horse and just rode right over all of us. He was committed, all right. Did you meet Campobello?" Surprised at Hawk's local knowledge, Jason only nods. "He's with CISEN, with whom we have a working arrangement. I understand Campobello is a real old pro, but maybe not a good company man. He had some kind of run-in with CISEN management."

"He's protecting Manwaring."

"CISEN and SEDENA are at sword's point. Just like us and DIA. SEDENA would do anything to suck up to DIA, so CISEN spites them by looking after Manwaring. It's classic agency behavior."

"Manwaring knew who I was."

"Did he, by God!" Hawk turns this over. "What did that suggest to you?"

"Someone told him."

"Who knew besides you and me?"

"Ben Noble. Maybe Sid after I asked about Miriam. Maybe he mentioned it to someone else."

"Like Werner. You see why I don't want you parading your assignments with others?"

"Sir, may I ask a question?"

"You never hesitate to."

"Why shouldn't Colonel Werner know of my mission? Or Sid? Are we concerned with a leak?"

Hawk only gives that a lifted shoulder. "It's always a consideration here. Whatever he reports goes on to DIA, so they know everything he knows, but he doesn't know what they know." Jason waits but Hawk goes no further.

"Manwaring did agree I could see Miriam. In a week or two."

"You could embarrass us if you run afoul of SEDENA there. The Mexicans don't like finding us in their country any more than you Canadians do."

"She'll be expecting me."

Hawk doesn't answer, only cocks his head slightly, unconvinced but ready to hear more. Jason searches for fresh ammunition. "Manwaring said we have a Sealed Sector for Mexico. It might be helpful to me to visit with them. For background."

Hawk's eyebrows go up at this. "Now you sound more like a CSIS spy than a man after Miriam Ashbury. Forget about the Sealed Sectors. I asked you to record Manwaring."

"They searched me and took it away."

"You don't seem to be much of a secret agent. But at least you got in. He might have refused to let you through the gate."

Not every house in Mexico has a gate. So Hawk's not forthcoming about his familiarity with the locale. "General, Manwaring doesn't want to hear of Miriam leaving Mexico. That was pretty clear. So I need to spend some time with her. She has to convince him it's best for her after I get her to agree."

"She's living with Manwaring. Sounds as if she's happily settled there."

"It might not be what you think. Maybe more of a father-daughter relationship."

Hawk's amused. "Really? Like your own attachment is just brother-sister?"

"We were very close friends," Jason says, not hiding his irritation.

"Turning an attached woman is serious spy craft, Jason. Doesn't sound like your style." Apparently having had enough fun, he becomes brusque. "I'll consider whether it's worth more of your time. Back to work."

Rescuing Miriam will be a substantial campaign, given Manwaring's attitude, and Hawk sounds short on patience. More leverage is needed.

Jason rejoins Archie's staff. He finds himself struggling again to clear the wisp of doubt that has begun to cloud his view of SECOR, now because of Manwaring's tirades. Just concentrating on the process helps. Hours of problematic intercepts hold his attention, none of them really stimulating. He listens to some crank bad-mouthing the administration.

"I think we've got enough," Sid says. "I'll slate him for detention."

Jason's mind is still smoldering—Miriam's danger, Manwaring's mania, Hawk's condescension. Now Sid's casual dispatch of a borderline suspect whips it into flame. He has to choke down a cry of protest. He's not free to challenge Sid; he needs him. But he gags over the words, *"Why not jail them all?"* with just enough sarcasm to draw a sour look from Sid and a shocked one from Archie. Jason turns away.

When he comes out on the street later, his surly mood still percolating, all seems normal. Most people are driving, just a few walking, a couple skateboarding, and a cyclist goes by. A baby carriage passes, guided by a backpacking mother. No one looks dramatic, maybe just stressed like most ordinary Americans, fussing over their own concerns. Jason watches the passersby; they all seem like everyday citizens, but maybe some are afraid to look over their shoulder. Bil, who was a young lion in Canada, is full of fear in California; Manwaring needs an armed guard at his hip; Sid believes the focal point of security is intimidation. What have they done to the legendary confidence, the American swagger?

There's neither a sun nor a blue sky; only a solid, light-gray ceiling like a high fog, and it smells like soot.

# THIRTEEN

BEN NOBLE IS WAITING IN HIS ROOM. JASON EXPECTS A CALL from him after that e-mail warning him off Mexico, but his unannounced materialization on the only chair, slouched there in his topcoat, is a reaction far in excess of departmental peeve. He doesn't greet Jason, but merely gazes at him with the expression of a parent who has just received a summons from the school principal.

"Whatever I've done, I'm sorry," Jason says. "Won't you take off your coat and settle in?"

Instead, Noble makes for the door. "Let's get a drink." In the lobby he bypasses the lounge, and in the street they find no local bars. They settle for coffee in a grim and almost deserted café. "SECOR chose the hotel?" Jason nods. "You have to assume you're bugged."

"You think SECOR doesn't trust me?"

Noble shrugs. "They're not sure of you because of that camp." With a look of doleful resignation, he fiddles with his cup. "I knew this would be trouble." He stretches the moment in silence while Jason tries to pin down the cause of his grouchiness.

"You can't imagine what a shithouse you've landed me in." The volume rises above his normal hush, signaling a lowering of control, which alarms Jason. Noble gets up, doffs the topcoat and flings it on the bench with an operatic flourish, then falls back into his seat, apparently restored. "I've been besieged since I sent your decodes to the A-D."

"About Manwaring?"

"I told you not to go for a reason."

"I was already gone." Noble snorts derisively. "Hawk insisted I go. He wants me to coax Miriam Ashbury back to the States."

Noble leans across the table in the guise of an admonishing parent. "We sent you here to stay quietly out of the way, learn about the real world of security, and maybe find out a bit more about detention camps. You do remember your mission?"

"I think I hear an echo of the A-D."

Noble sighs. Poor Ben! He's so much more focused on higher management than on his own people that he can never produce the effects from one that would satisfy the other. Now he lurches to his feet and walks to the counter, holding out his cup for a refill from the surly owner. Jason remains seated as Noble then stands beside him, cup in hand, too preoccupied with his message to sip from it. "We've been given an informal note that a Mexican agency has reported the presence of a CSIS agent."

"Informal?"

"A formal advice would get DFAIT down our throat. And so on. They're showing us a professional courtesy. But also telling us to keep out."

"How would they have found out?"

"SECOR, maybe. You didn't tell Manwaring you worked for us?"

"He already knew."

Noble sits down again and leans across the table. "How could we know your old girlfriend was involved with Manwaring? You didn't tell us. SECOR didn't tell us." Jason decides not to respond. "What d'you think Manwaring is up to?"

"Talking. Ranting. Lecturing his friends. He put on quite a show."

"Talking's fine. In Mexico. No problem there. Subversive activity would be quite a different matter." Jason abruptly recalls Hawk's *we believe he's in touch with a network here.* Noble lowers his voice. "Manwaring may be working with American expats in Canada. No real evidence yet, just straws in the wind. Didn't Hawk alert you?"

"Not Canada. He mentioned an American network. Just

a hypothesis."

"This is classified. I shouldn't discuss it with you but you've already opened the door." He pauses, perhaps still reluctant to trust Jason. "SECOR called the A-D. Washington SECOR, not L.A. They're concerned that a hostile group is organizing in Canada, primarily American immigrants."

"Why is that a shock? I've met Americans at home who detest this administration. Why wouldn't they get together?"

"Okay, they can get together. Our concern is where SECOR is going with this. Are they using it to build a narrative that Canada is encouraging dissidents?"

Jason asks, "What about their man in Ottawa? Any help?"

"He probably knows nothing about this—it's coming from Washington. On the other hand, he could be in Ottawa to look for confirmation. Maybe Hawk's using you for the same reason. Or maybe this is a caper dreamt up in Washington just to pressure us."

"Wow …" More than red meat, almost dripping blood. "What do we do now?"

"Never mind *we*. What *you* should do is become a turtle. Don't stick your neck out in any direction. Obey SECOR orders without asking questions. Make notes of everything you learn but *don't comment*."

Once again, a twinge of panic. "I'm not being recalled to Ottawa, am I?"

Noble feigns disgust. "Your General Hawk signals that your work is worthwhile. Some evaluation. The A-D called him.

He got an earful. He insists on keeping you a few weeks more. Is there some way to get out of this Mexican caper?"

"Hawk thinks I can bring in Manwaring."

"Really? That would be good for business between us. Just so long as you bring him into the United States. We can't allow him in Canada. The administration would vaporize us."

Jason knows he should shut up at this point. "Are we going to help SECOR … identify this group in Canada?"

"*Of course not.* We're strictly neutral. We can never choose sides in American politics. Don't bring that up again." The rebuke sinks in for a moment. "Tell me about Werner. What's his function at L.A. Station?"

"What's our interest in Werner? How do you even know about him?"

"Let's remember how this goes, Jason. I ask and you answer. Not the other way around. You should practice doing this with me so you know how to behave in front of the A-D."

"He's a liaison from the Pentagon."

"Interesting. Is he curious about your role?"

"He detests me. Also CSIS."

Noble nods his head. "We manage to get along with SECOR, but not DIA. They can't stand civilian agencies. Does Werner know you saw Manwaring?"

"No one's supposed to know except Hawk."

Noble mulls this over for several moments. "D'you know what command he reports to?"

"Someone in the Pentagon. Why?"

"There you go again." Noble pauses and then speaks barely above his whisper level. "There's some static out there that senior officers resent the army being ground up in all these campaigns. Be alert to anything you hear about Werner."

# FOURTEEN

JASON CONTINUES TO PUT IN LONG HOURS AT THE STATION, walking home in darkness. This night, rain has been promised, but none has come, just a sifting of gentle mist, enough to make the sidewalks slick and cause the glow from streetlamps to blur into periodic flares along a dark tunnel. He's thinking of Miriam. He's become addicted to her presence on these evening walks.

The old hotel sits just outside an area of even older houses, most converted to warrens of apartments above the threadbare businesses at street level. He's discovered, on his occasional strolls, that English is a second language hereabouts. He's sometimes the only person on foot, everyone else in cars, but in the stores or strip malls he could be in Mexico, the aisles crowded with Spanish speakers. There's a smattering of other languages, some Asian, and he even catches Arabic phrases among the babble. It's a serious neighborhood, not much laughter. He can see in the shops that money is well husbanded.

As he crosses an intersection, down to his right he can see the revolving flashers of SECOR patrol cars and a little crowd of onlookers. He pauses to watch. It looks like a raid. He walks the short block toward it. The group of bystanders is on one curb, two vans at the opposite. Two men are about to be hustled into one van, both handcuffed.

"What's happening?"

"Muslims."

"How do you know they're Muslims?" he asks the speaker, an older man in work clothes.

"'Cause they're pickin' them up here every night. They're all 'round here. They even got those little drones up to watch 'em. SECOR doin' their job, right?" Jason wonders if they're victims of Archie's vigilance, troubled as he often is by its insensitivity. Someone calling a family member in the Sudan. Maybe reacting to some homeland account of American brutality. Maybe just a few passionate words, but now internment.

More people are escorted out of the house, two women and four children, not yet teenaged. He starts to cross. As soon as he steps off the curb, the SECORs react. The small drone hovering over the crowd will have sounded an alarm. Two of them move out to meet him, hands on pistol stocks.

"Get back to that sidewalk!"

"Easy, Sergeant. I'm a Class Three SECOR agent. Let me show you." He lifts his necklace clear, carefully. "I'm with L.A. Station."

"We don't need any help. *Sir*." The prisoners have paused by the van. He hears one of them speak to the other in Arabic.

"I speak Arabic, in case it's needed."

"They know enough English to do what they're told."

"The women and kids too?"

"That's a problem for the station. Our job is to get this family out of here. They've been reported."

"Reported?"

"Sending money to a terrorist organization."

Very plainly dressed, they don't look as if they have money to send anywhere. The one who spoke is examining Jason closely. "You speak our language," he says in Arabic. "Can you help us?"

"You sent money to terrorists?"

He's perhaps forty years old, has a dark Middle Eastern complexion, and an untrimmed moustache. He wears a rough shirt and pants that are stained with something like concrete dust. Could even be another stonemason.

"Not true! We sent *hawala*[7] to my parents, not to terrorists."

---

7   *hawala:* An old custom to transfer funds free of banks. An *hawala* agent in L.A. would receive the payment and notify a colleague in Pakistan to pay it out. Widely used for transfers to the home country and handouts to the new one.

"Sir, you can't talk to these prisoners." The sergeant is angry. He motions the prisoners into the van.

"Sounds like a misunderstanding to me, Sergeant. He says they only sent money to the family."

"They all say that."

"All?"

"We've been clearing this whole area. They're all doing it. Now please get out of our way."

He carries away with him the image of the man climbing into the van, his expression dissolving from hope, as he listened to Jason pleading for him, into desolation as he is pushed through the door. The rest of the family is then crammed into the second vehicle. Jason has an uneasy night going over it.

He's called into Hawk's office early the next day.

"I understand the latest exhibition of your free spirit was choosing to butt into a SECOR operation." He seems pleased with the shock value of this opening.

"Oh. That. I just thought they needed a translator."

"Mounted on a white charger, I presume? You embarrassed this station." But he seems more amused than reproving. Jason has an image of some irritated local commander, far beneath Hawk's level, having ventured to criticize one of the general's staff, giving Hawk the opportunity to hone his sarcastic edge.

"You haven't mentioned this latest escapade to your fellow analysts, have you?"

"Not directly," Jason prevaricated.

"Watch your step around the office, Jason." Hawk leaves no doubt that's the final word.

Hawk's television set is muttering away over his shoulder—the president in attendance at a mass funeral in Arlington Cemetery. This is not customary; the party avoids mention of casualties and prohibits pictures of coffins, with all media obliged to cooperate, but an exception has been made today—a mass burial of the first lot of American servicemen killed in the Sudan. However calculating the rationale, such ceremonies are always moving—the pageantry, the solemn ranks, the lowered flags, the pathos of the Last Post, the lament for the young men who are to disappear into those somber pits, after failing to kill some other young men, who became their executioners in a place of no significance to the mourners.

The president is in military uniform. He's taken to dressing as commander-in-chief lately. He's backed up by a row of cloned generals in rigid tribute.

"We remain steadfast," he intones. *Steadfast* has become the catchword to characterize both the chief executive and his administration. "We must bring these people out of their medieval culture and into the world our enlightened democracies have created, or else we will be burying these courageous young Christians for decades. We must win, and we are winning, but the price is terrible. I can only console the families of these heroes by reminding them …" And so on.

"He can really carry it off, can't he?" Hawk smiles, but (it seems to Jason) rather derisively. "Of course, he's a professional actor."

Jason is shocked at Hawk's tone, almost mocking. "I didn't know that. He was on the stage?"

"Minor television stuff. He really found his métier, though, as a motivational speaker for business gatherings. Made a fortune at it."

"How could he get from there to a nomination for president?"

"He was what they needed—someone who could appeal to American families who were losing their sons and daughters."

They watch the ceremonial conclusion. Representatives of the families approach the president, some breaking down, but others seem to draw strength, even dignity, from his presence. Jason hides his astonishment at Hawk's attitude. Maybe there are limits to Hawk's loyalty, and an actor/president might be outside them.

Hawk has always referred to the party as *we*; today it's *they*. Probably just his mood, watching a funeral. Or another of his ploys, testing Jason to see if he rises to the snide bait. Jason keeps his mouth shut. Hawk switches off the set.

"Just don't do it again." Hawk turns to his paperwork. Jason hesitates. "Something else?"

"Sir, I might be out of order but … could we find out whether the old man who was detained with me was released?"

It's hard to surprise Hawk, but this does. He lifts his head sharply and stares at Jason. "What for? Is this man of interest to CSIS?"

"Just to me. He helped me in detention. I got to know him. He has absolutely nothing to do with terrorists or even protestors. He's an old man who came here forty years ago. He's the kind you Americans take pride in—immigrants who come here to make better lives and who become loyal Americans."

Hawk leans back in his chair, and gives full attention. "Just when I'm getting comfortable with you, you drop something like this on me and I realize you're really somewhere else. It makes me wonder what else you've been up to."

Jason's not pleased to be seen as inscrutable. "You read me fine, sir. This just got to me. I was frightened in that camp. It was pretty scary. This man was a rock. I owe him. He's done nothing at all to justify detention and he's still a loyal citizen in spite of it all. We should get him released."

Hawk takes many seconds to digest this. "I'll be damned. Release a prisoner—an *American* prisoner—on the say-so of a CSIS agent? Can you imagine the alarm bells?"

"I'm sorry, I may be out of line. I just thought for once we could … do the right thing."

"The *right thing*. That'll be all, Jason. Better not ask me again to do the *right thing*."

Jason walks away, mulling a fresh impression of Hawk; it puzzles him. He's seen Hawk as the embodiment of the service he commands, the arch-SECOR, committed to the administration, dedicated to imprisoning terrorists even those only slightly suspect. L.A. Station, only one of several SECOR sites, has nonetheless many times the size and potency of the whole CSIS apparatus. He can compare Hawk then to his own A-D (whom, admittedly, he has only seen twice and not for long): no questioning, no backing-off, no half-heartedness. He sees total commitment between leader and project.

Once Jason has accepted that view, he assumes that he understands Hawk and can at least respect his actions as consistent with his beliefs. He's even warmed up to him, as a person of opinion but not guilt. Not one whose views he can ever share, but one he can make sense of.

He's begun to like Hawk, while losing some respect for SECOR, partly because the single-minded actions of Sid and even Archie seem to override natural justice, partly because of what he's seen on the street and in his hotel, and partly because some of Manwaring's ravings have a core of common sense. But he hasn't wavered in his view of Hawk. Now, he's not so convinced.

Re-assessing Hawk bothers Jason. It offends his training, which has drilled him to beware of preferences that could be caused by any tilt toward the liked over the lesser liked, the generic roots of bias.

He begins looking harder for some more balanced construct that would explain Hawk's attitude. He's a little troubled by where this speculation seems to lead him, but he keeps on pondering.

# FIFTEEN

JASON HAS BEEN SO ENTRANCED BY THE ELEGANT ARCHITECture of SECOR's functions that his critical faculty has been overwhelmed. Now, he begins to see it as more like the Roman Catholic Church during its medieval supremacy, an intricate machine that ran without any lubricant of human compassion, a seeker of sin, or even thoughts of sin, with or without substance. SECOR agents are in love with the process, with little concern for its excesses.

One of its roles is to censor the news. "They're setting up for another raid," Sid tells him. "They're a damn nuisance. The uniforms handle most of it but we always get a shitload of analysis."

"Raiding what?"

"Local newspaper."

"Can I go?"

"Ask Hawk."

"I need to go along. CSIS would die to be able to intimidate the media. They dump on us all the time."

Hawk looks ready to intimidate anyone. "You people need a Defense of Canada Act to handle the media."

"Working on your media technique here can hold off my recall."

"Recall? Isn't that up to me?"

"If the A-D says come home, I'm gone. And of course your man in Ottawa would be coming back here."

Hawk looks only a little put out at this blatant threat. "Bullying journalists puts me in a good mood. Lucky for you."

They pull out of the basement garage to lead the small convoy awaiting them in the street. As they whip along, several more vehicles with SECOR logos funnel in behind them until they must resemble a NASCAR pack as they sweep by, wailing and bleating.

"We're raiding the *Los Angeles Courier*?" It's one of the more prestigious American dailies, though somewhat hobbled nowadays. It's about as 'liberal' as a journal dares be under the eyes of the regime. Maybe even that's too much, or why the raid?

Their assault force wheels to a stop in front of the building, blocking traffic both ways, and dozens of gray SECORs flood through the various entries. Hawk goes in the main entrance at a dignified pace, Jason at his elbow.

"Please take us to the publisher's office," Hawk demands politely of a distressed young receptionist. She's gawking at the wedges of agents fanning out from the lobby to corridors, stairs, and elevators.

"Mr. Mackintyre is expecting you?" she manages as they shoot up to his level. The question is a reflex; she's too frightened to keep silent.

"If not, I'd be surprised."

In fact he's outside his office door in a jam of associates, several of whom are trying to talk at once. A couple of Hawk's agents are ahead of them, and he's scanning the warrant they've served on him. "For God's sake, Silas," he cries as Hawk approaches.

"Mack, you published a story that two so-called protestors were shot by SECOR and a few more wounded. Publication was prohibited because foreign interests organized it all. And you didn't check with us first."

"We didn't need to. We had a man there and he reported what he saw. We didn't even cover it in the print edition. Only on our website."

"Indicating you were aware it was illegal to print it."

"Some of us think it's a newsworthy event when our government shoots some of its own citizens. I seem to recall you once represented civil rights victims in court. Before you were co-opted by Big Oil."

Hawk merely inclines his head in recognition. "As a matter of fact, I won two of those suits. Of course, that's before we had a terrorist threat and were forced to license protests."

"Oh, for Christ's sake. There's no more danger from terrorism at a protest than there is from a political rally in downtown Washington."

"Recent history disputes that, Mack. That's why we issued an order to ban publicity on this one."

"Damn it, Silas! Every news outlet in the world had that story. Right across the border the Canadians had it in headlines."

"You also ran an editorial referring to the eviction of Muslim families from a sensitive district. You called it 'ethnic cleansing, American style.'"

"What do you people call it?"

"We don't expect a newspaper with a tradition of good citizenship to accuse the administration of ethnic persecution. When it's simply protecting its citizens."

"Good citizens respect due process. By that standard, the administration doesn't qualify."

"Well, we're not too concerned with what a publisher thinks, only with what he makes the public think."

Mackintyre seems to tire of scoring points in front of his staff. "Oh, come into my office." He leads the way into a corner room, venting his anger by slamming the open door against the stop, thrusting back his wheeled chair, and banging an open drawer shut. Hawk watches the performance with amusement.

The room is untidy, littered with the paraphernalia of the trade. Two computer monitors, stacks of printed texts, printouts in the customary bindings, many photographic enlargements, all tossed on desk or tables as if hastily scanned. A dozen photos, some of Mackintyre with another person or group, are hung about the walls. The president is shaking hands with him in one. Jason is amazed to focus on a shot of the publisher with Hawk, out of uniform. As he sits down, Mackintyre catches him looking it over. "I keep it up there to remind myself that we used to be friends."

"I'm still a friend, Mack, but you should know better than to put me in a bind."

"Hell, Silas, you could have overlooked that story. The administration shouldn't mind a few barbs. Accept a little criticism with grace." The sarcasm is overdone.

"Nicely put, just as your lawyer wrote it."

"Who is your spear-carrier here? Couldn't he afford a uniform?"

"Jason Currie is a Canadian observer."

"The Canadians are with you?" He runs his glance over Jason with something close to disgust. "I thought you people still accepted the media as a functional component of a democracy. I hope you're not here to learn how to handle it like SECOR."

"As a matter of fact, that's exactly why he's here," Hawk says. "Canada has been a weak sister in our mutual struggle, but their security service is determined to stiffen them up."

"Sir, I hope you don't swallow that whole," Jason says.

"Don't worry, son." Mackintyre leans back and folds his hands together as he continues to evaluate Jason. Hawk perches on one corner of the desk while Jason remains respectfully erect. "I'm quite familiar with Silas's playful deceptions. Besides, I speak regularly with Canadian editors. You people enjoy a lot more honesty in the news than we're allowed here."

"Careful, Mack," Hawk says, but it comes out as mockery.

"You were a better lawyer than you are a general, Silas. You can't even keep a straight face when you make a phony charge. Are your minions actually searching this building? Tell me what you're looking for. I'll help you find it without your ham-fisted agents screwing up our deadlines."

"More articles about protests. And the names of whoever's tipping you off to cover them."

"We destroy any data like that." Mackintyre is a little triumphant. "We learned to protect our tipsters after your last visit." Hawk absorbs this for a moment and then goes to the hall. Jason can see him instructing a subordinate there. He jumps on the opportunity.

"Excuse me, sir, you two behave like role-players. What's going on?"

Mackintyre regards him with suspicion. "I wonder why Hawk brought you along. What's your status in Canada?"

"Analyst. Not very senior." Mackintyre nods, waiting for more, clearly skeptical.

"How do you come to know General Hawk so well?"

"We're members of the same church. Since boys."

"What church?"

"It's a conservative old Episcopal congregation. You Canadians would call it Anglican. Not fundamentalist. That's what you're asking, isn't it?"

"I was just curious about General Hawk's background."

"No kidding. I'm beginning to get curious about yours."

Hawk re-enters. "Don't contaminate Jason, Mack. He already has the idea that all Americans are Christian crusaders. Canadians tend to look for simplistic causes of complex relationships."

Mackintyre looks from one to the other and back again in exasperation. "I know this is a treat for you, Silas, but most of us are not amused when SECOR comes calling. This particular sweep may be just a lark, but your people are seriously changing this country. The reason this young man is curious is because the administration has made religion a factor. And my old friend Silas Hawk should be ashamed to be where he is. It was bad enough when he was a lawyer for Big Oil."

After that, they stop twitting one another. Hawk and Jason leave the publisher to smolder. They move about the building, Hawk overseeing the search. He calls it off after an hour with nothing of use uncovered. En route back to the tower, Jason asks him, "Will they be penalized for the article?"

"It will add to their file. They could draw a temporary suspension." Jason feels a sidelong glance measuring him. "You surprised me. I've always heard Canadians were noted for conformity."

"Yes, sir. But we don't necessarily conform to the same ideas."

Hawk snickers. "Jason, that's a definition of non-conformity. Not well accepted at SECOR. Did you learn anything at all?"

"That it wouldn't work in Canada."

# SIXTEEN

HE'S AWAKENED BY THE HOTEL PHONE. "IT'S FOUR-THIRTY!"

"I know what time it is," Hawk's mechanical voice says. "At five you'll be picked up by a SECOR patrol."

SECOR station works around the clock, so Jason's not surprised to find it fully staffed at this hour, but with strangers, the graveyard shift, nearing its quitting time. There's a sprinkling of familiar faces, a number of them looking as he must, unshaven and hastily dressed. Except Hawk, as neatly turned out as for any workday. Maybe he never sleeps.

"The army sent us a file—from Khartoum. A Sudanese there, directing a cell here—right here—in California. Using coded e-mails. Sounds just too simple, doesn't it? Now we've got to verify it. Then the army will take all the credit. I've parceled out the e-mails. I want your take as well. We're tracing the addresses through the servers."

This is what he's craved for—real subversives, not just adolescent ravings. Not the thin gruel SECOR's been accepting as sufficient cause for internment. He's wide awake now. Hawk's staccato sentences and man-of-action tension are an added stimulant. "We're drawing together a profile. Should have that soon. You'll want it too. Helps to know his mindset."

"What kind of person?"

"University professor. Doctor Al Ansari. Religious. Advisor to the regime. Apparently eminent."

"Wow! Army intelligence must have lit up when they struck this. We're bringing him here?"

A little of Hawk's ardor evaporates. "That's not the way it works. The Pentagon's holding Sudanese prisoners in Sudan. For now. Probably to find any potential collaborators before they bury the rest."

"They'll have to make an exception for this one."

"DIA aren't giving up one inch of their territorial rights. They need our input to verify the data. Maybe to make arrests. Then if anything goes wrong it will be our fault. But they want all the credit. So he stays in Khartoum."

"We have to live with that?"

"Let's do our job now, then work out our next move."

The e-mail translations seem innocent. They were sent to numbers of Sudanese in California, clearly immigrants there, whom Al Ansari seems to have known personally in the home country. They would have been picked up as intercepts, but with Sudan's low profile before the invasion, they were probably dispatched to the great unanalyzed recycle bin. Al Ansari's advice was sought on some of the missteps of devout Sudanese in a hedonistic America. The responses were not much different from those a priest might give a penitent. The army's convinced that the pastoral advice hides coded messages. Jason turns to the originals, scanned and e-mailed from Khartoum, and begins studying every Arabic sentence.

Hawk approaches later. "Any progress?"

"These are very rough translations. On a word-for-word comparison they stand up, but they don't make sense as context."

"That's why DIA's sure they're coded."

"Pretty inefficient code. To hide a message you have to create a sensible cover."

"The army trains translators in a hurry," Hawk says. "Good enough for interrogation. Maybe not for this level—" Jason chuckles, and Hawk reacts sharply. "What's the joke?"

"I just realized this bit is a direct quotation from the Koran. Not in English—it makes no sense. In Arabic."

"A quotation used as code?"

"A quotation used as a quotation. He's giving advice by quoting the greatest authority."

"I'm glad you're having a good time, Jason. Here's the Al Ansari profile. Call me when you have something that doesn't amuse you."

Doctor Ahmed Al Ansari is a professor of history. He argues that a state cannot be bound by both a religious code and a secular constitution, but only one or the other. It's nearly the same conclusion reached by the Founding Fathers and recognized nowadays by every liberal country, but he stands it on its head by insisting that it precludes any committed Islamic state from embracing democracy. He doesn't condemn the democracies, but merely asserts that the individualism, which is inherent in such systems, is incompatible with allegiance to God and the Islamic community, the *Ummah*.

"Personally I would commit to the security of Islam over the ebb and flow of individual priorities," he has written, "but others will choose as their conscience and their teaching dictate. However, they cannot ride both horses. Submission to God's will cannot be subject to a majority of fifty percent plus one; it demands certainty, and so a doctrinal state is inevitably authoritarian." Al Ansari is hostile to the West, not because his analysis is at odds with Western thought but because of the choice he has made. He's an advocate of *Sharia* law, which has been gradually redefined in the West as compatible with support for terrorism. He is as well a passionate critic of the American occupations.

Hawk returns about noon. "We have one of them." After hours of meticulous transcribing, Jason has lost much of his zeal. Al Ansari's style is formal, his reasoning intricate, his advice concrete but always deferring to Islamic tradition, all of it difficult to translate with precision. Some of his references have sent Jason to his books. His desk is crowded—a Koran, an Arabic dictionary, several texts on Islamic practice, and piles of e-mails, originals in right-to-left format and the translations European style. "He was easy enough to trace. He's being interrogated now."

"What sort of person?"

"Lives in a slum. Works in a convenience store. Hardly any English. Neighborhood has lots of Arabs."

"Married?"

"Why's that material?"

"Martyrs are typically single. Some of the e-mails give advice on marital problems. Not sexual, just proper relations between spouses."

Hawk now looks concerned. "What're you coming up with here? We're looking for evidence. Not marriage counseling, evidence of conspiracy. Coded or otherwise."

"General, I've been reading this man's mail for—seven hours. I'm not finding conspiracy. What do the code-crackers say?"

Hawk also seems to have lost his enthusiasm. He sits on the corner of Jason's desk. He looks crestfallen. "No code system found."

"The other translators?"

"Not all as opinionated as you. But nothing useful so far."

"Could the army have made a mistake?" Normally Hawk wears confidence like a cape. Now he's troubled. His vulnerability opens a door of promise for Jason. A chance to help, something he's always looking for. A chance to firm up his base with Hawk. Maybe a longer tether on his Mexican mission.

"They'd never admit it. We have our neck out on this one, Jason. The army has an investment in this man. If we suggest their story is a crock of shit, the Pentagon will use it against us. They'll leak that we botched the follow-up on their coup. They'll make Ansari into Osama bin Laden. SECOR can't find its ass with both hands. This is a time bomb and it's already ticking."

"Sir, there's another way. Let me see the hard drive from his computer. We've only seen his e-mails. If he's running a cell there's bound to be something concrete. And he might be—we haven't found anything to exonerate him, just nothing to condemn him."

"There's no way DIA will let it out of their hands. Especially if we tell them we're finding nothing now."

"So don't tell them. We're hot on the trail but we need all the data. We back their story but we should leave no stone unturned."

"That would really make them suspicious."

"Just get us that hard drive."

"Keep working, Jason. I'll go after the Pentagon." He slides down from his perch and strides away, confidence somewhat restored.

It's near the end of a long day when Hawk comes by again.

"They agreed to let us download the computer. In Khartoum. Also to interrogate Al Ansari."

"But we need it here, not in Khartoum."

"Best deal on offer. I couldn't shake them."

"The army would have us under its thumb."

"They have us there now."

"We could say that we need more detail to prevent a potential disaster. Shift the responsibility. It's up to them to back it up."

"Jason, there's no way the army will release that hard drive. They don't want to give us anything to build on." The chance to get closer to Hawk recedes to the vanishing point.

But Hawk's not finished. "They're suspicious. They insist we have an army officer present. I've agreed and nominated Werner. He's here now."

"Oh. Colonel Werner is to head the mission, General?"

Whether Hawk's irritated with that or perhaps taken aback by Jason's effrontery, he only responds with a laser glare at Jason and turns away.

"General, we daren't use the army to translate. Their linguists start with not one word of the language and in six months they're rated fluent. You can imagine. I've been speaking Arabic since I was six months old. This is very sensitive material. You should take me."

"You've just been arguing against going."

"If we can't do it here, I'll do it properly there."

"Werner says they're competent. Here he comes now."

The Colonel strides over to them, snapping a salute at Hawk and a sharp glance at Jason. "Eric, Currie feels we need our own translator. He's volunteered."

Werner's surprised. "Currie? We can't take a Canadian civilian to a war zone. We've got our own linguists."

"Like the one who translated this, Colonel?" Jason waves his file toward Werner's chin.

"Forget it, Currie. You couldn't get permission from CSIS anyway. We'll be leaving in a few hours."

"Sir, my assignment is to report to General Hawk and follow his orders. Nothing about where."

"Nice try, but you're neither American nor military. They wouldn't let you off the plane in Sudan."

Hawk steps between them. "Easy, Eric. The army needs our cooperation. We need a sensitive translator. Incidentally, the file says Al Ansari hates Americans. We might do better with a Canadian. I've decided to take Currie. We'll tell CSIS later."

Werner manages to control his dissent, perhaps with difficulty, nods, and moves off briskly, throwing one last glare at Jason.

"You don't handle Werner very adroitly, Jason," Hawk says, not without a touch of malice.

"No, sir. I wish I had your talent for it."

# SEVENTEEN

"WE'LL BE MAKING A STEEP DESCENT TO MINIMIZE THE RISK from ground fire."

Jason's noted with relief, reading the latest communiqué, that Khartoum has been 'pacified' and the airport is in American hands, so he's anticipated an exciting but not really dangerous stay in an occupied city. So what's this ground fire? Before their mission has even begun, they've been misled, perhaps not for the last time, by military newspeak.

From L.A., they'd arrived at a massive base in Yemen, where the Americans have a series of encampments stoutly held against a largely hostile and sometimes murderous population, rather like the Roman legions in ancient Britain, holding the forts and the highroads, with all other territory too hazardous to penetrate. From there they've been transshipped in a smaller plane, crossing the Red Sea to the fresh theatre.

They don't descend; they dive out of the washed sky toward tilted brown desert, arcing across the windows. Jason's pressed hard against his restraining belt. Some quarter of Khartoum slides by, hidden under a smoke layer that rolls before the breeze like muddy water. The flash of an explosion lights it up. They sweep through a dust cloud, suddenly darkened. He feels the grip of pressure in his gut as they pull out and find their glide path. Banking into it, they pass low over another arm of the city, this one nearly free of smoke. Jason has been scanning through briefing notes—the city lies at the junction of the White Nile and the Blue Nile, and he glimpses both rivers briefly. Across one of them is Omdurman, where the self-proclaimed Mahdi was entombed. Winston Churchill as a young subaltern took part there in the last charge by British cavalry. Now once more there's a spearhead of Western power pricking at the resilience of Islam.

Miles of brown houses sprawl beneath. They're close enough to see the streets, only some paved, and all hazy in blowing dust, the citizens, mostly in white, trapped in chaos. There are knots of civilians, hurrying here and there, some loaded down with goods, either fleeing with their own or looting someone else's. Wrecked and burnt-out cars, trucks, buses, and military vehicles are scattered along the streets, some under rubble. And bodies, some attended and others forlornly deserted. Fleetingly, he glimpses an alley where dogs are tearing at a small corpse, possibly human. He focuses on a tank firing at a multi-storey building, the gun flash and the clouds of debris directly under the airplane window. Squads of camouflaged troops laden with gear snake along the edges of buildings. He doesn't know what to expect in a city said to be pacified, but not anarchy. He should feel a stiffening of fear, a surge of horror and of pity, the feelings of a civilized person facing savage behavior, but seen from the remote sterility of an aircraft, the spectacle raises no honest sentiment but rather the kind of fascination he might feel as a witness to a street accident.

On the opposite bench, Hawk and Werner are also staring down at the tumult. He can just hear Werner muttering, really disturbed. Hawk is calmer.

They taxi to a hangar. Another aircraft is discharging cargo there, power carts whisking the stream of supplies through the massive hangar doors. Most of their own plane is crammed with crated goods, leaving only abbreviated benches for priority passengers: six senior officers, five other ranks, and Jason. Now they all step out into searing heat.

"I thought the city was secured," Werner says to the lieutenant who signals them to his vehicle.

"Is that what they're saying in the States? Who writes that stuff? We're taking rocket fire every day. We had a mortar attack this morning. We can't go into the city except in force with armor."

"Their army is still intact then?"

"We can't find their formations anymore, but we have our

hands full now with irregulars, and they're worse."

"Usual story," Werner says. "You can't just hunker down here. You need to blast them out. You must have plenty of firepower."

"Yes, sir." He looks worn out. Jason admires his poise in the face of Werner's gratuitous advice. "If we had enough manpower to use it all."

"But we allowed for plenty of ground forces this time."

"Perhaps, sir. But they've stripped us bare for a major assault to the south."

The lieutenant has been eyeing Jason's drab fatigues, void of any identification except a Canadian flag patch, which SECOR has somehow provided. "You're not a journalist, are you, sir? We can't admit any who aren't accredited."

"If he were," Werner says, "do you think we'd have him on this plane?"

Jason's full of sympathy for the young officer. "I'm an Arabic linguist."

"We'd better get you under cover if the colonel vouches for you."

They drive by squads of soldiers stripping cargo planes and ferrying their contents to storage. Many are naked to the waist; the others' shirts are blackened with sweat in the desert heat. Nobody's lounging; there's an air of urgency. An ambulance races past. They pass an aircraft wreck, black, with a stench of burnt fuel. In the distance Jason can make out a line of three drones, one just preparing to take off.

A haze of smoke and dust hangs everywhere and has already crept under Jason's shirt and mixed with his sweat. More men surround the terminal, some of them installing blast shields over the windows. Inside, it's like a high-paced shopping mall, officers and men moving smartly among the command centers. The lieutenant leaves them at the end of a hallway, closed off by a detail of resting men. They enter a room with no windows.

A major sits at a table used as desk, hovered over by a sergeant. He comes to his feet, and both salute smartly.

"General Hawk, and this is Colonel Werner."

"Major Shragg, sir." He's amazingly tall—inches over six feet—and nearly bald. He has a neat moustache like the classical British officer. "Who is this civilian?"

"Our translator, Mr. Currie."

There's no change in Shragg's correct expression, but Jason's sensors pick up his disapproval. "And this is *our* translator, Technical Sergeant Brill."

"You're the team that interrogated Al Ansari?" Hawk asks.

"No, sir, we just identified him. My assignment is combat support, interrogating prisoners close to our action. He was brought in with a sheaf of e-mails found on his computer. Sergeant Brill found them incriminating."

"I did the translations myself, sir," the sergeant says, still at attention. "Some refer to earlier mail we didn't find. Why would a Khartoum professor be exchanging mail with anyone in California? So we copied them to your station."

Hawk bestows a manly military smile. "Good work, Major Shragg. Give me the name of your commanding officer so I can pass on my congratulations. We're ready to see the prisoner." More salutes as the major and his sergeant leave the stage.

It's now late in their day. Jason's sleepless and jetlagged. Hawk and Werner are no doubt the same. But time is pressing, so they prepare to face the suspect.

Al Ansari looks disheveled but still gives an impression of great composure. He's a small black man in traditional dress, a white robe. Jason puts his age in the sixties, maybe late sixties. His face is lined, almost in folds, and dominated by dark eyes that seem huge and nearly round, as if in permanent surprise. His beard is unimpressive, only a grizzled wisp. He looks over his trio of inquisitors with some apprehension but also curiosity. Hawk motions him toward the chair that faces the three others.

"Please sit down," Jason says politely, and Al Ansari does so while looking him over quizzically.

"You are American?"

"Canadian." Touching the flag on his arm.

"Explain to him that we come from the United States," Hawk says. "There are many Sudanese there, most of whom are good citizens. But there are also a few young men who are doing great harm to their fellow Sudanese by plotting attacks on our people. We would like him to help us identify them so that all other Sudanese Americans will be secure. No harm will come to these men."

"That sounds a little thick to me," Jason says.

"Just tell him!" Werner says before Hawk can comment. Hawk glares at Werner.

Al Ansari hears Jason out with the raised eyebrows of a skeptic. "Do the Americans tell you Canadians such tales?" Jason breaks into a chuckle.

"Never mind the witticisms," Hawk says, cutting Werner short. "Cooperative or not?"

"Are you prepared to help us?" Jason asks. "It would certainly improve your situation with the Americans."

"By help you mean betray young men who are dedicated to their community?"

"It sounds as if *he's* asking *you* the questions," Hawk says. "Tell him his religion is being dishonored by these extremists. They teach hatred of Christians."

"The general suggests Islamists are teaching young Muslims in America that Christians are the enemies of Islam. It's causing problems in his country."

"Ah! I sympathize with the general. Radical Christians are teaching *their* young men that Muslims are the enemies of Christianity, and that is causing problems in *my* country."

Jason translates this. Hawk's mildly amused, but Werner is exasperated. He leans toward Al Ansari and spears him with his glare. "Tell him if his own government could control their radicals we wouldn't need to be here."

Al Ansari notes Werner's anger, but replies patiently. "And his own government can do that in America?"

Jason decides to modify this. "He says it's difficult for governments to rein in militants. He suggests we must have the same problem."

"*Does* he?" Hawk regards the Sudanese with interest, holding up one hand to restrain Werner. "Tell him the problem may be only radical Islam, but if he can't help us sort out radical Islam from sincere Islam, we may have to consider Islam itself as the enemy." Jason translates faithfully.

"There is only one Islam. It is people who are radical or otherwise."

"He's playing with us," Werner says. "We need to use other methods."

The prisoner looks at Jason.

"The colonel demands more cooperation. It's unwise to trifle with these officers," he adds in a quiet tone of caution.

Ansari stares at Jason. "You come from Canada. *Your* country has no part in this war."

"He will try to be more cooperative," Jason says in English.

"Jason, this is an interrogation," Hawk says. "You sound as though it's a neighborly chat. Be a little more forceful."

"They're getting impatient," Jason interprets.

"You're an interesting intermediary," Ansari says. How much English might he understand?

Werner gets up and moves around, frustrated. Hawk is calm but has had enough. "I understand what we're dealing with.

We'll take a different tack tomorrow."

"May I talk with him, reason with him? He seems to be approachable. He doesn't sound like a fanatic."

Werner is scandalized. "Currie, you're here as an interpreter, not a goddamn—"

"Just a moment, Eric," Hawk says. "It'll do no harm for Jason to soften him up with a touch of humanity. Sometimes that helps to crack them."

The rancor between the two has become tangible. It's not the first time Hawk has contradicted his subordinate in Jason's presence, this time without coating his malice.

Al Ansari has followed the exchange intently, perhaps grasping the nub of it. "Doctor," Jason says, "these officers have been assured that you are a fundamentalist, with contacts in California who mean to attack Americans. Their duty is to protect their people. If you can show us that your American friends are ordinary citizens, with no such intentions, they will be spared a very hard time. And so will you."

"If I had such friends, how would I demonstrate their innocence?"

"Give us all their names and we will investigate them."

"By 'investigate,' you mean the way you're presently investigating me?"

"Certainly not. This is a war zone. In America we would merely ask others about them and examine their records. The general would be concerned if any were fundamentalists who might become suicide bombers."

Al Ansari's agitated. "There's that 'fundamentalist' again. We are profound believers in the authority of the Koran. Suicide! It is forbidden! Do you really believe that millions of Muslims would rather die to kill Christians? They only want to survive with their own families. Islam or Christianity doesn't make human beings so different from one another."

"But—but there have been *many* suicides, whether or not it's forbidden—"

"Those have no more to do with Islam than American wars have to do with Christianity. I don't support them, nor should you. It's not about faith; it's about leaders. Yours seem to be as misguided as ours. We have enough blood on our hands, but so do you."

"Jason, is there a single word of any use to us in that whole exquisite passage?" Hawk seems discouraged. Werner's disgust is undisguised; he stands with his hands behind his back, staring down at Al Ansari.

"Your associates have less patience than you do," Al Ansari says. Nowhere near winning his cooperation, Jason hurries on, trying a more provocative line.

"Some people in America believe that Arabs hate them and would destroy America if they could."

"Popular beliefs are easily contrived. There as well as here." How can he offer such a conclusion to two representatives of that leadership except as a taunt? He and Al Ansari both speak Arabic, though with different accents, so their minds should make contact, but for the filter of custom, the one indoctrinated in a community of prayer, where every phase of behavior, social, sexual, and familial, is shaped by teaching that originated in a desert culture thirteen centuries ago and has changed little; the other a product of an Enlightenment, the main thrust of which was to undermine and replace such doctrinal guidance. So they hear each other clearly, but their minds can barely communicate.

Al Ansari studies Jason with his huge eyes. His own reaction is being read. Despair settles over the professor, the gaze now overcome by a film of dullness. Al Ansari's tone sinks to a murmur, as if there is no point in talking to anyone but himself. "Not all Islamic countries are run by thugs masquerading as the faithful. Some of us are dedicated to the reconciliation of our religion with our obligations to the rest of the planet. We *will* be good citizens of this world but without compromising our faith."

Hawk says quietly, "Your sales pitch has moved him to defiance. I take it he's not buying?"

"Waste of time," says Werner. "He's just playing a game." They leave Al Ansari slumped in his chair, ready to be returned to his den.

# EIGHTEEN

JASON DINES ON COLD ARMY RATIONS, SEATED, AS IT TURNS out, beside the same, even wearier lieutenant who had received them. They sit on the floor in a faintly lit waiting room, surrounded by drained men. Some have found enough floor space to sprawl at length; others lean against the wall or slouch on their packs. A few are eating from their packaged rations. Some are sleeping or trying to. Among the bodies, a litter of guns and gear obliterates the tile floor. There's little conversation, just shared exhaustion.

"Have most of these men just come from the States?" Jason asks in a hushed voice.

"A few from other fronts. Mostly Stateside."

"How about you?"

"Seattle."

"I lived for years in Vancouver."

"Hey! Been there many times." His features brighten as he visualizes home. For a moment, he looks as young as he probably is. Jason is encouraged to ask a question that has been bothering him.

"Lieutenant, do you feel we're justified here?"

The boy disappears and the face tightens into adult reserve. "That's not a proper question, sir, you know that."

"Your commanders spelled out the rationale?"

"I know what our mission is. But we're trained to fight enemy armies. Going up against soldiers who look like civilians can drive you crazy. Sometimes we shoot the wrong people. Or get our own men killed."

"Must be incredibly frustrating. How *do* you sort them out?"

"Mostly by who's shooting at us. Look, I know what you're getting at. Sometimes Muslims can seem like Indians in the Old West. But most of us try to behave like decent Americans."

"Do your officers resent the army being used up in all these campaigns?" The lieutenant's head snaps back. He stares at Jason. "I've heard comments like that from officers in the States," Jason says.

"You won't hear them from officers in the field." He turns away.

Jason finds a corner of the floor with room enough to stretch out. Exhausted as he is, it's impossible to really sleep.

There are moments of stillness, encouraging his muscles to relax, suddenly split by bursts of distant firing or the *whump!* of a projectile. He feels too well protected to be afraid, but he's certainly alert. Someone stirs or turns over and then a dozen more bodies follow. Occasional feet tromp nearby and commands are passed along. It's the kind of night when he yearns for sleep but just as much for the night to be over to relieve the tension of insomnia.

When he rises at first light, quite a number of spaces on the floor have been vacated, by men summoned for yet earlier duty. He moves about the terminal, peering through those windows that still lack blast screens, able to glimpse the flights already landing. The nighttime firing has petered out and the day's hostilities not quite begun.

Hawk catches up to him. He's in a grim mood. Jason follows him wordlessly to an unoccupied corner. "Werner has convinced General Carmody that we're here to discredit the army's scoop. I got a dressing down from Carmody just now. They'd already given their version to the embedded correspondents here. Carmody doesn't want us watering down their scenario. And he doesn't like your participation."

"Because I'm Canadian?"

"Because Werner told him you've taken a button and sewed a vest on it."

Jason feels a cold draft of fear. There's no law here but the army. Even Hawk is impotent. Jason fidgets nervously and probably looks frightened, because Hawk softens his tone.

"Are you really certain of your interpretation, Jason? Nothing but parochial guidance?"

"Dead certain. We can demonstrate it. We can take Al Ansari through every e-mail on his hard drive and show what he's advising and why. None of it is threatening. What we've got is an overeager linguist using imagination for lack of skill."

"Whose superiors agree with him. That's our problem."

"I think I understand Al Ansari. He's a philosopher. He'd love to debate us all day long. He's also a sincere Muslim who abhors suicide. Give me enough time with him and I'm sure he'll clear himself."

"Jason." Hawk's hands signal a full stop. "Listen carefully. This is no longer about Al Ansari. It's about the army's take on Al Ansari. So far as they're concerned, his guilt is proven. That's already out there. Now they need SECOR to confirm it. Or, if we don't, pay the consequences."

"A dozen linguists would agree with me," Jason says.

"And they'd have a hundred. We can't get into a pissing contest with the army. The government has to be on their side. We rate about the same as traffic cops, necessary but annoying. Then there are their friends on the Armed Services Committee; they could crucify SECOR over this."

Jason suddenly snaps alert to how much trouble Hawk is facing, thanks to his reading of Al Ansari. "What can we do?"

"The shortest way out is to agree with them. Then detain a lot of American Sudanese. What we can't do is detain none."

"Even if there's no cell, no conspiracy?"

"Especially then. The army is scapegoating us. We have to be seen doing everything possible to verify their plot. Maybe we can turn the tables later. Then we accuse the army of sending us on a wild-goose chase. But we can't do that until we've turned over every stone and shown nothing was under it."

After conniving to come here to get tighter with Hawk, Jason's now in danger of alienating him. He needs to help, somehow. To be very cooperative. "Tell me what to do."

"Carmody made it clear you're not to translate for Ansari. Werner's convinced him you're shaping the answers. They're not keen on me being there, either. They prefer Werner. He's a SECOR liaison. So they'll let me be present, but Werner will ask the questions."

"You accepted that?"

"No choice. This is army territory. You and I are only here to dress up the story. As for you, they're short of competent translators—" He pauses, no doubt as the irony of this strikes him. "And you're available now. So, I've offered you to Major Shragg for the day since we're using his sergeant for the interrogation."

"I'll do anything I'm asked."

"One thing, Jason. Carmody told me Shragg's in line for a commendation for turning up Al Ansari. Watch out he doesn't get you shot out there. Here's Werner."

The colonel looks smug to Jason, but it's probably only

his customary confidence. "Have a good day, Currie. This will be a new experience for you, getting shot at. Keep your head down. You'll probably feel different about Muslims by tonight."

Major Shragg leads them into Khartoum. They have an armored carrier as transport and travel in a small convoy with a massive tank in support, so he's impressed that the mission may be hazardous. Their little column skirts the city limits until they edge into a quarter where both vehicles and foot soldiers are on the move. The rattle of automatic rifles becomes constant. Grenades and mortar bombs pop off now and again, none really close. They weave around debris spilling from half-destroyed buildings. A few desperate survivors claw through wreckage here and there. He can't believe they'll find anyone alive, but what else can they do? Most of the Sudanese are hidden.

Their task is to interview prisoners brought into a walled compound that the army has secured. It's the garden of a private house, much larger than most, and partially wrecked. Furniture and trappings have cascaded through the shattered walls. Remnants of what must have been a magnificent carpet are partly buried under the rubble, from which also protrudes one hand, with the rest of a woman's body suggested by a scrap of feminine clothing.

Three prisoners sprawl along the wall, young black men who wear no recognizable uniform. They stare at the

American soldiers, loaded with gear, with something between envy and defiance. All three are wounded. The major commandeers a damaged table for his notes and they go to work. One prisoner's hand is wrapped in a rough bandage, now rusty with dried blood. He's clearly in pain. The major chooses him first. "Tell him we'll treat his wound and give him painkillers if he cooperates."

It's a powerful incentive, probably contrary to international law, but perhaps that doesn't apply to irregulars. The men respond with eager answers but sparse information. Shragg dismisses them in disgust. They're moved out without receiving the promised medication. Several more are herded in, looking just like the first lot but in worse shape. One is supported by his comrades. He looks about sixteen. He's very pale. He holds one hand over his chest, oozing blood. The major singles him out. "Ask him how many are in that house."

Jason asks but gets no reply. "I don't think he can understand."

"Then make him understand!"

Jason repeats the question. The boy stares at him blankly and then seems to lose consciousness. His hand falls to his side and he slumps to the ground. Blood continues to seep from his wound. His comrades move toward him. Their guards nudge them back with leveled weapons.

"I think he's dead anyway," one of them says. Jason kneels beside him. The boy's chest heaves, barely. His eyes are open but without recognition.

Jason is swept with shame, as palpable as a shudder, kneeling over a subsiding life, trying to coax some morsel of information with the last gasp. Finally he whispers, "I hope you will find paradise."

The boy stares at this stranger, speaking his own language to him in a gentle voice, as if he might be a giver of relief, someone who could quiet the turmoil in his mind as his heart gushes out its last feeble spurts. Jason sees his hand move and understands he wants to be touched. He reaches out and holds the boy's hand. The spark dies out in a moment as he is overcome by the lassitude of death.

One of the guards spits. "Jesus Christ!"

Another says, "Aren't you gonna kiss him, sir?" There are a couple of snickers. The major swears in disgust.

They leave him lying there. The other prisoners huddle against the wall, abject, beaten men, choked with fear but also hatred. They stare at the Americans with loathing, at Jason with bewilderment.

"Perhaps they would have been more amenable if we'd given their buddy some help," Jason says angrily to the major.

"Christ! This is a battle zone. Our job is to get information. If we know which buildings are occupied, we can handle it with drones. If we have to send in men, some of them will get killed. We're not here to be nice to these *jihadis*; we're here to save the lives of our own men."

"What if they lie? Who wouldn't?"

"I'll interrogate, you interpret. They have plenty of incentive with him lying there dead."

They have that kind of relationship the rest of the day. The major and his men take him for a wimp, and he seethes over it. But he then admits to himself that he would probably feel the same way they do if he had been bushwhacked as often as they have. He becomes more cooperative and things go more smoothly. He manages to get some answers, whether useful or not. Some of the prisoners are so shaken they are incomprehensible to him. Others are defiant.

The Sudanese seem to him as alike as an extended family, while the Americans are a mélange of black, white, and Asian. The Sudanese are defeated, leaden with despair, while the Americans wear the confidence, even arrogance, of conquering warriors.

Late in the day, when they are all sweaty, dusty, tired, and frustrated, another detail delivers two prisoners, one mangled by shrapnel wounds. Jason once saw a deer shot by a group of hunters, still gasping, but bloody over its whole body; this man looks the same. His eyes are wild with fear and pain. He moans continuously, but only faintly, too weak to give full voice to his agony. His overseers have no pity for him. "His buddy blew himself up when we broke in. We had three wounded, one pretty bad. This guy was probably supposed to do the same, but he must have chickened out. We need to know if there are more suiciders in there."

Jason can get no response from him. He doesn't think he's

resisting, only unhinged, unable rather than unwilling. The major doesn't agree. "Pull him to his feet and walk him about. Shake him up." He screams as they pull him up. Two men can walk him with difficulty, his legs dragging. But he doesn't speak. The major steps in front of the dangling body and punches him in the side where one wound is welling blood and froth. The prisoner begins choking. "Now ask him!"

"He's beyond talking."

"Do as you're ordered, Currie."

"This is torture, Major."

"The Pentagon gave us the green light for enhanced interrogation."

"Can the Pentagon do that?"

"The Pentagon can do what it damn well pleases in a war zone. Now get on with it."

Jason looks to the guards to find if there's any support there. They're paying close attention—maybe enjoying the dressing-down. The remaining prisoner is left to watch the tableau, perhaps steeling himself for his own turn, screwing up his defiance. Jason knows he's a tenderfoot among veterans. These men are trapped in a world where bodies are ruined, comrades disintegrated. They're surrounded by closeted enemies whose hatred is bottomless. Who is he to question them? The prisoner manages a final moan and dies. Jason sinks down on a concrete block, miserable.

"Has this man been searched yet?" Shragg steps close to the other prisoner, ready for his next subject.

"We were just starting—"

"Well, search him now!"

Shragg steps away, but one step only. Before he sets the second foot down there's a white flash, followed instantly by the crack of the explosion. Jason finds himself on the ground, blinded by dust. He imagines himself wounded, but when he makes a tentative move to rise he's surprised to find himself intact. He gets to his feet, gingerly, nearly deaf and hurting everywhere.

He's the only one standing. Shragg, close to the prisoner, took the full blast up his back. It is split open, the outline of his ribs clear in the mangled flesh. All three soldiers are wounded. Two are now struggling to rise. The third stirs and moans gently. The prisoner is just a mound in the dust. As Jason's head clears, it comes to him that his tiff with Shragg distracted the guards before they completed their search, and now Shragg is dead.

A medic checks him after the wounded have been patched up and Shragg's corpse sorted into a body bag. "You're incredibly lucky. We'll check you out back at the base but nothing serious. Can you hear okay?" Jason doesn't feel lucky. If he were truly lucky he wouldn't be here in the Sudan.

Nightfall is approaching when they arrive at the terminal. None of them has any trace of good will remaining.

# NINETEEN

JASON'S LEFT WRIST IS CRACKED AND THE REST OF THE ARM bloodied where the skin was rasped off. He is bandaged with a light cast applied, the skin above the dressing turned ochre with disinfectant.

He spends the night in the mobile hospital in the terminal. Sleep is hard to find; his arm aches and, even more, his mind churns with remorse, tainted with self-pity. He moans over his too-clever move to include himself on the Sudan assignment; he now despises himself for his rancor toward Shragg.

When he's not lacerating himself he listens to those more seriously wounded. A few sleep, more stir fitfully, others moan, and some even talk. Medics come and go. During the night a group of critical cases are moved to an outbound plane. It's never quiet. There's no comfort in thinking of

Miriam, now further out of reach if he's alienated Hawk.

Finally he does sleep, uneasily, to be awakened by Hawk. He feels mindless, spaced out. Catching his reflection in Hawk's eyes, he must look the same.

"I heard about Shragg."

Jason can't hear of the major without choking up, whether from genuine sympathy or shock at his own near miss. "I believe I'm clear to get out of here now." They wait for a sling to support his arm.

"No progress yesterday," Hawk says as they settle in a boarding lounge half full of resting men.

"Why?"

"They manhandled Ansari and made him less helpful."

"Manhandled?"

Hawk shrugs. "Werner's job is to protect DIA's property rights. They just don't want Al Ansari exonerated. We go along or go home."

"What about the hard drive. We were promised access."

"With all that's happened, could it help at all?"

Surprising to find Hawk without resources. Perhaps the stonewalling from the army followed by Jason's close shave has made him decide to back off? His own self-pity evaporates. Something needs to be done, and quickly, to restore their position.

"It would give me a great deal of satisfaction if I could find anything at all."

Hawk's interest picks up. "One angle I could try—if we're

to cross-examine suspects in L.A., we should know what they were telling him. We only have his own e-mails."

"Sir, you've got to *demand* that hard drive."

"You seem to be full of piss and vinegar. Getting blown up agrees with you."

"It certainly sharpened my focus. Look, they must be concerned to give us no excuses. Drive home to Carmody that Al Ansari hasn't been helpful, so we must have more leads. Hit him hard. No hard drive, no cell to be found."

"I can handle Carmody." But he hesitates. "Remember, if I get that hard drive, you need to find something conclusive. Either Ansari's innocent or the army's story is credible. In-between makes us look like wimps." He hurries off.

Jason takes advantage of the empty bench to sprawl full length, tired and aching, and dozes quietly.

Carmody does agree to give them access to Al Ansari's computer. Jason labors over the dense Arabic the rest of that day and into the night. There are lengthy notes, probably for lectures, religious arguments, partly familiar to him, reams of personal records as mundane as his own files, and finally a little red meat.

"Just enough to warrant one more crack at Al Ansari."

With Carmody's brusque consent, they proceed once more to the room at the end of the passage. Al Ansari is brought in. Jason is stunned at his appearance. "What the *hell*—"

"Back off, Currie," Werner says. "We had to get rough

with him."

The Sudanese is bowed, stiff, and moving hesitantly. He shuffles along to the chair and sits down heavily, leaning on the back first to steady himself. His face is bruised. Blood spatters the white robe. He holds one hand in the other after he sits; the one he protects is discolored. He is calm enough, but when Jason meets his gaze directly, he can see terror fighting with resolution. In fear of pain, or more fearful of betraying his faith? Jason catches Hawk's eye. Hawk shakes his head.

"Understand, Currie," Werner says, leaning on each word, "you are seconded to an active unit and subject to military discipline." He lets that sink in. "We're recording this interrogation. Don't finesse his answers. If you're insubordinate I'll have you charged." The two guards watch the exchange with curiosity, not sympathy. Al Ansari looks from Jason to Werner and back again, perhaps with a little hope.

"I'm sorry to see you've been mistreated," Jason says finally to Al Ansari.

"I see that your body also has been violated."

"Just a moment!" Werner holds a cautionary hand in front of Jason. "We agreed you could ask this man specific questions on the content of his computer. No chitchat. Translate his replies word for word."

"It's impossible to translate Arabic into English word for word." Hawk signals Jason to tone it down. "But I'll try, Colonel."

He has five printed files and leads the Sudanese through them meticulously. Al Ansari answers carefully; the context of each is so clear, there's nothing to hide. The red light of a recorder flutters with each word and Werner strains to hear every one. He stops interrupting after a while. On the last file Jason tries to expand the exchange.

"This man asked your advice because he felt he was being contaminated by American customs?"

"Contaminated?"

"It was hard for him to follow Islamic customs there."

"I advised that if he chose to live in America he must accept their ways and yet remain a true Muslim. If he cannot find that path, he can return to a Muslim country."

"Very clear advice," Jason says.

"We've heard all that," Werner says when he hears the English version. "Naturally he would say that."

"It's also in his e-mail."

"It's in code."

Jason turns back to Al Ansari. "Please go on."

"I said he couldn't expect Americans to adapt to *our ways*."

"I think you've covered all the ground you need to, Currie. You haven't turned up anything we didn't know."

"Colonel, I did find some other files that we've never seen. I think you need to hear them."

"Probably just more of the same."

"Not really. I think you need to … *protect* yourselves by hearing the rest of this."

"*Protect* ourselves? Listen, Currie—"

"Eric," Hawk says, "let's not go out on a limb until we have all the data. Your career could be hanging on the outcome here."

Werner thinks that over. "All right, Currie. Keep it short."

Jason leans closer to the professor. He speaks with greater emphasis. "Doctor, I found an exchange of e-mails between you and World Horizons." He repeats the question in English. Werner makes an indecipherable sound. "Do you remember this exchange?"

"Of course. I'm old and frail as you see, but I remember my own words."

"He remembers," Jason says.

"Where is this leading?" Werner asks. "What in hell is World Horizons?"

"It's an NGO. Doctor, would you tell us how you came to receive e-mails from an American charity which is funded by evangelical Christians?"

Al Ansari almost smiles, the corners of his mouth lifting involuntarily. "That was some time ago. You have been very thorough. Their funding as you call it means nothing to me."

"Is it all right if we join this conversation, Jason?" Hawk's a little impatient. Jason repeats the question and response in English. Hawk leans forward, listening carefully.

"One e-mail?" Hawk asks.

"Just a minute," Werner says. "The army sent us all his e-mails and I don't remember anything about World Horizons."

"They only sent us the e-mails to and from the States. These were within Sudan. There are hundreds of local e-mails that were never translated. World Horizons has an office here. Maybe your translator didn't react to their title because it's in Arabic."

"What's the gist of their exchange?" Hawk asks.

"World Horizons begs Al Ansari to use his influence with the regime to support a cease-fire with the rebel groups."

"And his response?"

"He says he has already done that and will continue to do so. There's considerable to-and-fro for several weeks. It's all in Arabic. The tone is friendly."

"It could be a setup," Werner says. "All added afterwards to make him look friendly."

"Easy enough to verify. Let's ask World Horizons."

Hawk and Jason turn to Werner for his answer. It's some time coming. Al Ansari also watches with interest. "It's time to get General Carmody involved," Werner says.

Carmody has a war on his hands. He's unavailable. Al Ansari is returned to his lair. The general does not summon them until evening.

"Hawk, I don't need this kind of distraction just now."

"Colonel Werner felt you needed to be informed. This affair is certain to be raised in Washington. World Horizons is quite a force. The president's wife is one its sponsors."

"Christ!"

"General," Werner says, "we have to verify these e-mails

before we make any decisions."

"How do you propose to do that, Colonel? We're certainly not going to call a respected NGO and ask them if it's all right to use enhanced interrogation on one of their friendly contacts."

"We've only been questioning him, sir."

"Then why is he bloodstained?" Jason asks, and draws a cautionary glance from Hawk. Carmody chooses not to hear the remark.

"Look, both of you. Do we have anything at all to verify a plot in L.A.? All right, then. We're not going to stumble into an inquiry on why we mistreated an old man whom this charity takes to be a goddamn saint. Hold him in protective custody. Send him to the base and treat him like a guest. Advise World Horizons and let *them* take the lead. You can follow up at home. If you turn up nothing, let's bury the whole business. I'm not pulling any chestnuts out of the fire for DIA. Hawk?"

"I think that's a very astute decision, General."

"Now can I get back to my war?"

Hawk sends Jason home, along with a couple of hundred soldiers, some recovering from wounds, some ending their tour of duty unscarred, at least outwardly, all bound for the West Coast. They take up all of the four long benches that run from flight deck to tail.

It's not a triumphal flight for Jason. Despite the last-minute salvage of his relationship with Hawk, he is full of bitterness: over Shragg, over his helplessness with Al Ansari, and over his awakening to the nature of the Middle Eastern wars. There will be no undamaged survivors, not these men, not their country.

# TWENTY

THE SUDAN HAS SUCKED OUT WHAT REMAINED OF HIS ENTHU-siasm for SECOR, which now seems to him like the army's alter ego, each absolute in its own territory, and more determined to hold those limits than form any alliance. In tandem, these two forces and their lesser relatives all but own America, which shudders in a vise between them. Space-age armies in the field, seamless security at home, and paranoia on all sides. He can't reconcile this garrison mentality with the beaten irregulars he's seen in the Sudan.

Maybe it's time to go home to CSIS. After he finds Miriam.

But he hasn't even seen her yet. Hawk may never allow it. That thought leads on to a fantasy in which he would desert SECOR (and therefore CSIS) and escape to Mexico. From there ... but this mockery of a plan has no spine. They may not even relate to each other when they finally meet.

Werner has returned as well. The colonel has plunged into the search for Al Ansari's Californian devotees, apparently still intent on validating the army's original thesis, which Jason sees as pointless. Sid and Archie are supervising the assaults on his chosen targets. Jason would welcome a sympathetic hearing of his own tales, but even Archie is now cool toward him, despite his sling and his bandages. Werner may have soured their friendship.

Hawk had gone directly to Washington, which sounded ominous. When he does arrive at the Station, Jason gets to see him late in the day. He has one question to ask, though he dreads the response. "What happened with Al Ansari?"

Hawk, standing behind his desk and unpacking documents from his attaché case, pauses and turns his full attention to Jason. "So that's it?" He sits down. He says, quietly, "He died of a heart attack. Before World Horizons could even talk to him."

"*Son of a bitch!*"

Hawk is startled. "Not aimed at me, I hope."

"Did anyone else die of defiance after I left?" He needs a moment to let his anger drain, and Hawk allows it. "They preferred him dead."

"The army is no more responsible for his death than you are for Shragg's. Shit happens, more so in war. Do you believe there was anything more we could have done to change that man's fate? I may have the title of a general but I have no standing in the real military. We were just walk-on extras."

Hawk is right, but it doesn't help much. "We have to accommodate the hard truth," Hawk says, "that so long as this administration has popular support to make war on terrorists, this kind of thing will happen. That's our world. Now let's get on with it."

Hawk doesn't agree with the administration? "They must have given you a hard time in Washington."

"General Carmody has been heard there."

"You might not have gotten into it if I hadn't …"

"Maybe that's true. I took you to Sudan because I wanted an unfiltered reading of Al Ansari. How could I trust what the army told me? But I didn't expect you to be a loose cannon. You nearly sunk us. But then you bailed us out. On the whole, you did well, but you did it the hard way. A touch quixotic, but not bad for a man who'd never been around combat."

"Sir, what they're working on now is rounding up Al Ansari's contacts. Werner's taken over."

"He would while I was away. I'll let that pass for a few days, then shut him down."

"Werner's dedicated to proving the army right."

Hawk gives him a questioning look. "Be careful not to misread Werner."

"Sir?"

"He wasn't happy with what he saw. They're grinding up a lot of trained men and materiel."

"Anyway, you can imagine what use he'd make of me. Let me get on with Guadalajara. Maybe this time I'll get her to come back."

Hawk goes into one of his thoughtful poses, leaning back in his chair and turning his head as if listening to phantom advice. "A lot of Americans live in Guada. Maybe that's why Manwaring chose that area."

"Sir? I thought he was a fugitive. Presumably he'd avoid Americans."

"We're getting nothing on his network. Something different is going on. Something we don't pick up. Be aware that Manwaring has worked out an original approach. Don't be afraid to speculate. It might involve local Americans."

Jason tries his best to hide his sudden elation—Hawk *is* sending him back! "He doesn't get out much. He wouldn't know many Americans."

Hawk looks disgusted. "Whatever impression he made on you is just what he intended to make. Be a little more skeptical. You're not dealing with an amateur. He's probably using his live-in as a go-between."

"She's only been protesting in churches—"

"I'm sending you to Guada, Jason, but not solely to further your relationship with an old flame. Find out how he's operating."

On the plane south, Jason has plenty of time to mull over Hawk's behavior. Maybe he is too intelligent to be a single-minded zealot. This is the first time he has allowed some reservations to be seen. Maybe he was really pissed off by what he saw in Khartoum. But maybe he was just role-playing, testing Jason's limits after the debacle in Sudan.

"Yes, she's here." Manwaring regards him thoughtfully for a few moments, as if readying his pitch. "Miriam and I had a long talk. About you. About your offer to help her. About going back to Canada. I insisted that she make up her own mind. She wants to stay here." He sounds quite stressed.

"Whatever she wishes." Jason keeps his tone neutral. "I remember her as a woman who always makes up her own mind."

"She's quite determined." Jason nods casually. Manwaring looks ready to confront any challenge, but with none coming, he tapers off. "She feels safe enough with Felipe and me."

When Jason doesn't argue, he goes on, "Of course, Sergio and his people are always close by. So she's safer here than she might be anywhere else."

"I may talk to her now?"

Manwaring gives up and stalks into the house. Jason is suddenly nervous—boyishly nervous. He has invested so much in his image of her that he feels set up for disappointment. What if she turns out to be indifferent, even cold? She might be a stranger, not ready to welcome a brief lover. So many years since—maybe it's just a juvenile romp to her now, overtaken by years of marriage and their more adult sensations. Will she be at all the woman he has imagined? It's a throwback moment to adolescent angst. And then, there she is.

"I brought you fresh coffee." He's paralyzed for a moment, still seized by such fears. But she does look nearly as he has pictured her, though now more woman than girl. Her shoulders have broadened, her teenage body has become more matronly, she's more substantial. Her expression is no longer shy but now quite direct. She puts down the coffee and holds out her hand.

Shaky with relief, he grips it with his left, and then seizes the other as well. "This calls for more than a handshake."

She steps close, wraps her arms around his neck, and gives him a light kiss. "You've had an accident." She runs her hand over the cast, then takes the other hand, and leads him to the table. He submits, lightened by relief. They arrange themselves, taking time, each sizing up the other with little glances, adjusting to a decade of change.

She laughs. "It's just like a blind date." She seems to relax. "I heard your voice when you came before. I wanted so much to speak to you. But I'd promised Brendan to wait until he was sure it would be right to see you. So I hid."

"Right?"

"We weren't sure what we were dealing with. CSIS isn't a friend." She delivers this without trying to soften it. She looks directly into his face, challenging him to be forthcoming.

"Miriam, I'm not CSIS. I used my job to get here. I wanted to see you, to help you. CSIS was just a means to an end."

"But now you're working with SECOR. They're the perfect example of what's wrong with America."

"I'm not married to SECOR either. I have a temporary assignment and then I'm off home." He can see at once that these explanations carry no weight with Miriam. Her expression stiffens; she looks skeptical. Maybe she's wary that he seems to gloss over his professional roles. She doesn't respond. "If I hadn't worked for CSIS and didn't get a move to SECOR I'd never have gotten here. I just took advantage."

There's a barrier between them that he should have anticipated. He has been so concentrated on just finding her that he's ignored her history: she's a maverick, a dedicated protestor. She was courting detention when she fled here. Hawk will arrest her whenever he can. Why wouldn't she be suspicious?

"I guess I've been clumsy," he says softly. "Of course you don't trust me. I understand how you feel about SECOR. I'm not far from the same opinion. I hope we can talk about this."

He sits back and lets her work on it. Finally she reaches over and touches his bandage. "What happened to you, Jason?"

"Oh, I was in the Sudan …"

"The *Sudan*!"

"Just a few days. A SECOR job. They needed someone fluent in Arabic. Just to talk to one person. I … got close to the action and got blown up. Sort of. They sent me home—I mean … back to the States."

He studies her as he stumbles through this capsule of his adventures. She listens with full attention, just as he recalls her listening intensely to any of his youthful misadventures. She might be the older sister of that girl, but a woman of confidence now and not so easily persuadable. When he meets her eyes directly, it's the same Miriam looking out at him, but no longer under any spell. What does *she* see? A friend and lover or just an anxious-looking thirty-something who might resemble a person she'd almost forgotten? He's a little breathless, conscious now of how choked up with tension he has been.

She reaches out and touches the hand on the injured arm. "I know from the way you try to minimize it that it was a terrible experience. I'm so sorry, Jason." He is moved by her words; he tears up with no warning. He needs a moment to find his equilibrium.

He can see Manwaring through the parlor window, seemingly absorbed in his newspaper, but Jason imagines him to be only pretending to read, with his mind on the pair just outside and the potential outcome. His own satisfaction in finding Miriam helps him sympathize with Manwaring. Of course the old man would be deeply attached to her.

He finds something to talk about, to prolong the moment. "I spent a little time with Bil."

"Ah! When I saw him last, he was so furious with me. For protesting."

"He says he can't even call you now. His place is bugged."

She shows no surprise. " Would he even want to see me? After I left my husband, I went to Bil. He wasn't very …

comforting. He was worried. Over what they would think of me staying there. He was completely under the thumb of that outfit. So I knew to move on." Bil had seemed angry when he talked of Miriam; she's just sad speaking of him.

He's not sure where to turn, how to reach her, but she has no such hesitation: "I heard Ramona and you were quite a settled couple."

"I thought so too."

"It wore off?"

"She wanted more than I could deliver."

"Ah!" Her hair is the deepest brown—reddish as the light falls across it—and worn short of her collar now, not stretching toward her waist as he remembers. She wears very large glasses, large enough to cover not only her Middle Eastern eyes but her brows as well. When he saw her last, she was junior to him; now she seems more grown up than he feels. He's pleasantly intimidated. "So we're all three of us divorced," she says. "My parents would be scandalized." Her wide smile, which he enjoys now, is so familiar.

"What happened with yours?"

She isn't reluctant, as he is, to open up her marriage. "He was a lapsed Christian most of our time together. Then he got serious; he was 'born again.' I don't really know how—I was out of touch with his mind. I went with him to some evangelical services. It was rather exciting, everybody full of joy. Even if you couldn't share their certainty, you had to love their jubilance. They were so secure. But he couldn't be.

He just got more fundamentalist. I saw he was afraid of losing his faith if he didn't constantly parade it. He wanted me to convert. I couldn't, not with sincerity. I'm more political than religious. Besides, while I'm only a token Maronite, it would have broken my parents' hearts after what the family went through." For her parents, as for his own, though not devout, Maronism was their last bond to their past. "I got involved with a protest group. I got into it because I was so sick of all our wars. And the lies we were force-fed to justify them. So many people were willing to put their beliefs on the line. Thousands. Tens of thousands. It was intoxicating."

"But it got you into trouble?"

She smiles again. "You're thinking of protests back home. Trouble there might be a push from a cop, or a dirty look from a passerby. In the States, with no media, it's riot cops, dogs, pepper spray, clubs, and water cannons. Sometimes guns. Prison."

"Prison?"

"That's why I got my American citizenship. They told me it would help if I were arrested. Any protestor caught with a foreign passport gets thrown in detention, no questions asked. I'd been a resident for years, so no problem to apply. I even let my Canadian passport lapse."

Jason knows the downside: as a dual citizen she can never be sure of the support of the Canadian government if she is arrested. The Americans own her. No point in warning her now, but it adds another brick to the wall between her and return to the States.

"After one rally they were after me. I'd spoken in a church. Some of them stood up to Washington, but they're one group the administration tries to keep onside. I heard I might be charged. I told my husband. He called me a traitor." The words tumble out. Her emotion makes him uneasy. He has no such passion for political protest. Perhaps he should. She sounds a bit like Manwaring.

Felipe materializes beside them. He speaks to her in Spanish.

"I'm sorry. I have an errand for Brendan—urgent. He can't travel freely, so I look after some of his affairs." She touches him on the shoulder. "You must be exhausted. It's a long trip, and you've been hurt. I want you to go to my room—you know it—and rest for a while. I'll catch you later." Jason remembers Hawk's *probably using his live-in as a go-between.* So she is a full partner.

In the familiar room, he stretches out in travel weariness, but he's also exhilarated, as though he has jumped the hurdle and is finally running in the clear. Miriam is here; now it's up to him.

# TWENTY-ONE

"... THE WAR AGAINST TERRORISM AND THE DEFENSE OF Christianity. It doesn't matter what they think at Harvard or in the editorial offices of the *New York Times*, Americans have confidence in the administration for those two reasons."

Manwaring rules the table. Some moments, he seems to Jason to be quite mad. Perhaps all exiles are, railing over the indifference of a country that might never take them back. While he's holding forth, Jason wonders if Miriam and Campobello are ever turned off by arguments they must have heard so many times, but both of them seem to give their honest attention, so either they're better at holding their focus than he is, or Manwaring has the teacher's genius of presenting familiar ideas in always novel forms. Jason is less interested in his critique of the American mindset than in studying Miriam. She gets livelier as the dinner wears on, maybe inspired by their host's generous hand with the wine, maybe by the attention she has to feel from Jason's lingering glances. They sit cornered to each other, and now she reaches over, impulsively, and covers his hand with hers. Manwaring pauses, only for a second, but Jason catches his eyes on their linked hands.

"Fifty percent of the world's people would die to have American rights, and meanwhile the administration is changing America into the kind of country those people are longing to escape. Don't you see that?"

Jason shrugs, perhaps too nonchalantly because Miriam pinches his hand to caution him. "But Americans can still vote—"

"Pah!" He lunges from the chair and stands facing Jason, hands on hips, daring him to disagree. "Vote for whom? Look, Jason, the value of a vote is proportional to its power to change the regime. If you don't agree with their policies, you can throw the scoundrels out. Dozens of states can manufacture elections that they cannot possibly lose. If you can't replace the administration, you've lost; you're no longer a citizen of a free country. The spinal column has been extracted, and you're now a squid."

"But you *can* replace the administration—"

"With what? There's no effective opposition. Business adores the party. They contribute unlimited amounts, tax-deductible of course. The party enjoys a two- or three-to-one advantage in funds. Huge numbers are so turned off by our feckless Congress that they don't even bother to vote. Those who do, make their choice watching television, where money is decisive—"

"Enough for tonight, Brendan," Miriam's tone stops him mid-gesture. "Jason's not a political animal, and you've immersed him in it for an hour. Sergio has been polite as always, but there's a limit."

"I apologize for my fixation." He really does sound apologetic, almost chastened. He quiets and falls back in his chair. His voice sinks to a near-whisper. He turns to Jason. "I may be obsessed with the disintegration of America, but I can hardly believe that anyone should not be. The United States is the Praetorian Guard of our culture—the heart muscle of the western world. If American democracy sickens, Jason, Canadian democracy will soon be infected."

He stretches his feet out under the table and falls back into gloomy rumination. Suddenly, he looks exhausted. Campobello, eyes on Manwaring, rises and prepares to leave.

Miriam takes Manwaring firmly in hand and guides him up the narrow stairs, waving goodnight. Jason walks to the gate with Campobello. "He seems to wear himself out with his own arguments."

"Not from his words, señor. From his despair." He shakes hands with Jason in his formal way. "He was very influenced by your presence tonight."

"He seemed eager to bring me around to his view of

America. Is that what you meant?"

"I don't think he cares about your politics." He shakes hands in his formal way and leaves. Jason locks the gate.

The faint light reflecting from within is suddenly reduced, and then extinguished. Felipe is putting the house to bed. Jason lingers in near darkness, his mind on Miriam and Manwaring. Collaborators, oddly matched lovers, or both? Can this youthful Miriam be deeply attached to a much older man? He needs to know more of her role, her commitment here. He needs to understand the danger she may be in. Hawk's *think about his network* comes to mind.

The door closes softly. Light footsteps. The smell of her perfume as she draws close. "He went out like a light."

That moment in the Marons' backyard, the isolation of the darkness and the heat of pubescence pulling them together, comes back to him. Perhaps it does to Miriam too. He touches her shoulder. She responds at once. She slips an arm around his neck and returns his kiss. Not passionately but warmly enough. She presses hard against him. But instead of losing himself as he did in the Maron yard, he holds back.

She slips from his arm. "You must think I'm bold as a hussy." She's more pleased than contrite. "I just wanted to show you how happy I am. With your being here. All my old feelings are coming to life. Don't you feel that happening?"

"I ... feel a lot of things happening. You. Better than ever. Much better. But I'm not sure where it's all leading us."

She turns to leave but he grasps at her arm. She lingers,

uncertain, as he struggles to break free from his constraint. There's a long moment in silence. Words won't come. He pulls her to him and hugs her. Now she returns the embrace. Neither speaks, but a lot of years are slipping away as they stand there, recovering once familiar feelings. With his good arm around her back, his cast pressed against her belly, and his head buried against her neck and shoulder, he feels as awkward as a teenager at the school dance. But, basking in her warmth, he doesn't care to move.

Finally she slips an arm through his and leads him to the house. "I must get back to Brendan. When he's overtired he has very bad nights. We'll sort it out tomorrow."

Manwaring looks absorbed in his laptop when Jason joins him on the patio. He's staring rather crossly at his newspaper.

"Anything new?"

"Hmm."

"American news?"

"Final Report of the Committee on the Fire-Bombing of Churches. Not much to it."

Manwaring sees that Jason's not sure whether to sit. He gives his full attention and his manners are revived. "Why don't you join me?" He waits for Jason to settle. "The final word, after three years to analyze the evidence, is that their preliminary report is confirmed: the churches were set on fire by human agency, identity unknown. Some finding!"

"It was all over TV in Canada. Lot of discussion at CSIS."

Manwaring's interested to hear Jason. "Ah! What did CSIS conclude?"

"The veterans thought the timing was too convenient. The election followed within months. This administration got in by attacking terrorists, understood to be Muslims. The old dogs thought the party must have been involved somehow. I imagine most intelligence agencies had suspicions."

Manwaring's brows arch in astonishment. "The Canadian government believed the party firebombed our own Christian churches?"

"Certainly not. The government was told by DFAIT that Muslim radicals attacked the churches. DFAIT were given that by your State Department. It was accepted without question by our government. CSIS management cracked down on speculation."

"What do you believe?"

"Now that I've seen it close up, I believe this administration would do anything to win."

"There's a difference between speculation and evidence, Jason. We don't know who caused those fires." He says this so emphatically that Jason accepts the topic is closed, although he's surprised at Manwaring passing up a chance to pillory the administration.

"I'd like to hear from you about Sudan. Miriam told me." Of course she would.

"She hasn't heard the worst of it." He sketches his experiences, leaving out Shragg's final mission.

Manwaring is keenly interested in the interrogation of Al Ansari. "They may have destroyed a potential ally."

"Perhaps. He was a devout Muslim. He thought our kind of governance unsuitable for his people, but he wasn't a terrorist. He abhorred suicide."

"The administration is attacking the wrong enemy. The problem isn't Islam but the radical misuse of Islam to confront the West." They both fall silent, Jason dwelling on Al Ansari and the way in which their minds made contact in that little room. He's not sure what Manwaring's thinking—maybe just formulating another perfect aphorism.

Miriam rescues Jason. She's arranged that Felipe will accompany them on a tour around the city, an opportunity to spend time together. "On no account let anyone in if you can't identify them," she says, and Manwaring nods like a child eager to gain approval.

"Why such concern?" Jason asks as they get underway.

"Normally Felipe wouldn't leave him alone. But I can't go about unguarded either, so if you're to see anything here, we have to do it this way. Sergio will drop by shortly."

"Who are you so afraid of? Campobello mentioned SEDENA, but also 'others.'"

"Sergio believes the Pentagon's aching to get Brendan back. He escaped from DIA and they'll never forgive him. And there's the bounty hunters."

"Say again?"

"The Pentagon will pay hard cash. Lots of it. Not necessarily alive. Sergio thinks Brendan might be worth tens of thousands to a professional hit-man."

# TWENTY-TWO

GUADALAJARA IS AN ATTRACTIVE CITY. ALSO OLD. OLDER THAN Quebec City by seventy-six years. The two have common roots as European and Catholic outposts in the New World. Jason and Miriam walk around the Plaza del Armas and pass by the great cathedral with its yellow-tiled spires. There are lots of other walkers, well dressed, many women rather stylishly so. Quite a number of identifiable Americans. In her guide's spiel, Miriam mentions that the area has great numbers of American students, since doctors and other professionals can take recognized degrees at lower cost. "There's a huge colony here of expatriate Americans, it's said the largest anywhere."

"I've heard a lot of American vets retire here."

"It's cheaper and the weather's better."

"D'you run across many?"

"I've met one or two at the house. Friends of Sergio."

"His contacts extend even to American veterans?"

"American residents are intelligence targets. CISEN watch them for drug connections to the States. Sergio says that DIA is involved here."

"Why would they be?"

"Keeping an eye out for unrest in the army. Sergio says it's easier to pick up warning signs in the retired cadre than the active one."

There's plenty of traffic and a hint of pollution, but at this altitude the air is light and just pleasantly warm. They walk for an hour or so with Felipe behind, respecting their privacy. Whenever Jason glances back, he catches Felipe inspecting the passers-by, casting looks right and left, always alert. Perhaps they're being followed?

Miriam folds her arm through his and they walk in step like old lovers. He catches sidelong glances from her. What is she seeing? What is she thinking?

"I was thinking of our summers together," she says. She reads his thoughts the way Hawk does. "Long, hot days … sunning, swimming, talking, laughing." She pulls him a little closer. "When I was in my swimsuit, I'd catch you ogling me."

"I only recall being careful not to, with Bil there."

Miriam stands them lunch at a traditional restaurant where a mariachi group entertains tourists, just like them. They've left their car some distance back. Felipe goes to bring it as Miriam and Jason linger.

"Your professor is a very intense man."

She smiles. "My mother would have called him a grace-grower."

"A gray squirrel?" She's startled for a moment and then laughs merrily.

"A *grace-grower*. A person whose demands on you help you acquire grace just by putting up with them. We used it often at home. Bil and I dragged in quite a few grace-growers."

"Such as me, I suppose." She laughs again, but doesn't deny it. "Is he always so … worked up?"

"You're new, you're Canadian. He has to win you over."

Or maybe he's just hyper because of their interest in each other. "How did he get so passionately involved?"

"At Harvard he taught Heritage of American Law. The administration approached him. They were going to concentrate all those agencies into the new SECOR and they wanted to bulletproof it against court challenges. He drafted guidelines to keep the agency's powers just within the Constitution. The Justice Department used his work to see where the challenges would come from, and then tried to outflank them with legislation. They also used his reputation to sell the deal to Congress. He was furious and went public. Harvard was embarrassed. He was warned to tone it down. He didn't. Then the Justice Department charged him."

"With what?"

"Sedition, under the new Act."

"On what evidence?"

"Evidence gives them no problem. Brendan's case less than most. He'd released the names of Muslims in prison whom he knew to be blameless. That was actionable under the Act. But it wouldn't have mattered if he'd been innocent as snow. They have armies of lawyers who can find a case against anyone who crosses them."

Jason knew little of this in Canada. "At SECOR they said he was hurt by DIA. Is he okay now?"

"He's sixty-five, but his body's a lot older. He gets tired. And discouraged. And angry. At night, I talk to him. Cool him down. In ten or fifteen minutes he falls into deep sleep. Then in three hours or so, the dreams begin. Sometimes nightmares."

Miriam's patience with the compulsive lectures at table springs into focus. "So that's why you put up with it? But you're more than putting up with it, aren't you?"

Her direct answer catches him off-guard. "You mean sleeping with him? It's not quite what you think. Our relationship is more friends than lovers." She watches him turning this over, not sure how to reply. "He's more or less impotent. He's been ruined."

"Ruined." Jason thinks of his own affliction.

"In interrogating him, they destroyed his testicles with electrodes."

"My God!" He feels abruptly sickened and reflexively crosses his knees.

"He also lost most of his teeth before he'd had enough."

Jason stares at her for a moment before the significance of *enough* sinks in. "Before he broke?"

"He finally gave them some names. To buy time. False leads. When they came back at him, he defied them. That's when they threw the switch."

She waits him out as he soaks this in. "How did he escape?"

"They thought he was dying. That was serious—he was a prize catch. They took him to a military hospital. When he'd recovered a little, he got away."

"How?"

"In his guard's uniform."

"That old man took out a guard?"

"He garroted him with his IV tubing."

"He *killed* his guard?"

"He doesn't know." Jason must look horrified because she says, "Maybe if you'd been through it you'd be able to do the same thing."

"No wonder DIA is after him. Can't he be extradited?"

"He's been given refugee status. Mexico respects the Convention. The United States can hardly assure the Mexicans that he wouldn't be subject to torture if he returns, so he's not extraditable." Manwaring now begins to look more the heroic old militant than the ranting dissident. No wonder DIA—and Hawk—want him out of circulation.

They sit there awhile without speaking, Jason sorting out

his feelings toward Manwaring, which are increasingly complex.

"We should go. I have to stop at the American consulate."

"Why?"

"To turn my passport in. They're replacing it. The new one uses a chip."

As Felipe threads the car though traffic, there's a long silence. Then she says, "Brendan told me you were sent here to bring me back to the States."

"That's my assignment from SECOR. So long as I seem to making some progress, I may be able to come back here. But what I really want is to help you come home. To Canada. You'll be out of reach there. From either SECOR or the Pentagon."

"But your agency works with SECOR. Isn't that how you come to be here?"

"You've committed no crime, not so far as Canada is concerned. Protesting against the government isn't exactly promoted, but it is respected. You're still Canadian even if you're also an American citizen, and once you come home, you can't be sent back to the States."

"It would mean running out on Brendan."

Jason and Felipe wait for her in the lobby. When she comes out of the Consulate he can see the change in her. She's angry. He recognizes the face of a teenage Miriam after a row with her mother, eyes snapping under threatening brows.

"They stonewalled me. I'm on some list—only specified offices can reissue—and so on. They told me to go to the San Diego office. My passport will be revoked in ten days."

"It's a ploy to get you across the border. Don't even think of it." Ploy by whom, though? Hawk, taking a second approach? Maybe Werner has had a sniff of his mission to Mexico and has brought DIA into the mix?

"I have to hold a valid passport to keep my Mexican visa. Once some bureaucrat finds out it's revoked—"

"They won't have to find out on their own. Whoever set this up will tell them when they're ready."

"I won't let them walk over me like this." She's too rattled to get into the car. She walks a few feet, turns around, walks back toward him. Jason reaches a hand toward her. "Miriam—"

"Never mind! I'm not going to the States for a passport and I'm not going to Canada. I'll apply to the Canadian consulate here. They'll have to give me back my old passport. I'll be Canadian again."

The day winds down with no lecture at dinner. The passport episode is batted around. Sergio sees it as Jason does. "One passport is as good as another, señora. But do it quickly. Whoever arranged this will already have informed a friendly official. Some agency of ours will demand that you produce a passport to validate your visa. Clearly, someone wants you out of Mexico."

"I'll download the forms right now."

Manwaring's subdued, if not by the passport crisis then perhaps by the time and attention that Jason appropriates from Miriam. Once she has her application completed, she's a little triumphant. "Felipe can drop this off at the consulate tomorrow. Two weeks should do it. Whoever did it will be shocked to discover I'm a documented Canadian. Again." Her temper quite restored, she almost flirts with Jason under Manwaring's gaze. But he allows her to see him off to bed early.

An hour later she comes to Jason in her own room. They talk of their past, their families, the long summers together. They draw closer. He finally has nerve enough to confess to her. "That night I walked you home … it bothered me for years. I was so … guilty. You were Bil's sister and I took advantage of you."

"Why would Bil be upset?"

"Going as far as we did …"

She stares at him for a moment. "Did we actually *do* it?"

"You don't *remember*?"

She breaks into light laughter. "I remember being pretty high—both of us. I found grass stains on my panties next morning. They were under the bed and I was so relieved my mother hadn't seen them. Did we actually … in the *yard*?" She presses to him and whispers. "I couldn't remember. I thought I'd know when I saw you. By your attitude. But you were just like before. I couldn't *ask* you, could I? So I decided I'd imagined it. At least the juicy part. You'd be surprised how often I fantasized making love with you in my teens. So I thought it was the same thing, a fantasy. You were always very respectful, so I guess I thought you wouldn't have taken advantage of me." She's amused; he's incredulous.

"You really don't recall? You went on feeling yourself a virgin?"

"Oh, no! That went with that piggish Humphrey Smith. Long before you. It was a disaster. Mounted me like a toad. It took about a minute. I was terrified he would brag about it. But he was afraid of Bil, so I guess he didn't."

Jason is stunned—enough by her blackout but more by the discovery of Humphrey Smith, ahead of him. Humphrey Smith! Jason knew him as a feckless hanger-on of the bully squad, to be respected only when he was backed up by their presence. Chubby, awkward—how could she possibly …? "You can't *remember*? It was like an explosion."

"I knew something happened, but it was all out of focus. Imagine if Bil had found out." Now she reaches out and touches him on the thigh, raising the voltage between them. "You never talk about Ramona."

Abruptly he finds himself fighting for self-control, clenched by his mortification even while bursting to be free of it. He can feel tears burning the corners of his eyes. She moves close and pulls his head against her breast. Words begin to hiss from him like jets of expelled steam.

"I thought we were okay. Just the usual rough spots. Finally I realized she was laughing at me. She used me. She kept saying, 'I can't communicate with you.' So many times I got sick of hearing it and missed the nuance: I can't communicate with *you*. Then, finally, 'I can't communicate with you, not like Norman.'"

Miriam strokes his head. "Norman?"

"Neighbor. Fat, beefy, beery, but available. I asked her why she married me. *You were the only one who mentioned marriage*." His tears are spotting her shirt. He burrows between her breasts, hiding his shame from her, smothering the choked confession. The story struggles out—the blow-by-blow exchanges by which Ramona humbled him, the shriveling of affection, the belittlement, questioning his virility, and finally the paraded infidelities. Miriam hears it all without comment, only hugging and stroking him, her touch its own statement. "I can't shake it off. I'm like a teenager."

"You don't forget such things. You learn to see them for what they are."

"The last night ..." He can hardly get it out, stifled by shame, but desperate to eject the most poisonous memory. "She'd begun to talk of having a child. Only to taunt me. That I wasn't man enough to make her pregnant. We were both drunk. I tried to grab her. I wanted to hurt her. To rape her. We fell. Her on top. She got up. I just lay there, drunk, disgraced. She kicked me in the groin. Twice. She said—she said, 'you're not even a Canadian, you're a fucking Arab.'"

Miriam pulls him down. They lie against each other. Touching her raises only a little response in him. The knife-edge of lust is still captive to Ramona's scorn. The charge in his loins can barely raise a spark, let alone power an erection. He's fit only for cuddling. She seems to understand that. Now she has another lover who's unable to perform.

The heat of shame subsides. Then, they talk. For a long while, side by side. No more of his shortcomings as a husband; he goes on to his disconnect with Bil, then he dwells on his detention in the desert, and finally his regrets in the Sudan. As one experience is revealed he rushes on to the next, until the purge is complete. Miriam gathers closer, holds him and listens, curled against him, the heat of her flesh gradually stirring the juices in his own wizened body. She accepts it all with only rare comments, patiently witnessing while his anguish washes away. Lightened with relief, his mind finally rests, and he drifts in Miriam's arms. When he awakens in the early light of dawn, she is gone.

# TWENTY-THREE

ON HIS RETURN, HAWK IS OUT OF TOWN, SO JASON'S RELIEVED to avoid, for the moment, lying his way through another report. After some thought, he texts Noble: *Need status Miriam Ashbury passport from DFAIT. Urgent.* Noble responds next day: *Ashbury passport renewal application in process.*

Where might she go in Canada? If he can get her to go. She has no family there now; she has been away ten years. She'll need to be undercover for some time, certainly away from the media. Jason uses a public payphone to call his cousin, Adolphus Kouri (his father, Jason's uncle, never felt the need to anglicize his name).

"You want her to stay with *me?*" He's thirty years older than Jason. When he was a boy and his cousin was already husky and bearded, Jason idolized him, and he in turn treated

Jason as a protégé. As Jason matured, he had advice from him on all matters of consequence: sex, 'as much as you can get'; marriage, 'only if unavoidable' (his one recourse to it had proved a disaster); religion, 'save it till you're old'; friendship, 'no more than two or three, if you can find that many you can trust.' He held one job all his working days, as a millwright and maintenance supervisor, never ambitious to change, and took his pension at the earliest. Vancouver Island has enough metropolitan areas to comfort any city dweller, but Adolphus chose his retreat among the great trees, close enough to reach the nearest town but not for it to reach him.

Jason visited him there, a little surprised to find it literally in the bush, overhung by giant evergreens, a few acres of pasture to one side, with a ramshackle house and a small barn on either side of a corral. His nearest neighbor then was miles away. Over many holiday visits, Jason saw the buildings refurbished, the fences replaced, and a few horses installed. A neighbor built somewhat closer, then two, then ten, nearly all of them owning horses. Now he boarded about twenty animals and maintained a network of riding trails snaking through the trees to hook up with the old logging roads that wind up the surrounding heights. Too much for one man, Adolphus has two day-workers now, but so far as Jason knows, he's the only person who's ever shared the house.

"She needs a place to stay. I may not get back for a while. Naturally I thought of you."

"Did you, by God! You know there's never been a woman

in this house?"

"If it's too much—"

"Oh, never mind groveling. I know what my clan obligations are. Are you going to marry this woman?"

"It ... hasn't been discussed."

"Good. Don't bring it up. Is she bossy, does she leave things lying around, is she fussy about food?"

"Uncle Adolphus, she's thoroughly housebroken and very agreeable."

"You told me your Ramona was very agreeable. When is she coming?"

"Actually, she hasn't made up her mind yet."

"Oh, *she* hasn't made up *her* mind. Well, if she's not too proud, she can call me. Where can I reach you?"

"I don't think it's wise for you to call me here. Or Miriam. I'll try to call from time to time."

Adolphus gives that a moment of thought. "You didn't say what she's hiding from."

"She'll tell you all about it. She's very articulate."

"God help me."

His evenings are uneasy. He's not so keen now to put in extra hours at SECOR. But when he's in his hotel room, his work stays with him. He returns to the day's business—more and more data spewing out of the massed machines, more concentration squandered on mundane analysis, more Muslims detained on mild suspicion, more abuses of American privacy.

When he does sleep, the Sudan comes to life in his dreams, with white flashes and broken bodies in lunatic montage. Waking, his memory chews over the events more coherently, but never without an overlay of guilt. He walks to the tower to face the day's analysis with his mind already clouded.

Losing his zest for the job is one thing, but worse, Werner is always present. His experience in the Sudan might have raised doubts that he denies by ramping up his commitment. He shows it in furrowed eyebrows and, when he does speak, a raspy edge to his voice. Jason tries to stay well clear, not always successfully.

When the Sudan campaign comes up in one of their stretching walkabouts, Archie asks for Jason's input. He gets carried away enough to describe the interrogations.

"Wait a minute," one of them says. "You sound as though you're sympathizing with these people."

"They were being tortured."

"Tortured? What's a little rough treatment if someone has information that will save our men?"

"Besides," Archie says, "they'd certainly do it to our people. Remember that video of captives being beheaded."

"You need to distinguish between terrorists like that and ordinary people defending their own country."

This makes everybody uncomfortable, some downright hostile. Too late to shut up, Jason now spots Werner in the doorway, looking as if he'd swallowed a lemon. He strides over and plants himself in front of Jason.

"Our methods are not the problem, Currie. Canadians like you—and Americans like you—are the problem. We can't afford to pay attention to any of you wimps."

"Wimps?" Jason lets his frustration speak. "You think torture is heroic?"

"These people can never evolve into a society like ours. Their mullahs won't let them."

Jason's in front of a very unfriendly house. Werner has now pacified his demons. He strides off, to approving glances and even one or two kudos. Archie goes back to his desk. None of them will look Jason in the eye the rest of the day. He has been steadily losing his status as that interesting Canadian; now he's just that outsider.

Noble sends him another text message, coded: *CSIS assured Hawk your report of camp inmates has been secured. Also your visit to Sudan. Management prefers that you make no more trips to Mexico.*

*Prefers?* Puzzling. Normally, management did not prefer, they just commanded. Maybe the delicate touch has something to do with Hawk being 'assured.' Jason makes use of Sid's SCIP connection to call Noble. "Ben? I gather you spoke to Hawk. I assume you were planning to recall me." The moment of silence tells him he's right.

"Jason, the A-D's concerned you might be picked up by a Mexican agency. They've warned us, remember. You can imagine how the shit would fly. He's still livid that you went to the Sudan without clearance. What if you'd been killed? How could he explain that?"

"It would have embarrassed me too." He fingers the cast, thankful he's never reported the near miss. "Hawk won't let me come home. He needs me for a specific mission. That I'm uniquely qualified for."

"Where?"

"Mexico. Hawk's eager to bring Miriam Ashbury back here. She and I are very close friends."

"That kind of friends?"

"I've committed to Hawk to bring her. He's counting heavily on it. Trouble is she's very loyal to Brendan Manwaring. So it's taking a while."

"Tell Hawk you can't bring it off. That should get you home." When Jason doesn't answer, Noble takes a fatherly line. "I'd like to see you out of there, Jason."

"You think *I'm* at risk?"

"Certainly. What does Hawk want her for?"

"To help sort the innocent protestors from the budding terrorists. It's his pet project."

"Really? Doesn't sound like SECOR." Jason avoids any response.

He arranges to see Hawk later. "I hear Werner tore a strip off you in front of my staff," Hawk says, both chastising Jason and enjoying the outcome. "You should either keep a lower profile or learn to defend yourself."

"Ben Noble says I can't go to Mexico again. Did he ask you to recall me?"

"Damn CSIS! First they sent you to blunder into that camp, now they want you back when you're starting to be useful."

"Things were going well, too."

Hawk smirks, almost breaking into laughter. "I'm not sure you seem transparent because you're transparent or because you really do have something to hide."

"I'll tell Noble Mexico is out then?"

"Never mind the phony acquiescence. I know you're hot for her. Fine. You can pillow-talk her into coming back. Meanwhile, we still have zero sigint on Manwaring."

"Are we talking about an activist group or just political opposition?"

"Now you're going to tell me only one of those is illegal. Political opposition can develop into activism. Manwaring can tell you about that. Here's another possibility: could there be a counterintelligence caper going on? DIA using Guada retired vets. Loyal Ones. Trying to penetrate Manwaring's network, posing as activists. That would bring Werner into the equation."

"Werner? I can't imagine Werner pretending to collaborate with Manwaring."

"Werner does what he's ordered to do."

How to put these hypotheses to rest seems beyond Jason, but if they're helping him to Guada, he welcomes the attempt. "Noble also said he'd assured you that my report on the camp has been secured."

"He used some such euphemism. I asked him to shred it. 'Secured' just means stored on some hard drive somewhere."

"They'd never destroy it. Anything Canadian intelligence turns up that can be useful tends to get used. Maybe as a word to a minister, maybe the media. Maybe not now, but when it pays off."

"Sounds like any other intelligence agency. But if they keep it quiet awhile, it'll be good enough."

Knowing he should leave well enough alone, Jason can't resist a question. "But you can't hope to keep the camps secret indefinitely."

Hawk regards him in the speculative way of a person tracing a question back to its motivation. "Naturally there's some static out there. The families know their men have disappeared. There's talk in the mosques. But the numbers are unknown; the citizenship is uncertain. The administration has advised some imams that a public protest will result in a crackdown on their mosques."

"How many are we talking about?" He expects no answer, but an evasion may give him a hint.

"I just told you that's secret. Your CSIS seems to think it's about a hundred thousand."

*A hundred thousand?* Hawk can follow him putting it together. He's ready for Jason to ask the obvious question.

"How can they get away with it?"

"The rationale is that these people support attacks on our

country. If we left them free to grow into jihadists, we'd be failing our mission."

"But you're also sweeping up innocent sympathizers."

"Tell me an infallible method to sort one from the other."

"Due process."

"Now tell me who ever got elected by appealing to due process when Americans were under attack."

"So it all comes down to politics."

"And security. Some Americans believe we should hold out our hand to Muslims even as we attack their rogue states. Keep the good guys on our side while we take on the outlaws. But others believe that Muslims can't be made into good citizens. We don't accommodate seventh-century customs from Christians and Jews. Why should we respect them in Muslims?"

"What about free speech and religious tolerance?"

"Ah well. There's a whiff of hypocrisy about any administration, not to be taken too seriously. You're probably familiar with it in Canada, where you preach tolerance to the rest of the world and still treat your aboriginals like untouchables."

"What will you do with them all?"

"Leave them there. Maybe even find work for them. There's a proposal to employ them on defense projects."

"Slave labor?"

"Certainly not. After all, we employ criminals in conventional jails because it's good for them to be busy."

"The camp where they held me had Americans in those

cages. Not Middle Eastern POWs—Americans."

"I understand that's what you reported to CSIS."

"How will the administration justify it when it all comes out?"

"We had to close the door on all threats to our home base."

Hawk continues to be cool, almost matter-of-fact, while the prospect he is describing has Jason horrified. "Why are you laying this out for me?"

"Because I'm letting you go to Mexico, that professor's going to tell you the same things, and you should work out how to make use of it when he springs it on you."

Hawk opens his desk drawer, removes a manicure kit, and begins filing his nails. Jason watches in fascination. It's so quiet he can hear the scraping of the file. Hawk looks up from his task. "Anything else?"

"How long will it go on, General?"

"When there's a payoff. They'll probably be pushing Canada to take action. You people are still bringing in Muslim immigrants."

After this conversation, Jason decides to open a file, encrypted on his laptop. To win Miriam he has to support Manwaring, so he accumulates data on SECOR that could be useful to the professor, taking care not to identify his role in what he will share. Anyway, Manwaring seems to know more of SECOR than he does.

Later, when he leaves to walk home to his hotel, Jason's

mind is still sorting through it all like a slow CPU struggling to match up incompatible files.

It's another smoky evening. When he looks up, the summit of the tower is obscured in the turgid air. He'd always thought of the United States as a bright and colorful country, like Canada but with masses of people, everyone active, engaged, and confident. Now it seems darker. The atmosphere no longer brims with hope. It reminds him of Eastern Europe before the collapse of the Soviet Empire.

# TWENTY-FOUR

MANWARING HAS BEGUN TO THAW A LITTLE. AS WELL, THE professor clearly knows far more than Jason does of what's happening in the States. It's impossible to surprise him. Sitting in the morning sun with Miriam and her mentor, Jason opens up more of his closeted past.

"Miriam will have told you that I was held in a desert prison camp."

"Of course. You might have mentioned this earlier."

"Our first relationship was ... rather frosty."

"A SECOR collaborator would hardly expect open arms from a dissident. I understand that you waited until you felt more comfortable. Either with me or with Miriam."

Jason ignores the hidden message there. "You already knew of the camps?"

"I knew of them."

"They hold large numbers of Arab Muslims, many of whom are American citizens."

"Jason," Miriam says, "you're not really certain they're citizens."

"Just the one that I was held in, yes. Mostly Americans."

He has an easy choice: turn off Manwaring, turn off Miriam. They sit there for an hour, the sun casting long shadows across the room, the smells of desert shrubbery sifting through the open door on little riffles of wind, as he dwells on his time in the camp.

"As I thought," Manwaring says. "I knew their crackdown would have to escalate—if they're maddening Arabs in the Middle East, there would be repercussions among the same people in America. So they need to control it. And shore up their support from frightened Christians."

Manwaring sees the problem as Hawk did, but what appears a solution to one seems an atrocity to the other. Jason asks, "You already have an idea where they're heading, don't you?"

"You saw only one camp? For Muslims?"

"There are others?"

"Did you imagine the only so-called enemies of the State were Muslims? I was held in a camp in Arizona. I saw no Muslims. I know of another in remote Alaska, occupants unknown. There's one in our Pacific Islands, replacing an old leper colony. There are certainly more."

"How in God's name do they keep it all secret?" His frustration at his own ignorance bubbles over. Miriam looks shocked at his tone but Manwaring responds almost like Hawk, eyeing him ironically.

"What secret? The administration has chosen Muslim Arabs as their bogeyman. They're the enemy, and America must be defended. They have their reasons: to attack terrorism, to support Israel, and to defend Christianity. But mainly, to keep themselves in power. All of this is no secret. Other governments, like your own, understand the strategy, whether or not they approve of it. Ultimately it raises the question: what will they do about *American* Arabs?"

Jason turns to Miriam. "You're not surprised. You two have talked about this."

"Brendan's consumed by it. He often speculates on what comes next."

"Massive internment is what I heard at SECOR."

Manwaring nods. "That'll be part of it. Have you heard deportation discussed there?"

"*Deportation*? Unthinkable."

The professor laughs harshly. "You've made considerable progress in decoding the outer layers of the regime's psyche, but you have yet to penetrate to its soul. They'll concentrate on immigrants from the states they're occupying. Former citizens of those countries will become enemy aliens. Like the Japanese-Americans in World War Two. They'll be required to register. Many will go into detention. Their families are then a problem. What happens to their wives and children?

If they isolate the men somehow, their families could be with them. Then come the restricted areas. Only for American citizens and their families. Men who haven't been granted citizenship could still be deported."

"You agree with SECOR."

"I read the administration as they do."

"How will they go about it?"

"There'll be an act to register Arab Muslims. Not just immigrants, American citizens."

Remembering Hawk's summary, Jason can't challenge this. He looks to Miriam. She's harmonized with her mentor. "None of this should surprise you," she says. "You've just been telling us how SECOR sees it." This is all familiar ground between them.

"Can you—your supporters—do anything to change it? Is there any real opposition?"

"We can't discuss that with a CSIS agent." Manwaring leans back against his chair and contemplates Jason, perhaps considering how much to tell him. "A lot of things are going on in my country you're not yet aware of. American history is full of radical changes in direction."

Felipe enters. He nods to Manwaring; whatever his errand, it's been accomplished. A message to Campobello? Jason recalls Hawk's *maybe he's communicating through CISEN*. Manwaring excuses himself and goes upstairs with Felipe. Jason feels Miriam's eyes on him but when he meets her gaze she looks away. Does she still not trust him now, after the hours of unburdening on the last visit?

He takes her by the elbow. "Let's go outside. I need to talk to you."

Someone will try to stop Manwaring—DIA, SEDENA, some expatriate American. Canada is the urgent solution. Now that he has found and fallen in love with Miriam, he has to get her away, free from the Americans and their descent into self-destruction. Perhaps even in the forested hills of Vancouver Island with Adolphus. He wants out, but he wants Miriam out first. And what about Brendan Manwaring?

"Miriam, everything I hear makes staying here more dangerous. I've got to get you out."

"No chance, Jason. He needs me. I'm committed. We're joined at the hip."

"He can't even communicate with the States. It's all monitored."

"Jason, I want to trust you. But I can't trust SECOR. I can't trust CSIS. *You* don't even trust them."

"Miriam, my real interest is right here. Getting you out."

"Well, I'm not getting out. So stop fretting about it and think of ways to help us. Stop telling Hawk whatever you find out here. That would be a start."

"I have to play along. Or he'll cut me off. I screen everything I say …"

"Don't play with me, Jason. You're just an amateur. Those people at SECOR are professionals. They know how to extract what they need from you." The conflicted trust between them has all but evaporated. After a moment of cold silence, Miriam must sense this breakdown, because she softens her position. "If I were in Canada I'd have to *do* something anyway, so I'd end up in trouble there as well."

"Do something?"

"Demonstrate, paint slogans on walls, set up a pirate TV station, write letters, make speeches—"

"But that's how you got in trouble in the first place."

"I've learned a lot since then. From Brendan. How to go about subverting them."

"You sound just like him, Miriam. It isn't even your own country."

"It could be. If these people can't be stopped, they'll lean on Canada till we crack."

"Canadians wouldn't stand for it."

"Americans weren't supposed to either."

That pauses him. An image of the A-D mocks him. There's one who would be comfortable with this regime. "If you go on, the Mexicans will ship you back to the States."

"Sergio will protect us. Even if it means going outlaw. Let's just leave it for now. He'll be here for dinner."

Dinner is subdued, with Manwaring rather withdrawn. Sergio answers her soberly. "I can protect you to a point, señora, but your case is different than the professor's. He's a refugee under our safekeeping. You're a foreign resident, you were a protestor in the States. The Americans are always after us not to renew visas for people they call subversive. Sometimes they reach an official who can satisfy them, sometimes not."

"If I go to Canada they could still turn me over to the States. Jason, you know well enough how the Canadian agencies are backing down to them."

"You're a citizen. You can't be shipped to another country. The Americans can't get you out of Canada."

Manwaring has been following this debate with only passing attention, his mind perhaps still grinding over the inhospitable mix of facts, but now he joins in. "Miriam, you may not be quite safe anywhere. No one who attacks this regime will ever be quite safe. But here you have Sergio and CISEN. In Canada, I imagine agencies like CSIS would rather find a way to get rid of you."

Jason knows that some arms of the Canadian government are now wary of criticizing a regime that hunkers over Canada like a grizzly over a lamb, but he persists mulishly. "They couldn't get rid of a Canadian citizen."

"Unless she was indicted for a crime in the States that was extraditable. Canada would have its excuse. Could the administration manufacture one?"

No one at the table seems to doubt it, not even a dismayed Jason, fielding a meaningful glance from the professor.

Jason sits on the bed in her room for a long while, expecting her. There is one more string to his bow, but he hates to use it. Maybe Manwaring is wakeful; maybe Miriam's had enough of his entreaties for one day. She never comes.

# TWENTY-FIVE

JASON FINDS A TEXT MESSAGE FROM NOBLE ON HIS CELL: *DFAIT urgently request you call consulate in Guadalajara.* They're expecting him.

"Mr. Currie? Mr. Kendal will speak to you. Please wait while I find him."

It's some time before he's found. "Ah! Mr. Currie. Good of you to contact me. I'm here only a day or two on urgent commercial affairs. From Ottawa. We're extremely involved down here."

Jason recognizes the accent of private Canadian schools as refined afterwards in the Foreign Service, nicely rounded tones and impeccable diction, well seasoned with self-importance. "You have a message for me, Mr. Kendal?"

"The message, yes." There's a pause, perhaps while he

searches his memory, or his pockets. "Yes. I have been asked by Ottawa to meet with you. Today."

"Something wrong? Some relative?"

"Relative? Why no. Not a relative. Unless Mrs. Ashbury is now related to you in some manner."

"Something has happened that you need to talk to her about?"

"May I see you here at the consulate, together with Mrs. Ashbury?"

"What for?"

"A matter of importance. Your … agency assured us you would be cooperative. My instructions are to meet with Mrs. Ashbury personally."

They arrange to meet at noon. "You can refuse to see him. I have no alternative."

"I don't mind. I'm really curious what Foreign Affairs could want."

"You must take Felipe with you," Manwaring says.

"They'll pick us up in an official car. We're untouchable at the consulate."

"Take him anyway."

"Good of you to come. My name is Kendal. I've taken the liberty of booking lunch, just across the street." A social rather than official meeting?

The consulate staff is known at the chic restaurant. Kendal is greeted like an old lover by the longhaired, fiftyish hostess, who flirts with him in a melodious accent of uncertain provenance. She's attentive to Miriam and Jason as well, but obviously knows who's paying. She greets Felipe in Spanish while using English to the others, with instant perception of everyone's ethnicity.

Kendal strikes him as one of those people for whom the word *empathy* is academic; he has none and neutralizes yours. His eyes in finding yours glaze over with disinterest. He has a chiseled chin and as fine a nose as John Barrymore, high, very gently arched, statuesque. He seems to find himself to be under observation, a gathering point for the attention of others, especially women, and contrives to present his profile to whichever one of them he imagines to be admiring him, so that once he has to whisper to Jason, "Isn't that woman staring at me?"

He has long slender fingers and wraps them around each other as he speaks, as if he were washing his hands, and his gaze concentrates on Jason's forehead. When he listens, his hands are still but his eyes roam, disengaged from the speaker.

While Jason sizes him up in silence and Felipe is quiet as usual, Miriam tries to pin down his mission. Kendal evades her effortlessly while he settles in, orders, evaluates the other patrons, flirts with the hostess, and finally gets to the point.

"Mrs. Ashbury—perhaps I may call you Miriam?—you've acquired a reputation in the United States as an outspoken critic of the administration."

Miriam's nettled, but Jason says mildly, "Most Canadians

would share her views."

"Ah! Share her views. But most Canadians live in Canada, where their views on American affairs are never heard by Washington. You, Miriam, became an American citizen, a very different situation. So you've attracted *attention*." Miriam is now bristling. "Do you plan to go back to Canada soon?"

"Why is that of any concern to the Canadian government?"

"Well, we do have *national* interests to consider, don't we? You do understand?"

"No. I don't. Not at all. Does that mean you're asking me to keep quiet?"

Kendal doesn't like this response. He seems to pick up, for the first time, the hostility that Miriam takes no pains to conceal. "Perhaps you will be remaining here with Professor Manwaring?"

"That's no business of yours, is it?"

"Actually, it is. We received your application to re-issue a passport."

"It expired. Isn't it just routine to issue a new one? None of my particulars has changed."

"Oh, it's never routine to issue passports. Especially nowadays. There's the retina scan to arrange. That's obligatory now."

"So, make an appointment."

He smiles, the kind of smile that is a conscious facial movement without the slightest emotional stimulus to authenticate it. "Perhaps you could tell me where you intend to travel now?"

"It isn't required to have any travel plans to apply?"

"Of course not. But you have a valid Mexican visa. For the moment. If you intend to remain here, the Mexican government will insist on a current passport before renewing it."

"I understand that. That's why I applied. I expected to receive an appointment by now. For my scan."

"Quite so. But I'm afraid you're on a list of those who require clearance from the Minister's office. It sometimes takes several months."

"That's ridiculous. What's the point of having a consulate here in Guadalajara if it can't simply issue a passport?"

"The point, Miriam, is to protect our national interests. A passport to a sensitive individual is a matter for Ottawa."

"Sensitive individual! Don't you people have any role other than sucking up to the administration?"

"Come now, you don't really expect us to frustrate our largest source of international income. Our ally in the defense of North America?"

"Defense against whom? This administration is our greatest threat."

After that, luncheon is aborted. They've only managed the soup course. Except Felipe—he finishes his roll as well.

"My God, Miriam! The Canadian government doesn't even want to *see* you in Canada. They prefer you in detention—but in the States." Skepticism aside, Jason has taken for granted that, in the clinch, Canada will of course stand by any of its citizens. Now he grasps that this maneuver would fit comfortably with the A-D's vision of his duty, and was probably set in motion by him. Not just Miriam's been betrayed—Jason has as well.

"Brendan will know what to do."

"I'm afraid this message is unambiguous," Manwaring says. They've found him shut in the house despite the warmth of the day, faithful to Sergio's standing caution never to sit in the garden when he's unprotected. They've come home by taxi, Miriam unwilling to use an unfriendly government's limousine. "The Canadians have been coerced into delaying or even denying a passport. Mexico City could now refuse to extend the visa. Miriam could be deported. Not to Canada—to the States. She'll have to go underground."

He's jarred out of his customary single-mindedness, like a chess player confronted by an outlaw move. He's wordless for some moments, head sunk in morose reflection. Jason wonders if he's focusing on life without Miriam. Or perhaps on the sudden awareness that powerful enemies are circling, and much more closely than he's assumed. "Sergio will know what to do. He's coming tonight as usual."

"Of course I could see that you might not be safe here indefinitely," Campobello says. "Mexico is trying to keep the friendship of the Americans. So we have to be agreeable. Some people would give them more of what they demand, some less. Just like Canada."

"I'm not sure what all that computes to," Jason says. "Will Mexico renew her visa?"

"I would. But I won't be asked. She's supposed to hold a valid passport to have a resident's visa."

"So it comes down to Canada."

"Perhaps so," Campobello says. "You understand, of course, that this is preliminary? A message to Miriam to get out of the way. Professor Manwaring is the target."

Jason has an uneasy awareness that this activity around Miriam might follow from his own intrusions: asking Sid for her file, coming to Mexico, not just once, and especially being a guest at the home of a notorious dissident. Stirring the pot has caused it to bubble. "So going underground may not help?"

"Exactly. Miriam might be able to disappear, but Professor Manwaring will never be able to."

"Your agency can protect him," she says.

"We've been able to by keeping very quiet. Just Felipe and me and one or two of my associates."

"So what's changed?"

"Things are not so quiet now, señora." He looks directly at Jason. "The presence of a Canadian agent has altered the balance."

"Just Jason—being here?" Campobello has made his point and says nothing more. Miriam glowers but doesn't challenge him. "Bastards!"

"You could move to Canada, Professor," Jason says, not very enthusiastically. "You can both go there. You could go on working together."

"Could he even get in?" Miriam's slightly hopeful.

"There's a large American colony, mostly hostile to the administration, quite a few known dissidents according to CSIS. You'd be heroes among them. Once he's in, I don't see how the government could deport him."

"Giving up Sergio and his protection," Manwaring says. "Would you and your CSIS guard us? I think the Canadian government has just confirmed that they don't even want Miriam in your country. So they want me even less."

"How could he get past the border?" Sergio asks.

"He has to get into the country secretly, then demand refugee status. And he can't fly over American territory."

Manwaring grows tired and discouraged as the talk goes on. Miriam finally helps him to bed while Jason follows Campobello to the gate. "What are his chances in Canada, señor?"

"Not bad once he's past the border."

"His safety there?"

"He'll need protection. Anywhere."

Campobello hesitates to leave. "The difficulty with her passport is to your advantage, señor."

"It might be a break for Miriam if it forces her to go."

"*She* might be better off in Canada. But it's not a break for him."

Miriam comes to him later. They sit on her bed and talk. She's in a dark and edgy mood. In a reversal of their roles, she needs his support. They're isolated in a capsule of near darkness, sizzling with emotions—fear, anger, and their building feelings for each other, affection, maybe love, certainly desire. They whisper, but the words are as potent as a touch.

"Going to Canada—running away."

"Not when you have no choice."

"I'm not leaving Mexico. I'm not going to Canada."

"Just to spite them?"

"To do my job. To help Brendan."

"You can't help Brendan by getting shipped back to the States."

"They can hide me somewhere."

"If you go into hiding you can't do anything useful."

"Jason, why can't you help me?"

"I can help you get out of here. Let me get you home. Let me live with you and love you where we don't need a guard to walk down the street."

"Live with me and love me right here. You can join us." There's just enough light to make out her look—fixed on him, intense, begging for his help.

He pulls her close. "I only want to join *you*."

She puts her hand on his chest and pushes him back a little. Her other hand falls on his thigh and a sizzle of excitement surprises him. "If I went home with you, would you help me with my work?"

"Your work?"

"Brendan's work. Our cause!" Her voice rises with impatience.

"Of course I'll help you."

"Don't tell me you'll help as if we're washing the kitchen floor. Will you help me with our cause?"

"I'll help you with anything, Miriam."

She exhales a satisfied sigh. "Then let me help you now."

She moves her hand from his chest to his neck. She draws him to her. He's overwhelmed. He wants to respond but this is the moment of doubt. His body fights to break through the envelope. "Miriam. Finally. It's love." He's shocked to see little globes of tears reflect in the faint light, creeping down her cheek. His body awakens. *Do it!*

He can't remember just how it goes after he moves over her and into her. It's not leisurely, it's not elegant; it's urgent, a crude compulsion to penetrate. The congealed juices of mind and body thaw, quicken, and then surge out of him. He falls away, heaving with relief, spent, but clear. She rolls against him and holds him. He can hear her heart thumping. Or maybe it's his own.

After some minutes, he thinks of her tears. "I didn't hurt you?"

She murmurs something, then: "I was just ... relieved. That you finally let go."

After a while she says, "I have to check on Brendan." When she comes back, she says nothing. She pulls off her gown and slides into bed. She has the rounded body of a mature woman but the same heat as the girl on the back steps years ago. It's after midnight in the Maron yard and he can smell the dewy grass.

"I knew you needed me," she says. "But I need you too."

# TWENTY-SIX

"You haven't accomplished much. Unless you got what you were after from that woman. All you've learned is that she'd rather stay with him."

"Miriam will have to leave Mexico. She needs a little time to separate from him gracefully." It's getting more comfortable to lie, even with Hawk's gaze sweeping him for nonverbal giveaways. "I've learned more of what he knows about the administration's plans. He's well informed."

"But *how* is he informed? That's the key."

"I picked up a hint that Miriam has access to his net."

"We need more than hints. Nothing helpful from Manwaring? If you're not getting anywhere, there's not much point in going back. We'll find another way. If the army doesn't snatch him first."

"That's what it's all about? Getting Manwaring to spite the army?"

"You're the only one interested in her for her own sake."

Jason can't handle this brush-off without a little heat "I may not be much of a spy, but at least I found out their final plan."

Hawk has effectively dismissed him, but Jason's raw tone refocuses him. "Final plan?"

"Manwaring says it's not just detention. They're going to deport noncitizens."

"*Does* he? Where would he have gotten that?"

"I don't know. Yet."

"Your woman—did she know about this?"

"She said he was obsessed by what would happen. But even if they *wanted* to—"

Hawk tosses his head impatiently. "Forget the rhetoric. A way can be found. You need to get away from your high school thinking. Maybe they're all naive up there. Your man Noble seems about as sound as a wet sponge."

"Excuse me, sir. I'm not used to thinking in global terms. Canadians are pretty much absorbed in just keeping our own country out of your wars."

Hawk surprises him by overlooking the sarcasm and taking this as a serious comment. "Look, Jason, our society is the most dynamic in history. You would agree with that, wouldn't you?" Jason is working out a neutral response when Hawk goes on. "But there are still parts of the world held hostage by gothic regimes. At one time it wouldn't have concerned us. Nations didn't mess with each other's customs. We'd let them bumble along until they either smartened up or failed. But now that we're a truly global society, these outdated regimes are a drag on international well being. Follow?"

"I think I see where you're heading, sir."

"We need to promote reform worldwide. We have to help backward states learn how to govern themselves, to become producers of wealth rather than welfare cases. Either by friendly persuasion or if necessary by coercion."

Is there any ounce of sincerity behind the ironic smirk that could possibly validate such a romantic view of the national mission? Or is he making fun of Jason?

"History will look back on this period and compare it with the flowering of the Western world after the Enlightenment."

"After the Enlightenment came the revolution," Jason says.

"Damn! You don't rise above the pedestrian, do you?" Hawk sounds irritated but can't quite smother a grin. "I have to allow for you being a Canadian. You people aren't required to change the world, are you?"

"We're not sure that you are, either."

"Run along, Jason, go do your analyses."

"Still on Mexico—"

"Run along."

Archie never wants to hear Jason's doubts. He's a believer, unsullied by skepticism. He has faith, not just in his country, but more so in his religion. He's the only SECOR now whom

Jason finds in the least sympathetic. He is Jason's only retreat in an inhospitable workplace. So Jason listens patiently when Archie sometimes veers into his personal concerns. He now knows the family—the wife, Mame, the two kids—and all Archie's issues as a member of the board of his evangelical church. "We had a surprise guest this weekend. At the service."

He leans toward Jason, clearly pleased, and cracks his open-mouthed smile. Jason wonders again at the innocence that this SECOR warrior can sometimes project. Archie's voice drops to a near-whisper. "Anita Skye."

"The vice-president?" A news magazine is on his desk. Archie pulls it over. Skye's picture fills the cover page. She's in military camouflage. Her face, professionally preserved, looks younger than her fifty-something years, the hair still jet black where it escapes from the helmet. She's wearing two revolvers, both with ivory butts like General Patton's, and her hand is resting on one. Slashed across the page: 'The Crusader from the White House.'

"She was at your service?"

"She spoke to us."

"A political speech? In *church*?"

"Just a heads-up for supporters."

"Hopefully no new wars."

"Christianity *as the code of the United States*. Virtually an official religion. Like Islam in every one of their countries."

"Archie, isn't it part of your constitution that government

should have nothing to do with religion?" Archie merely smiles; he keeps any response to himself. "I'm always interested in how you see things. You're not as predictable as some people here."

"You're a maverick yourself, Jason, but my mindset comes from my beliefs."

"And Anita Skye shares them? Is that why she was there?"

"Partly. But also to tell fellow believers that the administration is listening."

"Listening?"

"She talked of the demands that our Muslims make. How they need to become a lot more American before they ask the rest of us for respect. My wife and I listened to it over again."

"Again? There's a recording?"

Archie hesitates. "There was no media coverage. But the church records everything, and the board got digital copies. I've been listening to it again as I drive in to work."

"Pretty stirring stuff? I've heard she's really outspoken."

"Plain talk. Not as grand as the president but more punch."

"Fascinating. May I hear a bit of it?"

Archie hesitates again. "I suppose it won't hurt. It's already summarized in this magazine." He fiddles with his smart phone. "Just the closing part."

Skye has a high, clear voice, almost too high. "We would never lack the courage to act when Christians are threatened—when *you* are threatened. We have made America into a fortress, and we're keeping her safe by engaging these enemies in their own countries rather than here. This is now the most secure country in the world.

"But Americans deserve more. We think our faith is one of the pillars of the Republic, a republic that would not have been possible without the faith of our founders. *We will defend that faith, whatever it takes.* We're preparing a program that will enshrine Christianity as the inspiration and code of the Republic. We're taking steps to ensure that alien doctrines will not be allowed to flourish as equals. What would you find if you went to live in a Muslim country? If people of other faiths come to live here, they should have no doubt that this is a Christian country and give due respect to the religion on which America was founded, and which we celebrate. We promise Americans that the beliefs with which we were all raised and which honor our history will not be passed over. We will not try to pacify those who hate Christianity by giving them equal status.

"I cannot be more specific today. You will be hearing more of our message in the weeks to come. When you do, please speak out to endorse it. Between us, we can and will keep America free, and *keep America Christian.* Thank you."

Jason's shocked. Archie looks pleased. "Archie, does Anita Skye really speak for the party?"

"Sure. She should be the next president."

"But this president is popular."

"He can't run again."

"And Skye could be the nominee?"

"She has the right message."

"Which is?"

"Don't back down to the Muslims."

"Would *you* vote for her?"

"Jason, if the party put her up, what choice would there be?"

"The other party?"

"They're not as committed. It would be like voting for the second team."

First, Hawk's ironic summary—almost a send-up—of American war aims. Then, Archie's presentation of Anita Skye. Jason's troubled by the smell of change. Their return to Canada for Miriam is being urged by the storm clouds building over the United States.

The vice-presidential story touches off an outbreak of comment. He reads some of the pundit jargon, and follows simplistic comments on television. "I'm all for freedom to worship, but this is a Christian country," is his favorite. The converging point of all the twaddle is hostility toward Muslims. The regime has eased the stopper out of the bottle, and the escaping vapor has a poisonous stench.

# TWENTY-SEVEN

JASON IS AWAKENED BY THE TELEPHONE. "SERGIO CAMPOBELLO. There's been an accident. To Señor Manwaring." He gives Jason a few seconds.

"Not serious?"

"Serious. The professor is dead."

Jason's groggy mind engages. "*Dead*! Dead how?"

"An explosion."

"Miriam?" he whispers.

"Survived. She's a little hurt. Felipe is worse, but alive."

"But … he was protected."

The momentary silence tells him that Campobello takes this as a reproach. "It's something I might have foreseen. I relied on the alarm system and the dog, but they attacked from outside the wall. For me, it's a professional failure."

"I'm sorry, Sergio. I'm sure you did everything—"

"We'll expect you later today."

He finds a very early flight. He's dazed, but knows he must get out immediately. Hawk will have this news shortly, maybe already, and will block any visit to Mexico. He sweats out the wait for takeoff with a nervous eye for a squad in gray.

Hawk might even be privy to the killing—but then he would have made sure of Jason. His mind is hearing footsteps. Can SECOR somehow locate him by his necklace, a kind of GPS? He weighs leaving it behind, but then how can he avoid interrogation on his return?

Once in the air, he then has leisure, too much of it, to work his way through acceptance. Like any other nonprofessional, he doesn't know how to handle violent death other than to tiptoe around it. It's easier to think of Miriam, nurse and confidante to the professor. He has seen how she warmed herself in the heat of Manwaring's passions. Her nature is commitment, and she focused most of hers on her mentor.

Manwaring was no rebel; he was a kind of loyalist. But he was beholden to an America that he saw being displaced by autocracy, and his own death is now a manifestation of his country's degeneration. However it was managed, Jason's certain they will find the administration as the inspiration if not the agent of the murder.

"America the warrior of democracy abroad has lost faith in democracy at home," Manwaring had mused on Jason's last morning with him. He went on, stretched out by his table in the shade, his paper and his coffee cup at his elbow and the dog at his feet, ruminating in that mood of despair over the decline of his homeland. His eyes were fixed on some point in the garden but his mind was visualizing a country he now saw as alien. "The last line of defense is always an aroused public. How do you bring it to life when the administration is feeding it barbiturates?" After some brooding he went on, very slowly. "America, which used to be the light of the world, has all but burned out in a final flare of intolerance. The city on the hill has become the ruins on the hill."

After a few more silent moments between them, Manwaring had surprised Jason.

"I need to speak to you about Miriam." He'd sat upright and leaned toward him. "I always understood our relationship would be fleeting." He spoke very quietly, no passion now, just resignation. "I know the danger I'm in—worse than I thought, now that I see what they can do. Her danger is almost as great. She will have to go. I will never reach Canada, but she can. You will make sure of that." He had reached out and touched Jason on the shoulder. "But please let me choose the moment."

Campobello is waiting at the airport.

"We have time, but not a lot." He sweeps up Jason's bag and sets a brisk pace out of the terminal.

"She's all right, but they could just as easily have gotten her. They meant to," he answers to Jason's first question. "She was just lucky. We think they used a projectile, fired through the window. It was open and screened. It passed through the screen and exploded against the head of the bed."

"But the wall is ten feet high. You can't see the windows—"

"They could have used a truck with a—what do you call it?—cherry picker. I should have had that window boarded."

"She's still in danger if they know she's alive."

"They will by now. But after all, he was the threat. She may be considered a loose end. But we'll take no chances."

"Good. Are *you* in danger?"

He shrugs. "Not as much as I used to be, and I survived. They've gotten used to not bothering much about me."

"Do you know who did it?"

"Not yet. Do you?"

"God, no!"

"We will find out. Perhaps they were able to use their friends at SEDENA, or perhaps they had clearance to manage it on their own." He pauses for a moment. "They must have known the house quite well."

"Sergio! Please. You can't really think that about me."

"You wouldn't do anything to hurt Miriam. Not knowingly. Maybe by accident?"

"I report to a general at SECOR. Mostly I lie."

Campobello seems to accept this. Jason recalls that Hawk knew the house was gated.

They drive to an apartment building in a newer section of the city and enter a basement parking area. Campobello puts Jason's bag into the vehicle beside them, an old, dusty pickup.

"We'll wait ten minutes. You'll lie down in the back."

"We're being followed?"

"We must expect it. They would have your flight number."

"Where are we?"

"I live here. Since the professor moved into my house."

"You own that house?"

"Of course. I was born there." He removes his suit jacket and tie and dons a beaten-up sombrero from the cab. "Now I'm an old farmer."

"How did you get her away? They must have been watching the house."

"I guessed there would be four men in two cars. I called two ambulances. We put Felipe in one and the professor in the other and sent them in two directions. After a few minutes I took Miriam to a private clinic in my car. I took precautions. No one was able to follow."

"So they were certain to be at the airport to follow me."

"Naturally."

In spite of Campobello's smooth professionalism in secreting Miriam, Jason's troubled. "Sergio, I've seen how this works. If it's DIA, they'll send as many men as necessary, regardless of your country's wishes."

"I agree she must leave here in time." He starts the motor and the old truck chokes out a cloud of diesel fumes. "But Canada would be difficult."

With Jason prone in the cargo box, they drive for some time, making several U-turns, before he's welcomed into the cab. "You're not afraid they're using a drone to follow us?" Jason asks.

"Not in Mexico. You're thinking SECOR, who are allowed to use them everywhere. Here we only have to account for ground surveillance."

Miriam meets them at the door of another apartment, a woman beside her. She looks quite calm, but when she hugs him he can feel the tension in her shoulders. "I thought you might not be allowed to come."

She has yellowish stains on her face over scraped patches. One arm is bandaged. As she leads him in, she limps against him. "Sergio said you were on your way, but I thought they might hold you."

"Look at you, Miriam." A stab of panic as he reads the signs of the near miss.

"Felipe's in hospital. I was lucky. The bed tipped over on me. It probably saved me from the worst of it. I was all wrapped up in the sheets. The ceiling came down on me—like a truckload of dust. I could barely move. Zorra found me. She was shaking, covered with dust and blood. We both huddled there. Expecting someone. To help." Jason catches the still figure of the Doberman bedded down in a corner, staring at him. "She slept in the hall. Outside his door. The door blew out. Missed her. She's spaced out." Perhaps like herself.

"I called. For Brendan. Then Felipe. Nobody came." She goes on awhile, words in short bursts followed by silence, as if describing a slide show, one image after another, her voice rising as she works through them. He watches her closely. She catches him doing that, stops talking and then smiles slightly. "You look worried. I'm not getting hysterical, Jason. I've already shed my tears."

The woman with her is a matronly lady with a Mexican complexion. "This is Señora Majorca. Juanita. It's her apartment." Sergio and she leave them alone.

She leads him to a couch. They sit very close to each other. She looks at him in that direct way of hers. "I want to tell you the rest." She seems less tense.

"Only if you feel up to it."

"After I crawled out—it took a while—I went to his room. It was dark, full of dust. It smelt burnt, smoky. Brendan, he was … mangled. His head was … dangling. There was a lot of blood …" She remained with the body until she heard Sergio below.

Juanita now comes to them and offers her a pill with water. "For the pain, Miriam."

"It's not so bad now." But she swallows it.

"It feels better to share your grief," Juanita says, leaving them.

"She's right, you know. I do feel better talking to you." She takes hold of his hand and pulls him around so that they face each other. She kisses him. Then she pushes away from him. "Now we have to decide what to do."

"You cannot continue your work from here, señora," Campobello says.

The four of them have assembled around the kitchen table. Miriam looks tired but determined. "Brendan believed we were gaining ground. There's another election in a year or so. We need to keep on building up opposition. You have the access, Sergio."

"I have been able to send messages. In a code I can't decipher, to a person I don't know, at a place with no name."

"You were communicating with Manwaring's network?" Jason asks.

"I sent messages for him."

"Without knowing who was receiving them?"

"The professor decided it was too dangerous for me to know." He's clearly disgusted—a professional deemed unsuitable for the risks of his profession.

"Then how can this network function now?"

Campobello eyes him coolly. "I think you should leave that to those who are involved."

"You should know me better by now, Sergio. Anyway, I'm not interested in your communications. My point is that Miriam can't do any good here now, so we should find a way to get her to Canada."

"When I'm good and ready, Jason." She gives him that look he's seen before. "There has to be a way. What if we simply send a message saying we're standing by for advice?"

"They would probably think it came from his assassins.

Their best plan would be to forget the Mexican connection for now and get on with their business." A dreary silence follows. The miasma of death lays over them like a blanket.

Finally Miriam gets up, looking frustrated. "I'm too tired to think." She almost stomps from the kitchen.

"She has been very quiet until now," Juanita says. "Worried whether you would come. Now that you're here and she has shared her grief, she needs to rest."

"I must get her away."

Campobello says, "You mean to Canada? Flying over the United States?"

"She could fly to Europe, then Canada."

"No American passport now, no Canadian passport yet."

"Can you provide a passport?"

"Certainly. Good enough for most uses, but not good enough to get past European security. Not with the Americans standing beside them. What do you think, Juanita?"

"Better to hide her in Mexico."

Jason avoids disagreeing, but believes Miriam is at risk anywhere in Mexico. SEDENA will track her down and DIA will abduct or kill her. Getting her to safe haven in Canada is his sole interest. For Sergio, it's carrying the pain of the professor's murder and somehow protecting his protégée. Juanita now sits quietly and awaits the outcome. Jason breaks the silence.

"Cruise ships! She could go by sea. There are cruise liners every day. They stop on the West Coast. Some in Vancouver."

"They pass through American waters. Their passenger lists are filed with SECOR."

"But they can't scrutinize ship passengers the way they do at airports. They can have over a thousand passengers. They unload like a mob. Will one of your passports be good enough there?"

"Probably. How good is her Spanish, Juanita?"

"Not bad, if she doesn't say too much."

Campobello busies himself on the telephone, rattling off instructions in Spanish, while Jason goes to Miriam with a tiny camera Campobello has given him.

Having purged herself of her feelings, for the moment, she sleeps. He stretches out beside her, facing her, listening to her breathing and watching the rise and fall of her chest. For now she seems dreamless, but he imagines the hellish visions lurking in her memory from which she may never find complete relief. Now she's vulnerable, lying there, unlike the Miriam he has become used to, in command of herself, and even of Manwaring at times. He reaches and lightly folds his hand around her shoulder. She stirs. He snaps half a dozen shots while her eyes are open. She hardly wakens. Her eyelids flutter and close when he says nothing.

"These will do," Campobello says. "I'll take some of you also."

"Why?"

"We cannot have your name recorded. You will also need a Mexican passport."

"I can't go with her on the cruise."

Campobello scoffs. "Of course not, but you must at least take her to the ship. She cannot go alone. You should be with her until she boards, then go back to SECOR."

"Do we have any cruises yet?"

"We have found three that will dock in Canada. Two in Vancouver, one in Victoria. They all make stops first in the United States."

"Vancouver's best. She can be anywhere in Canada in hours. Where do they dock in Mexico?"

"One next week. From Puerto Vallarta. It stops in San Francisco, then Vancouver."

"Is Puerto Vallarta very far?"

"Three hundred fifty kilometers. Five hours by car."

"They take pictures of all boarding passengers. She needs to change her appearance."

"I can supply a wig. Long hair. Juanita can find her local clothing."

"In Puerto Vallarta we could pretend to be a Mexican couple who are speaking English to practice for the cruise."

"The other risk is San Francisco. She could remain in her cabin."

Jason doesn't like this. "If most of the passengers go into the city, she should also. It would attract attention if she stayed aboard. In a group of tourists, she might be invisible."

"A single woman is noticeable."

"Not so much on a cruise ship. There will be dozens if not

hundreds of unattached women."

"In pairs."

Jason mulls this over. "Is it possible that Señora Majorca could accompany her?"

Campobello looks about to express his reluctance when the señora answers. "With pleasure, señor."

"It might be arranged …" Campobello frowns. "But I still have doubts. If they suspect she's on a cruise ship, she'll be trapped."

"Sergio, I know what they're thinking. It's urgent to get Miriam out of Guadalajara. I like the odds on the ship."

Jason cannot disappear from SECOR for long. He messages Hawk: *investigating Manwaring murder probably by DIA*. He hopes that might delay any reaction by Hawk, but the prompt response surprises him: *let Mexican agencies investigate concentrate on cleaning up loose ends*. Almost granting permission to look after Miriam.

# TWENTY-EIGHT

THEY SET OUT TWO DAYS LATER. HE IS BOOKED AT A GIANT American hotel, adjacent to the port, where they will be invisible. Campobello's passports identify them as Señor and Señora Castillo. He's also provided a passport for Señora Majorca, since her name could be known in the intelligence community. Miriam is dressed to look older so that the two ladies seem closer in age.

The final preparation is the removal of Jason's cast. "We cannot have either of you advertising your identity with your wounds." Sergio cuts through the plaster. "Juanita will bandage it. You must wear shirts with long sleeves. Same for her. Answer everybody in English, don't attempt Spanish. Just remember to speak English a little slowly."

They speed northward along the toll highway for hours before turning off onto the winding road into Puerto Vallarta, their speed now cut by half. Miriam, almost sullen, takes no interest in the countryside. Perhaps the final decision to return to Canada verges on betrayal of her mentor's cause. He tries several forays to catch her interest; she doesn't want to talk. Juanita points out landmarks and gets only polite acknowledgments. Maybe she feels guilty; so does he. He supposes everyone does when someone else is singled out for death.

The drive becomes wearisome in the heavy silence, short stretches of blind views between sudden curves. Occasionally she does make some remark, muttered more to herself than to him, which he can't make out over the road noise. Once he does hear, "There was no funeral." She must mean that her grief is unrelieved by what some call closure, felt after last rites, which has always seemed to him more the renunciation of guilt.

They crawl for miles behind a local bus choking out black clouds of exhaust. He's worn out, and she probably more so, when they finally see the towers of the tourist quarter rising against the Bay of Flags. He remembers Campobello's orders and speaks with (probably exaggerated) hesitation in English as they're received in the lobby, Miriam managing to hide her limp.

In their room, she strips in front of him and walks, naked, into the shower. He waits for an alarming time, unwilling to intrude on her mood. Perhaps she's cleansing her mind as well as her body, for when she emerges, wearing only a towel turban on her wet hair, flushed and smelling of soap, she finally smiles.

She throws herself on top of the bed and holds out her arms for him. Tender with relief, they make love slowly, sharing not only its intensity but also its celebration of life.

Ramona made love as if it were an exercise in a gym. Miriam, unhurried, allows her warmth to draw him in. Her hands shape him to her body. They unite, locking together smoothly, like a matched set, and move in sync to a shared climax. He's immensely satisfied. Neither wants to move. When they wake, the room is dark.

He escorts his ladies into the town center, away from the sterility of the tourist hotels. They saunter along the Malecon, busy with its mix of tourists and locals, and dine in sight of the bay. Miriam is now in some recovery cycle, not offering to mention Manwaring. She touches Jason numbers of times, his arm, his shoulder, his hand, seeking reassurance. Juanita entertains them with legends of the port. She's vibrant with anticipation of the voyage; her only regret is that Campobello has ordered her immediate return by air from Vancouver.

When they go to bed, Miriam curls hard against him, her need so evident he worries about her frame of mind on the cruise, and blesses Juanita's company.

The next morning, when they rise early and wait for Juanita to join them, Miriam is ready to talk about her life with the professor. "After Bil almost threw me out—I suppose he had no choice—I came to Mexico. I didn't know Brendan. Never heard of him. Remember, they weren't giving him any coverage in the States. I was thinking—seriously—of going back to university. I wanted to study politics and economics. I came to Guadalajara because of the university. I read about him there. He was well covered in the local media. Condemned in English and rather lionized in Spanish. Some American expatriates despised him. He's so private—you saw that—it was hard to meet him. Then one day I got a note from *him*. Asking me to visit."

"Manwaring knew you were in Guada?"

"More than that. He knew my whole background. He wanted to meet me as a comrade in arms. I thought he was starved for conversation with kindred spirits. When he suggested not long after that I move in, I was ready."

"And you became his right hand. And more than that." She winces, and he kicks himself.

"We never really got to be lovers. We tried, but it was no good. We were just bedmates. Not like you and me."

They take the local bus downtown and walk with the sea dancing beside. They take coffee in little cafes. They lunch on fresh seafood. It's a brief honeymoon before she sails, and they make the most of it, dining and even dancing on their last evening. And talking, always talking, sometimes of their past, pushed by Juanita, who seems fascinated by their Canadian upbringing and its contrast with her circumscribed Catholic childhood. Plenty of their history to share on the voyage.

In their room on their final night, he makes a last attempt to comprehend the mystery of Manwaring's communications.

"What will happen to his network now?"

She's surprised. "Why would it change? There must be others to replace him."

"You know these people?"

"Only a few by their pseudonyms."

"Some of them are in the administration?"

She pauses at this. Perhaps he has pushed her too hard. "Of course I trust you, Jason—I've no one else to trust now. But I don't know as much as you suspect. He was afraid I'd be too much at risk. I know it was done on Pacific Time. His key contact was someone who knew a good deal about government plans. Brendan had some kind of power over him."

"Power?"

"I mean it was more than friendship. More than an ally."

"An old lover?"

"I know it was a man."

"How did he get his messages through? SECOR picked up no signals intel."

She looks conflicted, afraid to break her promise, then whispers, "Sergio took the coded messages. Nearly every day. Everything went on their secure lines. Replies the same way. But he doesn't know any of the contacts. And I don't know where the other end of the chain was. I only did the encryption for him. And decoding. The digits are rearranged in series. It's tied in with the days of the month. It's indecipherable unless you know those two tables. I could send a message but I didn't know where it was going."

"Then you can't reestablish contact?"

"If I reach Canada, I'd be surprised if they don't contact me." *If I reach Canada ...* The thought that she might not spreads over him like a shadow.

The telephone startles them. Campobello begins speaking as soon as Jason lifts the receiver: "I can only speak for one minute. They're checking all the cruise ports."

"But how ...?"

"*Listen*! There's no time. You must get out of that hotel now. *This minute*! Don't pack. Take nothing, just walk out. Juanita will be at the car. Take the bus to Manzanillo. *Manzanillo*. Find a plain hotel. Juanita will call me. Go *now*."

"We're leaving here. They're on our tail," he says to Miriam, expecting a demand for an explanation. Instead, he receives one startled look and then she reaches for her jacket.

"Suitcases?" He shakes his head and she beats him to the door. They manage to saunter by the desk with a nod to the clerk, but taut with the fear of some peremptory challenge. Juanita is standing by the car in the parking lot.

"We must take the bus. The terminal is a short walk. We leave the car here."

They have a moment to grab the one suitcase locked in the trunk. The short walk is tense; unknown forces may be poised to descend on them ... At the terminal, they find the next departure is still an hour away. Juanita buys her own ticket and keeps away from them; no need to link them in the clerk's memory. Then they have only to hold down their tension, not easy as it jumps back up with every entry through the main doorway. Jason forces himself to avoid looking that way as travelers accrue. Miriam sits as close to him as she can. She touches his arm constantly for reassurance.

The bus is nearly full, even at this hour. It's first-class, so air-conditioned and comfortable. But the drive is wearing, the road two-lane throughout, often winding, and rough at times. Their driver presses ahead, with frequent highlights used to push slower traffic, though without much gain. It's almost four hours to their destination. Plenty of time to speculate on what's happening to them now, and what it's leading to. Jason constructs and then discards several plans. Useless to make any decision until they can draw on Campobello's expertise.

All the excitement of their getaway is drained by the tedium of the darkened journey. They arrive in a terminal nearly deserted, amongst fellow travelers who all look equally exhausted, beneath fluorescent lights, which leach the humanity from every face. There are only a few people to meet the bus, and Jason's relieved to see each of them quickly partnered with a passenger and on their way.

There is a nondescript hotel close by. They register separately from Juanita. She comes to their room at once. "We must call Sergio. But not from here. You should come with me, Jason."

The nearest public telephone is back in the terminal, now almost clear of clients. Juanita places a call that lasts only seconds. Then they wait. The phone rings about ten minutes later. She has a rapid conversation in Spanish before turning the call over to Jason.

"You've done well to get clear, señor."

"How did you find out?"

"Allies in the intelligence community. Her description has been posted in every cruise port in Mexico. DIA has called in a lot of favours to get such cooperation. Once they'd picked out your last-minute booking on that cruise they would soon have found your hotel. They will have been there by now. A narrow escape."

"Why Manzanillo?"

"It's our busiest port—many ships. We're looking for a cargo vessel to Vancouver or anywhere near. Many of them carry a few passengers. There's no common system to find fugitives on these cargo ships. She'd be anonymous."

"We thought she was anonymous in Puerto Vallerta."

"I didn't expect DIA to trade for help from a Mexican agency. No doubt with a generous reward. They must be crushed that they missed her in the house. She went from anonymous to wanted in an hour. Now she's a valuable prize."

"I'm very grateful." Campobello does not acknowledge his thanks. "Meanwhile I'm overdue in L.A."

"One thing at a time, señor. SECOR is not your first concern. You must move out of that hotel in the morning. It's too close to the terminal, in case they guess your route. But they'll focus on Puerto Vallerta until that ship sails. So you have until five o'clock tomorrow evening—that is today. Their next move will be to concentrate on other cruise ships. Meanwhile we will locate any vessel bound for Canada. You may be in Manzanillo for some time. Find some better place to hide."

# TWENTY-NINE

'… LOOSE ENDS NOT EASY TO CLEAN UP REQUEST DELAY …'

'… Use your own judgement but imperative you be here after three days …'

The exchange with Hawk is only slightly reassuring. Jason puts aside his apprehension over what might be forthcoming on that third day.

It all seems like a game, especially dealing with Hawk. Now comes the awakening: it's not a game. Jason thinks of Miriam when she spoke of Manwaring's head 'hanging from his body.' That leads him to the image once again of those scattered body parts in the Sudanese garden. Nauseous recollections, but with staying power. Miriam has been primed for such atrocities all along, she knew what was going on out there, while he has been consumed by fantasies of their common future. The two of them have been talking past each other; now, he finds himself forced to her vision, bleak, unwelcoming, but much tighter to reality.

They've ended up in a marginal hotel near the harbour. It's noisy: from shady clients coming and going at surprising intervals, from whistles and hoots, and loud machinery drifting from the port. Trucks rumble by under their window. A walk in the neighborhood is discouraging; Miriam attracts attention from people they'd rather not meet. Back in their room, they watch a dreary television program in Spanish. With all this free time and no progress, they're both heavy with anxiety. If Sergio finds no direct way out of this place, then what?

"There are lots of ships. Why not just take the first opening and go anywhere but the States?' she speculates.

"I'm not sending you off to Shanghai or Jakarta while I go back to L.A."

"I can fly to Canada anonymously from anywhere outside the States."

"Miriam, no one flies anonymously anymore. These people will have access through friendly contacts to most carriers. They will have identified your Mexican passport at the hotel. If you fly they'll be ready for you."

"If I fly direct to Canada there's nothing that DIA can do."

Jason's ready to grant this—getting her to Canada has always been the solution. But lots of flights from anywhere to Canada land somewhere else en route.

"Let's be patient and give Sergio a chance."

They pass an uneasy night: too much noise to sleep, too much tension to make love. When Jason goes down for an early coffee, the night clerk signals him.

"The *Federales* were checking. They were interested in you."

"How long ago?"

"Couple of hours."

Jason squares his appreciation with a generous tip. "We'll be checking out in a minute."

"Of course." Neither Miriam nor Juanita is ready but he panics them into a ten-minute departure. It's a nasty feeling—bundling out into the street without bathing, without breakfast, and without a place to go. There are no cruising cabs. They walk to a tiny restaurant where they can phone. Miriam distracts the single waiter while Juanita phones Sergio, and then hands the receiver to Jason.

"We're on the run again. Any good news?"

"Take your time and find a proper hotel. Some place the *Federales* won't be checking every two hours. Buy some clothes. Behave like people with money who never attract the police. Then be patient."

"Miriam wants to go anywhere that's available."

"I expected that. There are several possibilities, but I need one more day."

"Tomorrow," Jason tells them. "Meanwhile we're to live it up a little." They take rooms away from the port, in the tourist area, with its beaches and fleets of small pleasure boats. They stroll on another *malecon* in the evening. For a day they are vacationing tourists. Meanwhile they cannot relax. While they linger, the search for Miriam could be closing in.

"The best I can do," Campobello tells them the following morning, "is to drop you in Los Angeles."

"But she cannot be found in an American port."

"Listen to me. This is the only cargo ship we find with a vacancy. It's off-loading in Manzanillo tomorrow. They're dropping a pair of passengers there so they have an opening. But they go next to Long Beach and then back to Europe. This is not all bad. There is no way for them to pick her out."

"What a risk though."

"Nothing we might do is free of risk. They'll never expect her to enter the States. She walks off the ship. She goes through Customs. She has money. She has a reservation at a good hotel. She's only staying for a week. Customs see thousands like her."

"She'll be beyond our help. She's an American citizen."

"I know. But the day she arrives, she can fly on to Vancouver. They won't be checking flights from L.A. I will send a messenger tonight with a new passport and a reservation. There are lots of flights L.A. to Vancouver. I don't see how they can identify her. The only real threat is if they find she has been on this particular ship, so you must not leave any trail. Mention the ship to no one. Do not be seen at the ship yourself."

They bat it around for an hour, Miriam enthusiastic, Jason full of reservations, Juanita disappointed to become redundant. Miriam decides to go for it.

There's a very different feeling this night than the one before the cruise ship sailing. That was poignant, the finale of a tender interlude. It had firmed up their love, even while mourning for Manwaring. There was no fear then; now there's plenty. Jason struggles with it in silence, Miriam takes it in stride. He understands that she's used to it. Beside Manwaring, she's lived in fear for some time.

Miriam has no plans beyond reaching Canada, no friends in Vancouver. "My cousin retired to Vancouver Island. Why not stay with him awhile? You could come on to Ottawa when I'm recalled."

"When?"

"Whenever Hawk is sick of me. Sometime between tomorrow and months from now."

"Your cousin?"

"He's a bit of a curmudgeon, but interesting company. He lives like a hermit on an acreage in the bush. He's on pension and boards horses for the extra."

"He lives alone?"

"But he's civilized. Are you any good with horses?"

"I've never had to find out. It sounds a stretch."

"Maybe, but he's family. I've already warned him you might come."

The next morning the messenger arrives with her documents. He has Campobello's instructions that Jason and Juanita are to drive with him to Guadalajara. Their little group find the ship berthed near several frigates of the Mexican Navy. She's not as commanding as the great cruise vessel was, but with her decks piled with containers she at least towers over the navy. Jason and Juanita cannot be seen, so they study her from a distance, watching the pair of cranes begin to unload some of the containers to waiting float trucks.

"You can still back off," Jason says unhelpfully.

Miriam just laughs. "It was all settled when it was settled. I'll be waiting for you."

They share a long embrace, Juanita a shorter one. They cannot wait to see her sail. As Miriam disappears aboard, they drive away.

On his flight to L.A., he finds an editorial comment on Manwaring's death: "... killed in an explosion in Guadalajara, where he had been living after fleeing the United States. He was in contact with terrorists. A Mexican agency says the killing was related to the drug trade. Americans can be forgiven for thinking that Mexico shouldn't be harboring fugitives like this in the first place."

# THIRTY

AFTER HIS OTHER TRIPS, JASON WAS EDGY THAT HAWK WOULD decide to send him home. Now he's hoping Hawk will do just that. But Hawk's like an alienated parent, disapproving but not quite ready to forsake his property rights. Once Miriam turns up in Canada (at his cousin's!), he expects to be packed off to Canada in disgrace, but meanwhile he needs to keep Hawk's goodwill.

"Leaving the country without clearance—juvenile!" Hawk seems more annoyed than outraged.

"It was the middle of the night."

"Oh? SECOR closes down at dusk? We had the details before you got to the airport." Not from Campobello. Another source in Guada?

"You didn't try to stop me."

"I thought it might not be a bad idea to have our man on the scene. If you'd bothered to confide in me, I might have sent you anyway." He lets this rebuke sink in. Jason, braced for a dressing-down, struggles to read Hawk's direction. "We have the official version. Tell me what actually happened?"

Jason summarizes, not mentioning Miriam.

"So it was professional. Either DIA or their allies. Damn DIA! An American government agency murdering an American for political reasons. Typical of the military that the way to handle a problem is to kill someone."

Brimming with bitterness, Jason says, "Manwaring told me that SECOR has the same prerogative."

Hawk looks angry. "We don't have it and we don't need it. We're not murderers. We don't train men to be killers the way the military does. You should have known when he was having you on. He played games with you." He cools off before finishing. "Miriam Ashbury—you've avoided mentioning her—where is she?"

"Sergio Campobello took her."

"The CISEN rogue agent? And where is she now?"

"She was injured. She's still recovering. Campobello has her hidden."

Hawk breaks into a grin, rather sardonic. "You must take SECOR to be just like CSIS. We're tracking her now. We'll find her. What's her condition?"

"She's hurt. She's completely shaken. It was … just a terrible scene. Blood—body parts … she'll need time."

"She wouldn't be planning to fly to Canada, would she?"

Startled at this sideways leap, Jason scrambles. "She's very confused. She talked of going home. Some time."

"Because I understand Washington has revoked her passport."

"SECOR did that? Was that your doing?"

Hawk hears the anger. "Why would I revoke her passport when you promised to bring her here?" He waits for Jason who chokes off a response. "You didn't discuss Manwaring and Ashbury with Werner, did you?"

"No. Maybe Sid … they've been working together." They both weigh what's going on here. Jason has the sense that Hawk and he are engaged in a game where neither can say what he means. He hedges. "She doesn't need a passport to hide out in Mexico."

"With an expired visa? She'll be on some list. She would have been better off coming here with you."

"SECOR would have detained her."

"Temporarily. If she's a sincere dissident we might then have expelled her to Canada."

"You only wanted her to get at Manwaring."

"If we'd gotten him, at least he'd be alive."

This twist Jason can't handle. "He attacked that guard to escape, after being tortured for honest protests. I think he and the army were quits."

"I'm not making excuses for the Pentagon. Just pointing out how they operate."

"He believed there was a point of no return. Once it was passed, America could never recover."

Hawk brings the exchange to a full stop, turning his face away as in exasperation. "You missed his point. What he was doing was to paint the administration as ideologue, out of step with American tradition. Afraid to let people speak out. That's the weak point."

"The administration's weak point?" Jason is taken aback to hear Hawk demeaning his superiors.

"His opinion, not mine."

He motions Jason to leave. He seems more sobered than peeved.

Jason goes back to work with at least the hope that her route is still secret. In a few days, she'll be clear of United States territory.

All the staff seem to know of Manwaring's murder. Archie at least has some sympathy. "We heard you landed in the middle of it, Jason. Your family friend, was she all right?"

"She's alive anyway." He's never discussed his Mexican trips in the office after the original rebuff from Sid. "How did you hear about it?"

"Werner knew all about it."

Werner shows up that afternoon. He makes a point of stopping by Jason's cubicle, standing close to him as he labours over an intercept. "I hear there wasn't much left to bury."

"Your people made sure of that."

"It wasn't our people. He was a fugitive who assaulted an American serviceman, and we wanted him back, but not enough to blow up his house. That's not our style. I hope the Maron woman is okay." His tone is oddly conciliatory.

"How did you hear about it?"

"Contacts in Mexico."

Jason's made an effort to keep his voice down, but as Werner strides away, he notes the heads cocked in his direction; his involvement with Manwaring and probably Miriam is now office gossip. Werner sounds as if he's known all along.

He lost his standing some time ago but now finds himself shunned, by some who work with Werner, by others in genuine disgust at his trading with the enemy. Only Archie seems to resist the chill.

Noble calls, rather breathlessly. "Are you in the clear on the assassination?"

"Completely."

"The A-D was terrified you might have been there. Listen, CSIS must *not* be involved in any way in a killing in Mexico. Don't discuss Manwaring with anyone. You never heard of him. The A-D's trying to get you out of there but Hawk's being contrary. Have you heard whether your lady friend's okay?"

"She may be on her way to Europe." He waits for Noble to mention her revoked passport. He may not know of it. But he might also be testing Jason.

"We're preparing an analysis—for Cabinet—of recent comments there. Especially these new policies for Muslims. Foreign Affairs just regurgitate the schlock they get. They're terrified of inquiring too aggressively. Might lose their standing on the cocktail circuit. Cabinet is concerned if they're ratcheting up the pressure on homegrown Muslims. We could get a flood of refugees. They could even be legitimate. Admissible under the UN treaties. A nightmare."

"So get ready for them."

"Damn! That isn't the answer they want. What about SECOR? What new policies?"

"They've begun interning families."

"Begun? As in likely to continue?"

"And escalate."

"Cabinet will be petrified. Jason, you seem to get along with Hawk, for whatever reason. Can you get his personal slant? He's supposed to be online with the White House."

"I think I just gave you his slant."

"What about the massacre in the Sudan? Are SECOR intercepts picking up much reaction?"

"Massacre?"

"My God! They really smother bad news." Noble sounds admiring. "According to Al Jazeera, two hundred civilians. Yesterday. Apparently a revenge orgy after a chaplain was blown up. At least that's what the Arabic media are insisting. They're calling it the Khartoum massacre."

"The latest communique from Sudan reported that dozens

of Sudanese *guerillas* were wiped out when they tried to ambush an American column."

Another brief silence. "Will their media really swallow that?"

"I can hear your envy clearly. They have no trouble at all with domestic media. Foreign journalists are a problem, but none are credentialed and no one here pays much attention to foreigners. Including Canadian."

"Jesus!"

"That's profanity here, Ben."

"We heard that Anita Skye attacked Muslims in a church service. Would they go that far? It would turn off any friendly Muslims."

"She doesn't think there are any friendly Muslims. At least when she's addressing Christians."

"If you get anything from Hawk …"

"There'll be a lot more of it soon, won't there? Rounding up Muslim families?"

Hawk takes an instant to work out Jason's direction. "I've already told you more than you should know of their intentions. Manwaring must have as well. The more they campaign against Muslim states, the more American Muslims turn against them."

"Perhaps young men, but *families*?"

"It's not just our problem, is it? Canada has a large Muslim population. If they're stirred up here, you have a problem as well. I assume that's where this is coming from?"

"Our Cabinet is concerned."

"What they're working out is how to contain these people in this country while they pacify them in theirs. Isolation—registration—it's all on the table. They have to concentrate them somehow."

*Concentrate.* The word hangs in the air. They're both silent, eyeing each other. "How far will they go?"

"To the point where they win, and Muslims accept it."

He uses the secure line to call Campobello. "An army officer told me they had nothing to do with the incident."

"He may not be wrong. I found one of them. A man we know, a narco mule. We know he's been feeding information to SEDENA. They're protecting him."

"So SEDENA did DIA's dirty work?"

"Or it was their own idea. My information is that SEDENA was very concerned when a CSIS agent turned up at the home of Professor Manwaring."

"Concerned about *me*?"

"Concerned that Canada was talking to Manwaring. He was getting too hot."

Jason's nauseated. He needs to take a couple of deep breaths. Sergio waits. "Sergio—is it possible that my visits were enough—"

"More than possible." He disconnects. Jason's left with another helping of guilt.

When Hawk summons him two days later, Jason is spooked, bracing himself to hear that Miriam has been picked up in San Francisco. His mind flits through emergency scenarios. Contact the Canadian consulate? Beg assistance from CSIS? Ask Hawk, as a personal favour …?

"Ah, Jason." He's decked out in splendid grey, medals and all. *How does a lawyer earn medals?* "I hear you're persona non grata with your fellow staff."

"Yes, sir. They're annoyed with me for speaking in Latin."

"Werner says you've been ostracized over Manwaring. I told him you were simply trying it on with a comely divorcée."

"Thank you for taking my side, General." But needling is wasted on him this day; he's too benign to be nettled, a different Hawk from the last meeting. With those extra seconds of study Hawk affects, he picks up the anxiety.

"Your jabs have no punch today, Jason. Matter of fact, even Werner seemed a little subdued. He seems to be mourning Manwaring as much as you."

"I'll be all right once I get home."

"That may be a while. It would please Werner too much if I sent you back to Canada. He thinks Canadians should all be made into good Americans, like they tried to do with your friend, Nabil Maron."

Hawk reads his shock and continues with less sarcasm. "He was arrested. I think Werner set it up."

"General, Bil is one Canadian you *could* make into a good American. He and I split because he's become just like you people. Arrested for what?"

He shrugs. "Maybe because of his sister. Werner's working on it."

"He's a Canadian citizen!"

"Not anymore. He took the oath. Werner says the Pentagon's concerned over a leak on the Internet protocol. Maron worked on it."

"Manwaring knew about that process. Even I knew a little. Lots of people could have leaked it."

"Lots of them didn't have sisters working with dissidents in Mexico."

So Bil Maron, who really had become devoted to this new America, even to the extent of renouncing his birthright, has been sucked down into the whirlpool spun by Manwaring's assassination. With Miriam in flight, the Pentagon will be going public with a tale of brother-sister espionage, tied to Manwaring's treasonous network.

"Sir, we've *got* to help him. We both know he was never involved. How can we clear him?"

"I pointed that out to Werner, but he's adamant."

"Werner! He seems to be involved in a lot of activities besides liaising with SECOR."

"You've noticed that?"

"I could ask Ben Noble to get DFAIT involved." Hawk shakes his head, and Jason realizes as he speaks that a timid DFAIT would refuse to intervene for a dual citizen.

"He's army property, Jason." It's hopeless. Bil, God help

him, is on his own, without even his abandoned Canadian citizenship to speak for him.

"That isn't why I asked you here." Jason steels himself, but Hawk has a different kind of surprise. "Tomorrow is SECOR Day. We're having a Corps parade before the vice-president." Jason is speechless, still full of the two Marons and their hanging fates. "You probably noticed the dress uniform. Pity you don't qualify for one. All the staff will be in parade dress except you. But I've managed to hold a seat for you. Up in the gods somewhere, with the in-laws and the distant relatives, but at least it'll get you in. There'll be a hundred thousand."

"A hundred thousand SECORs?"

"Guests. A couple of thousand uniforms on the field."

"The field?"

"Jason, you're a little stunned today. The Coliseum. The V-P will take the salute and then address the ranks. You'll at least be able to hear her speech up there. It's considered the hottest event of the year outside Hollywood. You're privileged to get in. They turned down your consul, by the way. Also, no media. They do their own coverage so they can edit out any ambiguous bits." Jason manages only to mumble his thanks, insincerely, when Hawk hands him the precious ticket. He retreats as gracefully as he can, still simmering at the news of Bil and without having heard anything of Miriam.

# THIRTY-ONE

THE STADIUM IS SO FULL THAT JASON HAS TO LABOR UP TO THE very back row, and there find a space well along from the aisle, into which he can cram himself. It's the first day of full sun and smokeless sky since he arrived here. The air is crisp. The panorama beneath him is clear and colorful. And Miriam must be only a couple of days short of Long Beach, just miles from here. When he calls Adolphus later, he might have news from her. Good news, good weather. The tension of the last days begins to lighten, just like the weather.

The seatmates whom he disturbs are a pair of heavy men in jackets, and a family of three on his other side, the man with a baseball cap celebrating a local team, his rather dainty wife, and an elfin boy of about four between them. The two men seem like brothers—they look alike and speak alike, and loudly. They may need to be loud; the din swallows conversation. Others around him who are drinking (most are not) have beer in cans, but the brothers have a liquor bottle, from which they each swig from time to time, to the disgust of the lady to Jason's left.

The sunlight plays on myriads of flags, an unbroken row along the top of the stands, many more on the field below. Military bands are stationed along one sideline. One after another breaks out from its position, parades the length of the field, and returns to its stand. Along the opposite side are contingents of SECORs, all in battle dress with helmets and face shields, arms sloped, rifles at rest, waiting their turn to fall in behind a parading band. As one unit completes its circuit, it's succeeded promptly by the next. A ring of SECOR gray guards the entire perimeter of the field.

The bands are stirring, as always. But the ranks of the warriors are intimidating. When they move out, spears of light flash from their visors. Each unit becomes like a single marcher, every hand and foot synchronized, even the plastic faces cloned like robots. Jason fantasizes that if one should fall in the way of those merciless ranks, he would be trampled into road kill.

At one end of the field a stage has been raised, a star-spangled skirting hiding its supports. At the back of the stage elongated drapery, in red-and-white striping, flanks a screen of heroic size, televising the action, following the marchers, sweeping across the stationary columns, poking into the stands, mixing close-ups amongst the long shots. Matching screens ride high along the edges of the stadium. Media stars are singled out by the cameras, some drawing lame cheers as they are aggrandized on the screens. There's a pan over the field-level row of SECOR commanders, mostly generals. The shot focuses in to identify some, prompting a little applause. Jason finds Hawk, not central but not far from it.

The image is so immediate that Hawk's acid smile could be directed at him. Staring at the screen, dwelling on Hawk, he shuts out the commotion …

He dwells on Hawk's preoccupation with Manwaring's network. *How does he communicate?* Not just once: Hawk brought that up several times. How did he? And with what co-conspirators, either eminent enough or numerous enough to be of concern to Hawk, and perhaps even more to DIA?

He's drawn back to the surroundings. The last marchers have returned to their stations, the screens show the lyrics of "Onward Christian Soldiers," the bands crank it out with brassy relish, and the whole mass struggles into it, even the little boy two seats away, though he's drowned out by Jason's boozy neighbors. The singing rises with building confidence to compete with the zest of the musicians. There's satisfied applause as all get to the end, more or less in sync. The screens and the bands take up "God Bless America," through which they all stand. Everyone has hand on heart except Jason, at first, but he catches on promptly, even mouthing the words.

Then they wait. The hubbub of the crowd is a relief after

all the blaring and thumping. Preparations of some kind are underway around the stage, watched by everyone with rising expectation. The murmur becomes the buzz of a hive, sizzling with anticipation. Jason tunes it out …

Thinking of DIA brings back an exchange with Hawk. Werner! *He seems to be involved in a lot of activities besides liaising with SECOR.* Like a DIA agent. And Hawk's snide reply: *You've noticed that?*

Werner had been near the gates, noting Jason's arrival without comment, unfriendly as usual. Why is he so sour? Resentment of Canada and its gentler policies? Or maybe, it strikes him now, the CSIS connection worries him—a Canadian intelligence agency that seems to be getting close to an escaped dissident.

DIA's involved. Werner's involved. Hawk didn't even want Werner to know about the visits to Guada. But he did know. Hawk several times warned him of Werner: *remember that Sid works with Werner every day; you didn't mention your assignment to Werner, did you?* Even Noble asked about Werner—*there's some static out there that senior officers resent their army being ground up.* Werner would have been one of them.

The bands now launch "Hail to the Chief." But it's not the chief; it's the vice-president. When she appears, there's a cry of relief, like a primal howl. She stands waiting to be recognized, to let her presence capture every person's attention. She wears the uniform of a five-star general, cap included, and carries a sidearm. Jason is visited by a whimsical image of the prime minister of Canada in full military regalia—hilarious! But this country's second in command carries it off quite well. She looks as heroic as Joan of Arc.

Now she comes forward to the podium, slowly, looking about with studied grace, an anchor of composure. The camera focuses in on her face. When she smiles, like an accommodating parent, the sound rises. Now there's a new murmur under it. Gradually it takes over, growing as people identify it and join in, until nothing else can be heard but the voice of the crowd chanting, "*A-neet'a! A-neet-a! A-neet-a!*"

It hardens into a war cry. Those around Jason have started in hesitantly, looking about for affirmation, then with more confidence, finally with zeal. The trapped air of the oval shakes with the rumbles of "*A-neet-a!*" Jason can visualize the sound waves, pulsing upwards from the open Coliseum and rolling above the suburbs like cannon volleys.

It gets into his head. He's drunk with noise. He glances at the others—how are they coping? He's shocked to see the little boy—crying! Standing between his chanting parents, he holds his hands over his ears, wailing in terror. Jason touches the father. He turns, eyes glazed. *Your son!* Jason mouths and points. The man looks at the child in wonder, then at Jason with something like resentment. He picks up the boy and holds him high enough to see over the crowd. He chants in the boy's ear. The child cries harder. The father passes him off to his mother.

The giant face on the screen, smiling, then stiffens to become serious, then stern, then determined. The chin lifts, the jaw sets, the gaze focuses on some horizon others are too common to perceive—a heroic pose, the very image of a leader. What a role! What an audience! No wonder they are all intoxicated.

"Fellow Americans—fellow Christians!" She raises one hand to quiet them. It takes many seconds for the stir to decelerate—to a hum, to a whisper, and then nearly silent attention. Jason's head, still buzzing, begins to clear. He concentrates on the screen, on the heroic face. He savors the reassuring voice. So do they all.

"This *Christian* nation ..." (a strong current of affirmation) "... is in the midst of a great crusade, a war to preserve the furthest advance of human society, which is our Western democracy." She pauses.

"Our enemy in that war is radical Islam, an ideology which holds that *jihad*—religious war—must be waged against those who question its beliefs. *Radical Islam* tries to dominate Muslim societies. It is rule by force. It is a repudiation of our Western ethic, which is rule by consent. But it is far more. It is an assault *on our faith*! That is what makes it the most evil enemy America has ever faced." She pauses again. Jason's neighbors shift with anticipation ...

His thoughts drift to Werner again. He recalls Hawk's *maybe DIA see an opening to get into his network. That would bring Werner into the equation.* Thousands of veterans in Guada, loyal to the United States, but a few, maybe quite a few, resentful toward the administration, fed up with its disastrous misuse of the army for ideological pursuits. Many more in the States, even in Canada. Could there be an underground *within the army*, even looking to ally with Manwaring and his activist opposition? What if DIA's been working to infiltrate such a network? *Or even penetrated it?*

"Some will tell you that we are in this war because we have misunderstood the intentions of our enemies. But we know them too well. We are in debt to our old enemy, the martyr of Al Qaeda, Osama bin Laden …" She waits to allow amazement that they are in any way in debt to such a person. "We are in his debt because he stated the radical conviction so clearly that it can never be misunderstood. If we loved peace a hundred times as much, we could still not ignore his challenge, in his own words: *'This battle is not between Al Qaeda and the United States. This is a battle of Muslims against the global crusaders.'* Crusaders!—Christians like us! It is the same as saying: this is a battle of Islam *against Christianity*.

"If there is no way to compromise with this enemy, if there is no way except to surrender our beliefs, or to stand and fight for them, if war is the only right way for our Christian nation, then I say: *BRING IT ON!*"

They have settled back into their seats by now, but this pulls them up again. Some people shout their agreement; others merely applaud. Some people do neither and even look dubious. The brothers shout; the parents applaud; the child and

Jason are silent.

The crowd noise sinks. "But we have chosen to bring it on in *their* countries so that we will not have to do so here in our own. We are battling far from home so that we will not have to suffer war and ruin here. But we are fighting there for another reason: our Christian sisters and brothers are under attack. We are in the Sudan this very today to defend them."

General applause this time, wide support for this latest American front, at least among the kind of citizens who would be in this stadium. The nearest brother notes that Jason is not applauding. "What's the matter with *you*?"

Jason goes through the motions, clapping without enthusiasm. Then he finds his way back to his ruminations, shutting out the speech and ignoring the brother, who is now giving him as much attention as he does the speaker ...

But if DIA were close to breaking in, why murder Manwaring? Security agencies kill to open such channels, not to seal them. Jason groans internally. The assassination would have been a disaster. It even changed Werner—*he seems to be mourning Manwaring as much as you.*

The vice-president holds up her hand to quiet the crowd again. What a figure she cuts, standing very erect, with her peaked cap casting a threatening shadow over her eyes, her arm raised like one of the ancient prophets, very still as she alerts them that the core message is coming.

"But the Sudan, Somalia, Yemen—these are not the only battlegrounds between our faith and theirs. We are at war with an *underground legion* in our own cities." She waits for the phrase to take hold, for the idea to capture them like wind across a wheat field. "Yes! Here in America! Collaborators! Traitors! Not just immigrants—*American citizens*—people who have been welcomed here and granted a life far superior to the one they escaped, who have taken an oath of allegiance, who have sworn to uphold our Constitution, and who are *betraying us*."

The stadium becomes silent. Every face is turned toward the stage or the nearest screen. Jason sees uncertainty, then ripening belief, a gathering of fear. Indignation then begins to build. It continues as an undertone while the magnetic voice resumes.

"It is difficult for me to tell you this because it was difficult at first to accept it. So I have waited—evidence had to be gathered. We all know that this country was built by peoples of many lands, who came here and became good Americans. It is our heritage. It is very painful to find that some of those who were granted citizenship came here with the intention to act as *agents of terror*."

Heads are turning—people using the pause to have an exchange with the next person, seeking reassurance. They cannot doubt her words, but still …?

"Believe me, these are people whose loyalty is first to their own religion, which leaves no room for loyalty to our country. They are like the fanatics who become suicide bombers. They would glory in destroying themselves in order to kill

Americans, here in the United States, if we should let them …"

… Of course! *Of course! SEDENA must have acted on its own—a shock to DIA!* Sergio saw that too. So how does Werner fit? What if his real mission's not just screening SECOR—could he be coordinating the infiltration? He would have known everything about Manwaring. No wonder he'd be worried that a CSIS agent was meddling in his territory. No wonder Hawk's suspicious of Werner.

"We are here," the vice-president says, "to celebrate the United States Security Corps. Let me tell you: there is more to thank them for today than sealing our borders. It is SECOR that has unmasked the terrorists among us. They have uncovered one cell after another of Muslim subversives, men, even some women, and, if you can believe it, *even children*, who were hidden here long enough to become American citizens and whose mission all along was to act when ordered, to kill when signaled. We can all thank SECOR that they found these people and that those orders were never carried out."

As she speaks, her arm sweeps in the direction of the SECOR General Staff, who rise on cue to receive a volley of applause. No wonder Hawk was worked up. He probably knew the whole program, worthy of a new uniform. Jason's puzzled though by the 'terrorist cells'—found and destroyed—since he's seen none so far. He picks out Hawk's face in the row of officers. What must he be thinking? He's very bright—could he be comfortable with this overdone spectacle?

Jason grimaces in disagreement, but then notices the abominable brother pause his clapping and glare at him. So he applauds as well.

"I have to tell you we continue to uncover far more of these buried cells." The giant face looks out to them in appeal. "So what are we to do? Wait until one of them strikes?" The crowd reaction prompts the answer. "This is not an administration that will wait until Americans are killed in our streets! This is what we will do: we will build a *firewall around America*! We must stop these people. Our administration will allow *no more Muslims* into the United States."

She spreads both hands and bows slightly to the exuberant applause of a hundred thousand Christians. It's a cry of relief after the frightening buildup. It persists for a long moment, and she does nothing to turn it off. When it does die out, she pauses so long in the silence that another ripple of anxiety takes hold.

"But what of those already here? Many are good citizens. You may have neighbors who are Muslim and whom you know to be as American as yourself. But with the technology that we have today, we are confident that SECOR can separate the tares from the wheat. We will find the subversives and those who sympathize with them. Whether they are citizens or not, we will isolate them. We will not give the privilege of American constitutional protection to such dissidents while in their own countries and in their very creed they give no such rights to Christians."

So there it is, the solution Hawk had hinted at: *concentration*. The camps need not be hidden any longer; they are to become the manifestation of the party's vigilance. The more that is known of them, the more credit the administration might receive. Except perhaps for the methods used in separating the tares from the wheat, which will remain in SECOR's closet.

There is a long pause, so long that a few zealots begin applauding as if she were done, but she holds up her arm one more time.

"We must protect our country, and we must protect our faith. Otherwise, we could one day see a *Muslim become president of the United States*!" There is a wounded cry at this, as if a hundred thousand souls are abused. It rises from the stands like a moaning wind. She waits again for quiet. "So we will act, and I depend on you to support us. You won't fail me, will you?"

The whole throng is pulled to its feet by the appeal. There are some cheers, but most people merely applaud. The final passages of her speech have slightly chilled her audience, as no doubt planned. They are all to remember a serious occasion, not a celebration. There is some cheering and a few hats are launched sailing toward the field. Jason's family to the left huddle together in approval, the boy squashed between their thighs. To his right, he looks to see the brothers, nodding and sharing a last swallow.

The bands now strike up. The SECORs have re-formed in review formation. Vice-President Anita Skye descends from the stage to walk along the front rank, and then take the salute, a paragon of military style as she hears out the salvos and snaps her hand to her cap. She passes by the stands to reach in and shake hands with the principle SECORs.

She returns to the stage and raises both arms. "God bless you, and *God bless America!*" But she seems reluctant to leave. She stands there, waving, soaking in the steady din of applause. There's now another groundswell of chanting under it, coming from the field. It's picked up gradually by the lower level of the crowd and moves upwards until the entire coliseum has a single voice. He can't identify it until the nearest brother shouts it in his ear: "*No more Muslims! No more Muslims!*"

Around the rows it volleys. He sees fists raised, including those beside him. He watches the vice-president, to see if she might discourage it. On the screen, she inclines her head a notch, interested but not disapproving, then turns and backs off the stage, arms still raised. The chant deepens: *No more Muslims! No more Muslims!*

Jason pays no attention. He's so thrilled to identify Werner as the master infiltrator that he feels like laughing. He pictures Hawk's face when he shares his hypothesis—not so cool for once. The applause following the vice-president off the stage barely registers, nor the ugly brother looming over him, until he is grabbed by the shoulder.

"What the fuck's the matter with you?"

"Oh. I'm fine, terrific."

"Fine? You're laughing at her!"

In the next millisecond his sight is blocked out by the bottom of a bottle, followed instantly by an explosion of lights, softening and withdrawing into darkness …

His recollection of the aftermath is like the memory of a binge: unrecognized figures helping him down the thousand steps to the exit, maybe kind souls, maybe disgusted ushers; then a sort of van loading up with drunks and other outcasts. He has a dreamlike flash of a uniformed Archie Bear, turning away as he sees him. Ashamed to become involved? While Jason's trying to sort this out in his bleary state, there's an exchange between two SECOR officers. "That's the man."

"You're sure?"

"I'm sure he was speaking Arabic to that other prisoner."

Jason registers just enough of this to be alarmed. He reaches for his necklace and finds it gone, somehow pulled free. So when he sees Werner arriving, whom he has never been happy to see before, he exclaims, "Colonel! What a relief!"

Werner looks him over with no sign of familiarity. "Yes, I know that one. I'll deal with him myself."

# THIRTY-THREE

"DO YOU DO INTERROGATIONS HERE PERSONALLY, COLONEL?"

"Don't play smartass with me, Currie. You're in enough trouble now. I've been assigned to question you because this is my case." He's been taken to a camp somewhere. He has no idea where. A few of the prisoners were loaded on a plane, where he spent all his energy fighting pain. Then into a van, finally driven directly into some building. There was no ritual introduction as in his first detention. He was handed coveralls and flip-flop shoes, then led to a cell (not a cage), and left alone.

He's far from thinking clearly. Pulses of pain muddle his thoughts. His face, deeply bruised by that bottle, has stiffened and probably turned color. His concentration struggles to stay engaged. Now he's been led in manacles to this room. A guard remains with him. Werner strides in.

"To begin with, you need to give us Miriam Ashbury."

"*Miriam*? Why do you want Miriam?" He's shocked at the sound of his own voice.

"Because she can give us the key. Where is she?"

"What key?"

"Hawk thinks you've got her hidden in Mexico. She couldn't travel far—her American passport's been revoked and her Canadian passport hasn't been re-issued."

"Sergio Campobello's got her. He's got safe houses you'd never find."

"I can't help you if you don't cooperate, Currie."

"I don't know where she is. Does General Hawk know I'm here?"

"Hawk has his own problems." What problems? The remark wakes up Jason. His detention affects Hawk somehow? "You embarrassed SECOR. You embarrassed your colleagues."

Jason revives the image of Archie Bear turning away. Werner watches him with that expression that comes so naturally to him, probably from a lifetime of being mostly right and always obeyed. Self-confidence. Even arrogance. It irritates Jason. "I'll explain to General Hawk."

"Huh! He's not much more committed than you are."

"Committed?"

"Committed. That's the state of mind of a military officer when his country is at war. Hawk's just a lawyer. You're just a math whiz who knows Arabic. I'm a soldier." So that's why he's always angry—he *has* to be committed. Jason represents skepticism, doubt. Werner cannot allow himself doubt. The army has no such accommodation. It's taboo in his profession.

"You take it all as mawkish, don't you?" Werner's nostrils flare. Jason sees too late that he has touched off the famous temper. "Grown men wearing medals, tearing up over their flag? You think it's cool to sneer at us. People like you have prevented your own army from joining us. The Canadian military has a fine history. I know lots of your officers. They all think they should be fighting beside us."

It's foolish to provoke him; he might be the only way out of here. Nevertheless, "I guess that's why we let civilians make such decisions," Jason says.

"Civilians like you. You saw for yourself what we're up against in the Sudan. They hate us. If they had the means, they'd wipe us off the earth. If we leave them be, one day they *will* have the means. The Iranians almost did."

"I'm a CSIS analyst. Will you advise my people that you're holding me here?"

"CSIS! Another Canadian foul-up."

"What am I supposed to have done?"

"Not much, Currie: conspiring with terrorists in Mexico. Not to mention those Arabs in the Coliseum."

"I was assaulted. By two brothers."

"That's not how security saw it. You insulted the vice-president and they defended her." Werner looks confident, like a chess player with forced mate in sight. "By the way, they gave me this." He draws Jason's Class III necklace from his pocket.

"You set that up? Pretty mean trick, Colonel. Not what they teach at West Point."

"It got you here."

"May I speak to General Hawk?"

Werner chuckles. He isn't angry now; he's triumphant. He has no fear of Hawk. "Sergeant-Major Rightful will show you the drill." He gives Jason only a sardonic glance as he walks out, signaling the guard to take him to his cell.

Plenty of time then to analyze his situation. He's been carefully set up. All to find Miriam? Why is she so crucial? *Because she has the key.* The encoding system?

His own position? Prisoners in the United States used to have rights. You could demand a lawyer, which sets off a legal process forcing the authorities to make their case or release you. You could make a phone call (to Hawk, to CSIS). But under the Defense of America Act, once you're labeled a security threat, you have no rights and the authorities no limits. The contest becomes the State against the terrorist, about like the nutcracker versus the nut. No help is coming. He has to hold out until Hawk (hopefully) finds him, meanwhile shielding his lover.

After some hours, he's allowed out in a fenced enclosure. He can see much of the camp. It's eerily similar to the one where he spent that long night; it could even be the same one. His cell's in a windowless concrete unit, identical to the one where Hawk rescued him. Through the fences he can see the rows of plastic-roofed cages like the one he occupied. He can even hear the catcalls as the guards pass. In a distant exercise area for the open-air inmates, there's the movement of orange coveralls. His red outfit must identify the prisoners held in the concrete bunker, the select ones. A guard is housed in a raised cabin along the one adjacent wall. Otherwise he's alone but for one other inmate in red, a young black man.

"Hey, brother, you new here too?"

He's barely out of his teens. They fall into step together, wheeling around the tight little pen. "I don't know *why* I'm here. *Shit!* I only got to be Muslim 'cause we all did. 'N the names were so great. Nobody tol' me it was a crime against America."

"But there must be a reason …"

"Aw, we busted a construction shed. We took dynamite."

Enough of a crime to warrant interrogation in the special block? "Have you met other prisoners yet?"

"A few. All Muslims, like us."

"Actually, I'm Christian."

"Man, you a spy?" He laughs heartily. Laughter must be exceptional in that chill arena of bare earth beside that concrete wall because the guard leans out to scrutinize them.

"Mostly foreigners?"

"Shit, no. Americans, like us."

"I'm Canadian."

"Man! They hittin' on Canajuns now? You must be special."

"I'm afraid so."

After dinner, rice and an unrecognizable other that his tender jaw refuses, Jason stretches out on his shelf when the music begins. There's a hiss of static over opened speakers, and then the crash of electronic chords, introducing the loudest clamor he's ever heard. It lifts him from his shelf like an explosion. He paces about, searching for the source while it bounces from wall to wall. He can hear the metal door vibrating against its latch. He imagines the walls to be throbbing as the boom and whine pulses against them like a pounding heart of sound. It's without shape, without any character except intensity. Deaf idiots could have produced it in Bedlam. It's unbearably incoherent, it makes no contact with the concept of music understood by his brain; every iota of agreeability has been stripped from it; it's obscene, and it's very, very loud.

He's staring at the source, a tiny outlet in his ceiling, protected by a stainless mesh, when he's tapped on the shoulder and a voice shouts in his ear: "Mr. Currie!" Jason starts violently; the pain in his face flares into life.

It's a man in military fatigues, a black man. Jason recognizes his sergeant-major's rank. He's much bigger than Jason and clearly fitter, his spare frame and muscular arms exposed by a tight shirt with bulging sleeves. He's hatless but wears ear protectors. Jason covets them. He signals Jason to follow him. Once outside the cell, with the door clanging shut, the volume drops enough to allow him to be heard.

"Come along." Jason's not restrained by shackles or cuffs, but he suspects this man would never need their insurance. They pass through a couple of corridors. The music follows along, but now bearably through the sequence of closed doors.

They reach a room like a gym. The noise drops off. There's a tiny pool at one side, about the size of a grave, pieces of equipment that mean nothing to Jason, and a smell of sweat and something else, perhaps fear.

The sergeant-major is a bland-looking man, neither threatening nor inviting. His main feature is his hair—almost none, bald on top and the sides cropped stubble. He looks Jason up and down as if buying a horse, measuring his strength or lack of it.

"My name is Sergeant-Major Rightful. Call me Sir."

"Certainly, Sir."

Rightful shows just the shadow of a frown, so Jason is warned that he doesn't brook sarcasm.

"Now, there's no need to be afraid," he says, which makes Jason instantly fearful, with a quick twinge in the solar plexus. "This is just a demonstration. Colonel Werner has authorized it. We like our guests to understand the conditions here so that we don't waste each other's time."

He waits for a response, so Jason gushes out, "Yes, Sir!"

"Now, we don't do torture." What a relief. "But we are permitted by regulations to employ enhanced interrogation."

"What's the difference, Sir?"

"Practical. Torture is like breaking a man's bones. Driving nails into his skull. Cutting off body parts. It destroys a prisoner. There's not much recovery."

"And the other?"

"Stops short of destruction. It hurts, but you can recover. And we only do it until we have what we need."

"What if you never get what you need?"

"Ah, well. Then we'd consider the case a failure." He goes on in a friendly tone. "You're a very intelligent man, Mr. Currie, or you wouldn't be an officer in SECOR, so I won't have any trouble getting your cooperation. It's the stupid ones who make us work harder. So you don't need to be nervous. We're going to do this demonstration now. You'd be interested to learn that we do the same demo with our own people so that they understand how it feels to an inmate. Come over to the pool."

It takes only a few seconds, but the memory will be permanent. At the edge of the pool a sort of surfboard with belts attached leans against a lift apparatus. He knows what it's for, and his knees buckle. An aide materializes. Jason braces himself, preparing his breathing as they strap him in. The lift whirs and they edge him into the water. It's icy. Then down, down, chilled and shaking. They stop him just as he leans his head back to keep his mouth above the surface.

"This will just be a test dip. Just a few seconds. Don't be concerned." At this he is plunged down. He swallows one mouthful, then holds his breath. He remembers that it's possible for a man to do that for as long as three minutes. In seconds he begins to doubt this. Pain builds in his lungs. He has swum underwater often enough—this is not the same. With his eyes open, the cold water stings, so he closes them. But then the claustrophobia is terrifying, so he opens them. He feels that he's passing out. He bites down to resist opening his mouth—the pressure in his lungs tries to burst through. A haze forms in his eyes, the water seems to be darkening. He can feel his body bucking against the straps. He wants to scream.

"There, Mr. Currie, only thirty seconds. Just enough to understand. You see how it works?"

"Yes, Sir." He's plunged down again with rocket speed as soon as he speaks, no time to clam up. He swallows water again. He needs to choke but struggles not to. He is sure he will pass out. Then back up. He hangs on the board and throws up water, choking and vomiting at once. His mouth is scorched by stomach acid. He's out of control, the first time he has ever felt so helpless.

"You need to develop some stomach for this." The sergeant-major is looking at him with something like sympathy in his eyes. "That was just a finishing touch. You see, if you require us to use this form of persuasion, we wouldn't always *warn you* when you're going down. Sometimes we'd just surprise you." He shares this as an amusing wrinkle. There may be others that Jason doesn't want to learn. "Now that you understand the nature of our business, Mr. Currie, I'll leave it to Colonel Werner to do your interrogation. No need for me to see you here again, unless he tells me he considers you uncooperative."

His hands shackled now, the aide, whom Rightful calls Corporal Slick, leads Jason back to his chamber. Slick's narrow face almost comes to a point. His eyes bulge like black buttons. He reminds Jason of a rat. The barely muted music is still pounding through every cell door.

"One more thing before goodnight." Slick whips a black object from his pocket. Jason's smothered within a hood. Slick ties it tightly behind his neck. "Prisoners enjoy the music more if they have no distractions."

"How can I find my way around?"

"You'll have to learn, won't you? Have a good night."

Before the music finally stops, Jason loses his sense of time. It could be hours or days later. When he has maneuvered himself onto his sleeping shelf, all he can do is lie there and think, but the noise makes thought incoherent. He relives his moments of waterboarding. He tries to visualize what other indecencies might be practiced on him. Not knowing is worse than knowing. He allows himself to be shaken with fear. Then he grips himself and overcomes it with concentration. The cycle repeats as soon as he lets go. It exhausts him while prohibiting sleep. He even tries summoning up Ramona, once his unfailing negative diversion, but even her poison has lost its potency in the face of this menace. In time the sound loses its dominance. It becomes just a pulsing constant, almost like very loud traffic noise. It's turned off.

Rightful comes to his cell with breakfast. He removes the hood. Jason can tell from his expression what he must look like. He takes off the handcuffs. "So you had a bad night."

"Isn't that what's supposed to happen?"

"The point is that you'd be better off if you tell Colonel Werner whatever it is that he needs to know. You're a professional, so I don't need to spell it out for you."

"Your enhanced interrogation was never part of my training, Sergeant-Major. I'm an analyst, not a secret agent."

"I do have some good news for you. We could make use of your Arabic. We could make a deal with you. You might have a little bargaining power."

If it were anyone else, Jason would take it as toying with him, all part of the reward-disappointment cycle, but Rightful seems too out front to play such games. "I'm starved for good news."

"We have some Sudanese here. We know one or more are members of a cell, but we don't know which ones. We've identified the cell but not the members. We think they're among a group of ten Sudanese in one block. Most of these men might be just camp followers but one or two are genuine terrorists. If you can identify those prisoners, we won't need persuasion on the rest. Colonel Werner suggested you might help us."

"I'll bet he did."

Rightful looks disappointed at the sarcasm, as if Jason has looked down his nose at a personal favor. "A chance to save several men from a hard time, Mr. Currie. We had a prisoner die under questioning last week."

"You don't really imagine they'd trust some newcomer?"

"Maybe not. But you might hear enough to know if anyone there is different—their attitude, how defiant, how devoted. Colonel Werner says you have a talent for annoying people. If you irritate them, maybe one of them will brag about things to come. You'll want to pretend to be a Muslim." He's slow and precise in his speech, without emotion, and all the more convincing because of it. Jason understands why he was assigned as an interrogator. His absence of deception is a weapon.

"And if I can help?"

"You'll be excused from interrogation while you're assisting."

Jason tries not to seem eager, but the more time he spends away from Werner, the better chance Hawk may rescue him. "I think this is a very long shot, but if I can spare men from torture, I'll try."

"Very good, sir. But we don't torture here."

"Right. Enhanced interrogation."

# THIRTY-FOUR

JASON IS MOVED FROM HIS PRIVATE CELL AND ITS FRACTURED music into the general prison, units with individual cubbyholes for lockup overnight, but an open door in daytime into a common area. Pushed through the metal door, he's peered at by the ten prisoners already resident, some of whom look mildly interested in a newcomer, some nearer hostile, all silent, sizing up this newcomer with his bruised face.

"*As-salam alaykum.*"

There is a moment of hesitation before a single man answers. "*Wa alaykum as-salam.*"

He has no intention of posing as Muslim. Sooner or later he is certain to be unmasked—one inmate, at least, already knows he's Christian—and might not survive the discovery. He awaits a chance to expose himself during an afternoon when no one speaks to him. The terse conversation around him is in mixed Arabic and English. He guards his understanding of Arabic carefully. When he asks which of the lock-ups is his, he is led to its door by one of the less suspicious cellmates. There's a prayer mat and the Koran on his bunk.

"I must be one of the few Christians in here," he says.

There is a hush behind them, like the shutting down of an engine. "How did you come here then?"

"I'm Canadian. My people were from Lebanon and Egypt. We respect Islam. The Americans accuse me of helping a terrorist." He steps out of the metal closet and faces a tense group of silent men.

"*Did* you help him?" one of them then asks.

"He was just a loudmouth. I twisted his words enough to make him seem harmless."

"They put you in here for that?"

"They say I was trying to help him. When I denied it, they put me on the waterboard."

"Is it so terrifying?" a young man asks, or rather gushes. He's barely out of his teens, and so eager to be reassured that it overcomes the group reserve.

"It's frightening, but you'll survive it."

The boy's relieved, then abashed as he sees he has spoken out of turn. "Of course you'll survive it," one of them says. "You don't need a Christian to tell you that."

There's little conversation then, and that in Arabic, although he has seen that English is understood. Later, he's isolated further when one prisoner leads the afternoon prayers and everyone but him participates.

A meal is handed in. They share it on benches around the two tables. His face and jaw are a little less tender and he's now eager to eat something. There are no utensils except plastic spoons.

The man next to him smiles when Jason takes one. "No knives or forks," he says. "Not even metal spoons." Jason stares at him, uncertain. "They believe we are such brutes that we would kill them with plastic knives." He leans close and chokes out the words through a gust of laughter. He gives Jason a dig in the ribs. About half of the group smiles with him.

The hypersensitive security has made the guards into figures of derision. But not everyone is amused. Three men quit their bench and shrink to the furthest corner of the chamber, muttering remarks in Arabic. He cannot hear clearly but picks up enough to know it's aimed at him. So there are at least two factions here; one might include Rightful's targets, the other acts like a neighborhood gang making sport of a novice. After this exchange, most of them are more comfortable with him.

After evening prayers the guards arrive, paired for security. Each prisoner enters his coop and slams the door, setting the lock. One guard then tests each door while the other watches from a safe distance. A few insults in Arabic and English follow the guards out as the main door slams like a vault's. Now the community of the common room evaporates, and each man is sealed in his own space. The lights are dimmed.

Jason is better off than in his former cell but far from comfortable. He can hear bits of conversation among the units, but that soon dies out. Each man searches for sleep, but from the constant shifting most are unable to embrace it. Those who do add a medley of snoring to the uneasy night. Jason comforts himself with thoughts of Miriam, perhaps already safe in Canada.

They're allowed to exercise together for a half-hour, in a larger yard than the restricted one he has already used. "You're Canadian, maybe they'll send you back," one of them says in English as they fall into step together.

"It's my only hope," Jason says, quite honestly.

"My name's Saeed Habib. My family is in Canada, in Edmonton. Could you let them know where I am?"

"If I can get to Canada. How did you end up in here?"

"I left my family because my cousin was here. He could get me a good job."

"What's the charge?"

"Having the same name as my cousin."

"Where's your cousin?"

"I think he left this country."

"Accused of terrorism?"

"They accuse any Muslim. He pushed an officer down when they tried to enter his mosque. They had his name. They took me because we have names that sound the same to the Americans."

They're accompanied by a patrol of four unarmed guards who are also dog handlers. The patrollers are unfriendly and the dogs more so. They snarl at the prisoners as soon as they enter the yard. They follow beside as the group circles, and one bites an inmate who steps out of line. Why put the patrol among the prisoners when there are already guards in two towers, armed and out of reach? His partner explains: "We think it's just to frighten us."

An inmate is grabbed as they re-enter. Two guards haul him away, the dogs at his heels. Tension has eased during the half-hour circuits; now it thickens again. Those who do speak to him say little. When the prisoner is led back in he's semiconscious, naked, blood streaking his thighs. The guards leave him sprawled across his shelf, his red uniform tossed over him. All his mates can do is cover him with some of their own blankets and leave him to ride out his misery, regularly moaning.

"Why did they do it?" Jason asks his walking partner.

"They want names."

"What if you have none to give?"

"He could have given them names of people they could never find."

One of the prisoners, who leads the prayers, is qualified as an imam. "That is legitimate," he says.

There seems to be general agreement for a moment, then another inmate objects. "It's an affront!"

"He will be forgiven if no one comes to harm and the man

will survive."

"Better not to survive." Perhaps he's found one of his quarries.

The imam mutters to Jason, "That one wants to be a martyr."

"You disapprove of martyrdom?"

"Martyrs die in battle, defending the faith. Not in prison behaving like mules."

"You don't sound like a terrorist. Why are you in here?"

"Because I'm Sudanese."

Jason has a flash of memory: the discussion in front of a mosque that led to Archie having one of the groups detained. Perhaps this man is here for an act as innocent.

"Did you come to America recently?"

"Five years. I'm almost ready to become an American." He says this with a wry smile. "I came to this country because I was considered a radical in the mosque and might have been arrested if I stayed in Sudan."

The moaning finally quiets.

The next day the injured man is mobile though moving stiffly. Both sides of his face are bruised. He limps severely. He says little. Conversation is subdued on all sides, everyone studying the man, perhaps looking into their own future. But when the door crashes open, the guards drag away the same victim. He gives a howl of fear. Two or three others move toward him, perhaps to aid him, perhaps simply obeying the human reflex to respond to a cry for help. Instantly one guard levels a spray can at them and releases a cloud of stinging vapor. They all feel its burning droplets, but the closest are blinded. In the seconds of recovery, the prisoner and escort slip away.

Jason and others help wash the toxin from the faces of those hurt. The imam blinks his reddened eyes repeatedly. "This is not their worst. When we do the exchanges, we hear it from other prisoners. If you're stubborn like that one, they'll take all your clothes. Women will question you. They'll fasten your hands behind you so you can't hide your nakedness. The women will taunt you and laugh at your genitals and poke them with their clubs. Or set the dogs on you." Jason can't imagine a man like Rightful taking part in such behavior. Perhaps these stories are planted to intimidate the inmates. But what are the limits nowadays if waterboarding is actually in the manual?

The imam points out a man with a speech defect, nearly a babble. "He was thrown by the giant they call Attila, a pet of the warders." Attila is the champion of the 'wrestling matches,' in which pairs of prisoners are forced to wrestle with the victor promised some privilege. "He was raped by Attila. The guards made him do it. It was a party. Even women guards. After, he tried to hang himself." His attempt at suicide had only wrecked his throat.

This day passes in tension waiting for the return of their unlucky comrade. By evening prayers, it's clear he will not be coming back.

"There are some you must watch," the imam whispers to him as they wheel around the exercise yard. He gestures to a trio on the opposite leg. Jason recognizes them as the would-be martyr and his two cronies.

"They distrust Christians?"

"They hate Americans, and Canadians will do as well."

"They have no weapons."

"Their hands. Don't let them crowd you in the yard. Take care in the shower."

The nearest guard and his snarling dog edge over to them. "No talking."

Later, they're marched to the shower, five at a time. Mindful of the imam's cautioning, he backs into a corner. Within seconds, two of the militants have crowded him against the wall. They have only fists. Jason crouches and covers his face with his good arm to save his tender jaw. One of them then hits his unprotected abdomen with a wallop that seems to squeeze through all the way to his spine, exploding the air from his body. He goes down in agony, heaving like a fish, unable to concentrate on anything but sucking in air. A couple of barefoot kicks skid off his ribs. By then the remaining pair are muscling the attackers aside, angry voices rising over the rush of the water. Abruptly the noise ceases. The guards enter and turn off the water. Everyone backs away, leaving Jason slumped and soaked in the corner, still wheezing. All five are then held there, naked, dripping, and chilled, until Sergeant-Major Rightful arrives.

"Who attacked you?" He's much more threatening, perhaps to protect Jason.

"I can't be sure. Everyone looks alike in the shower."

"You come with me." Still wet and bowed, Jason follows him to the interrogation room. "You don't seem to be making any friends in there, Mr. Currie. Anything on the two who attacked you?"

"How do you know there were only two?"

"The guards were cautioned to keep you under observation. We know which of them did it."

"You stage-managed the whole thing? What if they …?" He's stunned at such pitiless calculation. The terror of that moment when glistening bodies closed around him, the eyes of the two fanatics scorching him with hatred, wells up now in a hot wave that melts his slender residue of strength. He sinks to the floor, utterly wretched.

"It wasn't such a risk." Rightful looks at him, crouched there like a weepy child, with neither sympathy nor disdain. "Colonel Werner only permitted us to use you if we kept watch to protect you. He doesn't want anything to happen to you."

# THIRTY-FIVE

JASON GOES BACK TO HIS SOLITARY CELL. THE CONCERT crashes into life soon after. It must be evening because he's given a meal, but in the unvarying light and with no watch, it can be any time they contrive it to be. As the noise floods his mind, his grasp of time dissolves. He can't relax, he can't sleep. He can think only with great effort.

He works at building defenses: images of Miriam, her face, her lovely body, the warmth of her nearness, and her confident voice. Then her attitude: the battle-readiness in her expression when she confronts the administration. He can hold on to these images only with painful concentration as they fight the surf of sound. He moves from Miriam to math, easily visualized. Simple progressions: if a sequence begins 10, 12, 14, 16, what is $S$, the total of 20 terms? Where $n$ is the number of terms, a is the first term and d the difference between terms, $S=n(2a+(n-1)d)/2$ ; $S = 580$. Carrying the numerals sharply in his mind holds back the sound for precious moments. He moves on to geometric sequences, first in full numbers, then in fractions. The assault is muted enough to allow his overheating brain cells to quiet down. He survives. Finally he even sleeps. The intense concentration wears him down and he slips into a trance, lulled by the music of insanity.

Some time later the speaker is turned off. The silence wakens him. The rodent-like Slick appears at the slide in the door and issues him his breakfast mush. He's taken to the private yard for exercise. What a joy to have silence and natural light, to breathe clear air! It's as sweet as waking from a disheartening dream into the warm grip of the morning sun. Perhaps they arrange it just because the relief is so great that withholding it might then make it easier to break him.

There is one other prisoner in the quadrangle, and when he turns in his circuit, Jason recognizes Bil Maron. He's in an identical jumpsuit, red priority. He looks so changed as he approaches, and Jason has been so stressed that he even questions whether he has projected Bil's image onto some other prisoner's shape. When he's close, Bil shows no recognition, only glances at Jason with a blank expression. His face is gray, his athletic gracefulness has morphed into a round-shouldered shuffle, and his confident look has been replaced by stress. He comes close enough for Jason to reach out to him.

"Bil!" He jumps back and fends off the hand. He stares at Jason, who notes the guard above them leaning from his platform. "How did you get here?" Jason asks the question, but the same one's in Bil's eyes.

"Because of Miriam."

Jason grips his hand and holds it.

"Keep moving!" the guard barks.

They fall into the tight circle, which is all the yard allows. Bil walks with his eyes fixed on Jason. No doubt this was arranged to pressure him—or both of them—so they're likely being recorded. They do a full circuit before Bil says any more. "They blamed me for a leak on our research. DIA. Their take was that I passed data to Miriam."

"But you haven't been in touch with her for years. What are you accused of passing on?"

Bil stares at him, nervous. Suspicious? "Doesn't matter. Research on brain signals …"

Jason tries to laugh, for the microphone. "Transforming brainwaves to digital signals? Some leak. We had a briefing on it at CSIS months ago. Our military liaison knew of it, but they were sure it would go nowhere. They told us your tests failed."

Bil misses a step. "I wasn't surprised it failed. Anyway, the whole concept's been published in scientific journals. They claim I leaked it to Miriam."

"Don't buy that. You're here because of Manwaring's murder."

"They *killed* him? What happened to Miriam?"

"She disappeared."

"Maybe home to Canada? God! I wish I were in Canada! I wish I'd never left Canada. It's all so unjust. I've never done a thing against the party. Never uttered a word."

"Other people in here are just as innocent, Bil."

"Then why …?"

"They need to show results, genuine or not."

"Jason, help me get out of this swamp. You're with SECOR—*can* you help me?"

"I'll do whatever I can. I'll try to get across that you've had nothing to do with Miriam, not for years."

While he ponders what other comfort he can offer, the entry to the yard cracks open and they are swept back to their cells.

"Happy to see your boyhood pal?" Werner's at his caustic best as he surprises Jason.

"So you arranged that? He's innocent as an angel, Werner. He hasn't talked to Miriam in years. Have a look in your own ranks if the army's panicking about leaks."

Werner smiles, almost jovially. "Think hard about your own situation. That's what you need to do. You've dug a hole for yourself, and your friend Maron, and you need help to get out of it. Listen carefully." Sergeant-Major Rightful, sitting in the interrogation chamber on a bench designed for other purposes, judging from the shackles attached to it, follows their match with professional interest.

"You and Maron can stay here forever," Werner says. "Forever might not be very long for Christians among these Muslim fanatics. You've already seen how that can turn out. The only bargaining chip you have is that woman. Let's talk about her."

"You're offering to release Bil if I help you put Miriam in here? Honestly, Werner—a man from a family of West Point alumni—why do you allow them to use you this way?" If Werner doesn't understand Jason, Jason has the same difficulty with him, because this is exactly the wrong tack. Werner's pleasant look darkens.

"Because it's my job! You don't speak that language, do you? Soldiers doing their job whether or not it's pleasant. Or *rewarding*. Or *fulfilling*." A full measure of contempt saturates that last word. There's no apt response to it. "I've been trained to do the job that's given me and not worry about whether it will round out my résumé or make me feel *gratified*."

"Werner, Miriam has no significant information. You must know that. This is just some kind of vendetta because the army screwed up with Manwaring."

"He almost murdered one of us. He deserved a death sentence."

"So your people killed him. You're quits."

"*We didn't kill him.* I would have cracked the whole network if SEDENA hadn't decided he was too dangerous. Why would we kill him?" He stops abruptly, just as Jason begins parsing what he's just learned.

"Okay, you didn't kill Manwaring. But the point is the same, Werner. Miriam had no part in his network."

"She was with him for over a year. She must have known what he was doing."

"What he was doing was just talking a lot."

"We need to have what she knows."

"I can't help you find her."

"You've made up your mind that we're in the wrong no matter what I say, haven't you? You come from a country that's done very well while it was defended by American arms, and then you piss on our flag."

Jason catches Rightful's expression: disapproving. "Colonel, I respect your sense of duty. It's just not mine. Let's just agree to disagree and get to how Bil and I can get out of here."

"Give us Miriam Ashbury."

"She's not mine to give, nor Bil's. They're not even on speaking terms. Anyway, neither of us knows where she is. Manwaring was scrupulously careful *not* to endanger her by contact with his network. Suppose I give you my word, as an intelligence officer of an ally, that I know she has no knowledge of subversive activities in your country?"

"We wouldn't believe you."

"Sooner or later you'll have to advise CSIS that you're holding an agent. They'll insist on interviewing me."

"They don't know we've got you, and we're not telling them. We know you're helping American traitors in Canada. And now you've gotten CSIS involved in Mexico as well.

We're not giving you access to your superiors until we know who we can trust."

Jason's amazed. Werner may really believe that a Canadian agency would dare to help American dissidents. If only he knew Jason's superiors, or *their* superiors. After working alongside SECOR people for weeks, Jason can still be astonished by the level of American hysteria over security.

Werner shows a tight smile; he's sure he's hit the mark. "CSIS is helping them stretch their communications into Canada, aren't they?"

"Werner, that's just insane. CSIS is scared to death of the administration." The Pentagon, with its many tentacles into Canadian agencies, would have no such delusion, so Werner's alone in his paranoia. He must not have notified anyone up the chain that a CSIS agent is in detention.

"We know CSIS has a register of Americans who hate the administration."

"Werner, for God's sake! There could be such a list somewhere—we've all heard that. But only of Americans in Canada who oppose your administration. It was probably pressed on us by your own people. Whatever they expected CSIS to do with it, I doubt they're doing anything." Werner looks more annoyed than thoughtful, so he doesn't accept this. But the Pentagon would know it's true. Werner can't be keeping his superiors informed. Trying to be a lone hero and win his first star?

Werner still looks confident. "Meanwhile, I have you. I've

discharged my obligation to explain what is required of you as a prisoner under interrogation. Now we get to what is required of me when you fail to cooperate. You've had enough chances. We'll start this afternoon, Rightful." He strides out, with his back straight and head high. Jason has a nervous flutter in his stomach. He hasn't handled his last chance very well.

Rightful concurs. "Provoking the colonel was unwise, Mr. Currie."

Jason is returned to his cell, hooded and shackled again. The blare resumes from his speaker. Another wrinkle then—the cell light, sensed through the hood, begins to flutter off and on without any rhythm. It's so distracting he closes his eyes. That makes the noise even more potent. Might prisoners go quietly mad, lying immobile on their shelves, unable to shut out the assaults of noise and light? Can he hold himself together? His mind is trained in logic. He's a concentrating machine. He can never be brainwashed into submission. He tries to persuade himself that fear is their ally and defiance is his, but he's not altogether convincing. He pushes back the panic in his mind, but it's still there, waiting to take over, perhaps leaving his intellect in ruins.

The next summons arrives with the twist of a key in the lock. He's marched in shackles and hood to, he assumes, the usual chamber, where Rightful's voice greets him. "Good day, Mr. Currie." *What time of day is it?* "You're one of six subjects. Don't speak except to answer questions." That order is repeated in rudimentary Arabic by an unknown translator.

Rough hands remove his coverall. The arms open like a hospital gown's so that it comes off while he's shackled. His underwear is snipped off as icy shears threaten his groin. He's pushed back, staggering, until he feels the touch of the wall against his shoulders. He can hear the rustle of similar stripping mixed with grunts and gasps. A naked body brushes against him. A dog growls, very close, almost at his knees. It seems to pass among the prisoners. He hears a whimper of fear. There's a moment of suspended action.

Then, chaos. A blast of water knocks him to his knees. It's powerful enough to press his shoulders against the wall. It could be stripping his skin. It pins him, crumpled, gasping, for several brutal seconds, then passes on. A scream next to him pierces his ears, then other cries, wails, moans. The water's turned off. They're all panting. He's hauled to his feet. He's disoriented. He's very cold. Someone beside him is crying.

"That's just a taste," says the Arabic speaker. "There is much worse to come. You must tell us which one is your leader. Where are your explosives? Who else do you speak with? You will be released when you've spoken."

"They will never release us!" a voice cries. "Tell them nothing!" Instantly a command is barked and the dog goes wild. Its snarls blend with human shrieks. Jason remembers the bloody thighs he saw. He turns to the wall and presses against it to protect his genitals. A horny hand grips his shoulder and spins him back. The dog is called off but continues to growl. Having tasted blood, perhaps it slavers for more. Someone is sobbing nearby.

"Take that one out." Rightful's voice.

"Tell them nothing!" someone shouts, followed by the thud of a blow. A few seconds later, there's another water assault.

They get easier to bear as the shock effect lessens. Jason survives three. After the third, one of the unseen others breaks completely, blubbering and begging. He's also taken away. The hood is snatched off Jason's head. Rightful sizes him up. "Not bad, Mr. Currie. No whimpers from you. Yet. But this was just an introductory exercise."

"Oh? When will the next session be then, Sergeant-Major?" His attempt at coolness is spoiled by his stutter; he's chilled and trembling.

"Perhaps in an hour, perhaps tonight, perhaps tomorrow."

Slick appears and leads him back to his nest, still unclothed, shivering, and shackled. Slick tugs the hood on and secures it. Then he slaps Jason hard, on his sore jaw. Jason yelps. Slick laughs and leaves him to his cold, naked misery, comforted only by the raucous disharmony spewing from the speaker and the pulsing of the light.

Later, the sound stops and the light steadies. Jason's hearing gradually returns. There's a single set of footfalls, a clanging door, a second pair of passing feet. Going to interrogation? Then a long silence. Returning footsteps, one set heavy or shuffling. A defiant refusal or an abject surrender? When the door slams, the guard's steps approach his own door and stop. He braces for the crunch of a turning key. The steps resume and depart. This treatment is repeated irregularly, but the intimidation diminishes with repetition. After a while the sound assault resumes and the lights flicker, almost a relief after what seems like hours of straining at slight sounds.

The next day, or maybe the same day, there's another water game, hood, shackles, unknown companions. This seems to be a green and compliant group, not yet hardened, because after a single barrage and one dog attack, one of the group breaks, then a second. Jason feels a moment of smug superiority until he considers that a man might have a horror of dogs, like the revulsion some feel for snakes or spiders. Rats always bothered him. If they had set rats onto him, might he have broken?

After this session, he's allowed his red uniform again. It feels as luxurious as mink to his naked flesh. He knows he's being set up, but at least his body can recover somewhat before the next onslaught.

He's also permitted a walk in the private yard. Bil's there—clearly the reason for this privilege.

"I've told them everything I could think of." He's even paler and edgier, but unmarked, probably because he's answered every question. No reason he shouldn't. Jason doesn't mention his own trials, though Bil's sharp look at his face tells him they've left traces. "They told me you won't tell them where to find Miriam. Is that what it's all about?"

"Bil, I don't know where Miriam is."

"You're right to protect my sister. But if you know she's out of their reach somewhere ... Nothing else will get us out of here."

"They told you I refused?"

"Of course they did. Isn't that why you're still in here?"

"I don't know where she is. If I did, I wouldn't tell them, but I don't."

They stop walking and face each other. It's a surreal moment for these boyhood friends. Bil was the leader, Jason the follower. Now Bil's beseeching Jason. Bil smiles wryly, perhaps with the same thought. "How could it have turned out this way? Begging your help, when you've protected my sister, and I was ready to turn her in."

"I think they had a long time to brainwash you, Bil."

"Maybe." He seems suddenly more comfortable with himself. "Well, you should do what you need to do. I suppose they'll finally get tired of me. I have no way to help them. Once they realize that they'll probably send me back to Canada." He's an American citizen now. Jason knows they will never turn him over to another country. He belongs to them—he's American property, even if devalued. Jason himself might have a better chance of repatriation, and the unfairness of their two positions decides him. "Bil, sooner or later Miriam will surface. Perhaps in Canada, where she'll be safe. DIA can interview her there, with a lawyer present and

CSIS riding shotgun. I'll help CSIS arrange it."

Bil's face lights up as if the sun had touched it. It gives Jason a wrench to see him for a few seconds as he had throughout their early days, radiating optimism. "That could do it! So, after they're convinced she's no threat, you and I can get out of here. Good for you, Jason!" He gives Jason an almost ecstatic hug, thrilled with sudden hope, and Jason returns it, but with reservations. The guard looks down on them without expression.

# THIRTY-SIX

"SO YOU'VE DECIDED TO COME ACROSS?" WERNER SEEMS unenthusiastic, maybe even disappointed.

"I want to make a deal."

"I'm listening."

"In time, Miriam will find her way to Canada. It might take a while, but she'll turn up from somewhere. She'll be interrogated by CSIS. Your people can interview her with CSIS present. And her lawyer. Bil and I will be released to Canada. I'll act as a go-between to arrange it."

Werner absorbs this for a few seconds and then snorts. "Don't take me for stupid, Currie. How could they have a network without secure communication? She knows how they did it. She knows their contacts in the States. And maybe you know as well." After a moment he adds, "Maybe even one of your colleagues."

There's a hint of surprise on Rightful's face. Werner waits to coax a reaction. Jason says nothing.

"You don't often have nothing to say."

"Was that a question, Colonel? As far as I could see, all my colleagues have unquestioning loyalty to their country. Just like you."

That draws the usual hard look. "Let's get back to Ashbury. We want her here; she's no good to us in Canada."

"*If* she goes to Canada, you can't get her out without making your case in our courts, and you have no case."

"Sure we can. If CSIS gets her, they can whisk her across without a hearing. They've done it before."

This could be true. "They might if she were an agreed terrorist, but they'll know she's clean. So why risk a public enquiry?"

"Because they'll know we have you." Werner has a tight smile of triumph, sure of his winning position.

"You've *told* them I'm here?"

"Not yet. We'd prefer to pull our own chestnuts out of the fire. With your assistance. If you continue to be a pain in the ass, we'll trade what's left of your hide for hers."

"*Why*, Werner?" He's shaken and blurts out the question in frustration. Werner cocks his head, intrigued.

"Because you and that woman don't deserve a free pass to Canada." Werner is studying him closely. He seems pleased. He must see uncertainty. "Maybe you're beginning to come round. Let's get back to work before you relapse."

Then it's back to the waterboarding pool, but this time not in demonstration mode. After they strip him, he's plunged under, he thinks three times, but after the second he's lost, barely conscious. Curiously, he's not terrified. Having done it once and survived, it's then just bearable if he keeps his head. Through plugged ears he can hear the muffled voice of Rightful. "This is useless, sir. He knows how to handle it now."

But Werner insists on one more, longer this time. As he comes round and finds himself choking and spluttering, Jason realizes that he had passed out and swallowed water. Werner strides out.

"Two very stubborn men." Rightful shakes his head. "More like two dogs tugging on the same bone." He leans very close to Jason and looks into his eyes. "You stood up pretty well, Mr. Currie, but this session was amateurish. He's too impatient. In interrogation, we should never be impatient. We need to take enough time. We need to truly understand our client. We need to get his cooperation."

Still coughing up water, Jason manages; "If he's an amateur, why is he here?"

"Because he wanted to be. He seems to hate you."

Slick leads him to his cell, very cold, still bare-naked, soaking, disoriented. Slick fastens Jason's hood, shoves him down on the shelf, and lashes his knees to his neck, hands manacled behind, then leaves him to the concert and strobe-like flashing of the light. He's perhaps as miserable as a person can feel without specific pain. That comes later (not much later), as the cramping sets in. Ultimately, everywhere hurts, as the combination of cold and spasms spreads throughout his muscles.

He's amazed at his own obstinacy, his discovered endurance. He's been facing some portal in his mind through which he might pass in surrender; it's been almost levered open several times. Now, there is a shield in front of it. Whatever the stimulus, his fear for Miriam, his loathing for Werner, his compassion for Bil, maybe just his own terror of being forever broken, of never recovering the soundness of mind that's his persona, he has found a line of defense beyond which he must not allow them to penetrate.

He reviews Werner's words for hints: *how could they have a network without communication? She knows how they did it.* He lacks the two tables she mentioned to break the code. If his code breakers can't work them out, they can't access the network? Maybe Werner can't wrap it up without Miriam.

As the pain penetrates, he loses focus on Werner. He goes to his mental routines. He concentrates on his breathing first to dispel wandering thoughts. When his mind clears he rehearses more math sequences. Then he does translation routines, from English to Arabic to French and back to English, with bizarre results. He replays chess problems. He creates a cycle of these games and tries to repeat each item in sequence but adding some new step at the end so that the chain burns up more minutes with each repetition. It's exhausting, so much so it must wear him out, because he finds himself wakened by a kick to the kidney.

"Son of a bitch was asleep!" he hears Slick say to an unknown partner. "Wake up, sweetie! Your presence is requested." He undoes the neck rope and tries to pull Jason to his feet, but the leg muscles won't function. He collapses, crashing against Slick. They both fall, Jason on top. He manages to knee Slick but only weakly. Slick gets in two or three punches. They stumble along to the chamber, Jason still hooded.

"Her precise location now, Currie. Name of her host. Contact information." Werner sounds business-like, determined. No fooling around this time.

"Sorry, Colonel." Jason's shocked at the sound of his own voice, hoarse, almost a croak. "Memory loss from mistreatment."

"Shit!" Jason hopes that means Werner is shocked that he's still holding out. But maybe he's just annoyed by the flippancy. "Okay then. Fingernails."

"Just one, sir. One at a time is most effective." That's Rightful's advice.

They choose the little finger on the left hand. Rightful (Jason believes) extracts it slowly. Jason hears his raw voice shriek as the nerves are electrified with pain. He faints. Perhaps only for a few seconds. Then he throws up. All over the hood.

"Jesus! What a filthy mess!" They make no effort to clean him, only give him a fresh hood. The seconds of full light are so blinding he can't focus. The smell inside the new hood makes him wretch, so they snatch it off again. "Christ! What a fucking pain you are!" Slick's disgusted. "Let's shove him in the pool. I can't stand the smell."

They strap him on the board and plunge him in. It's a relief to be merely drowning rather than losing more fingernails. When they haul him out, he's barely conscious. Werner stomps out, exasperated. Jason is left on his board to recover like a patient on a gurney while they move along to a newly arrived group of six prisoners, hooded and handcuffed, and all naked.

"Which one of you is the leader?" the interpreter demands of them in Arabic. "No answer? Then we have a treat for you." Jason is shocked when a female guard enters. She's a dowdy fortyish, more forbidding than attractive, but only a voice to his fellow victims in their hoods. She stands close to one and murmurs to him. They're all startled at the sound of her voice. She touches his testicles. He jumps back. He shouts something that might be "whore!" in Arabic, and that sets off a howling blend of curses. The woman laughs and goes down the line, touching, poking, even slapping one rump. The revulsion is intense, with profanity Jason hasn't heard since boyhood. The group huddles for protection like chickens under a circling hawk. Slick and the translator snigger in contempt. The woman becomes more aggressive as her targets shrink from her. She fondles one man's genitals. He falls to the floor to escape her. She touches him then with her toe while he tries to roll away, shrieking at her.

"That will do," Sergeant-Major Rightful says, detached as always. "Explain to this lot that we will interview each one by himself in an hour. Keep that man." The one pitiful keeper, whimpering slightly, is shoved down on a wooden bench. Jason now focuses on a menacing control panel behind it. They clamp electrodes onto his fingers, his toes, and his testicles. Slick throws the switch for a second. The man's body jumps, and he screams, then sobs hoarsely as the power is cut. There's no attempt to get information. This must be only a conditioning session.

"The colonel thought you might benefit from just being an observer, Mr. Currie," Rightful says. "It will give you an idea of where you're going after you run out of nails." Fear. They want him to look ahead and be afraid. If he's not afraid it may not work.

Abruptly that generates an image of a day in primary school when his teacher sent him to the principal's office for discipline. Corporal punishment—the strap—was no longer permitted, but the prospect was almost as terrifying without it. His desk was at the back of the room, and it seemed a long walk to reach the door, his feet almost too heavy to shuffle. He could see the ghoulish fascination on the faces of his classmates. The high hallway was miles long. Then he sat on a bench with the staff throwing glances, curious rather than sympathetic. Finally, trembling, he went before the principal. *It was the fear.* The principal never raised his voice.

His pulse levels; his terror quiets. He has to fortify himself for another bout. It's the moment when another person might summon up his faith. He has only his discipline to fall back on. Now that he is sure that fear, more than pain, is their most powerful weapon—fear of pain itself, fear of being unable to bear pain, fear of breaking, of weeping or screaming, of losing control, and of never regaining control—he has to look fear in the eye, and the pain will be bearable, maybe. He has to concentrate on this *now*, because they must see him as nearly broken and will follow up before he can recover.

Rightful stands beside him as the naked inmate is marched out, still blubbering. Jason regards his impassive face. How do they all feel about their day when they get home? Does the victim's groveling quiet the whispers of guilt, the mistreatment having been suffered by a mere drudge, a nonperson? Does Rightful chat with his wife of his resourcefulness in the chamber? Does Werner brag to his West Point son of his triumphs? Or are they each very quiet, warning off questions?

"Mr. Currie." Maybe military indoctrination is Rightful's filter, watering down the revulsion he should feel. He's been trained to kill; maybe he allows that torture is, after all, less than murder. "You will have to accommodate Colonel Werner sooner or later. You've seen how far we can go. Not the woman—not in your case. But we *will* use the electrodes. I urge you to give him what he needs."

"I don't know how."

"You will have to give him whatever you know of the

woman. I don't wish to see you broken." He really seems sympathetic. But maybe he's just applying the psychology of his trade, softening Jason's resolve, making the next round more productive.

There's a break before that round. He gets one meal, so maybe it's overnight. He's allowed his coveralls again, but the hood goes back on. Slick stares as he removes it, so Jason wonders what he must look like now, unwashed, unshaven, unsleeping. His finger throbs steadily, possibly infected; his guts are in turmoil; his head aches. Every muscle is seized up. He can't be confident that he will hold out. He can't entirely quiet the fear that beyond some point his mind will be destroyed. Maybe they know what they're doing in leaving him awhile.

Then he's hauled once more to the chamber and strapped this time to the wooden bench, without his hood. "Make sure you put one electrode on that little finger," Werner says. He is grimmer this time. He also looks worn, which gives Jason a shot of strength.

He needs it. Fire explodes through his body. He feels himself heave up into a rigid arc. He hears his own scream. He blacks out. As a little light returns, he seems to see wire cages and orange men. Scraps of sentences in minimized Arabic. Faces full of want. The stonemason prays nearby. They fade and then he sees Bil, then Miriam with Bil. He is near them himself, out of view. They're all young. Something is being said but he can't make it out. A dark figure comes forward.

It's Werner. His image persists but the others dissolve. Jason edges into wakefulness. Werner is still in his face. This time he's real. "You were out for minutes."

Jason can't see clearly, but he can smell the singed flesh. His wounded finger might be in flames.

"Don't be so goddamn stubborn," Werner says, almost pleading. Then, "Give him another shot." Longer than the first. He comes back through a shroud of mist, with lights flitting like fireflies under his closed lids and a thousand bee stings on his body. He's afraid to move. He hears their voices. He opens his eyes.

"Colonel, there's no point in pushing him further. They just lie when they're broken. We've got all he's going to give us for now. We should leave him for a week. Then he'll be more susceptible for the next round." Rightful sounds sure of himself; how many prisoners has he evaluated under 'persuasion?'

Werner's look shocks Jason: he's actually white. With hatred? With fear of failure? There's spittle at the corners of his mouth; his eyes are wild. Is he cracking up? Maybe torturing decent people takes as much from the doer as the done. Werner moves about the room. Jason recalls an expression of his mother: he's *beside himself*. He feels a surge of hope, the first since they brought him here. *Werner's losing! I must be winning!*

Werner ignores Rightful. "Speak up, Currie! Damn you, you're wearing me out. If you won't talk about Ashbury, tell me about Hawk."

"Hawk?" His throat makes it come out like the voice of a

frog, startling Werner.

"He took special interest in the Sealed Sectors, didn't he?"

"Why would he?" Puzzling.

"There you go again. He sent you to Mexico. He must have briefed you on what the Mexican Sector was working on. That would be natural, wouldn't it?"

"The Mexican Sector?"

"He went in there often. Did you ever go with him?"

"Not allowed."

Werner stops his pacing and comes close to Jason. "It's not about you and me. I'm just trying to carry out my mission." He waits as if hoping for an answer. A long moment passes, Werner looking down at Jason, who must seem bewildered, Rightful looming over them both.

"Son of a bitch is proud of himself! Needs a lesson." Werner bites on his words and spits them out. His voice is unrecognizable. "Get Attila."

"That's not appropriate for a SECOR officer, sir."

"Rightful! Sergeant-Major!"

"Sir?"

Jason thinks of Al Ansari: a decent man whom Werner persecuted to his death. Now he's crushing Jason. How much can an officer like him stand before he destroys himself?

"Don't question me!" The sergeant-major shrugs and stays quiet.

Slick's at his elbow. "Not complaining of your treatment, are you?"

"Leave him be," Rightful says. He probably despises Slick for taking pleasure in inflicting pain. Rightful only takes pleasure in doing his job.

"What's needed here is humiliation. Get that dumb giant."

"Not appropriate, sir."

"Rightful! Don't contradict me. Get Attila."

"Sir, the Attila procedure will serve no purpose. After what he's already handled."

"It will serve the purpose of bringing him down a few pegs."

"Sir, this man will break in time. But he won't be of much use to us when he does. We need a different program. More patience. Then more of his cooperation."

"I'm out of patience. Do what I ordered." Werner's voice is grating. His face is sweating. Rightful studies his superior, perhaps weighing at what point he can refuse a direct order. Jason watches with fascination.

"Time for you to meet Attila," Slick whispers in Jason's ear.

Jason tries to register something Werner just said. His thought process has slowed to a crawl. He goes over Werner's words. Then he gets it.

"What mission, Werner?" His words must sound like some foreign tongue. Slick backs off, staring at him. Rightful cocks a glance at Jason, shakes his head once, and then goes to the wall telephone. Werner comes over and looks down at him again, all but spitting at him.

"What mission? Breaking into their goddamn network."

*I had it all wrong.* His revelation amuses him. He must show it because Werner's eyebrows form an arch of surprise.

"He's *laughing* at me!"

Werner doesn't filter the opposition's data. He's not working with a covert officer corps. *He didn't hold me just out of spite. He had to get Miriam because he can't break in without her.*

The dumb giant appears. Not quite a giant, but certainly huge. His red suit, no doubt the largest made, has a couple of buttons left undone to allow it to stretch across his chest. He's well above six feet, neatly bearded, almost bald, and either black or a deep Mediterranean bronze.

"Get their clothes off, Rightful." Slick and the sergeant-major help Jason to his feet and tug off his coveralls and underwear. He can hardly keep his balance. Attila strips off his own coverall. Naked, he's even more imposing: bulging shoulders, back and belly free of fat rolls, legs solid as columns. It's impossible to imagine this man being felled. He looks Jason over, barely able to stand facing him, and speaks almost apologetically, in Arabic.

"It would be better for you to give them what they want, brother."

Jason replies in the same language. "I'm unable to do so."

"They will force me to shame you."

"Why are you here?"

"Wait a minute!" Werner almost shouts. "Never mind debating him."

"How should I know? They took every man in my building. I don't know these terrorists."

"Are you a true believer, brother?"

"Enough, Currie!" Werner sounds desperate.

"Truly. But I must overcome you. It's the way in here."

"I hope you will be gentle."

"I will be gentle. God is great."

It doesn't take long, but the struggle is surprisingly tame. If Jason were at his fittest he could never hold off this monster, but as he is now he cannot even resist him. After a clumsy attempt, brushed aside by Attila, he's whirled around and hugged from behind. He cannot break free. The giant forces him down until he drops finally to his knees, then flat out. Attila pushes him into a hump and mounts him, but with a gentleness more of a lover than a rapist. After the desecration his body's already endured, it seems a minor violation. Jason hardly notices pain. But it's what Werner needed, because he crows, "How did that feel, Currie?"

"If you'll drop your pants, Colonel, I'll show you."

Jason rises to his knees. The fist arcing at him magnifies in size instant by instant until it fills his sight. The knuckles are the size of knee bones. He glimpses the ring with its military insignia zeroing in on his left eye. He turns his head. It wrecks on his cheekbone. He falls backwards, feet trapped under him. He struggles to roll over, tries to push himself up with his hands. He slides down again. The concrete floor, glazed with water, blood, and smelly secretions, is as slick as a skating rink. Werner and Attila seem to be waltzing beside him. He sees them only through a pink haze of blood. Slick and Rightful are skidding around them. It's a scene from Bedlam. He's frozen in wonder as he looks up at the whirling figures.

The naked giant throws Werner back toward Jason. He skids past, taking desperate steps to regain his balance. Jason manages a weak kick that just hooks around Werner's knee. It's enough to make his feet slide out from under him. For an instant he seems to be suspended like a levitating body until he hits, head first, with a sullen thud, quite loud. He cries out, the sound dying at once to a low moan like a fire engine's siren winding down. Jason looks into Werner's eyes as they lie opposite. Werner extends one arm a little. His finger tries to point at Jason. His eyes cloud. The whistle of escaping breath ends in a final heave. Then silence.

Rightful has cornered Attila and slugs him with his club. The giant slips to the floor. Rightful stares down at Werner. "*Jesus! I think he's dead!*"

# THIRTY-SEVEN

"I AM CAPTAIN CONSTANTINE."

Miriam takes his hand and looks him over. The captain is intimidating. He's well over six feet and carries plenty of weight without being paunchy. He has a bushy black beard, which works with his overhanging brows to make him look like a pirate in uniform. Meanwhile, he looks *her* over and she can immediately feel his interest. He likes women. He signals that as well by prolonging the handshake and adding a squeeze of intimacy.

"Most often, we have boring guests. Then sometimes something lively, like you. You are 'specially welcome."

"Well, thank you. I'm only going as far as L.A."

"Time enough to get to know you. Three days, maybe four. You will join my table for dinner. One other couple. Excuse me. I must go ashore. We may be delayed here one day and I must protest to the authorities."

She decides his accent is Eastern European even though his manners are more Mediterranean *boulevardier*. She doesn't like that 'one day.' One more day for the pursuers to close in.

She has been on cruise ships—deck pools and carpeted dining. This could hardly be more different. The bridge is in a sort of pod astern that also holds living quarters for crew and guests. From the bridge deck, she can now look down to the rest of the ship, which is completely taken up by stacked containers. The metal stairs down to that level are gated off, so passengers are not welcome further No wonder, it's a working area—as she watches a container is being hoisted by a gargantuan crane which then gently deposits it on the bed of a flat truck on the dock.

"My name is Leonidas and I will be your steward." He's an attractive young man in casual clothes who materializes from the metal pod. "Let me show you your cabin." He speaks English well, with an intriguing accent. She's astonished at the cabin—she has expected something like a metal capsule with a bunk swinging with the roll of the ship. It's the size of a decent hotel room, and as well furnished, private bath, a couch in addition to the bed, neat, clean. And noisy at the moment as the crane grinds away continuously.

"It's not often we have a single lady aboard," Leonidas says. He waits for an explanation.

"I must go to Los Angeles. But I've always wanted to take

a trip on a cargo ship, so I'm taking advantage to do it this way." Leonidas nods dutifully, suggesting he can't imagine such a motivation. She needs to hone her story for any other inquisitor, not to give any suggestion of being on the run.

Now she must face being alone. While Jason was beside her it was easy to hold her feelings under control. Now, she has no backing. She's out on her own, there are empowered agencies seeking her, and they're the same people who murdered her mentor and master. She allows herself to return to the sight of his body, carved into her memory so that she can never escape it. She sees again that head almost parted from the torso, both bloodied, none of the once familiar intensity in those open eyes, whose only message is the lack of any human presence. She runs that over and over in her mind, like she might run her tongue over an agonizing tooth. She plumbs as deeply as she can into the darkness of her horror. Some panic surges up, she mouths the bile of anxiety. But after fighting it down, she quiets gradually. Now she feels very tired. She lies down and almost immediately slips into sleep.

There's a kind of happy hour in the officers' lounge before an early dinner, the 'guests' mingling with the Captain and his staff. She's the center of attention immediately. Captain Constantine puts a propriety hand on her shoulder and introduces her to his officers and the other travellers. They've mostly been aboard from the Mediterranean on. All but one person.

"Señor Acosta—he also boarded in Manzanillo."

"Oh, I didn't see you come aboard …"

"Just today, señora." She's terrified he'll break into a spiel in Spanish, trapping her in her limited fluency, so she contrives to stay as far from him as the lounge allows. There's a middle-aged couple who, she hears from them, have several other trips on their record. There's a single gentleman, Signor Giordano, with a neat greying beard and flawless manners, fluent in precise English, who brims with curiosity as he hovers over her. A pair of not-quite-young men in casual dress are not so interested in anyone else. She decides they could be gay companions. She navigates through drinks and dinner with a keen awareness that a single lady on a voyage like this needs a better narrative. She feels Constantine's gaze on her too often. She's taken this as the normal interest of an overactive male appetite, but begins to wonder if it could also be suspicion. Maybe hiding out on a cargo vessel is a ploy not unknown to a man of his experience.

They get underway next day, finally. She can feel her tension drain as they slide past the headlands and face the open sea. "It is a relief always to be clear of the last port," Signor Giordano says. He stops beside her outside the bridge.

"You've seen many other ports?"

"Oh yes. I've even been to America before. I've been to the Orient. I hate flying and I find cruise ships too touristy. So I contrive to make my way like this. I'm an old man with plenty of time to see the world without the stress of airports and line-ups and indecent haste."

"I think you're very lucky to have found your *métier*."

"And you, madam, I hope you also find comfort on your journeys."

She realizes she must be completely transparent.

She has more luck with the couple—the Medfords of Edinburgh, also experienced sailors.

Lilah Medford's less interested in Miriam's motives than in the captain's. "You need to be careful with that man," she says in a pleasant light brogue. "I've seen this before on other trips, the hand on the shoulder, then the waist. They always think single women on vacation are vulnerable. But you look like you can handle it."

"I don't take it seriously. He's just checking me out."

"Maybe."

She hears Señor Acosta speaking in quite fluent English to the captain so she makes a pre-emptive strike to protect her identity. "You're also going to L.A.? You speak English almost like an American."

"So do you, señora."

"I work in the tourist industry. We hear more English than Spanish."

"Interesting. You work in Manzanillo?" She evades his questions easily, since he doesn't press for answers.

The ship plods across a not unfriendly sea and life settles into a pleasantly humdrum routine. Miriam finds her stress level tapering down as the hours pass. The container cells restrict walking routes on board, but she gets enough exercise climbing steep metal stairs. Watching for whales and porpoises, and occasionally locating some, is part of the routine. She hasn't had time to fortify herself with reading stock, but she finds a library donated by former passengers, mostly softcovers, romances and mysteries and a few classics. She indulges herself. When the weather is too hot or too sunny for reading outdoors, she retreats to the air-conditioned lounge. The gentle routine of the ship encourages rest; she naps in her lair and its cool comfort. She's invited to the bridge and finds it as digitized as an airplane flight deck. Captain Constantine gives his permission for a tour of the lower decks, guided by Leonidas. Most of the space is used for separate cells stuffed with still more containers, but she's fascinated by the Engine Room, giant engines labouring smoothly beside banks of gauges and switches, with the noise too much for Leonidas to cope.

Mealtimes are set within tight parameters so she meets officers and guests at every one. The remainder of the crew (of less than twenty) she hardly sees. They have their own dining quarters and lounge on a lower deck. All crew including officers are on shifts.

The ship's route is parallel to the coast of Baja California, which is in sight at times. She watches it crawl by, counting the days and then hours until they reach Long Beach. Her anxiety returns thinking of it. It's the only point of danger—could she be identified in some way? If she is, there is no escape route from the United States.

"What happens when we reach port?" she asks Signior Giordano.

"Oh, it's very different here. In Europe you can just go ashore, pretty quickly pass through Customs, especially if your country's in the EU. In America, they're more hyper. We're all under suspicion as potential terrorists. Customs come right on board. Sometimes they search the whole ship. They'll want to see your luggage. If you're leaving here they'll want to know where to, are you ticketed, do you have friends, the whole gamut. If you're not debarking here, you're not allowed in the port premises so the only way to visit shore is to call a taxi and there's not always time for that if the ship has a short turnaround."

"Are you leaving the ship in Long Beach?"

"Everybody is. All the passengers."

"Perhaps we could share a cab?"

"Certainly. I'm going to the bus terminal, then on to San Francisco."

It's not all smooth. When she awakens in the dark, which happens frequently, she can begin to question her own motives. SECOR and DIA and all those other agencies mock her frailty. What can a single person *do*—other than submit—in the face of the cynical mesh in which they hold America?

She becomes tiny and feeble and is swept by despair. She pictures Manwaring. She cries for him and for herself. She mourns for America. When she has binged enough on grief, she rallies by concentrating on Manwaring's courage. He endured so much, he lived with fear at his shoulder, yet he never wavered. They reduced him to a nearly headless corpse, but he had never surrendered. She can draw strength from his image as long as she hangs on to it. When she lets go, the despondency creeps back over her.

On her fourth morning she wakes to find the port in sight. Breakfast is handled briskly; all crew have plenty to do on harbour days. She organizes her meagre possessions and waits in suspense. Giordano's remarks about Customs have bulked them up into a giant roadblock. Her own experiences of border crossing haven't been pleasant; she has always ended up with an unfriendly agent whom she imagined to have dealt with deception every working day so that his nature was permanently flawed. She awaits the test nervously. The ship glides into its berth and is secured. There they are, waiting on the slip. They board immediately.

"Mexican citizen?" She just nods.

"Purpose of your trip?"

"Visiting my sister and her husband."

"They live where?"

"San Francisco."

"Their address?" She produces her notes and reads it off. "That's right downtown, isn't it?"

"I didn't think so. She said it was miles from downtown."

"How are you travelling from here?"

"By bus. From the terminal here."

"You have tickets?"

"Not yet."

"Why did you come here on a ship? It takes a long time and it's no cheaper than flying."

"I get anxiety attacks on a plane. Last time I took a bus from Guadalajara to San Francisco and it was a terrible trip. People opened the windows because it was so hot, then we had dust inside. It took forever. So when I found I could take this ship from Manzanillo I thought it was a gift. I even changed my dates to fit."

"What do you do for a living?"

"I'm the Maitresse d'Hotel at Buen Provecho in Guadalajara."

"What is that?"

"It's a high class restaurant. I greet customers and show them to their table."

"Oh, a waitress. Please open your luggage." It takes only a moment to sort through it. "This isn't much luggage. How long are you staying with your sister?"

"I have to be back in two weeks."

"So how are you returning?"

She sighs, exaggeratedly. "By bus. But at least I'll get an air-conditioned bus this time."

He regards her thoughtfully while she tries to look worry-free. "It's not usual for a woman to travel alone on a ship. We don't see that."

She grins. "That's what everyone told me. But I've had a

good time and people here have been quite kind, so it turned out to be a good idea."

He gives her a badge to clear the customs gate, and leaves with a slightly troubled expression.

She's still nervous. Maybe she could be stopped at the gate? She wants out quickly. She finds Giordano, also cleared. Cabs have been called. The crew and Captain are all fully engaged so they find their way to the pier without goodbyes.

She's standing there with Giordano, waiting for their cab, when she sees the Customs crew coming along the pier. Two of them flank Señor Acosta. He's handcuffed. As the group passes he gives the two of them a surly glance but says nothing.

"Can you imagine why they arrested him?" she asks Giordano when they're underway.

"Leonidas told me about him. His documentation wasn't right. Apparently he was really a Canadian with a fake Mexican passport. Trying to slip into the States. Leonidas says they're always watching for Mexican drug connections. Anyway, it took a little pressure off the rest of us. Customs kept up their quota."

At the bus terminal, she leaves the Italian sitting at a table, sipping coffee and waiting for her to return from the ladies' rest room, but she's already outside and boarding a cab en route to LAX.

There remains only the wait for takeoff, two hours when something might perhaps go wrong. Time barely crawls by as she holds down her tension. She cannot read, she cannot eat, she cannot find any distraction. The flight is called. She doesn't rush to the gate; she wants to be midway in the queue, not eager, not laggard. But there's no officialdom waiting inside the gate. Only a long breath of relief. Then, they're airborne and she's on her way out of danger. Her body is like a spring suddenly released, limp. She curls up and falls asleep. No one sleeps soundly on a plane, so she dreams. She's at the table with Manwaring and Campobello, listening once more to the flow of opinion, enjoying the robust sarcasm of the professor. Jason edges into the scene. He seems vaguely antagonistic, she pictures him and Manwaring snarling at each other, but they must somehow reconcile because they snap out of sight. She's shaken awake by the stewardess. They're in their glide path. When she raises the blind she's staring down at the Fraser River.

Now another Customs to clear; this one is much less threatening. Passengers move readily through the gates in the more relaxed atmosphere of Canadian entry. She steps up to the counter on signal.

"*Señora Martinez*," says a soft voice, all but whispering. "My name is Noble. If you don't mind, we'll go this way. Please."

# THIRTY-EIGHT

JASON PRIES OPEN HIS EYES. LIGHT BLINDS THEM, SO HE CLOSES them again. Then he edges them open just enough to acclimatize slowly. When he can focus, he finds himself staring at Hawk. Now dressed like a lawyer, he's seated on the corner of Jason's bench-bed, watching him intently.

"I had a hell of a time finding you," he says. Jason's not ready for clear thought. Why is he hard to find? He lets his eyes roam. He's still in his cell.

"Because it's a military prison. Not SECOR territory." Hawk is reading his mind, as he always seems to. "SECOR has you as AWOL but I knew Werner had you somewhere." He gets up and leans his slim frame down to inspect Jason's face, with professional interest. "I see Werner was at the top of his game. You look like shit."

"How does Werner look?"

"He looks very dead."

"*Dead*?" Jason's shaken to hear this. Werner's been the anchor of his attention. Now he's adrift.

Hawk runs his eye over Jason's cheekbone, scraped raw, and the one closed eye. "You're a bloody mess … this whole business is a bloody mess."

"Don't blame me."

"Of course I'm blaming you. You made a spectacle of yourself at the Coliseum and that gave Werner his chance."

"He'd have got me anyway." Jason's face is stiff and he slurs his words. He must sound as if he's barely coping, because Hawk looks alarmed. "He kept on about Miriam. He had me convinced, but it wasn't just her he was after. Not in the end."

Hawk becomes very alert, like an animal whose ears have just stood up. Finger over lips, he motions for caution and points to the mesh in the ceiling, now silent. Jason nods. Hawk is quite tense, something Jason hasn't seen before. He hesitates. "Things are moving faster than expected."

Jason tries to lever himself up. He manages it halfway, propped on one elbow with his back jammed against the wall. "D'you have a helicopter or did you drive?"

"Where do you think you are?"

"In the desert?"

"Eastern Washington. I used one of our planes."

Jason has trouble relating to this simple fact. He's a thousand miles from where he imagined himself to be. Hawk continues to study him watchfully. "Why couldn't you give Werner at least something to protect yourself?"

"What he wanted ... was to break me. After he had Miriam." Hawk seems to bite down on a retort as he sees Jason flagging. The cell door grinds open. Rightful enters.

"Rightful, this man is a SECOR officer," Hawk snaps erect, brimming with authority. "You had no business holding one of our officers. He was entirely within his rights to refuse to share information with you. You know the protocol. Each agency looks after its own."

"Strictly speaking, sir, he's not a SECOR officer. He's CSIS, according to Colonel Werner."

"Don't give me that legalistic crap, Sergeant-Major. He's seconded to SECOR."

"General, Rightful really tried to stop Werner—"

"You stay quiet, Currie." Not very gently.

"Sir, I'll ask the commandant for permission—"

"Never mind. I'll see the commandant myself. And for God's sake, get him into sick bay and have him attended to." Hawk leaves Rightful there and strides out, every inch a general.

Rightful looks down on Jason. "I understand where he's coming from, Mr. Currie. I warned Colonel Werner that we might have no jurisdiction. The commandant will probably be relieved to get a SECOR off his hands. Just go quietly."

He comes close to the bench and examines Jason for a moment. "I'm almost sorry to see you go. You were getting really interesting. But of course, Colonel Werner was too impatient." Jason can only nod. Rightful, far from stewing with guilt over his miserable assignment, must actually be proud of his workmanship. Maybe that's the only way for him to survive in here.

Jason's wheeled to sick bay. After bandaging and shots for pain, he falls into deep sleep, secure for once that he will not be kicked awake. He's better when Hawk and Rightful march in, late in the afternoon.

"You're being released into General Hawk's custody, sir."

"Out of here?"

"You're SECOR's property, Mr. Currie."

# THIRTY-NINE

"WHAT IS THIS PLACE?" MIRIAM ASKS.

"It's a private house."

"You don't mean a 'safe house?' Has CSIS been reading cold war novels?"

"We're actually quite up-to-date, señora." Noble's untouched by her sarcasm. The more he sees her anger, the easier it is to avoid any sympathy.

"You can't hold me here." Noble doesn't reply. He's wasted much of a day interrogating her with no useful result. She has answered his lead-in questions, though tersely, but as soon as he's begun slipping in more meaty attempts she just shuts down. He realizes now that he's dealing with a very strong will. He's begun to appreciate Jason's fascination with her.

"Don't call me señora. You know who I am."

"You adopted that identity and I'm afraid you're stuck with it, señora."

The A-D enters the room. "Arrangements completed," he says to Noble.

"I don't know who you are," Miriam says, "But you seem to be in authority here. I'm entitled to appear before an Immigration official."

"Señora, you are an illegal alien." The A-D says coldly.

"You can't deport anyone who's landed without a hearing."

"You haven't landed. 'Landed' means arriving at Customs and Immigration. You never got that far. You'll be escorted onto a plane to Mexico."

"Which will touch down at some point in the States. That's it, isn't it? Which government are you working for?"

"I think I understand my obligations to *this* country, señora. They don't include giving safe haven to terrorists."

"*Terrorists*! Is that the CSIS designation for any American who stands up to the thought police?"

The A-D turns to Noble. "Handle this personally. Confirm to me that you have actually seen her onto the plane and watched it take off." He strides away, stiff-backed as befits a general. Miriam sizes up Noble, who stands quietly, almost sheepishly.

"You're supposed to be a friend of Jason's."

Noble takes the chair beside her. "We have a considerable wait. Let's be comfortable."

# FORTY

OUTSIDE THE PRISON, JASON FEELS LIGHT AS AIR, AWAKE AS A sunrise—out of his dungeon, out of noise and pain, and almost free of fear. He tries to dance up the steps of the sleek little jet, but his stiffened body stumbles and he has to crawl the rest of the way. Once aboard, Hawk removes the token handcuffs. With the flight deck door closed the cabin is both quiet and private. The engines start up and the seatbelt warning light comes on.

"How did you spring me?"

"The commandant didn't even know they had a SECOR officer there. He couldn't wait to get shut of you." Jason falls wearily into his seat, fastens his belt, leans back, and closes his eyes. The engines rev up, the brakes release, and they begin to taxi.

Hawk leans across. "So you worked it out? I knew Werner had at least a sniff of the operation. The question is how much did he tell his command?"

"They'll know he's dead. If he named you they should be closing in on you right now."

"No sign of that so far." He's too tense to sit. He gets up and then takes a second seat behind Jason. "Werner told them that he had the network in his sights. Did he grill you about me?"

"Not until the end. He pretended it was all about Miriam. You duped me into suspecting Werner and his mythical veterans in Guada—I can hear your snicker. So I did swallow the bait. But when he showed me he had no real access to the network, I knew it had to be you."

"I always saw you were smarter than you were letting on. You knew about the camps before you got here."

"Not who was in them. Or how many. Where are we heading?"

"I told the commandant I'd deliver you directly to L.A. Station, but we're on our way to Bellingham."

"Why Bellingham?"

"It's close to the main crossing into British Columbia."

"Then what?"

"That's what we have to decide, isn't it?"

"They'll be looking into Werner's death."

"Rightful reported it as an accident." Now they're aloft, Hawk gets up and sits on the arm of Jason's seat. He stretches his legs across the aisle as if they've been cramped. He flexes his arms. He must be shaking off tension, setting himself to think clearly. Jason watches him, not sure what he's dealing with.

"But someone there knows what Werner was working on."

"I suspect the commandant will cover his ass by reporting that Werner held a SECOR without clearance and that you've now been released to me."

"Then what's the next move?"

Hawk considers this as if it tastes bad. "They just might go to SECOR HQ and blow it all open."

"Or they could decide Werner was on a wild-goose chase. Then they'd wait for more evidence."

"Werner gave them something more solid than suspicion. I'm guessing they were ready to move and he had them hold off until he broke you and got Miriam. It would have been a terrific coup for DIA, given SECOR a black eye, and made Werner a general."

The thought of Miriam in Werner's hands is agonizing to Jason. He must show it, because Hawk pauses and then goes on in a gentler tone.

"You never understood Werner. He *hated* what he had to do. But he did it thoroughly because he was indoctrinated to obey orders."

"Then why did you choose him?"

"He was imposed on me. He was there to watch me. The Pentagon liaises with each of our stations, but in fact all their officers are there to keep files on our commanders."

"But there's more to it than that. Werner thought I was here on some secret mission."

"It's all about Manwaring and his network. How did they communicate? Werner suspected SECOR's system was somehow being used by the Manwaring net. When you showed up, he thought CSIS was being added to the chain. Then I sent you to Mexico and he was sure of it. He was after Miriam because she might know how it worked; he wanted to break you to see how CSIS tied in. But Manwaring's murder threw him. He was looking for DIA to snatch Manwaring, maybe even Miriam, so he could break into their network."

"Why did you let me go to Mexico in the first place?"

"You wanted Miriam. That gave me a chance to open another channel to keep in touch with Manwaring in case we had to shut down the network. I never wanted her back in the States, far from it. But when you needed to find her, I also saw an opportunity to test you, hoping to find a potential ally. You could have been the same kind of Canadian as your director, obsequious toward our administration. So we kept you away from Miriam on the first trip to feel out your reaction. After that it was just a matter of more visits and Miriam."

Jason remembers Hawk's routine carping over his slow progress. Another deception, like Werner with the phantom vets. "When I saw them in Mexico, I knew they could never be lured back to the States. I thought you must have worked that out. So I began to speculate on why you really sent me there. But you sidetracked me with Werner." Hawk's slight smile is an acknowledgment. "How do you know what Werner was reporting?"

"I have my sources. But he caught me off-guard with you—he took advantage of your behavior at the Coliseum to get you into a military prison. I had to cash in a lot of favors to find you."

"They could move as soon as they hear you've got me with you."

Hawk straightens up, pauses, and then moves a few feet to another seat as if his body is trying to keep up with his racing mind. Jason's own attention has sharpened. "There's a Sealed Sector for Mexico. That's it, isn't it? You were passing Manwaring's messages on from that Sector, all on secure lines."

Hawk gives him that look of his. "When did you start looking in that direction?"

"When you began using 'they' instead of 'we' for the administration. Mathematicians are used to definitions that never change. You changed one. It got me thinking."

Hawk falls into thought for a few moments, then pulls the telephone from the seatback, looking more decisive now. He speaks rapidly in Spanish. Jason can hear the last word enunciated three times. Hawk disconnects.

"Warning that Sector," Jason says. "Code word repeated three times. What now, Silas?" It's the first time he's used the Christian name.

"Disappear."

"DIA will come after you. SECOR as well when they find both you and their Mexican Sector disappeared."

Hawk makes another restless move back to his original seat. "When the camp commandant reports that you're loose and with me, it will find its way to someone Werner was working with. They'll go to SECOR Command. There'll be an alert out for me. L.A. Station will be swarmed."

"Hence Canada?"

"Would I really be safer there? Some Canadians may detest this administration, but your government's comfortable with it."

"Luckily, they don't have the same power as yours. The trick is to get refugee status and then lots of publicity before the bureaucrats smother you. Maybe we can manage that."

"What about your Miriam? Isn't she still in Mexico?"

"She got out on a cargo ship."

"Ah! So that's what you were lying about when you said Campobello had hidden her. I wondered if you'd thought of that."

"She's on Vancouver Island by now."

"Are you sure? DIA made a major effort to find her. Werner got them really fired up. They'll have approached Ottawa. Remember they got her passport revoked."

Listening to Hawk's mastery of agency thinking, Jason suddenly panics over Miriam. "I should call my cousin."

"Do it then, but be careful what you say."

On the second try, he gets through. "Adolphus? It's your

cousin."

A slight pause. "How're you, cousin?"

"I wanted to be sure you got that package we sent you."

A longer pause. "It hasn't arrived yet."

"But—we sent it some time ago."

"Maybe it's still in transit."

"Damn!"

"Should we change our plans for the reunion?" Adolphus asks.

"I'll have to let you know." Jason meets Hawk's enquiring look. "She didn't show."

They can feel the plane settling into its glide path. Jason glances down at Bellingham Airport. The near desert country of eastern Washington has given way to the lush coastal belt. It's raining, not unusual here.

"I'll have to go. If I leave her to CSIS she could be quietly extradited. It's been done before."

"We'll both go."

"You might not be able to cross."

"It's your border. Find me a way across it."

As the plane taxies across the apron, Jason calls Ben Noble. "Ben? Miriam Ashbury seems to have gone missing."

"Where are you? Where have you been? SECOR says you're a fugitive, possibly working with dissidents. The A-D doesn't know which way to jump …"

"Never mind all that—what's happened to Miriam?"

"Where are you, Jason? Sounds like an airport."

"I'm with General Hawk. What about Miriam?"

There's a considerable pause. Noble then goes on very carefully. "Listen closely, Jason. We know nothing about Miriam Ashbury."

"But ...?"

"*Listen*! We *are* holding a woman named Señora Castillo. She has a passport that CBSA says is phony."

"My god! This is Kafkaesque. *You* know who she is. *I* know who she is. DFAIT has her photo on file. *Why is she in custody?*"

There's a substantial pause, Noble possibly reckoning how much he's authorized to say.

"We've verified that her passport is false. She's scheduled to be sent back to the United States because that's where her flight originated."

Jason feels the chill of helplessness. He can now visualize the web of bureaucracy being woven around Miriam, pulling her back to an American gulag. Hawk gets up from his chair, approaches, and sits again on the arm of Jason's seat, leaning in to eavesdrop. Jason mouths the words '*exporting her.*' "Ben, whatever your deal with the Americans is—you can imagine how DIA feel about her—you have to go through an extradition hearing. You'd never get it past the court."

An even longer pause this time. Jason braces for bad news.

"She entered Canada as Señora Castillo. With false documentation. CBSA can simply refuse her entry. She arrived from the United States and would be returned there."

"Ben, this is some kind of game. What's the A-D after?"

"Getting you out of there, for one thing. You're wrecking our relationship with SECOR. You're with General Hawk? Whereabouts?"

"On a plane."

"We've been trying to reach Hawk. He's somewhere unknown on a classified mission. I take it you're the classified mission?"

"I'm travelling with him."

"Under arrest?"

"Why—no. I'm okay."

Noble sighs. "So it's worse than we thought. Hawk's in trouble as well."

"Let's get back to Miriam."

"You're ignoring the long reach of the administration, Jason."

"So it all comes down to Washington's weight and Ottawa's weak spine."

"That's not the way the A-D sees it."

"If she's returned to the States, CSIS could be in worse trouble. She'd have to tell them that we've been strategizing with dissidents in Mexico."

Noble barely pauses. "We'd counter that you're a rogue agent and we're charging you." He gives Jason a moment to think this over. "I have to call you back after consulting with the A-D. Give me a couple of hours."

"We won't be available. I'll call you tomorrow morning and

she'd better be there." Jason sets down the phone and turns to Hawk, "We're both blown. He has to cover with the A-D. He wanted two more hours."

"In two hours they'll know that Mexico Sector has suddenly shut down. We'll both be classed as fugitives."

"Well, that will clarify the A-D's problem. He needs to get me out. We can trade for Miriam."

The intercom from the cockpit breaks in, "General, SECOR patrol at the airport are asking what assistance you require. A driver, other officers …?"

"Report that I'm in civilian dress on a classified mission and should not be recognized. Stay clear."

They can hear the intercom click off. "That will get back to L.A. Station," Jason says.

"In time."

They taxi to the terminal. Hawk leads the way right through to the exit. He hesitates for a moment, and then sets off at a brisk pace toward the parking area. Jason realizes they are following someone only when the woman ahead stops at her car and waits for them. She's erect, almost at attention. She salutes Hawk. They get in without speaking.

# FORTY-ONE

BLAINE HARBOR LIES A TOUCH SOUTH OF THE BORDER ACROSS the bay from White Rock in Canada. The two are only four or five miles apart, so it's an easy crossing point, and therefore under watch from the Corps. The little harbor is part of the Port of Bellingham, but the much larger shipping and cruise terminals are miles further southeast, with this segment home only to commercial fishing vessels and pleasure craft.

They're in the clothes their contact has provided, two sports fishermen at the tail-end of the salmon season, warmly dressed against the chill dawn of the strait, well equipped with fishing gear. Their silent driver pulls away.

"She's military, isn't she?"

"Serving officer."

"With plenty of nerve."

"All our people need that."

In the predawn darkness they move along the dock, tackle jingling and squeaking, counting slips to their boat. There's enough light from a distant standard to identify it. There are muted sounds of other early arrivals. One commercial boat starts up as they pass, with a throaty explosion and a cloud of diesel vapor, then quiets to a steady purr. A light flares and they're in its beam.

"Identify yourselves!"

A uniformed SECOR bars the dock. They produce driving licenses and fishing permits. "Idaho? What're you guys doing out here?"

"Salmon fishing, what else?"

"You're too late for the main run."

"That's what I told my boss—like he cares. Anyway, we'd be happy with one fish. Can you help us out here? What are they hitting on these days?" Jason makes salmon talk. Lures, location, depth, and speed. The guard is an authority on all points and happy to spend time talking to anyone on his lonely round.

"Good luck to you, then."

Their boat is a twenty-foot inboard. The plan is to move out with the fishing fleet, locate the SECOR patrol boat, and watch for an opportunity to cross the line. They spend a half-hour setting up their gear. The friendly SECOR passes once and stops to chat.

As daylight rises, several fishing boats and a few pleasure craft straggle out, and they follow. Jason, with his boating experience, is at the wheel, and Hawk is hunkered down in the cabin door to protect against the bite of the breeze. Leaving the marina, there's an immediate starboard turn to pass through the harbor entrance. Directly ahead and barely a mile away is the international border. Beyond it is the pier at White Rock. And right in their path is a sleek SECOR patrol vessel, crawling along. A single gun is mounted on the forward deck and a pair of machineguns on either side of the bow.

"Are they here to stop people entering or leaving?"

"Both."

"Who'd have thought they'd use guns to keep their own citizens from leaving."

"SECOR screens outgoing citizens. Some they interrogate, some they detain."

"Not possible to use your necklace?"

"Now you don't sound so bright."

All the boats turn sharply to port as they near the patrol, and Jason follows. The fishing fleet then disperses, heading away from the border.

"Would they really use the guns if we made a run for it?"

"Without hesitation. The administration is hounding SECOR to tighten our side of the border. Blowing up the odd vessel reinforces the message."

"Then let's get the lines out and behave like fishermen.

We'll have to wait till they move on. Meanwhile, we're under observation."

Jason sets the two trolling lines, weighted from the downriggers to the depth their friendly SECOR recommended, and they troll slowly west, almost paralleling the border, but also getting further from White Rock. The sun peeks over the horizon. More boats join them. In time, there are pleasure boats fishing or on the move in all directions, gathered into pods at the hot spots, identifiable from the flashing of the sun's rays off net and fish as they are landed. They stay clear of these fruitful clusters, keeping watch on the patrol, but nonetheless hook their own salmon.

"What do I do now?" Hawk cries when the rod's vigorous bobbing and bumping alerts him. Jason lifts the rod from its holder and passes it to him.

"Bring him in, General."

He does, only because the fish is well hooked. The line goes slack twice as he allows the rod to straighten. "Keep the rod tip up, damn it!" Jason shouts.

Jason lifts the net. They admire the silver shining fish.

"Now what?" Hawk says.

"Remove the hook gently and release her."

"But it's my first salmon."

Jason holds the fish just below the surface to allow it to recover. There's a whip of the tail and they watch it vanish into the depths. "We only keep what we can eat. I don't suppose they teach that at SECOR."

Hawk grins. "At SECOR every catch is a keeper."

Apart from that excitement, they have the peace of the fisherman—little tasks, checking the lures, adjusting their depth, changing speed, but time to draw in the beauty of the northwest coast, the San Juan Islands on the western horizon, to the east the mirage of Mount Baker, its great white dome floating high above its fir carpet. The strait teems with life, flocks of birds on the surface as well as in the air, many hanging near the fleet for food; sea lions can be heard from time to time; an eagle skims the surface nearby and snatches up an injured salmon in its talons.

The music of a gentle sea encourages Jason to meditate on their prospects. Once they slip into Canada, what then? Freeing Miriam. If Noble delivers her, good enough. If he hedges, Jason has some bargaining power—public opinion, if he breaks the story immediately.

Hawk's a different issue. There'll be brutal pressure from Washington to bury him. Detention with no access to the media is likely. Maybe even a secret extradition. Easing across the bay, the motor purring quietly, the day growing warmer, he weighs their chances.

Hawk has also become pensive. Jason, waiting to hear his thoughts, recalls their first meeting at the camp, Hawk's cool mastery of the moment, and his own naiveté. Now, he sees him as uneasy, almost vulnerable, needing help. They need each other's help. He decides to push one step further. "Before we cross the line, we need to prepare ourselves."

"I'm thinking about it."

"We have to tell the same story."

"If we get the opportunity."

"I'm coming to that. We'll make the opportunity. You can expect to be vilified by the administration as soon as they find you're in Canada. You'll be every kind of radical, turncoat, and subversive. You'll be either atheist or worse: a covert Muslim. You were a bosom pal of a murderous activist. I'm just getting started."

"I can think of lots more."

"That's what I'm getting at. You'll have to stay one move ahead of them in order to hold public sympathy. Also to disarm anyone who wants to send you back." Hawk appears to get the point but Jason spells it out anyway. "You need to make an immediate statement. A confession. Admit to anything they can make stick, right away. You can see where I'm heading."

One of the rods jumps. Hawk uses the opportunity to stall while he thinks over Jason's advice. "False alarm. Must have had a hit to pull the line from the downrigger." Jason nods and waits while Hawk winds in, resets the line and lowers the lure again. "Why do I get the feeling you know what that is?" he says finally.

"I believe I do. The church bombings."

Hawk looks dismayed. "When did you work it out?"

"Manwaring didn't want to talk about it. He should have raved about it. He should have publicized it. Miriam said he had power over his main contact. I hadn't put you in the picture yet but decided the power might be related to the bombings."

"You reported this to CSIS?"

"No. I assumed Manwaring had a plan to use the information. I thought he or Miriam would tell me how in time. Silas, why did you get involved? It was such a dirty business."

Hawk nods his head in reluctant agreement. "Of course I see that now. I have for a long while. But in those days, we seemed to be in real danger. Congress was frozen. We had to get emergency powers."

"So half a dozen empty churches seemed a bargain."

"Turned out to be a bargain with the devil. Once I saw where the party was going. That's my story." He's a little defiant but Jason can identify the regret in his tone.

"How did Manwaring find out?"

"I had helpers. One of them had an acute attack of conscience. He went to his old law professor, who turned out to be a member of Manwaring's network. They used it to get to me. I was pretty sick about it anyway, the way the administration was carrying on. I was easy to turn. The Mexico Sector was my idea. It took a year to change the staff."

"Convinced dissidents all?"

"Mostly people Manwaring knew. We only needed one shift."

They both pause to let their relationship stabilize.

"How was Manwaring planning to use it?"

"We were going to break the story as the election campaign got underway. Brendan believed it would break the party's hold."

"So you were going public anyway?"

"Never in doubt."

"That's just what you have to do when we get there. Get it out so they can't surprise us later. But when you admit to the bombings, you'll be the most despised man in America, at least for a while."

Hawk falls silent for a moment, perhaps weighing his future. "I have no choice. Now Manwaring's dead …"

When they've trolled about a mile, they circle back. The patrol boat has moved west along the borderline but not as far as they'd like; it still cuts them off from White Rock. A drone passes overhead and moves slowly off along the borderline. "I'm wondering if they're all on high alert because they're expecting us to break for Canada. We can't stay out here all day. The boats will start thinning out. Most of them will be gone by noon." A few of the anglers are already heading for port, perhaps limited out. Jason watches them to gauge the reaction of the patrol. "They're holding their position to keep an eye on the rest of us. Our best chance is to start back to port with a few other boats, then make a dash for it just before we get there. By the time they get after us we can be across the line."

"How fast can this thing go?"

"Full out, maybe twenty knots."

"And the patrol?"

"At least forty."

"You're the math whiz. If we're doing twenty with a half-mile head start and they're doing forty with three guns blazing, how do you rate our chances?"

"Better than staying here till they single us out."

Jason goes into the cabin to call Noble's cell number.

"Ben? I'd like to speak to Miriam, please."

"You can't imagine what I've been through to arrange this. Most of the night."

"Terribly sorry, Ben. Now can I speak to Miriam?"

"I'm all right. Just good and mad." He's so relieved to hear that voice, full of fight just now, that tears start from the corners of his eyes. He misses her words as he's choked up.

"… Talking among themselves about sending me back. I never expected to be treated like a terrorist in my own damn country. They even pretended I wasn't who I am. But now they're telling me that something might be arranged. Ben Noble says so but he sounds very ambiguous. Is that all CSIS doublespeak or do you have something going?"

"Working on it."

"Where are you?"

"We're on our way home."

"We?"

"Hawk's with me."

"So that's what you've been up to. Is that good news for

our side?"

"Emphatically."

"You're not in danger—?"

"Nothing serious."

"I know what that means. Take care. I need you, Jason." That sends a little charge through him.

"Where are you now?" Noble asks.

"Near White Rock. You can meet us there in an hour. At the pier."

"Wait a minute—" Jason disconnects. He calls the Vancouver offices of three newspapers and a press agency, all with the same brief message. "This is a CSIS officer. We expect a senior SECOR officer to defect from the United States this morning. Be at the pier in White Rock in one hour." He disconnects.

"They may check with CSIS," Hawk says.

"Unlikely. They've barely enough time to get here. CSIS wouldn't talk to them anyway."

"For whatever it means for your future, one or all of those calls may have been monitored."

Jason manages a jaunty smile. "That's significant only if we survive this trip."

# FORTY-TWO

THEY TROLL SLOWLY TOWARD PORT. SEVERAL MORE BOATS PASS en route to the anchorage. Jason watches the patrol, calculating its timing. It makes passes of about ten minutes in each direction, parallel to the border. He estimates its cruising speed at seven or eight knots, so each pass is about 1.2 nautical miles. If they start their run at the nearest point between Blaine anchorage and White Rock, they need less than three minutes to cross the line. If the time lost in noticing them, turning and getting up speed is—a full minute?—and they time their dash to begin with the patrol at its maximum distance, they could be in Canada when the patrol is still nearly 2,000 yards short of them, though within firing range. If the reaction is faster than a minute, or they can't do 20 knots—well, the patrol will be on their tail. Will it cross the boundary to close the gap? The patrol boat swings their way again. It continues at the same sedate pace.

The light chop they've had all morning is being stiffened by a freshening wind. The western sky is darkening a little. There's a smell of imminent rain.

"When d'you reckon?" Hawk asks. Jason's not sure whether he sounds tense or a little high on adrenalin.

"When it reaches the far end of the next pass. We need to be nearer port."

Hawk winds in and raises the lead balls on the downriggers. Jason falls in behind another boat heading home at half speed. They wave to him and hand-signal a good catch. He waves back and holds palms up to indicate a shutout. The patrol boat draws nearer. Then it begins its turn away. He gauges the distance to his takeoff point. The wind continues to rise, now directly into them. He steps up speed, passing the boat in front with more exchanges of friendly hand signals. He motions Hawk to come up beside him.

"You'll need to hold on with this chop building. At full throttle it will get rough."

"Where did you learn all this seamanship stuff?"

"Living in Vancouver."

"I've learned something about Canadians from you," Hawk says after standing there, watching Jason. "In the end, you did shake the fruit out of the tree. You gave me the final push."

Jason turns to Hawk. They face one another. "What have you decided?"

"I'll follow your advice. And Manwaring's plan. Americans will learn that I was in charge of the task force that burned those churches, and that I was under orders from the party that now runs the administration. And I have evidence." He offers his hand and they shake on it. Their relationship has become finally that of two friends.

The patrol is almost at the far end of its beat. They're approaching Blaine anchorage. "The drone is out of sight. We'll never get a better chance." Jason swings the bow toward White Rock and opens the throttle. The motor roars, the prop grips hard and pulls the stern down, the bow lifts higher, and they leap ahead. Jason adjusts the shaft angle and they plane high in the water. Hawk grips a stanchion with both hands as they bounce through the rising waves. Spray flies into the cockpit. Now it's beginning to rain so they're pelted by both fresh and salt water.

Within seconds, the patrol boat heels sharply as it snaps into a tight turn. Its bow waves mount—it's picking up speed. Men scramble down the deck and look to be clearing the machineguns.

A neat row of tiny splashes ahead looks like a leaping school of herring. They can't hear the machineguns over the roar of the engine and the wind. Jason wheels the boat sharply to starboard. Hawk's almost thrown but re-grips. Now port. He changes the timing and angles of the turns to be unpredictable. There's another line of splashes, falling just short. The zigzagging helps, but it's eating up more time. He can see one of the towers marking the border. At this weaving pace it's still a minute away.

"Make sure that vest is tied firmly. We might end up in the water."

In the distance, maybe three or four miles away, he sees the familiar maroon hull of a Canadian Coast Guard cutter, coming hard. If they have to bail out, they'll at least have a chance … a mixed blessing. Hawk could appeal for refugee status, but Canada might yield to pressure—safer if he gets to White Rock. They need the media as witnesses.

He turns back to Hawk. He's watching the Canadian cutter also, and he's laughing. Not chuckling, laughing outright. Hawk punches him in the shoulder. "They're all after us! *We're outed! We're fucking famous!*" He shakes with laughter. So now does Jason. They stand by the wheel with the air roaring by and the rain and spray streaming at their faces and laugh.

The engine rises and falls as it labors through the chop, the hull thudding against row after row of crunching waves, with one vessel overhauling and the other oncoming, and howl just to hear themselves laugh. Jason feels crazy but exhilarated.

But he's also beginning to be very tired. Prison, torture, days of stress, sleeplessness, their early start after a wakeful night, and now the pounding of the boat at high speed, all piling on to wear him down. He sucks it in and braces for their final run.

Running his eye along the shoreline, he finds the border marker. "We're almost across."

"Great!" Hawk bellows in his ear. "I've always wanted to visit Canada!" Splinters of glass dance across the shelf in front of the wheel. There are three bullet holes in the side window. He glances at Hawk, praying he's not been hit. Hawk's staring at the border marker, oblivious.

"We're over the line!"

He turns to look back. Patrol is still coming hard. She skims across the boundary without slacking speed. Bullets thud into their hull. One zings off something metal—their engine? He leans on the throttle, but it's already at max. He swerves more desperately to and fro, like a fish darting from its pursuer. Now the air horn hoots angrily from the converging cutter. Then more hoots, almost continuous. He glances at the patrol—*the bow waves diminish*! She's turning broadside.

"We're in the clear!" A stream of pink water sloshes past his feet. His eyes follow it to Hawk. He's sagged against the bulkhead, one hand pressed against his chest. His jacket shows a pink stain. Between his fingers he squeezes bright red blood.

"How bad?" Hawk shakes his head. "Lie down! I'll get you in."

The Canadian cutter has veered toward them, still coming hard. "We'll go inshore—too shallow for them." With the tide out, the beach inshore is very wide, confirming the gentle slope of the bottom. He wheels in as far as he dares. The cutter heaves to. Seconds later, they can see the activity on deck. "Launching their zodiac."

Here inshore the waves are gentler, beaten down by the

rain. They skim along parallel to the beach with the pier dead ahead. He has a moment to study Hawk. He's much paler. His eyes are locked on Jason. There's no expression, just hanging on.

Seaward, the zodiac is underway, riding high, with two men erect, gripping its stanchions as it flies over the waves. It sets a course directly for the end of the pier—to cut them off.

"It'll be close," he shouts. They now ride smoothly in the quieter water. He leans down to Hawk, "Once you're ashore"—but what to say? Hawk can't bolt up the stairs and surrender himself.

They've almost reached the pier—500 yards of trestle reaching out from shore with a boat anchorage at the deep end crossing it like a T. He glances left; the zodiac is poised to leap in front of them. He looks at the pier, where a handful of suited men watch, some shooting photos.

It's time to ease off the throttle, but he must reach the pier before he's cut off. Where to discharge Hawk? He cuts inside the cross of the T, forcing the zodiac to round the end behind them and lose a second or two. The high pier is just ahead, a line of moored boats on the lower slip to his left. He's going too fast to stop in time. He pulls the wheel hard to the right. The boat stands on edge as it tries to follow. He cuts the engine. The boat sluices sideways until it crashes into a pillar under the pier. Hawk's flung into the water. Jason has just enough time to glimpse him grabbing the foot rail of the dock before the zodiac slaps into his starboard bow and he's also thrown in the water.

He holds his breath. He has an instant of recall; he's on a board till Rightful pulls him up. But there's no board and he's not being pulled up—he's sinking. Why doesn't his lifebelt push him up? He tries a swimming stroke. He's so weak now it hardly moves him.

He gets mad. After what he's been through, this isn't fair. He can't drown just when he's triumphed. He needs to reach the media, lined up above him. He kicks angrily and his body makes a weak move upward. There's another man in the water now. He tries kicking again but it's getting harder. The other man grabs at him and then wraps his arm firmly through Jason's armpit and around his back. They ascend like a slow elevator.

"You've committed about a dozen infractions," his gasping rescuer says when they surface. But he's grinning. "It was a hell of a run, though."

There's Hawk, being pulled onto the slip. Jason flounders out of the water while both guards maneuver Hawk onto his back and tear at his jacket. Jason staggers to his feet.

They have the jacket open, now the shirt. Crouched beside Hawk, Jason throws a quick glance up the stairs. Four or five journalists are lined up at the threshold of the high pier, looking down at the tableau on the slip. Two Mounties hold them back from descending. On the first step down, the A-D is standing, glowering at him.

"Ambulance on its way." One of the Guards is applying

pressure to Hawk's chest. Jason can still see a dribble of frothy red blood, oozing out. He touches Hawk's hand. The fingers close on his. He can hear the siren coming down the pier. The little crowd parts to allow the stretcher team down. When they carry Hawk up the stairs, Jason beside him, Hawk is still holding his hand.

Without speaking, Hawk dies that evening.

# FORTY-THREE

JASON TRAVELS ALONE ON THE FERRY TO VANCOUVER ISLAND. Miriam has crossed a week earlier to find Adolphus.

He stays on the open top deck for the hour-and-a-half voyage, soaking in the saline smells, savoring his release. He has been cross-examined daily since White Rock, hundreds of thousands of words, dictated, transcribed, edited, then fed back to him for more detail, and finally buried in some secret file. Hawk's legacy has meanwhile become a sensitive issue. He's an heroic defector, murdered by a SECOR patrol. But in the United States he's a traitor, well documented now as a member of an underground opposition. Jason can imagine the tug-of-war ongoing between the centers of power in both Ottawa and Washington, each determined to own the final version. As threatening as the United States can be to its punier neighbor, Canadian journalism cannot quietly allow Hawk's exploits to be buried in infamy. Too much is in the open now. Perhaps the media will dig out the rest. The Canadian government has been taciturn, possibly to give the administration room to craft a scenario that will give it maximum covert.

The A-D is in a complicated position. His group has uncovered the plot to bomb Christian churches in order to discredit Muslims. But it's also given the Cabinet a massive headache. All kinds of back-stories are probably under construction to encourage the proper distribution of praise or blame to any of the competing parties, CSIS management, Cabinet staff, and the Office of the Prime Minister.

So the A-D has been rather testy. Jason has recounted the whole sequence of his American sojourn, the workings of SECOR, the visits to Manwaring, the Sudan trip, the detention, and every conversation he could reconstruct. Hawk's been their main focus, but they've also harangued him for details of Miriam's activities, which he's filtered carefully.

Much of his recital has grated on the A-D. "You *sympathized* with Al Ansari, didn't you?" "You considered Manwaring to be a *patriot*?" His manner has hardened into reproach as they went along. "You let Hawk lead you by the nose. He *used* you, and you didn't know it was happening." His treatment in detention gets no sympathy. "What did you expect when you refused to give up that woman? Enhanced interrogation is legal in the States."

"I didn't expect to be raped. Sir."

What they might do to Miriam has kept him on edge. Near the end of the week there was an unintended enlightenment. "Those gutless wonders in the Justice Department have declined to prosecute her. They're not sure what to charge her with. She could be lionized by the media—so the Americans would be even more frustrated with us. Meanwhile, she's hiding out somewhere on Vancouver Island."

Without much hope, Jason made his pitch for his boyhood friend, brother of his lover. "Is there a way to get Nabil Maron out of there? He's blameless, just caught up in the administration's paranoia. We have to do something for him."

"Paranoia?" The A-D had glared at him, poised between amazement and disgust. "Good God, Currie. Don't you think we've spent enough of our political capital? He made his own bed."

"By becoming an American citizen so he could work for the American military?"

The A-D had turned to Noble. "You see what happens when you rely on such people?"

So Bil Maron is beyond help. And Hawk is dead.

The A-D has the last word. "You're on sick leave until you recover, then on indefinite suspension. Someone else can decide what to do with you. Currie, you're a disgrace to the service."

"Yes, sir. I always thought I'd have trouble meeting your expectations."

It has been a couple of years since Jason has seen cousin Adolphus. He speculates on how the dour bachelor will have received Miriam. He's an intelligent man who has no patience with shallower wits, so he has always found more cause to scowl than smile. He must be well into his sixties now, a terse loner who will have challenged her amiability.

As Jason emerges from the passenger walkway, he spots Adolphus beside Miriam, beard grayer, maybe not quite so straight-backed as he remembers, but still a sturdy figure. He's half a head taller than Jason, looking down on him with snapping eyes.

"You look awful," Miriam says. His gap-toothed jaw is still a little swollen, a fading purple and yellow patch lingers where Werner's ring caught his cheekbone, and his little finger, minus its nail, is still taped. When she hugs him he begins shaking. He's losing control, afraid to speak. Adolphus watches wordlessly as she holds him and both shed a few tears.

"We've been contacted!" Miriam whispers as she holds him.

"Contacted? *We?*"

"We're on the team now, Jason. And they need us."

"Oh, that kind of contact." He exchanges glances with Adolphus, who shakes his head, runs his gaze over Jason without comment, and simply wraps one arm around his shoulders for a firm hug. He leads them to the same pickup truck of other visits, even more in need of a paint job now, its bed sprinkled with chaff, a sack of feed propped in a corner.

Jason can hardly look away from Miriam as they start up-island. Or keep from touching her more than Adolphus's presence allows. He manages to whisper, "You smell of horses. It's very fetching."

They drive slowly, Miriam chattering blithely about the ranch, the horses, and working with Adolphus (who is wordless).

But Jason is thinking of her brother. *I have to tell her about Bil. Not just yet. There'll be a time for that. Later, not today.*

This is not the end of this story.
It may be only the beginning.

*Follow at www.fearfulmaster.ca*

# ABOUT THE AUTHOR

ARTHUR LAWRENCE GREW UP wanting to be a poet. As a young man he was pushed into the working world, setting literature aside and spending his energy becoming an organization man. This took him from his home in North Toronto and let him experience the rest of Canada.

Forty years later, he retired as a Vice President. He and his wife Dorothy happily resettled to Vancouver Island, where his creative instincts re-emerged through books.

*Fearful Master* is his first published book.